C000069934

A Pilgrim's Heart

Nordun's Way Book Two

Also By Elles Lohuis

The Horse Master's Daughter (*Nordun's Way* Book One)

Echoes of Home (*Nordun's Way* Book Three)

Download your copy of the hand-drawn map of Nordun's travels, specially commissioned for the *Nordun's Way* series books 1, 2 and 3 at
www.elleslohuis.com or scan the QR Code.

A Pilgrim's Heart

Nordun's Way Book Two

ELLES LOHUIS

Black Peony Press

First published by Black Peony Press in 2022
ISBN 9789083240831 (Hardback)
ISBN 9789083240817 (Paperback)
ISBN 9789083240800 (E-book)

This book is for all who dare to live and love without fear,
and light the way forward.

Contents

Prologue

Tibet, Eastern Kham
The Year of The Wood Rooster
1412 (1285 AD)

There comes a time in your life when you'll face a real danger, a blatant violation of everything your heart knows to be true.

And in this moment, you'll have a decision to make—either you stand in your truth and brave the consequences, no matter what, or you'll turn away and spend the rest of your life living between bitter blame and lame absolution.

This time has come for me.

One

The sun throws her last beams of burnished orange through the kitchen window, elongating Father's shadow—he appears taller.

I look up, my feet pointed at the stove.

It's only the first day of my new life and I'm already exhausted. For sure, I never knew sorrow and joy could coexist so close to each other, occupying the same space, living in one tender heart.

This morning my grandmother went back to her monastery, my home for so many years as a novice nun. I decided not to join her again, but to return to lay life instead—the life I was ripped away from many years ago. A gnawing ache has nestled itself deeply into the hollows of my heart. How I'll miss them, my dearest sisters in solitude. Will I ever see them again?

I don't want to think about it. I've made my choice.

I've decided to stay with Father at the stables, my childhood home, and with my dear Karma, who came for me this afternoon. We met only a few moons ago and our love is still budding—we have a lot to discover and explore, the two of us.

Excitement and fear collide in my chest. A strange unknowing rushes through my veins. I have no idea how to live in this mundane world just yet, but my heart has called and I'm taking the leap.

"The ngakpa has requested us," Father says.

A sigh escapes from the depth of my chest. It's been a long day.

My hands cap my knees, and I raise my weary body. I was looking forward to an early night, but it seems we're heading to the village, Father and me. Dusk's already setting in an orange haze, heralding the night. I wonder, why go so late? Father's expression doesn't give away the answer to my unspoken question.

"I'll have to clean myself up." Dust flies around as my hands brush my skirt. Sangmo and I have just finished clearing my uncle's quarters for us to move in. I run my fingers through my unruly hair—I don't want to show up like this at the ngakpa's—it's disrespectful. "I'll be right back."

I rush off for a quick wash.

It's a short enough walk to the village. Father's pace is swift and silent. My mind drifts to our last meeting with the ngakpa. It seems so long ago, but it was only a few turns of the moon. How things have changed. How *I* have changed.

No more an aspiring nun in my grandmother's monastery, but the heir to my father's stables. A female horse master. Who would have thought? Not me, that's for sure. The ngakpa's divination did, though. Maybe that's why he wants us to come. I shiver, my legs stubbornly stiff as I try to keep up with Father's solid pace.

The bitter breeze lashes unforgivingly into the fluttering prayer flags. A high-pitched whistle resonates in the billowing sky. Looks like a storm is approaching.

The ngakpa's house if there, the first on the left, shrouded in darkness. Unlike the last time I was here, nobody welcomes us at the gate.

"Are you sure he's home?" I halt, but Father's already put his shoulder against the heavy door. A loud creak. The stench of stale soot hits our nostrils as we enter the dim hallway. My stomach tightens. Something's off. It's too quiet in here.

Father strides ahead, not bothered a bit by the suffocating atmosphere. Sheltered by his broad back, I follow.

A sudden ring drowns our hollow footsteps, and I almost jump—the ngakpa's prayer bell. He's home. *Good.* I take a deep breath to steady my speedy pulse. No need to be so nervous. All went well.

Father pauses for a moment and turns, a reassuring nod. Yes, we'll be fine.

The scent of heavy incense oozes behind maroon drapes. As we step in, spicy white whirls sneak their way out. A sole butter lamp—a big one—casts its flicker on the small shrine in the middle. I blink as my eyes adjust to the gloomy surroundings and the tangy fume of smoldering spices and herbs.

"Please, come." A thin voice resounds from the far-left corner of the room—the ngakpa's in his seat. I step forwards and lower my body three times to the shrine. Father follows.

"Sit, sit," the ngakpa's raspy voice urges. "So sorry to have you come this late."

He shifts in his cushioned seat. His fingertips spread lightly on the tops of our lowered heads as we take our place opposite him. A murmured blessing and a prayer, the rhythm not known to me but nevertheless comforting, smoothens the jagged edge of my nerves.

"I hear you had a fruitful journey." A string of bone prayer beads rattles around his thin wrist. He adjusts the white scarf around his narrow chest.

"Yes, gen-la." I look up. "Thanks to your excellent guidance."

He folds his hands in his lap. His narrow gaze rests on me. The pile of twisted locks on the top of his head sways in sync with his body. His eyes close and he gently rocks from left to right, to left, to right.

A strained silence fills the space between us. A slight exhale breathes from his lips. He seems to sink further in his seat. Is he in meditation?

My fingers fumble with the red string around my wrist, the blessing cord that my sisters tied to remind me of the Buddhist path.

"I have a request of you both." The ngakpa's voice is hardly audible. His eyes are still closed, the lines around them deepen.

I lean forward. A request? I glance at Father and my eyebrows raise. What could that be?

Father frowns. A concerned look crosses his face.

"Where to begin?" A faint shadow of sorrow moves over the ngakpa's face. "Khandro-la has left this morning." His shoulders drop.

Khando, his wife, left? A shiver shoots up my spine, my nerves raise to a high alert. My intuition served me right—something *is* off.

"She's not coming back." He opens his eyes, and his distant stare meets mine. "She's taken something with her." He rests his long tawny fingers on the side of the small table between us and leans across. "I request your help to retrieve it back." His eyes flash a dark plea from me to Father and back.

"Of course, gen-la." Father nods without hesitation. "Anything we can do." He clears his throat. The incense must bother him too.

"It's a matter of utmost discretion." The ngakpa's hands draw over the table. "You are the only ones I can ask." His eyes, like tiny black beads, pierce my gaze, and then turn to Father. "Even though I'm already in your debt, Palden-la." His voice becomes a muffled resonance in the pearly opaque surrounding us.

"Oh no, gen-la." Father straightens his back. His large hands open towards the ngakpa. "There's no debt between us, and if there is, it is us who owe you."

I raise my chin. Father's right, the ngakpa has always served us and our village with his prayers and rituals.

"Yet I am, Palden." The ngakpa's face folds into a quiet, solemn look. "For it has come to me that my wife aided your brother Tennah so many years ago, causing grave misfortune to your family."

My jaw drops. A sudden rush of blood swishes in my ears. Khandro and Uncle—together?

"Khandro-la." He hesitates. His fingers spread on the table. "She aided Tennah with a spell that caused Lhamo's untimely passing." He whispers her name ever so softly. *Lhamo*. My Mother.

"And now she has left and taken the spell." His hands glide over to the book in front of him, a thin pile of long, browned pothi pages. "It's my family's, written with the blood of my ancestors." His fingers longingly stroke the tainted edges of the brownish paper. "So powerful."

A spell book. I lean in. So this is the ngakpa's ritual book then? And Khandro took a spell out of it to cause my mother's death. Together with my uncle. I swallow hard, the heavy incense a sticky layer in the back of my throat.

"The spell does harm in their hands." He shakes his head, and the grayish coils wave in a slow motion on the top of his head. "I... wè...need the page back." His fingers clamp again around the edges of the small table between us, a pale blue shines translucent on his knuckles. The significance of his words slowly penetrates my mind. *Khandro-la and Uncle, together, gone with the spell that killed my mother.*

My sisters were right all along—and now it's confirmed. Uncle had a hand in mother's death with a snake spell. No wonder he left in such a hurry before I returned with a wild horse to stake my claim at the stables.

My temples throb. My thoughts swirl to clear the mist in my mind. *Focus.* My gaze fixes on the long pages. What now? From the corners of my eyes, Father's robust frame is a still composition.

"Yes, this requires our utmost discretion." Father rubs his chin. "Any idea where they might have gone to?" His quiet manner, his steady voice, it eases my panic—not all, but it certainly helps.

"Lhasa," the ngakpa says. "West, to Lhasa." His eyes on the book, the bone beads roll from his wrist.

Lhasa. My heart leaps. Lhasa, Land of The Gods, home of the Jowo Sakyamuni Buddha statue, the most revered object in Tibetan Buddhism. Yes, Lhasa would be the perfect place to hide.

So many visitors and pilgrims, nobody would notice two strangers from the East. *Lhasa*. Often my grandmother told me about her pilgrimage to this magical place. Oh, how I long to visit Lhasa myself in this lifetime. If only I get the chance—the merit this pilgrimage would bring.

"Give us some time, gen-la." Father's steadfast voice interrupts my wandering mind. "I promise we'll find a solution."

With a shrill sigh, the ngakpa leans back in his seat; the bone beads an ominous rattle in his hands.

"I know you will, Palden-la." The ngakpa closes his eyes. "You've never let me down."

His whole body sags. The leathery lines on his face relax and the beads in his hands quieten. A soft murmur from his lips beckons us—time to go. Quietly, Father and I make our way to the door.

"I'll see you soon, Nordun." The ngakpa's croaky voice stops me in my tracks. His eyes burn on the back of my head. I turn around, only to see I must have misheard. Still seated with his eyes closed, it's the serenity of his posture and the soft glow on his face that gives it away—the ngakpa's in deep meditation. I shake my head. My mind's playing tricks on me. Or maybe it's the tiredness of the long day taking over.

A sharp draft from the doorway dissolves the fleeting incense. The gleam of the butter lamp reveals the bloodshed images on the thangkas around me. I've seen them before, even so, a shiver runs up my spine and my feet haste into the hallway. Father's way ahead of me by now.

We walk home together under an indigo sky with a lone star shining proudly. The pale light from the waning moon is just enough to guide our way. The wind has died down—it's turned into a crisp and quiet evening. The only sound is the crunch of our footsteps on the gritty path. How I wish my mind were as calm as this vast evening sky—so many questions grind around without end. I glance at Father, walking beside me.

"Did you not know?" My heart's pounding. I don't want to upset Father, but my curiosity's getting the better of me—as usual. "About Uncle?"

Father shakes his head. "There were rumors nasty ones." Melancholy rims his voice. "I was devastated, Nordun. I missed your mother so much. I was only too relieved when my only brother showed up in that time of need, so I ignored that nasty talk."

I nod as I remember Father from that time, the immense change he went through. Grief brings even the strongest of men to their knees.

"I was happy to see my brother, despite everything that had passed between us." The moonlight casts a shadow on Father's solemn face. I don't dare to ask, but I've never known what happened between Father and his brother. I heard about a bad fallout, long before I was born. They made up when mother died. That's the only thing I know. And now betrayed by his only brother? My heart sinks as I think of Father's fate.

"I'm sorry," I say. "About all this." My muffled words—they're useless. Even so, I must voice them. It's the only way I can express myself right now.

"Me too, Nordun," Father says. "But I'm more sorry for all the time lost." His head bent; his voice grows thick. "For letting myself be blinded by grief, and for being so selfish that I abandoned my own blood." The rawness of his voice rips through me. I squint.

All these years, I thought he didn't care for me. I take in a deep breath. No use going there again. The crisp air clears the last traces of haze from my head.

I halt and turn to Father as we enter the gate to the stables. "What now?"

"We can't let this go." His toe kicks up loose pebbles. "We have to retrieve that page before it does more damage." His eyes flicker, an ominous gloom as he stares over my shoulder towards the darkened courtyard.

"And Uncle?" I cringe the moment I say it. *Uncle.* His evil deeds weight heavy on both our minds. An iron fist clamps tightly around my heart. My ribs tighten. We both know what will be done with Uncle. I shouldn't have brought it up.

To my relief, Father ignores my useless remark, his gaze fixed over my shoulder.

"I see word has gone around." His chin points towards the house. "So soon."

I turn to see the stark silhouettes of two horses in the courtyard. They're not ours. *Visitors.*

The grinding of our hasty footsteps quiets my pondering thoughts. I don't have to wonder for long. As the trees throw their lanky shadows in the moonlit courtyard, I recognize the voices without a doubt. *They're here.* Grandfather's family has arrived.

TWO

"Good news travels fast." Father's arms open to the visitors in the courtyard. "It's wonderful to see you, brothers."

Two men step out of the shadows and I recognize at least one of them—Dendup, the man with the sharp nose and red tassels in his hair. He's the one who requested that I meet my grandfather's family a few weeks ago.

It was the first time I'd ever met this side of my mother's family.

Seeing Father put his arms around Dendup, it looks like Father knows them well.

Of course he would—they're my mother's blood relatives. I just never realized Father was this close to them. After all, our families had a grave fall-out.

I was told my grandmother's brothers killed my grandfather Rapten after he eloped with Dechen, my grandmother—who was pregnant at the time. Grandfather's family never sought blood revenge, which was quite unusual. They also never claimed the child—my mother—who was raised by Grandmother's family. I was always under the impression that this tragedy caused the families to avoid each other at all costs.

But what do I know about Father, let alone the rest of my extended family? He stashed away at my grandmother's monastery when I was about five or six—I was so young—and I never met any of my relatives as far as I can remember.

Father beckons me into the courtyard, pride gleaming in his eyes. "Nordun, come."

I stumble forward, as clumsy as ever. How things have changed over the last few weeks. Going home to ask Father's permission to become a nun, I've gotten to understand him in such a different way. The grief-stricken, troubled man who abandoned me after my mother's death is no more.

Sure, Father's still filled with regret over his actions in the past. As humans, we always struggle with forgiving ourselves and letting go, don't we? My heart expands as I look at him now, standing here in the yard, full of confidence and hope for the future again.

Long white scarves sway over the men's outstretched arms. Khatas. Not to welcome me this time, but to celebrate my victory of bringing home a wild horse, tamed.

"Happy to learn of your fortunate return, sister." Dendup offers the khata around my neck. The sliver of moonlight that cuts across his rugged face reveals genuine joy.

"Thank you, brother." My head bent, my fingers fumble with the ends of the khata. I'm not sure of the exact family connection but he must be close as he's sent to represent the family.

"Our grandfather sends his regards," the other man says as he joins the khata giving. "He, wè, are most honored to be family."

A warm glow spreads through my body as the man's honest delight touches me. After so long, I'm finally part of the family. I've done them proud. I've proven to be a worthy successor to my father, the next in line to be the horse master of these stables. And the fact that I'm a woman taking up the position doesn't seem to be a concern to them. Being nomads, some of their women also ride horses, like Sangmo, my cousin.

"Please, come in," Father says. "You've made a long journey. You must be hungry."

Father ushers the men into the house. To the kitchen I notice, not the formal room. *Good.*

With the stove crackling away, tea is served and a generous amount of food is passed around, a fitting welcome for family.

Karma's hand touches my shoulder as he joins us. With a blushed smile, I look around. I don't see his sister Sangmo anywhere. Well, I suppose she's still tidying up our quarters. That girl doesn't stop working.

As the men want to hear all about my journey to the Four Sisters Mountain, I fill the teacups and let Karma do the talking. After all, I would never have gotten there in the first place without his help.

Normally not a man of many words, this time Karma goes all out recounting how he intercepted Uncle's three sons from preventing me from getting the wild horse. The story of tricking the two cousins by getting them drunk is quite hilarious. The aftermath of the tale, however, when he fought off the third cousin who came around with a gang of his mates, really gets the men roaring.

My heart surges. *This man.*

He throws me a meaningful glance, conveniently leaving out the bit about the drinking, the gambling, and the two women of leisure hanging around his neck. I guess he doesn't want to embarrass me, something he does so easily as he's everything I'm not. Confident, worldly, with a wicked sense of humor—he's experienced in all the ways of this world—the world I've just entered and started to explore.

"So, they haven't been seen since?" Dendup raises his cup to Karma with a wide smile. "Well done, brother. That's how we take care of our own."

As I fill the cups with another round of tea, I hold my breath as the conversation takes an inevitable turn.

"And Tennah left?" Dendup's eyebrows draw down.

There it is. The iron fist clenches tight around my heart again. A sunken silence fills the air.

Father's big frame caves. His eyes dart over men's heads. I know—Father doesn't want to tell, for the consequences will be grave. *His own brother.* But he has no choice.

"I guess word has already reached you." He clears his throat and takes another sip of tea.

"I've sent word to the family." Karma glances from Father to the men and back. Not to me—he doesn't dare to, for I know what's coming.

"I had to." He lowers his head, and my heart drops to my stomach. Yes, he had to, but Father...

Carefully, I glance at Father, his body hunched, his gaze flung into nowhere. He's a strong man, but how much can even a strong man bear?

"There's more." Father shifts in his seat. "Nordun and I, we've just come from the ngakpa."

My pulse quickens. My hands wring around my cup.

"Seems his wife's involved in this too," Father says, his gaze drowns in his cup. "She provided Tennah with a spell to accomplish his evil deed and now they've run off—together."

Dendup and the other man don't move a muscle. Did they already hear about the ngakpa's wife? How?

My face flushes. I get up for more tea. The handle of the kettle slips in my sweaty palms.

"Where to?" Dendup hands me his cup but keeps his eyes on Father. I pour him another one without spilling.

Father slowly slurps his tea and gives himself some time before responding.

"Lhasa," he says. "The ngakpa thinks they went to Lhasa." He looks up and a somber stare meets us.

"Lhasa." Karma straightens his back and raises his chin towards the men.

"Then Lhasa it is." Dendup clicks his tongue. He turns to Father, a curt nod. "The family has decided."

The kettle weighs heavy in my hands. The stove hisses and roars. Tears burn in my eyes. *The family has decided.* They're going to Lhasa.

"We'll take care of it," Dendup says. "Karma and I."

No! Not Karma! A wave of nausea heaves in my stomach. I stumble, and steam rises as tea slushes over the sizzling stove. My lungs collapse. *Focus.*

The stench of burned milk sears my nostrils, the arid heat of dung scorches the back of my throat. With all my strength, I direct my senses to stay present. The kettle bangs back on the cooker. I take in a deep breath, fighting the panic filling my being.

They're not saying it, but I know exactly what it means. They are going to Lhasa to avenge Mother's death—Dendup and Karma are going to Lhasa to slay my uncle.

"We'll leave tomorrow." Dendup waves his hand. "We'll waste no good time to get this done."

I dig my heels in the hardwood floor to steady myself—another deep breath in and out. It's not working, I'm lost. I gawk at Father. My face's on fire by now.

Say something. My mouth opens, but the words stay stuck deep down my throat. What to do? I need time. Time to think.

"Let us do the proper preparations first," I blurt out. "We need prayer, and guidance from the ngakpa as we don't know how to handle the spell."

All eyes are on me now. My hands dig in a rag, my feet rumble around the stove.

"Please." I stretch my arms to Karma, his face void of any expression. My eyes widen, I can't believe this. How can he sit there so calmly when he knows he's going off to murder a man?

"Nordun's right." Father's voice—raw and unsteady—cuts through the tension like a blunt knife, causing frayed edges to linger between us. "It's a long, arduous journey. It's better to prepare well."

The men sift in their seat. Dendup throws Karma an odd glance while the other man gulps down his tea.

I hold my breath—again. My lungs explode in my chest. *Will they?*

"You're probably right." Dendup shrugs after a pause that seemed without end. "We'll leave the day after tomorrow."

A sigh of relief gushes from my chest. *Good.* This gives me the time to better my case.

"Nordun." Father throws me a sharp look before I get the chance to open my mouth again. He pushes his cup aside, and he points at the big jug on the shelf.

The cloth drops from my hands and I step back. A bitter taste fills my mouth. *Revenge.* So it's decided then, just like that.

I snatch the jug from the shelf and hand it to Father. Too flustered to pour the chang myself, I clear the teacups, their clatter drowning the lone cry inside of me. *No killing, not Karma*—but as the chang flows, I know my desperate words won't be heard.

Three

L hasa—the first thing on my waking mind.

My chest contracts at the thought of going. What brought so much joy yesterday evening frightens me in the early morning after. My hands weigh heavy on my chest as my eyes open to the stark darkness covering the room. The wooden ceiling is a blur from afar, but my mind is sharp. How quickly genuine enthusiasm turns into crippling anxiety when we let our mind rule over the call of my heart.

Prayer—that will focus me, give me the courage to step on my path again. Now that I'm not in the monastery anymore, I've been neglecting my daily prayer and meditation. Being with my sisters, following the monastic rhythm, day-to-day life was simple. Over ten years of a meticulous routine of prayer, study, and work—how quickly I've let myself fall out of this, becoming lazy and sloppy with practice.

I stretch my arms over my head and let my thoughts go over the past few weeks. A lot has happened, a lot has changed. Leaving the monastery as a nun, learning the ways of the wild, traveling for days at an end. Getting to know my father and family again and now settling back at my childhood home as a lay person. Sure, I can use all of this as an excuse—in the end it's my own mind making up stories to justify my lax behavior. It's exactly as my grandmother said: *either we master our mind, or our mind masters us.*

Sangmo's even breath is the only sound in the room. I slide the blanket to the side. Time to ground into my lay practice. My eyes catch the frays of my sleeves as I smoothen my hair. What was a soft, moss-green chuba a few moons ago now is a caked, drab gray tatter. I haven't changed since I took off my monastic robe in Sonam's kitchen. My fingers straighten the reluctant, coarse creases in vain. I guess it's also time to get my own lay clothes. I wonder if Father kept some of Mother's clothing? She always dressed well.

My heart warms at the thought of mother—my memories of her are returning, one by one. Her eyes, full of love and joy, have never left me, but the pictures of her and me together—they faded with her passing. It was only when Sonam took me to his family to learn the ways of the wild horses I remembered. Mother and Father training the horses, with me running around in the pen. Father's powerful arms lifting me in the front of the saddle—mother's slender hands gripping me tight. So much joy, so many wonderful memories coming through after so many years.

For a long time, there was only the one, the haunting one. I wince, for it was the one of Father carrying Mother home. His arms clenched her soaking wet body, his face wrought with desperation. Mother's face a pale blue, her limbs lifeless...

They'd let me think she'd drowned while riding her favorite horse. An accident, they'd said. The horse wasn't tamed yet, they'd said.

I swallow a lump of what seems like ceaseless sadness. Turns out it wasn't an accident at all. Father's brother put a spell on mother's horse. A snake spell, causing the horse to balk at the sight of water—and that's where the snakes live. It wasn't the horse that killed her—father's brother did.

My ragged fingernails catch the hem of my scarf. *Uncle*. His malevolent stare, his sour breath—my intuition was right that first time we met. His deeds are evil. The apparition of the phantom-snake twice—here at the stables and in the cave—it was all Uncle's doing. He let me think I was losing my mind.

Good thing my grandmother's teachings are solid, engrained in my mind. All those years at the monastery, studying and living side by side with seasoned Buddhist practitioners has been my saving.

The thin yarn rips as I wrap my scarf tighter. That's a sign. I need some new clothes. Traveling all the way to Lhasa, these won't hold.

Lhasa. The knot in my stomach tightens. Time for prayer.

Dawn peeps through the eastern window of the prayer rooms. A few rays of soft blue yellow caress the polished shrine. The butter lamps cast the last of their wilting flicker on the magnificent golden Buddha. With the sweet fragrance of fresh flowers lingering around, the place is kept immaculate, as Mother always did. I guess Father found solace in Buddhism after all.

My knees sink in the thick woolen carpet. Three prostrations, a little incense, and I sit down on a mat. The jade beads slide between my fingers and my mind turns to prayer—*Oṃ tāre tu tāre ture soha.*

It was Green Tara who appeared to me right here after I sought her refuge from my reoccurring nightmares. These haunting dreams I had since childhood all make sense now. The crack of a lashing whip claps in my ears, the stench of frantic fear hits my nostrils. I still cringe at the memory of the stallion in that pen, his body drenched in sweat, his wild eyes agonizing as he stood there trembling, tied up and beaten down by my cousins. How could I turn my back on suffering like that? The only way to get rid of my nasty cousins was to take up the challenge, to catch a wild horse so I could become my father's legal successor to the stables. Leaving monastic life behind was the only way.

Growing up in the monastery, the immense benefit of being a nun... I miss it. I miss my sisters in solitude. I shift in my seat. This mundane world, other people, even my family—I still feel so awkward around them. My heart knows—my home is out in this world now, with Father at the stables, and with Karma, my love. Yet, I wonder, will it ever feel like home out here?

My shoulders drop. My mind releases all the stories. Silence pervades my being as the thoughts fleet away. I immerse myself in the vastness of all that is and sit with my eyes closed—being here, being now.

A slight draft deepens the whiff of lingering herbs and carries a soft voice all around. "I'm always here." It's Tara. I open my eyes, hoping she will appear to me the same as last time, but there's nothing but the traces of incense curling up.

"You still possess the same persistent, loving heart and the genuine desire to help all sentient beings. Nothing has changed, my child." Tara's voice again, a whisper on the breeze.

The smoldering wicks of the fading butter lamps burst a high hiss. I hold my breath, and the jade beads squished in the palm of my hand. As I fix my eyes on the crackling sparks, I feel it again—a little breeze. Tara's here. Gratitude fills my heart and I slowly breath out, emptying myself to receive whatever she brings for me.

"Nothing has changed." Her truth floats in the swirling curls around my head. "Good practice, practice that is of benefit to all, is—and will always be—taking action in this samsaric realm." My vision blurs ever so slightly, a soft gleam surrounding me as I focus on her voice. "Nothing has changed, Nordun. You are able and ready to do whatever is needed."

The doubts, fears, and worries that weighed down my heart all melt away as the truth of these words lightens my being. Tara's encouraging words are like a warm balm, soothing yet strengthening me, like the first time she appeared to me.

"Remember, Nordun." There is a raw, almost daring edge around her voice now. "Act from a pure heart and act swiftly... for all good things will be done."

A cool gush turns the air, inciting the dwindling butter lamps to flare one last time before they extinguish with a whisper. With the early rays of soft blueish yellow warming to an ochre orange, she's gone, taking with her whatever weighted down my heart.

As the impact of what just happened settles in my being, my mind turns to the last time I was here. The time Tara encouraged me to take up the challenge of bringing a wild horse home.

I guess this time it's off to Lhasa then, despite the objections my father and the rest of the family will make. Dendup and Karma might stir up a protest, but it's crystal clear to me—it's a terrible thing they're planning to do, and they don't see it themselves. They don't understand the consequences, not for themselves, and not for the rest of the family. It's all up to me now.

I raise my eyes to the golden glow of the Buddha. A surge of adrenaline shoots up my spine. I'm coming to Lhasa, no matter what.

Another few morning prayers and then I'm down, drawn in by the smell of fried momos and fresh baked bread from the hall to the kitchen. With the stove roaring, the kettle steaming, and the frying pan sizzling, the kitchen's in full swing. Father has a few servants around the house, but it's clearly Sangmo who's in charge of this kitchen. She's made herself at home here, much quicker than I have.

"Good morning." Sangmo's intense brown eyes radiate that innate nomadic wildness. She's back to her old self again.

"Dendup and Karma have already left to see about a caravan to join." She pours me a cup of tea.

A twinge of disappointment pinches at my heart. He's already gone. I would have loved to see Karma, as we didn't part on good terms last night. He made it clear he didn't like me objecting to the family's decision. I left the kitchen as soon as the chang started flowing and didn't get the chance to explain myself.

"Palden, happy to see you join us for breakfast." Sangmo throws me a meaningful glance as Father steps in.

I get it—she needs me to open the conversation.

"It's good to see—and smell—a woman's touch here." Father sits himself beside me, relishing in the savory aromas surrounding the many pots on the stove. Sangmo chuckles as she hands him a fresh cup of tea. What a change for Father, having Sangmo and me around after living with Uncle and his three sons for so long.

"I can get used to this." Father slurps his tea with a smack of approval. His eyes wander to the frays of my sleeves. "We've got to get you new clothes." He tugs my scarf and pokes his finger through the hole.

"Oh, that's just a tiny rip." I inspect the wool closer. "No bother to repair."

Father frowns and shakes his head. "Don't want people to think we've fallen into hard times now, do we?" His eyebrows draw up.

I tie the loose threads together. My sisters and I, we mended our robes and scarves until the cloth got too thin to keep the cold out. In this world, it seems to be all about outer appearance—something I'll have to keep in mind.

"Maybe go up to the storeroom and see if there's any of your mother's that you like?" Father says. "For now?" His voice wavers. "We'll get you new clothes of course, but just for now." He shifts in his seat, his eyes on the food Sangmo's put in front of us.

"Sure." I smile. "We'll have a look, won't we, Sangmo?"

She offers me an enthusiast nod. Sangmo loves clothes. She decided early on that I don't have any dress sense. That was clear when we sorted through the pile of clothes at Sonam's, replacing my nuns' robes.

Sangmo frets around the stove, a cloth in her hand. I see what she's doing—our bodies deal with worry in the same way.

"I guess we need to discuss the living quarters," Father says. "The building needs some refurbishing."

Sangmo sits herself opposite me and gives me another profound glance. "Oh yes, for sure, but it's fine for now, isn't it, Nordun?" The stealthy glance, the pressing tone in her voice—she wants me to bring up me going to Lhasa and her staying with Father.

"Well, there is something else I would like to talk about." I put down my tea and turn to Father. An alertness glints in his gaze. "Since I've decided to stay here at the stables, I'm thinking about how I can keep up a good practice—as a lay practitioner."

I suck in a deep breath.

"I want to live my life for the benefit of all sentient beings. That hasn't changed. In fact, I've only become more determined—seeing all the suffering around in this short time out here."

My thoughts go to the dilapidated dwellings I spotted along the road, sheltering so many families scrambling to make a living from a measly plot of land. And the tea caravan crossing our road in the intense midday heat—the sweat pouring from the porters' faces, the steam rising from the animals' rugged frames. I've never witnessed so much misery, all to provide our daily cup of tea. The thought of my own ignorance about it makes me wince.

"Being of benefit to all, purifying past karma and gaining further merit from positive actions—it's very different as a lay person," I say, and my voice dims a bit. "It takes time for me to get accustomed to my new position, as you may call it." My fingers circle around the rim of my cup. "I feel it would be good for me to make a pilgrimage, a pilgrimage to Lhasa, the most holy of all." Another audible breath fills my lungs.

I glance at Father, immovable in the corners of my eyes. My mind sharpens. I'll have to do better if I want to convince him, I see.

"I can't just leave all these years in the monastery behind." I straighten my back. "First, I need to revalue what I know and find new ways to use this." A profound knowing fills me, radiating its warmth through my skin. "A pilgrimage would be the way forward for me."

I lift my flushed face to meet Father's eyes. I don't want to rant, for it won't work, but the words keep coming, and there's no stopping them.

"A pilgrimage will bestow me with the blessings from all those who have gone before, the sages, the learned masters. Their examples illuminate the mind and will inspire me on ways how to deepen my lay practice. At the same time, a pilgrimage will gain so much merit for all sentient beings." By now my cheeks are on fire and my eyes fever with tears.

"This is important to me, Father." A tinge of desperation surges through me as my eyes search Father's for understanding.

My knuckles wound white around the cup; I feel it in every fiber of my being—a flush of adrenaline rushes the words I just spoke through my veins. *This is important to me, Father.* It's my deepest wish to establish a strong lay practice and gain the merit for all. I didn't realize this heartfelt desire seated inside of me. I simply need to go to Lhasa—not only to prevent Karma and Dendup from committing the gravest sin. Yes, Lhasa came to mind because of the family's decision, but there's so much more to my heart's desire, so much more layers if I'm open and honest with myself.

With an enormous sigh, I fall back in my seat, Father and Sangmo staring at me.

"I'm sorry." My mind blank by now, I wipe my sweaty palm on my skirt.

"Don't be. Your grandmother raised you well." Father puts up his hand for a moment, a waiver. "Your wish is something I've never experienced myself, and something I most likely never will. I'm not an educated practitioner like you." A pleased smile nestles in the corners of his mouth. His calm gaze makes my heart leap. I underestimated Father. He understands much more of me than I ever thought he would.

"I'm proud of you, my child," he says. "But I'm also worried as the journey to Lhasa is far, and dangerous." He shakes his head and rubs his chin. "It's already late, snow can come any time, maybe soon."

My cheeks still burning, I shoot to the front of my seat.

"Yes, yes." I stumble over my words. "But Dendup and Karma are going to Lhasa now. They'll keep me safe." I catch my breath for a moment and gulp down the rest of my tea.

"I'll talk to them." Father tugs the sleeves of his chuba. The flicker of sorrow on his face hurts my heart. "It's not all up to me, you know?"

I cast down my eyes and clench my teeth. No, the family made that clear.

Father puts up his cup as Sangmo pours another round of tea. "I was looking forward to having the two of you here." He throws me a meek smile.

Time to change the subject, I guess.

"Well, now that you mention it." I turn to Sangmo, bustling around the stove again. "How about Sangmo staying here until I return?"

With a sharp turn, Sangmo jumps in. "Yes, I love to help, as I do know a thing or two about horses." Her face lights up as she plops down on the seat opposite us. "And I'm sure you can use some help you now that Uncle and his sons…" Before Sangmo can finish her sentence, Father raises his hands.

"Sangmo, it's not me you have to ask," he says. "I'm delighted to have you here, but won't your family miss you at their home?"

Sangmo's cheeks rage red as she mangles the ragged cloth in her hands.

"Uh." Her eyes avert at me with a sense of despair. "I'm with child, so I don't think my family minds." Her voice fades as she steers away from us to the stove.

Poor Sangmo. My heart goes out to her, seeing her squirm like this.

"I see." Father raises his eyebrows and takes another slow sip of tea. "And you don't think marriage should be arranged?"

"No, no marriage." Her eyes cast down, Sangmo's voice is anything but compliant. "I don't want to be a second wife." She looks away again, her jaw set.

"I see." Father's as quiet as ever. "You're more than welcome here, providing Karma agrees, of course." He nods towards the door, and my heart skips a beat. It's Karma's standing in the doorpost, his arms crossed, his legs wide.

I don't know how long he's been there, but the rigid look on his face says it all. He's not amused—and that's an understatement.

"Nothing for me to agree on, apparently." His eyes glare an icy green, his hands ball into fists. "Sangmo always does what she wants, anyway." He turns on his heels and strides off, the echo of his boots resounding in the hallway long after he's left.

I bite my lip and look at Sangmo. She shrugs, takes up her cup, and blows the fatty foam to the sides.

"Ah well." She nips at the hot tea. "The worst part is over, he'll come around." The relief in her voice matches the light shine in her auburn eyes. From her pocket, she draws a fresh peach and cleans it with the cloth.

"Let's eat," she says, and sinks her teeth into the fleshy fruit. "I'm starving." With juice dripping along the corners of her mouth, she throws me one of her big grins.

I can only frown. This girl never ceases to amaze me.

Goes to show you—I still have a lot to learn about the ways of this world.

Four

The ngakpa's house is within walking distance, but I feel like riding today.

"Hey boy, you're looking good today." The stallion trots towards me, his frame slender and strong, his neck curved with grace. As I run my fingers through his coarse mane, he lets out a big huff. "I hear you." I put the halter around his head. "Let's go for a ride."

I've only been home for two days, but I miss being out riding. The horse did too—his hooves trample a melodic rhythm as I get into the pen.

A small step up and out of the courtyard, we ride into the rolling hills. Leaping on all fours, the stallion is in the mood to boot, and since I can also use some release, we'll take a detour, conquering the steep end of the slopes. With the breeze on our back, the horse's legs soar, sending clumps of grass flying up and around our ears. In no time, we've reached the top of the hill and circle around a few times to catch our breath.

My eyes scout the horizon. There's not a single cloud to be seen. The tops of the mountain range glister a perfect crystalline against the vast blue yonder. My hands tighten around the reins. That's where I'm going—where *we* will be going. To Lhasa, Karma and me.

I catch myself smiling. He might have stormed out of the kitchen this morning, but he hasn't left my mind for a moment since. All the way to Lhasa, together.

My mind spins. *A pilgrimage.* What a grand chance to gain benefit, and a fortunate opportunity to change the family's fate. The iron fist around me cuts my breath to a shallow wheeze. I'm sure Father will convince Karma and Dendup to let me come, but how I can accomplish what I really have set my heart to do?

My eyes on the shimmering peaks, I take a sharp breath in and spur on my horse. With a joyful leap, the stallion dashes down. The fast gallop clears my mind of any doubts that might have been lingering on. For now. And that is enough.

Here it is, the first house on the left—the ngakpa's house. How different in today's light. An open gate, white smoke rising from the chimney... He's home for sure. I dismount and lead the horse through the gate. There he is at the door. His thin frame stands tall, his long black hair coils over his shoulders. I've never seen him out like this.

"How good to see you again." He gestures me to follow him in.

My hastened footsteps resonate in the hollow hall. He glides to the kitchen, his long red and white scarf beaconing the way.

"Tea first." Milky steam rises from the kettle as he pours the two cups set on the low table beside to stove. "Tea always sooths the task ahead of us—which is not an easy one this time."

With the ngakpa's eyes on me, I nod and wrap my hands around the cup. The heat penetrates my palms. My shoulders sag and I take a moment to ground myself, collecting some of my scattered thoughts.

Here I am, in the ngakpa's kitchen, ready to prepare for a journey—again. Who would have thought? Not me!

"Happy to see you're continuing your practice as a lay person." His voice is low, a nod of approval.

He knows. The heat from my teacup spreads, rising through my arms, up my neck, into my cheeks. He knows I'm going to Lhasa.

"It's your personal responsibility to take this journey of purification and merit making in this lifetime," the ngakpa says. "Good, good. It helps not only you, but benefits all sentient beings." Slowly he sips his tea, a content slurp as I struggle to swallow mine.

"Yes gen-la," I say. His gaze, so insightful—it's impossible to hide from. "Now that I've seen the suffering out here, I'm even more determined."

He tilts his head to the side. His long coils sway in a slow motion behind.

"The years in the monastery have put you in a favorable position," he says. "Now it is up to you to further your practice." He must detect the apprehension in me, for he gives me a reassuring nudge.

"Nothing has changed, for you are gifted with a compassionate heart and the sincere desire to serve all sentient beings. Your determination more than compensates for the loss of monastic discipline you so fear." Before I get the chance to think about what he's actually saying, the ngakpa jumps to his feet. "Come, come, no time to waste."

Again I follow him, this time to the prayer room. As we enter, my feet stall.

The thin red curtain is drawn. Golden beams of sunlight flood the room. Garlands of fresh greens crown the shrine, their sweet fragrance carried on the soft breeze from the open window. Bright hues of yellow, red, and green drift on the pearly swirls of incense, reflecting the rich ribbons cascading from the ceiling and sides of the shrine. The once eerie thangkas now reveal the dazzling depictions of our trustworthy companions on the Buddhist path. This space, which yesterday instilled a sense of dread in me, now welcomes me to step in.

"First we pray," the ngakpa says. "Then we see."

Seated on his cushion, he folds his hands. His eyes close and I join in prayer as the invocations to the Three Jewels, Palden Lhamo, and other Dharma protectors flow from his lips. The prayers, followed by meditation, set the stage for the divination, requesting the deities to reveal the journey ahead of us.

As the ngakpa opens his eyes again, he unwraps a set of the bone dice from their cloth. The dice roll in his open palm, their pale white shine reflecting a shimmer in his tawny face.

"When you return, you'll learn the way of Mo." His voice leaves no room for questioning. "It will be of benefit to all, helping to overcome the obstacles in this worldly existence."

My eyes widen and I blink. Did I hear that right? Did the ngakpa just say I should learn divination?

"You want to be of benefit, right?" He leans in, his voice stern. "Then learn the way of Mo, for it allows us to see what might come." His face drops as he closes his palm around the dice. "And used with the proper motivation to help others, this selfless act of giving enhances our practice on the Bodhisattva's path."

I open my mouth for an advanced practice like Mo, so out of reach for me, but the ngakpa raises his hand, the dice a muffled thud in his closed palm. Meeting my eyes, his relaxed gaze lingers to his closed palm, and then draws back to me.

"Your grandmother taught you well," he says. "Your meditation practice is firm, and you have a deep understanding of emptiness and the interconnection of all things. You will learn fast, the rituals as well." He throws the dice on the cloth between us, their clicking sounds a ringing in my ears.

My body tenses. My eyes are still on the ngakpa's palm, now empty in the space between us. Beads of sweat form a thin veil on my forehead. My mind turns over his words. A firm meditation, a deep understanding. *Me?* I'm only a beginner on the path.

"Ra Tsa." His raspy voice jolts me out of my thoughts, straight back into here and now. I lean in, my eyes on the dice, the stark lines on the gleaming bones—RA TSA. My lips form the two syllables, as the ngakpa's recitation resonates in the room.

"It will take strength, that what you wish to achieve," he says, his long fingers on both sides of the dice. "And strength will arise in you, just as a fire is increased when touched by the wind."

I'm at the edge of my seat now. The ngakpa's words stir the unnerving unease in my mind. His eyes on the dice, his hands now glide to the edge of the table. He unwraps a clothed book as his eyes turn into a dark gloom.

"All what was lost will be obtained in the West," he says with a tone of determination.

So, we will find Uncle and the spell in Lhasa. That sounds good.

"But be it by force," he adds, his voice raw and uneven.

Force. I bite my lip. Of course, Uncle will not give up the spell willingly, and I don't dare to think of my family's resolutions.

The ngakpa turn the leaves of the unbound book, nearly until the end. Following the lines with his index finger, his body sways back and forth as he reads in silence.

Still at the edge of my seat, I clench my prayer beads tight. My eyes are fixed on the ngakpa and his book. When the swaying stops, the corners of his mouth turn up ever so slightly. My heart skips a beat. It must be a promising sign.

"Good, good." His smile broadens. "As the strength of your power is increasing, nothing will harm you." He looks up. A pensive glance graces his eyes. "The protectors are guarding you, but you will need to make more offering."

A wave of relief washes over my body. Of course, I will do the offering, for no harm, that is good.

"Whatever aims you have..." The ngakpa pauses for a moment and looks up to meet my eyes. "... these will be achieved." He presses his lips tight. I cringe as the iron fist closes around my heart again.

I bow my head. *He knows.* He knows I'm going to Lhasa to try to prevent the killing the family has ordered. Will he tell them?

His eyes burn on me. I twist the string of beads in my numb fingers. Will he try to stop me? Then again, all my aims will be achieved, the divination says. That should be a relief, but at this moment my chest is about to cave in.

"You know Nordun." His voice is gentle. I glance up, my vision a blur. "It is not easy to take responsibility for the behavior of others, or for the karma they have collected." His eyes still on me, the ngakpa's fingers line up the yellowed pages. "It's only the brave that take up the responsibility to help the sentient beings that are blinded, those who cannot see."

My breath stalls. My mind grasps the meaning of his. A lightness floods my being, for these are not words of warning—these are words of approval, of encouragement. My being sighs with relief.

"It's not by violence or argument that one can change one's fate, it's only by the strength of the heart," the ngakpa says. I raise my chin to meet his eyes. "Only when our hearts keep faith in the essential goodness of the others, and act with the purest intention, only then one can govern one's destiny."

Relief settles in my being as the ngakpa's words resonate their truth in me. He's right. I won't be able to convince Dendup and Karma with words, let alone with my physical strength. The only way for me to change what's planned is to act from my truth, to act from a boundless compassion. And how to do this, I don't know yet.

My hands release the beads and roll them between my fingers at the rhythm so familiar to me. All I have are my good intentions and faith in the goodness of the others—that's enough for now.

His eyes closed, the ngakpa's in meditation again, receiving the last instructions for our preparations. The clicking of my bead settles my mind. I ease back into my seat. It only takes a few moments before the ngakpa sets his reassuring look upon me.

"Yes, it is foretold. All is favorable, and your strength will increase," he says. "The power of the Dharma Protectors is with you, as is your special meditation deity."

A smile comes to my face. That will be Green Tara, the mother who's always come to my call.

"The offerings to praise and appease are clear." His hands wrap his white scarf tight. "Let's prepare for a fortunate journey."

He sums up the list of necessary items, from special incense to shavings of precious metal, all that needs to be offered. It's a lengthy list, a lot of work, but the gratitude in my heart makes the work light and quick. All I'm thinking of is how fortunate I am—I'm going to Lhasa—so soon.

The sun has already set on the Western peaks. Her flaming red accompanies me as I walk out of the gate, ready to go home. The work here has been done. My mind turns to the stables, where Father and the family are preparing their own. I wonder how Father has convinced them to let me come. Father's good like that—without a doubt.

"Long day?"

Karma's voice jolts me out of my thoughts. His tall frame leans against the wall—he's been waiting for me. "Thought you would like some company riding home."

There's a wide-open smile in those gorgeous green eyes—his face doesn't show any signs of anger left from this morning.

"I do, especially from you." I turn on my heels, wanting to pinch myself. Did I just say that?

"Good to hear." His voice rings with cheer—he's not hiding any of his feelings for me.

A little leg-up and off we go, out of the courtyard, into the hills.

"So you're coming to Lhasa then." He throws me another one of those cheeky grins.

My heart leaps. *Yes!* Father did good.

"I am," I say. "Thank you for letting me." My eyes stay on the horizon. "Now that you and Dendup are going anyway, it's a wonderful opportunity for me to do a pilgrimage."

"Pilgrimage." Karma's voice holds a daring edge. His horse slows down the pace and pauses. "No other reason for you to come?"

My hands clutch the reins. My stomach hardens. *He knows my intention! How?* My mind blanks in the frantic search for answers.

"Nothing to do with me then?" he says.

I glance at him from the corners of my eyes, making sure not to face him. Is that a grin? Yes, it is! He's teasing me, hinting at something very different—and I thought the worst, as usual.

"Ah well." I lean back in the saddle, trying to look casual as my heart beats loud in my chest. "That too." And I'm not lying, for this journey is more about Karma than he—or I—will ever know.

"Good." He slows down his horse even more and leans towards me. "I was hoping so since I came here for you, Nordun."

The emerald of his eyes draws me in. My heart surges. *That man!*

"I came to be with you, but the family's decision has to be respected." His lips pressed together, his stare sets in the distance. "Lhasa is a long way, but know I'll return to you, for sure."

His words seize me with an unknown longing. Oh, how I wish to be close to him right now.

"I know," I say. "But this pilgrimage is important to me." I halt my horse.

"I understand." He turns his horse beside me. "That dogged determination of yours, how I love it." He laughs and stretches out his hand. "Well, it's one of the many things I love about you."

I let his hand cover mine—strong, safe, warm.

"Just a few weeks ago, you could barely hold yourself on the back of a tame mare." He squeezes my fingers. "And look at you now."

My hand drops to my side as he stirs his horse to back away from mine.

"Come on." His teeth bare into a grin. "I'll dare you to a race!"

An enormous roar of laughter fills the air as he spurs on his stallion.

Dashing off at full speed, I don't hesitate for a moment and follow in pursuit.

It's a futile attempt, as he's so much faster, but it doesn't bother me at all.

I know he'll be waiting, as patient as ever for me to get there.

He'll be waiting at the stables—for me.

Five

Karma beat me, but I'm not too far behind. He's just dismounted his horse as mine scurries into the courtyard.

"You're getting better by the day," he says, an appreciative smile on his face. "Once you've been to Lhasa and back, who knows, you might even be able to keep up with me."

I catch my breath and pass up the opportunity to react. Swiftly, I slide off my horse.

"Loser takes care of the horses." He hands me the reins of his horse and gestures to the back of the house. "Looks like you're going that way, anyway."

Over his shoulder I see Father. He's waiting for me at the pen.

"Yep," I say and try to hide the feverish excitement of our encounter with a casual nod. Racing home in Karma's trail, it hit me—he rode out to meet me at the ngakpa's, ensuring me again that he came here for me, only me. "See you at the house."

My knees wobble, yet there's a spring in my step as I stride to the pen, a horse on either side. How I wish I weren't still so awkward around Karma.

Father's at the entrance of the pen, facing the last of the warm afternoon sun. He's looking so much stronger, and at the same time lighter, with bright eyes and a healthy tan. Yes, it was the grief of losing Mother that weighed Father down, but I can't help but wonder what part Uncle played in Father's despair as well. I shudder as my mind turns to Uncle and his sinister influence.

What this dark magic can do. And the ngakpa wants me to learn these rituals?

I take a deep breath in. I don't think so!

"All preparations done?" Father says. The gate swings open. The horses bolt in.

"Yes." I sling the halters over my shoulder. "All is done." Checking the latch twice, I secure the gate and throw my arms over the beams to admire the horses frolicking in the pen.

"I'm sure the ngakpa gave you excellent advice." Father glances at me. "Lhasa's a long journey."

My ribs tighten. Father's voice sounds calm, but his eyes breed a restlessness. I catch myself deliberating whether Father knows about my intention to go against the family's decision or if he's just worried about my safety. My temples throb. I'm not used to hiding my true intentions. It's costing me my peace of mind, hollowing me from the inside out.

I lean further in over the beam. Yes, Father's always been good at assessing people, especially me. He could always tell when I had snuck out as a little girl. I used to visit my little pony in his stables at night—it would have been impossible for him to have seen me climb from my bedroom window.

A smile breaks on my lips as I think of all those times. As well, it could have been the dried grass eternally stuck in my unruly hair or the dried smudges from my pony's nose on my cheeks that gave it away. With those awry thoughts, I shrug away my doubts and turn to Father.

"He did." I swallow, the last bit of unease stuck in my throat. "The ngakpa's divination was favorable, and we did all that was asked for." I frown as my finger catches a splinter from the rough beam I'm clinching.

Father nods and turns his gaze over to the pen. The group of fierce young stallions releases their energy left after a day of training.

"The horses are in great shape," Father says. "With one exception." He lets out a big laugh as my little pony, staunch and stocky, scampers along with the cavorting stallions. His bristly manes sway as the mischief makes his way over to us. He's always looking for a sweet treat and a firm scratch behind his ears.

"Time to put him in the barn," Father says. "He'll cause trouble if I leave him out here at night." With his round belly and a shiny coat on the pony, it's clear Father's taken good care of my childhood friend. "He's forever on the hunt for something to eat or somebody to annoy." Father opens the pen and I take the pony by his manes while sneaking him the little tsampa ball left in my pocket.

"Did you know he used to escape after you were gone?" Father says. "I had to get him from the village many times, eating everybody out of home and hearth." The rascal hops at Father's friendly slap as we make our way to the barn.

"Tennah suggested keeping the pony in. It calmed him down but never tamed his wild nature," Father says as he opens the barndoor. "This little scoundrel knows very well when to keep quiet, but his true colors, his tireless curiosity, shows whenever the chance."

We both laugh as his tiny hoofs trip into the shed, sweeping up the loose hay with a somewhat indignant huff.

"Just like you, my child." Father closes the door behind him. "I tried to keep you away from horses, but here you are." He leans back, and the barndoor creaks under his broad frame. "And the way you just came riding in on that stallion, you're a natural and it shows." He squeezes my shoulder. The pleasing gleam in his eyes warms my heart.

"Still, Karma beat me." I shake my head. Father's right, my true colors are showing as I played myself down just now. I always do.

"Karma's been in the saddle his whole life." Father stretches upright. "His life revolves around horses and riding—he's a wanderer, you know." His eyes narrow. "Karma's always on the road. He can't seem to settle down, no marriage, no children as far as I know of." He pauses. I shift my weight from left to right, my hands dangling along.

"But he takes good care of the family business, and he'll take good care of you." He rubs his chin. "That's most important to me."

I take in his words with care and wonder. *A wanderer.* What does Father mean to say?

"Thank you for letting me go to Lhasa, Father." I bow my head. He's made a tough decision and I'm most grateful for it.

"Be honest now, could I have kept you?" He chuckles and starts walking towards the house. "The three of you will go to Kandze tomorrow and join a caravan there. Dendup's arranged it."

Kandze, tomorrow. A surge of adrenaline rushes the late afternoon slump out of my body. It's real, I'm going to Lhasa—with Karma.

"Did they mind?" I say. They must have.

"They didn't." Father says. He stops and turns.

No? I stumble. A blush spreads all the way to my neck as I meet Father's amusing gaze. lips.

"It took little to convince them," he says. "I guess that's Karma's doing."

I flinch, my eyes to the ground. Of course, Father knows about Karma and me. What did I expect? Father's not blind. I tug the sleeves of my shirt. Everybody must know by now. It's me who still hasn't gotten my head around my attraction to Karma. It's me who's still in denial, not knowing what do to with it all.

"I've known Karma to be a good man, a responsible man," Father says. "That's why he got upset with Sangmo." My cheeks still burning, I glance up. "But he's more angry with the man whose child she's carrying." Father sighs and shakes his head. "Not taking responsibility, Karma would never do that. He's a man of his word."

My body relaxes at Father's praise for Karma. Father's always been an excellent judge of character. If he talks about Karma in this way, how can my attraction to Karma be wrong?

"I asked him to make amends with Sangmo," he says. The last light of the day softens the lines on his face, matching the mellow tone in his voice. "Lhasa's a long way and with Sangmo pregnant—anything can happen." His eyes gaze in the distance, a melancholic dark amber drowning in a silken tangerine sky.

My heart goes out to Father. The passage of time has not lessened the weight of his grief, it has just taught him how to carry it better.

"Karma and you." Father turns to me. "The two of you are very different, yet you seem to be quite a match."

The blush spreads again.

"I think so." I meet Father's eye. "But so much has changed for me. I'm not sure of anything these days." The blessing cord is a smooth touch under my fingertips as the memory of Karma's hand enveloping mine lingers in my mind. "I need time. Can't make a decision like that."

My mouth dry, I bite the bottom of my lip. I want to be honest with Father. There have already been too many things between us left unsaid for far too long. At the same time, it's difficult facing my own inner turmoil. I'm allowing my emotions to control me, giving them the upper hand. So much for a trained mind, Dechen would say.

"I see." His voice quiet, Father puts weight on every word. "When I met your mother, I had every reason not to marry her. She was so young, engaged to my best friend." He leans in. "Still, my heart knew this girl was my true love and there was no way I could talk myself out of it." An endearing, almost apologizing smile graces his face as his hands rest on my shoulders. "Be willing to trust your heart when you feel moved, my child, for it is only the heart that knows true love."

As his words resound in my ears, my mind wanders to that first night at the camp, when I first encountered Karma coming out of the shadows. The flutter in my stomach as those emerald eyes captured me, the tingling shooting up my arm as our hands touched. A sudden chill runs a shiver down my spine. I pull my scarf close. Coming from a place inside of me I never knew before, there was—and still is—something so feral about my feelings for Karma. It scares me, it really does.

"But remember." Father's voice is gentle, but his hands squeeze my forearms just enough to give him my undivided attention. "Karma's loyalty lies with his family duties—no matter what."

No matter what.

"Sure." I understand what Father's telling me. Karma's bound and blinded by family loyalty. He can't see it. Every muscle in my body tightens at the thought of Karma's fate. Lhasa is a good idea.

"Now, get yourself some clean clothes before tomorrow." Father points at the frayed ends of my sleeves. "You better prepare, as prayer's good, but it will not keep you warm."

He laughs as I grimace, a quasi-surprised expression on my face.

My head is light, my mind at ease—how good it feels to have Father back again.

"Will do," I say, and stride off to the quarters that are now my own.

There's no fire lit yet. Sangmo must have dozed off. With the sky turning a dusty purple, there's just enough light left to notice her puffy eyes as I enter the room.

"Want to get some new clothes?" I bounce beside her on the bed. She shoots up, her eyes wide.

"Am I already showing?" Her hands clasp her stomach.

"No, silly." I chuckle. "Clothes for me on the road. I'm leaving for Kandze tomorrow. I'm sure I can buy some there, but I can't arrive looking like this." I spread my arms, the threads dangle from my sleeves.

"Where?" Sparkles light up Sangmo's eyes. The thought of clothes and pretty things always perks her up.

"The storeroom." I gesture to the back. "Father's kept some of my mother's."

Sangmo sucks in her cheeks. "You're fine with that?"

"Why not?" I shrug. "It's just clothes, and it would be a pity to let them go unused."

And with that, I leap off the bed. I know where Father keeps the clothes. He tried to hide them from me after Mother's passing. Told me he had passed them on to less fortunate people around. But I know Father's far too attached to Mother's possessions to ever give them away. Mother had an immense wardrobe and by the number of bags Sangmo and I encounter in the storeroom, I guess Father kept all of it.

"Oh my." Sangmo sifts through the clothes. "Your mother had great taste ."

A pile of colorful, bright fabrics dazzles in front of me. Yes, Mother had great taste. Sifting through, my hands stroke the soft fur trimmings, the rich embroidered brocades, the delicate woven silks, and the intricate knitted wools. My thoughts drift back to my days with Mother. Short days as I was so young, yet happy days as her smile left me.

"You and Karma," I say. "You're good?" I raise my eyebrows at Sangmo and hold a turquoise chuba that would suit her, especially with her skin tone.

"I guess," Sangmo says and shrugs. "He's letting me stay here until you're all back. After that, he'll marry me off." Her shoulders hunch as she turns away, pretending to inspect the lining of the turquoise gown.

"I'm so sorry." The slick brocade slides through my hands. With their parents gone, Karma's the one who decides over Sangmo. He can do as he pleases.

"I don't want marriage," Sangmo says. "And certainly not as a second wife."

Her words pierce tiny holes in the gauzy air that has overtaken the storeroom. Her lips pinch into a thin white line. She spins, and the dress crumples in her hands. As she raises her chin, her eyes flash the darkest shade of burnished brown.

"Marriage. You've seen what it's like cooked up all day with a bunch of children." She throws her hands in the air. A cloud of turquoise silk floats midway. "Don't get me wrong, I love children—and I'm sure I'll love this one when I survive." She puts her hands on her belly and my mind blanks for a moment at the thought of her passing.

"Don't!" I grasp. "Don't even think about it."

She shrugs and blinks. A teardrop, ever so small, escapes from her brooding dark gaze.

"I need my freedom, sister." Sangmo sounds hoarse now. "More than anything." She tosses her head in her neck and stretches her arms.

"This place, with the horses, the mountains, the vast blue sky, this place is perfect." Her body stiffens, her arms drop to her side. "This is all I want, but I guess it's not my karma." With a silent sob, she runs her hands through the pile of clothes.

"You're so lucky," she says. "Palden lets you decide for yourself while Karma..." She opens her mouth, but then stops short. Her eyes dart over the pile. "Karma's the best brother, but he's too protective." A purple gown, silky and sleek, catches her attention.

"He's always on the road, family business he says, but in reality, he does whatever he wants." She holds a purple dress up to me, her face pinched. "It's not fair."

"It's not." I take the robe off her hands and put it on the pile. Far too flimsy for the road. "But it's whatever the family decides, right?"

A bitter taste comes to my mouth. It's not fair for women to have no say in their destinies, like it's not fair for Father to have no say in our own brother's fate. *The family has decided.* I'm trying hard to steer my mind away from harboring rancorous thoughts as Sangmo interrupts my futile attempt.

"He's fond of you, you know." Her hands rush through the pile, her face flushes.

"What?" That look she gives me, that glassy stare. She's up to something.

"Karma—you can convince him not to marry me off." She picks up the mauve robe again and hops from one foot to the other. "You're smart, you can!" A big smirk comes over her face. "Lhasa's a long way, you'll have enough time to convince Karma not to marry me off." Her hands hold up the same purple dress. I shake my head.

"Lhasa's a long way." I scoop the thin dress out of her hands again. "And a cold way, so help me and pick something warm and decent, please." My voice is half-pleading as my hands churn through the pile.

"Only if you try to change Karma's mind." Her hands grip mine—strong, decisive.

"I promise, I'll try." I give her hands a firm squeeze. "I sure will."

A small pang of unease stretches across my heart as I'm hiding my truth again.

If only Sangmo knew my plans to change Karma's mind—and so much more.

Six

The chuba we settled on late night yesterday fits perfect. Woven from the softest yak khullu and lined with sleek fur, this long coat will keep me warm on the long, arduous journey ahead.

"Now that's some color," Sangmo said when I pulled the coat from the pile—and it is. Like the bright blue poppies dotting the high slopes in late spring and early summer, the coat is the richest hue of blue, instead of the everyday black.

As my hand runs across the fine down, my mind wanders to those early summer days when I used to pick poppies with Choezem, our amchi from the monastery. A tinge of melancholy tugs at the soft corners of my heart. Get those bright ones, she used to say, for the brighter the color, the more potent the medicine. And of course, those bright ones always hid themselves on the most remote patches of our mountain.

With Sangmo finishing the braids in my hair, and me staring at the last of my tea, I'm almost done. My bags are packed—warm clothes, a prayer book, and a few other personal things. The men will take care of the rest.

Now that I peer at my small bags, a last moment of panic strikes. I wonder if it's sufficient—I have no idea what I'm supposed to bring. I've seen my sisters pack for pilgrimage, taking not more than a blanket, a prayer book, a day's provision, and the trust that the rest would be provided for them as pilgrims on the road. So confident in their ways, so steady in their faith. *It's our state of mind that's most important*, my grandmother always reminded my sisters upon leaving. *No need to pay so much heed to our bodies, they're only temporary vessels.* And with that, they always returned—well, except for one or two.

"You're all set now." Sangmo clicks her tongue and runs her hands over my tight braids. "This will last you for weeks." Yes, I'm all set, except for that restless feeling in my stomach. Prayers done. What more to do?

"I'll get your horse," Sangmo says. "You finish your tea. It will be the last good cup before the road." She throws me a wink and scoots out of the kitchen.

My own horse. I'll be taking the stallion I got from the Four Sisters Mountain, the one that proved me to be the rightful heir to these stables. My teeth grind the briny residue of tea in my mouth while my mind's trying to ease the jitters in my body.

"You're ready." His voice subdued; Father stands in the doorway, shoulders low. His hands hide in his pockets.

I shake my head and get up.

"I'm not sure if I'll ever be." I throw a faint smile his way.

His gaze lights up as it catches the blue coat. He takes a step forward. "You're so much like her. She always told me you took after me, especially with the mischief you were up to, but look at you now." His hands straighten the black fur along my collar with a comforting stroke.

"I got this coat for her in Chengdu, just before you were born." The dark in his eyes thaws into a wistful amber. "It was one of her favorites." He fumbles with the edges of the fur. His gaze drifts off into what must be bittersweet memories, but he quickly regains himself.

"Your company's waiting." His hands drop to his sides.

For a moment I hold my breath, but then I give in. I smother my awkwardness with the overwhelming surge of love in me and throw my arms around Father.

"Thank you," I say, and I mean it. Going to Lhasa, it's not something many fathers would allow their daughters to do, even if it is for pilgrimage. My face presses against the prickly wool of his chuba. His arms hold me in a tight lock.

"You'll be fine." He pulls the fur line hood over my head. "More than fine." His eyes gleam with a proud glow of a light amber now, the recognition I've always been longing for. "It's still cold out."

I nod. The rim of the hood throws a shadow over my hazy eyes. *Good.*

Silence accompanies us out of the courtyard. The mist muffles the rhythmic thuds of our horses' hooves. Dendup and Karma ride in front, trailing two packed horses each behind them. Seems like there's also trade planned on our trip.

My stallion follows with an eager prance, not used to being at the tail end. It takes all of me to keep him in reign as we boot up the hill towards the village. The ngakpa's standing at the gate and we ride in. The weisang is lit. We dismount for our blessing. A column of white smoke curls straight up, despite the stiff wind. It's a fortunate sign, just what I needed—it clears the last of the unease out from my body and mind.

As we're about to leave, the ngakpa ties a ribbon to the halter of my horse. He gestures me to come nearer and I bend over the neck of my horse. The ribbon flashes a bright blue between us. His gaze pierces into mine.

"Remember Nordun," the ngakpa says, his voice raspy in the billowing breeze. "It's only by the strength of the heart that one can change one's fate." He folds his hands and I bow my head. An extra blessing for the road.

With the ngakpa's words in my ears, I lead my horse out of the gate and follow Dendup and Karma over the mist covered hills.

I spur on my horse. A twinge of anxiety settles in the pit of my stomach. Somehow the ngakpa's words have stirred the pound of my restless mind again. With a deep breath in, I set my eyes on the road ahead and banish all doubt from my vision. No use letting my thoughts wander ahead, as I can't know what's coming. All I can do is to be right here, right now. And as my body gets attuned with the rise and fall on my stallion's back, my thoughts settle in sync with my prayer. *Om mani padme hung.*

Karma and Dendup are skilled riders. Their horses blaze their trail with ease as we move from the soft, open grasslands into the rocky terrain down the lower valley. They're no match for me. I've only started riding again a few weeks back, but they're taking good care of me. They've set a bone-rattling pace, but make sure my horse keeps the right trail down along the crossing streams. I also suspect we stop more frequently because of me, letting the horses replenish in the creeks, and resting in the shade of the hemming shrubs ourselves. Traveling this way, protected and secure, leaves me the opportunity to observe and open my eyes and heart for whatever comes my way.

And that is quite a lot. Traveling to the Four Sister Mountains, trying to avoid my uncle's revenge, I had to steer away from the main road, taking mostly the hidden pathways and secluded mountain trails. Still, encountering the caravan with its beasts of burden and seeing the dilapidated dwellings housing many families trying to scrape a living off a tiny piece of land firsthand was such a humbling experience. The entire journey left me with a profound sense of gratitude for my own fortunate position.

Now, traveling the main road, passing the many villages, the suffering of so many becomes even more apparent to me. It hits me hard. Elderly scuffling down the sides of the road, clothed in nothing more but rags, mothers bend over with babies on their breast and a fully loaded basket on their back, animals sagging through their hooves by the strain of excess overload, all trying to make a living, all trying to get through the day. As my mind registers the reality in front of me, my stomach knots. Traveling along, not knowing what to do. For a moment, I feel gutted, and totally useless.

Of course, I've seen suffering before. My sisters and I prayed for the sick and the death on request, visiting the many houses of the rich and the poor. Somehow, those encounters didn't hit me as hard. They were always brief moments in time, and in those moments, I felt of value, being able to do the requested prayers for the sick and the passing. Traveling through it, I'm part of it and I can't turn away. The suffering is all around.

My mouth dry, my mind feverish—I can't lighten the load for them in this samsara. Over ten years of study in the monastery taught me well not to fool myself. Our physical bodies, our families, our loved ones, our whole life here, it's fragile and ever changing. All I can do is pay attention, see clearly at this very moment, and act out of love on behalf of all beings.

With this realization I focus on the one thing I can offer and let my lips form the words over and over again—Om mani padme hung—may all being be free of suffering.

Seven

"We'll stop here for the night." Dendup points to the homestead, a little up on our left-hand side.

Good. The shadows are already lengthening—darkness is not far away. I pet my horse on his neck. He shows no signs of fatigue, but I can feel the tiredness seeping into my own bones. It's been a long day in the saddle, with many still to go.

"You're doing good, sister," Dendup says as we saddle off in the small courtyard. "Just let those reigns lose a bit." He clasps my hands and inspects the grooves in my red rubbed palms. "They're going to be sore." He clicks his tongue. "No need to hold on so tight. Trust yourself." He shakes his head.

Feeling a blush coming up, I quickly step back and clutch my hands to the side.

"And if you fall, one of us will pick you up." Dendup's grimace melts into an infectious smile, and I can't help but laugh along with him.

"Thank you," I say. "That's a real comfort."

Dendup's smile grows even wider as he gets on with the bags. What a pleasant man he turns out to be. Although aloof at first, he's been putting me at ease all day with his jokes and funny remarks.

"He's right, you know." Karma's hand rests on my shoulder. "You're a good enough rider." He turns to take the bags of my horse, but I'm ahead of him.

"No, please." My arms are around the bags. "I'm a burden enough on the two of you. I'll take care of my horse." With a big swing, I pull the bags off the horse's back, but their weight catches me by surprise. *This is not the load I packed!* My heels dig in the sand. I stumble back, but Karma's arms are quick to catch the bags and me before we hit the ground.

"You're not a burden, sister." Dendup leans across the back of my horse. "You're family." He cocks his head to the side and glances at Karma. "And so much more to some of us." With a quick wink, he saddles off his horse.

I cringe, the blush on my cheeks spreading down my neck.

"No use denying that." Karma's face is so close now, the loose strands of his hair brush my burning cheeks. My knees weak, my thoughts run all over the place. No, there's no use denying any of it. How I would love to lean back in those arms again.

Stop it. I turn away and wrestle myself from Karma's tight grip while desperately avoiding his emerald eyes.

"You're welcome," he says with that teasing tone of his.

Oh my, when will I ever get to be myself around him? Then again, who am I anyway as I've never been around a man? With a dry thud, my bags hit the floor.

The inn's packed, but it seems it was expected. Huge soup cauldrons on the stove spit out a healthy steam. Servants fly on their feet to feed the hungry guests. Dendup's already secured a pleasant spot for us. It doesn't take long before we're served with gigantic bowls of thukpa. The heap of flatbread to match is gone within the wink of an eye. We munch the food away, silent and fast. While the warm brew releases the tiredness in my bone, I lean back, my body nourished, my mind at ease.

"Sister, listen." Dendup puts down his second bowl of thukpa and draws close. "I know this is not your first time on the road, but the coming months will not be anything you ever experienced." He wipes his mouth with the back of his sleeve and sighs. "A pilgrimage... Your intentions are noble, but we'll encounter plenty of people who have something very different in mind."

In an instant, my stomach knots, squishing a sour brew against the back of my throat. *A pilgrimage, noble intentions.* I lower my eyes. If only they knew my actual intentions.

"Especially with a beautiful young woman like you," Dendup adds. Karma gives him a sharp stare. "Well, she is," Dendup says and shrugs. "And somebody's got to make her aware of it, and the dangers it brings on the road."

A blush creeps up again. Young, yes. Beautiful? I've never thought about myself like that.

"Promise you'll stay close to us. Don't get out of our sight." Dendup leans in even closer. He's the eldest. I can't be disrespectful. I meet his eye and clear my throat. Traces of sour acid sting the back of it. "Kandze's busy. We've got a lot to do." Dendup's hand waves at Karma. "And to be honest, we're not used to traveling with a woman, so you've got to stay close to us." Dendup straightens his back. "And do as we tell you."

I nod and glance at Karma. *Do as we tell you.* Where did I hear that before? My thoughts run over to the inn at the Four Sisters Mountain. Right. Karma telling me to stay back while he distracted my cousins—and himself—with drink, gamble, and women.

A slight smile comes to my mind. I have to admit; he took good care of me.

"Honestly, Nordun, we want to keep you safe with us," Karma says, while Dendup catches the eyes of the servant for another bowl of soup. "And if you're anything like the rest of the women in our family..."

Karma doesn't finish his sentence. He and Dendup burst out laughing, with me joining them an instant later. Sangmo already told me about some of the strong-headed women on my grandfather's side of the family, putting their foot down and going against the family's decisions in the camp. I can only imagine what they must think of me. Heading into the mountains, catching a wild horse, and claiming my stake at the stables. Although Karma should know me better by now. I pull up my sleeves. The warm brew has done its work on my weary body.

"I promise," I say. "I'll listen and follow you." And I mean it. They know best.

"Good, that's settled then." Dendup leans back and surveys the room. "Let's get some decent mats." It's not much later that I'm under my blanket, stuck between the slumbering yet watchful bodies of Karma and Dendup. With prayer on my mind, I drift off in a dreamless sleep as soon as my head hits the mat.

The next day, the three of us slide into a steady routine. Karma leads the way, my stallion frolics behind, and Dendup and the packed horses close the row. And so we ride for another day and a half at a fast pace towards Kandze. My body light, my mind at peace, I actually enjoy the ride and the company. Somehow, the little talk Dendup gave me on our first night cleared a lot of my initial unease about traveling with the two of them. Focusing my mind on prayer, something that comes so natural to me, makes the ride even more pleasant. I'm doing good—for the benefit of all.

As the shadows lengthen over the snow-capped peaks of the majestic Gongga Shan range, we ride into the wide valley with its green hills and rocky ridges. The rough Rongcha river frothing and crashing on the left of us leads us into Kandze. We're not the only ones arriving as we join the steady stream of traders, travelers, and pilgrims alike into the lively market town. Dendup gestures for me to ride between him and Karma, an order I'm more than happy to follow through, as it's getting crowded.

I raise myself on my horse, craning my neck. On the street in front of me, people are pushing themselves in front of the stalls lined up along the road. They seem to sell everything from fresh vegetables to colorful clothing. Further ahead, a herd of yaks and mules kick up a cloud of dust.

"Right here," Dendup steers our horses to the side. "We're avoiding the middle, staying with friends of ours tonight." He leads us into a small homestead, just off the main road, where a servant awaits us in the courtyard.

"Nice one." A young fellow takes the halter off my horse.

"Thank you, but I insist," I say. I'm taking care of my horse, as skillful riders do. No matter how tired, how weary I might be, my horse comes first. Karma's fingers squeeze my shoulder with approval.

"Come, let me show you." He slides his hands along my stallion's legs. "Sharp pebbles can leave the tiniest of cuts, growing into nasty infections on the road." His thumbs pry the horse's knees and back.

I nod. I get it and take extra care under Karma's watchful eye.

Though the sun's already set, this town's buzzing energy keeps my spirits up. After tea and a copious meal, Dendup and Karma head out to check our departure tomorrow. After some humming and hawing, they let me come along. The market's still packed as if the day's not nearly at an end. Foreign faces everywhere, strange words fill my ears while Dendup and Karma go about their business with men looking dark and broody. Karma changes tongues with no hesitation.

"Oh, he's always got a knack for that," Dendup says as I ask him about the foreigners' language. "That's the only reason I tolerate him with me on the road." He ducks as Karma's hand slaps his back.

The two of them laugh along as we push our way further to the main junction where Dendup is meeting a friend.

"Can you teach me?" I turn to Karma as we wait for Dendup to finish.

"The foreigners' tongue?" Karma frowns. "Sure, all you have to do is listen and look. Language is so much more than just words." His hands warm, he tucks a strand of loose hair behind my ears. "But try to see with eyes that have never seen before."

He catches my gaze, drawing me in with those emerald eyes of his. "View with eyes that know nothing, with eyes that are new, because what might look familiar to you might be something completely different." He scouts around and points at two moody strangers standing away from us. Their voices are harsh, their hands cut the space in sharp gestures between them. It looks like they're ready to break into a fight. "Now, if you didn't know better, you would bet your life they're in an argument, right?"

I nod—it certainly looks like it.

"What if I told you they're sharing a glorious memory together, recalling a tale long ago from their homeland?" Karma squeezes my hand as I study closer to the two standing there. "And it involves a beautiful, but oh-so-nosy woman from a faraway land."

He keeps a straight face as I turn in surprise. "What?"

But the teasing gleam in his deep green gaze says enough. He's leading me on.

"Karma!" Eyes wide, I swat my hand in the air.

"Yes, well," he says. "That last bit I made up, but the first bit, I swear, it's all true."

I shake my head and take him in. *This man!* I'm not sure what to believe here.

"You know very well things are not always what they seem," he says. "You've studied the Buddhist philosophy and understand our obscurations." A gentle but serious shadow crosses his face.

"I do," I say, for I've studied the many obscurations in class. Greed, ignorance, and hatred—they all cloud our mind. They prevent us from seeing clearly and lead us to do foolish, even harmful, and destructive actions.

"It's like that." Karma's voice carries a soft yet thoughtful edge as his arm slides around my waist. "Just try to suspend all your judgement on this journey. Let go of all that you think you know and come with a new, a fresh look on this road." He pulls me closer. "Then you'll see and understand what you were looking for—and the foreign language too."

Eight

I stand back while keeping my eyes and ears on the two temperamental foreigners. They're trailing off, still deep into their heated conversation. *Interesting.*

Dendup calls Karma over. I'm left to stand on the side—what do I know about these affairs? My fingers slide the jade beads across as my eyes trawl around. *Om mani padme hung.* The traders are packing up their stalls in the dusky pink sky. Last-moment buyers are hassling them to get the best deals at the end of the day. *Om mani padme hung.* A lost yak feasts on scraps left by the side of the road. A pair of red robes skirts along, disappearing into the narrow alley next to me. My eyes pick them up as my heart weights down with a tinge of regret. These women used to be sisters. I step back to catch some more of their sight, but they've moved into a small temple hidden down the alley. My heart skips a beat. *A temple.* That's what I need.

My hand pulls Karma's sleeve. "I'm going to the temple for a moment." He's in conversation, but I get his attention. His eyes dart over to the alley and back to me. He nods.

"Dendup." I catch Dendup's eye and point at the alley. "I'm waiting in the temple." His hand signals back, and I am off.

The flame of a big butter lamp flares as I close the door behind me. I blink, my eyes adjusting to the dark. Shreds of white smoke curl in the sparkle of the golden buddha. With the faint echo of the bustling town behind me, I lower myself and slide full length on the rough wooden planks, three times.

A peaceful warmth fills by body as I surrender to the Three Jewels. Slowly I circumambulate the Buddha statue, my feet in sync with the clicking of my beads. My lips form the prayer—-*Om mani padme hung*—but my mind's with my sisters on the mountaintop. It feels like a lifetime ago, and in a way, it is.

As I sit in prayer, a lone pilgrim strolls in. He prostrates, makes an offering of tsampa, circumambulates the Buddha statue, and goes again. I stay to myself in the corner, at peace with the here and now. The memories of my sisters fade as prayer fills my being. With a few more pilgrims coming and going, I've lost track of time. It must be almost dark. A few more prostrations to finish. Another pilgrim rushes in, slamming the door in my shoulder as I'm about to leave.

"Sorry." I hop aside. The man positions himself in the doorway, his hood drawn over his face. I skirt aside and slip under his arm into the alley.

"In a hurry?" A grubby hand slams me against the wall. Another slides under my coat. Fear strikes me as his sour breath hits my nostrils. *Chang.* He's drunk. My fists clench, every muscle in my body tenses to push him away. He's too strong. The rough wool of his overcoat grazes the edge of my jaw. *I'm trapped!* Cold sweat breaks on my forehead. My heart beats so fast it hurts my chest. I gulp a big breath and open my mouth to scream, but nothing comes out. His body heavy upon me, my lungs collapse, and my heads starts to spin.

"Get away from her, you fool!" A sharp voice in a heavy accent slices through the air.

"Or what?" The man turns, his one hand still under my coat, the other now loose on my shoulder.

I push. My bones crush under his weight, but he's not budging. Panic has overtaken my body, and I wrestle to keep my mind from imagining the worst-case scenario.

Crack! The sound of a whip crashes through the alley. A high-pitched yelp follows. In an instant, the dead weight slides to the side, taking me with it. My head smashes against the wall as my legs fail me. I go down, scraping the white plaster of the wall with me. Sharp gravel lodges into the palm of my hands as I push the squirming man with all I have. He rolls beside me. I heave, grasping for fresh air.

"Better watch it, sister." A tall shadow speaks, and a long whip coils from under a wide-sleeved coat. "Don't want to get yourself in a position like that, most unpleasant."

I glance up. It's a woman. Not as tall as her shadow, but absolutely statuesque. My whole body shakes as I stare at the woman hovering above me. Knee-high boots under a sleek coat, she bares her white teeth into a grin and rolls the whip back under her coat. I recoil. Was that a knife flashing underneath? She moves closer, her hands on her hips.

"You shouldn't be running around in the dark, not here."

The dim of the moon reveals her perfectly round face as she tips her head to the side.

My arms around me, I steady myself as the drunk beside me scampers off in the dark. The woman extends her arm. A slender, yet firm hand pulls me up. My legs shake and my mind has blanked. I keep staring at her.

"Nordun!" A harsh voice snaps me out of my daze. It's Karma, rushing into the alley. He stops in his tracks as he faces the woman beside me. For a moment, the two stare at each other, their bodies stock-still in front of me. I hold my breath. What is this?

"Well, well," the woman snaps. Her heels take a sharp turn. "If that isn't Karma." Her feet plant wide apart and her eyes flash a bright blue in motion. "Heard you were around, alright."

The haze in my mind evaporates. My eyes go from Karma to the woman and back. She knows Karma. Who is this woman?

His eyes still on her, Karma steps forward.

"Lanying." His voice steady, his eyes dart over to me, then back to her.

Lanying.

A sudden rush of blood shoots to my head, my temples throb. So, Karma knows her too. My mind's at full speed, trying to make sense of this all.

He turns to me. His jaw set, his gaze bounces back and forth. "You're good?"

"Oh, I see." With obvious hint of disdain in her voice, the woman raises her chin. "You've found yourself a new one, then." She snorts and pauses for him to react.

He doesn't. He stands there, unmovable, his face a pale white.

I'm nailed to the ground, my head exploding by now. *A new one?* What is going on here?

Then she takes a step back and lashes out at him. "Isn't she a bit too young, a bit too green to your taste?"

As my jaw drops, Karma's face flashes a bright red.

His eyes spitting fire, he bites back at her, but now in the foreign tongue.

What follows is a heated conversation in a language I don't understand, but I'm sure contains some nasty comments. Karma's voice carries a low and vicious tone, while Lanying's voice echoes a shrill shriek through the alley. The outrage on their faces, the fury in their gestures, it makes me want to run and hide—but where to?

"Pah!" Lanying's spit splatters right at Karma's feet. She takes one last look at me and storms off, leaving Karma and me in an awkward silence behind.

My mouth opens, but it's in vain. Karma's hand clamps tight around the back of my arm. He steers me out of the alley. Not a word is said between us as he marches me back to our guesthouse.

Not a word is said that evening; I made sure of that, for I went straight to bed.

Nine

They must have been lovers. That's the first thing that hits my mind as I wake to the hustle and bustle of goods loaded into the courtyard. I've been tossing and turning all night.

I could pretend that the busyness around the house kept me from a sound sleep, but I'd be fooling myself. It was my own ridiculous thoughts, my own disturbing emotions around Karma and the woman, and what happened between them in that alley last night.

I can't believe he acted like that. First fighting in front of me with the woman who actually saved me—who knows what would have happened if she hadn't been around? Then refusing to hear me out and parading me to the guesthouse like I was some disobedient little girl. No way I was having any of it. I went straight to bed, never mind missing my dinner.

The woolen blanket itches my nose as I throw myself on my back, my eyes at the ceiling. Who does he think he is?

They must have been lovers, and he's angry I found out. My mind's pushing on. Sure, he wants to keep me safe, but he's not angry I was at the temple. I told him I would be. He's angry I found out about Lanying.

My mind races back to the alley. Lanying—the way she looked at him, so full of contempt. The way she spoke to him, so furious, yet so passionate. And then Karma biting back at her, so livid. That's not the way people act when they don't care.

The blood rushes to my head and a dull thud swishes in my ears as I realize—they still care.

They're still lovers and he's angry, I found out. My chest tightens. I try to stop my feverish thoughts from taking off. This is not happening. I throw my blanket to the side and draw myself on my elbows. I will not get myself into a frenzy over this. Today I'm leaving for Lhasa. I'll need to focus my mind on making merit on the road ahead, not on Karma and whatever he has going on with that Lanying.

Besides, I could be wrong—what do I know about these things? Maybe there's nothing going on—anymore.

I sigh and stretch my limbs as I roll my head from side to side. Plenty of mats, but all empty. Good, an excellent opportunity for undisturbed morning prayer. I fold the blanket to prepare, but alas, there's a knock on the door. It's Dendup calling me in.

"Heard you bumped into an old friend of ours," Dendup says. His eyes are puffy and reddened. I sit down next to him in the kitchen.

Bread and tea are present in front of me, but my appetite's still missing. My hands wrap around the hot cup. So, he knows about Lanying.

"Better stay away from her. Trouble follows wherever that woman goes." He slurps his tea and pops a tsampa ball in his mouth. "Doesn't know her place either." Dendup's eyes are now on me.

"Hmm." I carefully blow the fatty foam in my cup aside. *She came just in time, though.* The words are on the tip of my tongue, but I swallow them. No need to go into the incident with the drunk man. Dendup probably doesn't remember I told them I was going to the temple.

"Her family can't control her." He gulps down his tea and wipes his mouth with the back of his hand. "They've given up on her years ago and let her roam now under the pretense of running the family business."

So, Lanying's in charge of her own. My eyebrows raise. "She seemed pretty put together to me." I shrug and take a sip. My eyes meet Dendup's over the rim of my cup. He throws me a big smirk as his teacup lands with a bang on the small table.

"Don't even be thinking about it, sister." There's something gruffy in his tone. "Stay away from that woman." He slaps his knees and gets up. "Time to go."

I swallow the last of my tea and stuff the bread in my pocket. With my lips pinched and my chin raised, I stride out the door.

The tiny courtyard is jam-packed. Bags, packs, people and horses, all shadows moving in the dewy morning mist. I make out my horse, already saddled. Karma's beaten me to it.

"Good morning," he says, his voice weary, his eyes a faded moss green. He hands me the lead of my stallion. The leather burns in my clenched fists. I give him a curt nod. There's no way I'm backing down as I did last night.

"Got you something." He stretches out his hand for me. His open palm holds a small turquoise pendant on a leather strap. It's a conch shell with its ends clasped in finely engraved silver. It looks like the intricate shell is carved with one slash straight out of an azure blue sky. *Wow!* It's one of the most delicate pieces of jewelry I've ever seen. Yet, the tiny shell exudes a robustness that is hard to miss.

"I saw it in the market yesterday and thought of you." Karma's voice sounds thin.

My eyes widen at the sight of this little beauty, piercing its bright blue hue through the flimsy morning light. The conch shell represents the Buddha's voice, the deep and pervasive sound of the dharma, awakening us from the slumber of ignorance and urging us to work for our own welfare and the welfare of others. A warmth spreads through my body. A symbol of truthful speech and strength, how perfect on this pilgrimage. And how thoughtful of Karma. I look up from his hands into his eyes, a flimsy emerald shimmer coming through.

"Please don't wander off again." He ties the ornament around my neck. "Stay close from now on." His eyes on the pendant, his fingers linger on my throat in a tender caress.

A blush spreads across my cheeks. "Will do." I clear my throat and unclench my throbbing fists. My fingertip runs over the stone body of the shell. It's hard and surprisingly soothing to the touch.

"Nordun." Karma grips my hand. "What happened?"

A burning sensation rushes up my arm as he spreads my fingers, exposing the bloodstained lines on the palms of my hands. I cringe. This doesn't feel good. Fiery, festering lesions streak the inside of my hand. Dirt and gravel have lodged in the already abraded grooves of my palms, causing them to infect overnight. It must have been from my fall in the alley yesterday evening. I yelp under Karma's stern stare. I try to pull back my hand, but it only hurts more.

"You silly." He grabs my other hand. It looks just as bad. "You checked your horse, but you forgot yourself." A thoughtful smile breaks through as his fingers stroke my palms. "Your heart's in the right place, but you have to take better care of yourself."

I cast my eyes down. "It's fine." I try to wriggle my hands out of his. "We've got to go." But Karma's not budging. His eyes scout over my shoulders.

"Wait." He scoots over to his bags and pulls out a clean cloth. "Come, boiled water's the best." He urges me into the kitchen, and he cleans out my wounds while I stand there, toes curled up in total humiliation. So much for the determination I set to meet Karma with this morning.

With my wounds dressed, we say goodbye to our generous hosts and ride out of the courtyard towards the edge of the town. We're not the only ones up so early. My jaw drops as we approach the herd of horses and mules. There must be hundreds of them all lined up along the road.

"I've never witnessed any of this." I turn to Karma in awe. This caravan is so much larger than I've ever seen.

A surge of energy shoots through my body as I raise myself in the saddle. My eyes dart over the colorful cacophony of people, beasts, and burden. The lead mules are decked out with bright plumes and ringing bells, signaling the caravan's arrival. Tinkling charms and tiny mirrors are tied on their halters to ward off evil spirits and ghosts.

All mules are loaded to the hilt with a variety of goods packed and checked. There's prized tea from Yunnan, pressed in brick and cake form, wrapped in tight bamboo sheaths and sown in waterproof yak skin, precious salt from Yanjing, bagged and plunked into bamboo carriages, dried pork and noodles from the locality, tied in formless bags, there's copper, sugar, and so much more in those bags and packs, I can't make it all out.

And then there's the company we're keeping on the road. There must be at least one mule keeper between ten to twelve fully loaded mules swarming round, checking their prized possessions for the take-off. There's a whole score of monks from the local monastery riding their horses, a dozen or so individual pilgrims on food travelling, and I spot even a few entire families joining the caravan, their youngest ones strapped on horses. My eyes trace the lengthy line to the front. *Lanying.* Her horse trots next to what are obviously the caravan leaders on their horses. As soon as she spots me, she raises her hand and yells.

"Good to see you, sister." She steers her horse over to me and bares her teeth into a grin. "Glad you're coming along." Her long overcoat, the darkest cobalt blue, flows along the flanks of her stallion. A sharp turn exposes her fitted trousers and a long knife, running the length of her thigh bone. As my eyes catch the handle poking underneath the heavy wool, I can only imagine the competent ferocity with which she will yield its blade in times of trouble. She casts a condescending glance at my company. "Talk later." And off she is, throwing an obvious wink my way.

"Tsss." Dendup shakes his head. From the corners of my eyes, I see Karma spurring on his horse, a stoic look on his face. I'm not sure what to make of it all.

What I am sure of, though, is that I'm not letting myself be carried away by it all again. Whatever it is or was between them, it's not mine. I lean back in the saddle and raise my hand. "See you later."

Soon we're moving along, but not before we circle the weisang lit by monks of the neighboring monastery. Two piles of smoldering cypress and juniper branches release their shreds of dense smoke. The bright white columns whirl straight up. *Om mani padme hung.* A low buzz of prayer resonates in the air as we move through. As the crisp, clear aroma of the penetrating smolder stings our eyes, we rid ourselves and our animals of any negative forces, ensuring a safe journey for ourselves and our animals on the road. Only when the last animal emerges out of the blotted air is the caravan ready to hit the road.

As fast as the three of us came to Kandze, so slow, we now move out with the caravan. Traveling in numbers is best, Dendup told me, but it feels like we're crawling instead of riding. My stallion trots won all fours. With my hands still sore, I'm having trouble reigning him in. Pretty soon he's going to balk, I'm sure of it. I sit tight, as we're both on edge.

"We'll pick up speed soon, you'll see," Karma says at the look of my anxious face. By the tone of his voice, I know he's not letting me out of his sight.

"Maybe let him loose a bit and ride up front?" I almost beg to be let go. With a wince, I pull the reins tighter.

"Ah sure, what harm can that do?" Dendup's cheery voice comes to my rescue. "Let the colt cavort a bit. He's got too much energy, it will do him good." He waves at me, a sign of release. "Just don't disturb the mules on your way."

His words fall on deaf ears. I'm already off to the front, my horse's ears twirling with delight over our newly gained freedom.

And while my horse releases his energy, I sit back in the saddle, taking it all in. I'm on pilgrimage to Lhasa, with Karma and a caravan. I shake my head. Who could have imagined that a few weeks ago? Not me, that's for sure.

"But when the karmic wind blows, we will be moved, no matter how strong we stand." My grandmother's soft voice resounds in my ears as my mind travels back to her. "And sometimes we're moved towards what we least expect."

Well, that's a sure truth.

Ten

Karma's right—we pick up speed, but our pace is nothing compared to the days before, when we rode with only the three of us. I understand. We have a long way ahead of us, and the beasts are loaded to the hilt. This pace provides excellent training for me, anyway. It demands me to reign in my enthusiastic stallion and my persistent impatience at the same time.

We settle into the steady cadence set by the headmen and their lead mules, supported by the vocals of the muleteers. The rhythmic tunes their throats blast out seem to work wonders in keeping up the pace and the spirits of our company.

Their vocals are also a great warning ahead for the small villages we pass through. Hearing our caravan approach from miles ahead, the locals prepare tea and meals and get ready to do some trade.

Most of the caravanners like to hold on to their goods, though. The nearer to Lhasa they get, the higher the value of their cargo, especially the prized tea and salt.

Being totally unaware of it before, I've come to understand that the caravan trade is a sort of shrewd game of manipulating supply and demand. At least, that's what I've observed over the last few days.

There's still so much I don't know about the workings of this mundane world. I settle back in the saddle, my eyes scout over the line of tireless men and mules kicking up the dust ahead. Then again, I never had to know.

"No need to fill our mind with things that bear no meaning to our lives," Dechen used to say, and she was right. My life as a nun revolved around study and prayer, working for the benefit of all sentient beings. Everything I needed was provided for.

However, now that I've been out of the monastery, I realize how ignorant I've been. Of course, everything was provided for. Dechen, Ghedun, and some of our senior nuns took care of that. They made sure the necessary bonds were formed and reformed, again and again, with our patrons, our generous donors.

I shift to the front of my saddle. How come I never saw this before? A shallow sigh slips from my lips and I cringe as I recall my carefree, or rather careless, attitude at the monastery. I was reckless with the food, the tea, the treats... with everything. My finger slides under the bandage and I scratch my aching palm. So many times, I spilled our provisions or let it go to waste, never thinking of its origin and the arduous labor my grandmother and others had to put in.

I straighten my back and twist my head from side to side. Now that I'm going to run the stables, I'll have to get to know this mundane world. A dull throb hits my temples. Just the thought of it makes my head hurt.

"Easy, boy." I tighten the lead on my frolicking horse while I reign in my straying thoughts. *Om mani padme hung.* No use thinking ahead. Lhasa's still far away, let alone my return to the stables.

And as the muleteers hum their songs, I chant my mantra—*Om mani padme hung*—countering the futile inner chatter of my mind and gaining precious merit for all at the same time.

With the steady pace we go, the caravan doesn't take many breaks during the day. The head muleteers seem to know exactly when and where to rest. We stop early enough at a big caravanserai to unload and feed the animals before dark sets in. Unlike the mules that are free to roam, Karma takes my horse and ties it to his.

"Your stallion's not used to this life on the road yet." Karma fastens the lead. "I bet he's sorry he came along by now and try to sneak off at night." Karma throws me one of his teasing looks, but I know by now this one's only halfhearted. Something else is occupying his mind.

Talking about my horse or somebody else? The words are on the tip of my tongue, but I swallow them. All day he's been keeping a close eye on me while at the same time observing Lanying from a distance. I've seen his eyes—and his mind—wander back and forth. Something's up. For whatever reason, it's obvious he doesn't want me to talk to her.

"Come on." Dendup's calling from the doorway. "I've ensured us some good seats."

And before I get a chance to say anything else, Karma's determined arms whisk me away into the caravanserai's kitchen.

While the three of us spend the night in comfort on the mats in the caravanserai, the muleteers keep near their cargo. They make themselves comfortable in the courtyard or the open fields, even sleeping on top of their precious goods. The atmosphere during the day is more than friendly, with everybody in the caravan sharing their meals and their conversations, it's the opposite once night falls. As the darkness turns trust into suspicion, the weary mind spins friends into foes. I can't help but wonder how strange the workings of our human mind.

It's an early start as we get up the next day. Dawn has not thrown her blue hue in the kitchen yet, but the roaring stove glows a fierce orange, providing us with all the light we need this morning.

"The road's good here, so no bother to walk in the dark," Dendup says as I rub the sleep out of my eyes over my first cup of tea. "Besides, we want to hit the river before midday."

I shoot up. "River?" My voice pitches. "What river?" My stomach churns the rich tea straight back along my palate. I almost gag.

"No worries." Dendup pours us another cup. "We'll have it crossed before you know it."

But his upbeat tone can't reassure me. *We need to cross the water.* Wide awake now, my mind's flooding. The aching memory of my mother's drowning sweeps right through.

My hands clench into fists as that vague, foolish fear I've had of water ever since her death roars its ugly head again. *Don't be silly.* I've crossed water before. My fingernails dig into the frayed bandages on my palms. *I can do this.* After all, fear is nothing but an obscuration, a projection of my untrained mind.

Just a few days ago, I faced my fear and conquered my demons there at the Four Sisters Mountain. I did that—o crossing a river should be easy, right?

I glance over the rim of my cup at Dendup's cheery face.

Besides, I've got my family right here with me. With a soft puff, I blow the steam off my cup, and as my breath settles, so does my mind. But not for long.

With our road winding and drawing nearer to the swiftly swelling stream this morning, the dreaded crossing's never far from my mind. I'm trying hard to suppress the unsettling feeling in my stomach and turn my thoughts to Green Tara, mother of all Buddha's. *Oṃ tāre tu tāre ture soha.* Tara has never failed me in times of trouble. A prayer to her always protects, even strengthens the weak and weary mind. In the corner of my eyes, however, I notice the river growing wider and wider. I can't help but wonder: *How will we ever get across to the other side?*

With the sun throwing her smallest shadow on our path, it must come up to noon. My mouth dry, I turn to Karma. "Are we there soon?" My voice is steady, but my fidgety fingers give away my anxiety.

"Next turn." He points ahead. "Can't wait, can you?"

He laughs at my grimace.

I guess I'm not fooling anybody but myself. As our part of the caravan coils around the next bend, I see it. The crossing's up ahead.

The first mules are already unloaded. Their packs and bags are pile up on the banks of the river. My eyes whiz to the wild foaming water. *What's that?* I crane my neck as I spot a few tiny black dots in the white spew of the rolling water. *Boats?* These must be boats!

I've never seen them before, but as we get closer, my suspicions are confirmed—the drifting black dots are actually yak skin boats. As the roar of the raging river hits my ears at full speed, cold sweat hits the back of my neck, and I freeze. Sensing my fear, my stallion balks on all fours.

"Easy." Dendup's already dismounted and takes my horse's halter. "There's a first for everything." He pats the stallion's head. "We'll help you two across."

He throws me one of his typical cheers, but his reassurance has no effect on me—not this time. With the reins slipping from my hands, every muscle in my body tenses up as I slide off my horse. My mind blanks as panic floods the void inside me. *Focus.* I twist my fingers in my horse's coarse mane to steady myself. My heart's pounding as I turn to Dendup.

"Thank you." I clear the fear that has gripped itself to the back of my throat. My shallow breath races with the speed of my heartbeats by now. *Focus.* I draw a deep breath and settle my eyes on the boats being loaded up at the banks of the river. The head mules are the first to be carried over by these bobbing vessels—nothing more than tied up wooden frames clad with yak skin.

My stomach churns. I clasp Karma's forearm. "Will it hold?"

"It will," he says, his hand on mine, a close grip. "Here, for his ears." He hands me a few pebbles. My eyebrows raise as I roll the wet stones in the palm of my hand.

"His ears?" My eyes dart from the pebbles to my horse's twirling ears and back.

"Yes, his ears." Karma takes the pebbles from my hand and tucks them in the stallion's ears. "It blocks the sound of the river, calms him down." The horse puffs a loud breeze in protest at first, but the twirling stops. It works.

"Need some too?" Karma tucks a loose strand of hair behind my ears. His eyes flash with that familiar tease as his hands stroke the back of my neck.

"No thanks." I pinch my lips. Everything's always a joke to these men. I have to admit, though, the tension in my body lessens ever so slightly. Or was it his subtle touch that makes me feel at ease just now?

"Come, sit." He pulls me down on a big bolder next to him. "It will take a while for our turn." With one hand clammy in his, I watch the spectacle of men and mules and struggling boats in front of me. My other hand is on my prayer beads, sliding them slow through my stiff fingers as I call upon Tara, to ensure a safe crossing.

Oṃ tāre tu tāre ture soha.

Eleven

With Karma and Dendup taking care of our horses and bags, all I have to do is sit tight. They've secured me a spot in the corner of the boat. As it turns out, even "sitting tight" is quite an ordeal.

My hands clasp around the side pole of the boat. I hold on with all my strength, but I'm no match for this force of nature. The fast-moving current beats merciless on the side of our vessel. I'm tossed between our solid leather bags and the jagged wooden frame of the boat.

Cold sweat beads on my forehead. My stomach rises with our vessel on the waves of the water. Giant boulders break the river's surface, causing a relentless spray of white foam to lash down on us. I shiver. The bitter cold invades every bone of my body, completely paling the scorching midday sun.

While my eyes search for safety, Dendup points to the other side. He's trying to tell me something, but his voice is lost on me. I don't know what's more deafening—the waves crashing with a vengeance against all the sides of our boat or the beat of my heart rushing in my ears.

There it is, that familiar fear striking my body again, turning my thoughts to the worst scenario of drowning—a horrific death. *Focus.* I know what's happening. I've been here before—my mind playing the same tricks on me—over and over again.

Sweat lashes down my back by now. I have to wrestle myself out of this suffocating grip of anxiety, but I'm blanking completely. Even the icy water gathering on the base of our boat, sloshing around my numb ankles—I feel it, but it doesn't really register with me.

Clenching my teeth, I draw upon the last bit of strength left in my body. *Only a steady, well-trained mind will be capable of warding off the obstacles you will meet out there*—my grandmother's words flash like a lightning beam through the void in my mind. *That's it!* It's useless to simply ignore these destructive thoughts—they're too tenacious. I've got to fight. I press my tongue against the roof of my mouth, and a sweet iron taste seeps through. I need to crush my fears, annihilate them with all force.

My knuckles whiten. I gasp for air and pull myself up from the rugged frame. *Oṃ tāre tu tāre ture soha.* While my lips form the words, I close my eyes and call upon Tara with all that is left in me. *Oṃ tāre tu tāre ture soha.* My temples throb. I fill my mind with Tara's chant, praying her beautiful vision will come to me again.

My mind's eye turns to the corners of my being. *She's here!* Her familiar, radiant green spirit hovers right in front of me. Her loving smile soothes my shivering body and mind as she draws nearer. With her right leg extended forward, she's ready to leap into action, wiping out all the false illusions that have nestled themselves deep inside of me for too long.

As the timber frame pounds into my battered body, Tara shines her crystal green light on me, filling my heart with a quiet, yet compelling calm. The bright hue permeates me, strengthening my body and clearing my mind. *I'm protected. I'm safe.* A vivid clarity settles within me, my body relaxes. My fears are only a projection of my mind. It's not real. My grandmother taught me well and Tara is on my side. I can do this.

My arms fling around the frame. I raise myself to face the raging river. *Oṃ tāre tu tāre ture soha.* With the ice-cold spray lashing down on me, I let the water run its course, sweeping clean my body, and turning my mind to a more positive outcome.

Any perception of time slips away as our tiny vessel braves the mighty river. I have no idea how long it takes us to reach the other side, and I don't mind. What I'm sure of, though, is that I'm the first out, wading to safer shore as fast as my weary legs can carry me. Drenched to the bone, I sink on all fours. The silty sand curls up between my fingers as my assurance. *We've made it.*

"That was a pretty rough fare for a first time." Dendup's hand reaches to pull me up. "At least you kept your food in. That's more than I can say of most of us." He nudges his head at Karma.

"Really?" My knees wobbly, I grab Dendup's hand and pull myself up.

"Oh yes, my first time crossing the water like this was not that smooth." Karma secures our horses to the side. "But then again, I do remember a certain someone who couldn't hold his food in that same fare either." He throws a smirk over his shoulder.

"True." Dendup snorts. "But that wasn't because of the boat." The two of them burst into laughter. I totally understand, for I've seen how Dendup's taken with the chang.

"You rest and stay with our horses." Dendup points at the approaching boats ferrying the rest of our caravan across. "We'll help some families with children across."

I spread my waterlogged coat over the sun-drenched boulders. It's going to take most of the day for the whole caravan to be ferried across. I'm fine with that. With nausea still ruling my stomach, I feel like I've been turned inside out and upside down. I sit myself next to my drying coat. I'm not going anywhere for a while.

Carefully I unwrap the sodden, blood-stained bandages from my trembling hands. A bit of air will dry them out.

"So you made it, sister," a familiar voice says. It's Lanying, looking put-together as ever, with her hooded cloak enveloping her lean physique. Her white teeth flash a grin. "Not that I doubted that for a moment. Those two are guarding you well."

Her eyes fix on the shore where Karma and Dendup are unloading the vessels. I open my mouth, but before I get the chance to say anything, she lands herself beside me and puts her hand around my neck.

"Pretty." Her eyes mirror the blue pendant as her fingers slide across the leather cord. "But not nearly enough to keep you safe on this journey. I've seen them look at you." A small disdain graces her lips as she curls them ever so slightly. "Here, take this."

I flinch as she pulls a small silver sheath from her cloak. "It's small, but has proven itself to me more than once." She presses the elaborate engraved sheath in my hands and draws out a small bone handle dagger. Its slender curved blade shimmers with an icy blue between us.

"Thank you." I clear my throat. "I mean, for yesterday. If you hadn't been there..."

She waves her hand. "Oh, but I was, so no bother," she says. "We sisters, we look out for each other." She looks me straight in the eye. "He won't always be there to project you, you know."

Her blue eyes pierce into mine. My cheeks burst into a flash. She's talking about Karma.

"Neither will I, so take it."

She slides the dagger back into its sheath and tucks it under the belt of my dress. It finally registers with me. She wants me to keep the knife!

My thumb circles the smooth top of the bone handle. "I've never handled something like this before." My breath shallows as an iron fist tightens around my heart. *And I never want to.*

I search for something to say—I don't want to offend her. She means well, but I don't want a knife. Not ever.

"It's a tough world out here for us women." Lanying lowers her voice. "Trust me, I know what I'm talking about." She grabs my hand and secures my sweaty palm around the cold silver sheath. "Don't hesitate to yield this blade whenever your instincts tell you to."

The harsh grimace on her face, the cagey tone with which she speaks those words, it drains the blood from my face.

My mouth opens in vain. She's gone as quickly as she appeared, a sudden breeze flailing the tail end of her cloak.

I'm left trying to wrap my head around our encounter. This woman just handed me a knife. My eyes lock on its translucent grip, a clear shine on my side. And on top of that, she encouraged me to yield it whenever I feel like it. Has she gone mad?

Better stay away from her. Dendup's words ring in my ears. *Trouble follows wherever that woman goes.* I blink. Maybe Dendup's right. Maybe I should stay away from her. *Then again...*

In the corner, I see Dendup and Karma approaching. The loading's finished—we'll be leaving soon. With one fluid move, I pull the dagger from under my belt and slip it in the inside of my dress. I'll hand it back to her as soon as I get the chance.

Flinging the now-dry coat around my shoulders, I hurry to the company waiting at our horses. In the meantime, there's no need to upset anybody—right?

Twelve

With the shadows already lengthening, there's not much time left in the saddle and I don't mind. The boat frame has left its malign mark on my ribs, reminding me of the rough passage with every shallow breath I take. A fresh cup of tea and a warming stove—that's what I'm looking most forward to now.

Our lodgings have my prayers answered. The tea's like it should be, rich and creamy. By the look of my slurping and chewing companion, the copious food's undoubtedly of the same quality, but I've left my appetite on the billowing waves of the afternoon. I have no desire to dig in. With my taste for tea satisfied, my blanket's the only comforting thought left. Fortunately, Dendup and Karma decide on an early night. *Om Tara.*

The dreamless sleep has cleared all remainders of yesterday's venture. After a hearty breakfast, we're on our way again, bright and early. A sprinkle of rain—an auspicious sign—guides us out of the village, onto the open road.

"Any surprises today?" I relax back in the saddle. Dendup's chewing on an apricot from a rather big bag, a generous gift from our most friendly hostess at the caravanserai.

"Nah." He spits the pit to the side. "Plain riding from here on." He nods ahead. "For a few days, anyway."

My eyes scout the horizon. The snow-crowned peaks of the magnificent Cho La range have been in sight ever since we left

Kandze. At this pace, however, the peaks are not getting any nearer.

As it turns out, this day does bring a surprise, albeit a pleasant one. With the sun at its peak, the road opens up to wide plains, carpeted by swaying long grass and abundant wildflowers. We've hit the fertile higher grasslands, the summer haven of the local nomads and their yaks.

I shift back in the saddle. My horse leaps at the sight of this luscious expanse, his frolicking hoofs pound the warm grass. A pair of sheltering pheasants rush out of the grass at the approach of our caravans, their shrill call a futile protest to our sudden appearance. While the mules plough through with the long grass swishing under their bellies, the breeze carries the sweet smell of crushed herbs all around. What a refreshing relief from the dust cloud I've gotten used to riding in.

"Time for a break." Karma signals ahead.

The front of the caravan has already halted near the small creek. With sweat sticking my shirt to my back, I slide off my horse and let him dash into the stream. A spray of crystal-clear water scatters under his hoofs.

The little ones have already found their refreshing treat, leaping across the stream with their hands and mouths full of juicy berries. Smudges of dark maroon and the brightest of purple streak their hands and faces. I scoop the water in my burning palms and run it over my heated face, down my neck. There're no trees at this height—the only shadows to be found are the scattered clouds drifting overhead.

"Come, sit." Dendup unpacked our lunch, a nice spread of sliced meat, baked bread, creamy yogurt, and some ripe fruits. I raise my eyebrows. Where did he get all this fresh food? We left so early this morning.

"You must have treated her well then," Karma says to Dendup. He slices a piece of the bread and hands it to me. I take a moment to catch on, but then my jaw drops. *Men!* I gulp down the cup of water in front of me and cringe. These two have gotten comfortable with me over the last few days, but I'm still not at ease in the company of men and their remarks—even if it's my family.

"Did you know these plains are the home of Gesar?" Karma pops a piece of bread in his mouth and leans back.

"Gesar?" I say. "King Gesar of Ling?" My mind perks up at the thought of this epic hero crossing these planes.

"Yep, Gesar the indomitable." Dendup's eyes gleam with admiration. "He lived right here on these plains, long time ago."

Who doesn't know of the great King Gesar? With his unequalled perseverance and extraordinary strength, this warrior king eliminated all evil and brought happiness to his people. My grandmother told us all about him in class. Gesar was not only a mundane warrior but also a spiritual one, as she used to emphasize. He overcame many difficulties at an early age.

Born as the son of the supreme god Indira, he was banished with his mother from this tribe by his uncle Trotung, a vain and pretentious man who wanted to rule himself. But Gesar didn't give up and became the leader of the tribe in the end, winning the victory in a horse race.

"King Gesar was intelligent, gentle, and courageous, a real spiritual warrior," she told us. "Of course, he was frightened, but knowing the inevitability of suffering, he overcame his fear and faced the many evil demons with success."

"Wow." Shafts of golden sun light up the vast grasslands around me, making this place seem even more magical.

Dendup wipes the yogurt dribbling down his chin. "Gesar's story must speak to you then."

"Yes, but doesn't everybody like the story?" I shrug at my companions.

"Sure." Dendup nods. "But not everybody has an evil uncle like Gesar had. I'm talking about an uncle who got him and his mother abandoned when he was very young. An uncle who tried all kinds of means to kill him."

An instant flush of heat runs up my cheeks. I lower my head with Dendup's and Karma's eyes burning on me. An evil uncle. My pulse races. Yes, I do have an evil uncle and they are on the hunt to kill him. Right now. My ribs tighten. The pit in my stomach swells.

"And not everybody claims the victory with a horse." Dendup's voice rings with cheer now. I glance up. "We're proud of you, sister. Let that be said!" He raises his cup and his face beams with pride.

A slight sigh of relief fills me. Dendup's genuine delight and the ease with which he shows it—it touches me. Still, I can't help but wonder: how does such a kind man plan such a horrific deed with seemingly the same ease?

"Thank you, brother." I clear my throat. "But my minor struggles and wins pale in the face of Gesar's magnificent trials and triumphs." My fingers fumble with the prayer beads around my neck. The absurd comparison makes me want to run and hide, but there's nowhere to go on these plains.

"Ah, still." Dendup glugs the last of the yogurt out of his bowl. "If his uncle had not been so malicious and scheming, Gesar could never have risen so high." He lets out a big burp and turns to Karma. "Same principle applies to everyone. No matter our trials and triumphs—it's our struggles that strengthen us, right?"

Karma's eyes narrow as Dendup slaps his knee.

"I guess you're right." Karma puts down his cup. "It is the struggle that strengthens us, no matter the motive or the magnitude of it." His voice drifts into the distance as a silent shadow moves across his face. "I'll better check our horses." He jumps up. "Can't have a euphoric horse on the road." And off he goes, making sure our horses don't graze on one of the many mountain herbs known for their sedative effects.

Packing the leftovers in his bag, Dendup shrugs. "It hasn't always been easy for Karma either," he says. "Still isn't." He pauses for a moment and rubs his chin as I frown.

"Sorry to hear that," I say. And I am, while also realizing I know nothing about Karma and his struggles.

"Blood relative or not, I've always considered him my true kinsman." Dendup glances over at the river. "But that's not the case with all in our family." His hands press tight on the bag, his fingers tie the string.

"Karma's got to prove his loyalty to them, time and time again." With a sigh, he slings the bag over his shoulder. "He's a good man, a strong man. They should be grateful to have such a fine man in our tribe."

My head light, I jump up. *Karma's loyalty lies with his family duties—no matter what.* A wave of nausea hits my stomach as I pretend to brush the crumbs off my dress. Seems like the family uses Karma to do the dirty work. Dendup just said so. I gag in silence as the bile rises in my throat. My empty thoughts leave me groundless as I try to grasp the meaning of it all. Karma's no fool. He must see this! Or is he so blinded by his infinite gratitude to them for saving his life so long ago? We all want to belong, but at what price? The blue above me blurs. My own family. *Why?*

"You good?" Dendup's voice calls from the distance.

I stumble forward. "I'm fine." My hands steady on my knees. "The heat's getting to me." I throw a slight smile. "Back in a moment." I flee to the river.

The crystal-clear stream cools my face and my temper. As the water runs over my bruised palms, my fingers trace the dark brown scabs on the places where the lesions festered so fiery. How fast the body heals itself, how miraculous we recover from what was so painful only yesterday.

"I don't think you're scarred for life." Karma's calm voice jolts me out of my musings. "Though it might be tender for a while." He takes my icy hands in his and envelops them ever so gently.

"It will," I say. "But no permanent markings of arduous journeys on the road on me yet." My heart expands at his intense gaze.

"Unlike you." I lower my eyes at the thin scar on his left hand. A fine bronzed line runs from his thumb to his wrist.

"Oh, is that what these are?" His smile broadens, his eyes still on me. "In that case, I've got many of them." His voice carries a mischievous hint, bringing that familiar flutter back to my stomach.

"Really?" I raise my chin in a futile attempt to defy the blush conquering my cheeks. He nods and draws me closer, his eyes a glistering green on me now.

"Oh, yes." He tucks a loose strand of hair behind my ear. "And it's my pleasure to show you." His lips—so near—brush against my burning cheek. "Whenever you're ready."

I gasp and hold my breath. The blood rushes to my head, bringing all my thoughts to an abrupt standstill. Suspended in time, my body's overwhelmed with the urge to draw close, to erase the distance between us.

A cry sounds from afar. "Let's go!"

I jolt back my head as Dendup's cheery voice pierces my eardrums.

"Best to keep that for later!" An amusing laughter graces Dendup's face as he hands me the lead of my stallion.

Please don't say that! I wince and drop my chin to my chest.

My face is still burning as Karma gives me a leg up. His hand lingers on my leg much longer than needed. A silly grin comes to my face, but my heart sinks as I think of Karma's fate and the family's unfortunate demands. A quiet roar rises inside of me.

I set my eyes on the shining peaks of the Cho La range ahead and spur on my horse. Lhasa was the best idea ever—no doubt about it.

Thirteen

Riding through the vastness of these grasslands, with their wide view and soft ground, suits me. The sweet smell of the warming earth, the faint hum of a lone dragonfly, the swish of tall grass against the horses' legs, the soft breeze billowing the thin fabric of my shirt against my back—it soothes all my senses and brings a little repose to my ever restless mind. My delight in riding these luscious planes must show, for when I catch Dendup watching me, he shakes his head.

"Don't want to get too comfortable, sister." He gestures to the Cho La pass looming in the distance. "She looks pleasing, yet she's deceiving." His voice carries a wary edge as he stares ahead.

My eyes follow his stare towards the magnificent mountain range. I've heard of Cho La's two faces but can't imagine them. "She's so lush, so green from this side." My eyes scan her shimmering peaks, rising out of the thick fir forest straight into the clear blue yonder.

Dendup shakes his head. "Just wait 'til she shows you her other side." He shifts his weight to the front of his saddle. "She's got the most jagged snow crags, the deepest frozen canyons and the most vicious hail pour-downs you'll ever encounter." His eyes narrow. "Nah, she's nothing but trouble."

My palms burn as I clasp the reins tight. There's no escaping Cho La. We'll have to cross her if we want to reach Lhasa. *Om Tara*. Let us pray she will grant us safe passage.

"We won't get to Manigangou until tomorrow, so best to enjoy this day." Dendup throws his arms in the air, his grin as wide as his reach. "We might just hit the end of the horseraces there. Should be fun."

Manigangou, our entrance to the Cho La Pass and famed for its horse-racing. I guess as a future horse master I should be interested, but to be honest, all I'm looking forward to is visiting the famed Yilhun Lha Tso. I'm not sure how far off a detour it is, but I've got my heart set on circumambulating this holy lake.

A warm glow fills my body as I think of all the merit accumulated by going to Yilhun Lha Tso. Yes, it will strengthen my spirit and cleanse away some of the unfortunate karma I've collected in the past.

I straighten my back and turn my gaze over to our caravan, searching out the pilgrims among us. For sure, there's many of us wanting to visit the holy lake. I glance at Dendup, his face still bearing that wide grin. If Karma and Dendup want to stay for the races, they can let me go to the lake in the company of the pilgrims. Right?

My hand swats a buzzing fly as my mind makes a familiar turn. *Right. Who am I fooling?* The two of them haven't let me out of their sight since the incident. I bite my lip and lean forward, searching for a more comfortable position in the saddle. *Ah well.* Then one of them might accompany me to the lake. After all, I am on pilgrimage and I can't pass Yilhun Lha Tso without paying homage. Turning to Dendup, I throw him my biggest smile. Not for me to worry about—I'll leave it up to them to decide who's coming along with me.

Rejoicing in the beauty of my surroundings, I turn my mind back to prayer. *Om mani padme hung.* How fortunate this precious life turns out to be today.

Manigangou tries to hide itself in the fold of the valley, but the myriad of prayer flags surrounding it gives it away. Vibrant and noisy, it turns out to be quite a bustling town.

Reaching our repose with the sun at her highest peak, there's not enough time left to visit the holy lake—not that I've discussed my planned visit with Karma or Dendup yet. There is, however, sufficient time left to deal with the authorities involved. Being part of a caravan, officials check and count our animals and goods every time we pass an officers' station. This time too, and it takes us a while before we can unload our horses in the courtyard of the inn.

"It's all about those damned levies," Dendup explained to me in Kandze. Every time the muleteers are checked at a station, they have to pay a percentage of the value their mules carry. That's another rule in the game of trade. The further the muleteers bring their goods, the more stations they pass, the more charges they pay. *Taxes.* The muleteers spit when they hear the word. Now I understand why.

As I walk my horse in the courtyard, Karma and Dendup are already unloading the two packhorses they brought on our journey. "Nothing of value, just presents for friends and family we visit in Lhasa," Karma sneered finely when we got our first check in Kandze. I didn't see what was in the bags, but he didn't have to pay at all.

"We're a bit like the monks," Dendup joked when I asked about it. "They're exempt from tax too." His smile hid it well, but by the tone of his voice, I knew he didn't want to elaborate on it. So I left it. I found out he told the truth, at least about the last part—monks don't have to pay tax on their trading goods, as the Mongol ruler whom they call Khan is a sincere supporter of the Dharma. *Om mani padme hum.*

My hands glide down my horse's legs, strong muscles ripple under a healthy skin. By now we're used to each other and the road we travel on together. He's still rowdy around other horses, especially in an enclosed courtyard, but nothing a small tsampa ball from my pocket won't cure. The stallion's lead secured, I sling my bag over my shoulder. As I glance up, I meet Karma's approving gaze.

"You go ahead, and get us some good seats," he says, stacking the bags. "We'll handle the rest of it."

As I head for the kitchen, I look back for a moment. Karma and Dendup have engaged themselves in a lively conversation with some officers. *Taxes.* By now I'm sure of it. Sonam avoided the tax stations when he took Sangmo and me on the back roads to his family's camp. And the visitors at that shady inn, they were all smugglers. My body tenses. My thoughts turn tricks on me again. And Karma? Is he a smuggler too? Is that why he's away so often?

The intense heat in the kitchen hits my face with a veil of instant sweat. A ferocious roar from the stove brings the many kettles on it, boiling to the brim. My body sinks into a cushioned seat, but my mind rambles on. *Taxes.* Is that why Sonam has gone missing? Did the officials find out? Did they catch him? The dull pounding in my head gets louder as my thoughts turn over all the horrible scenarios; penalties of prison, of mutilation, even death in the most gruesome ways. I've heard rumors of the cruelty with which the rulings are enforced. I shiver.

"Here sister." A small voice sounds from above. A tiny hand reaches out, and a cup of steaming milk brew drifts my way. In a haze, I take it.

"Thank you." My vision blurred. I look up. The cutest little face beams right at me. She looks familiar.

"I'll get you some bread too." And off she is, only to return a few moments later with a flat round bread. Now I recognize her. She's from one of the families traveling with us.

"You're welcome."

And gone she is, again.

Still dazed, I sip my tea. The comforting warmth brings an ease to my strained mind. Sonam is a man of the world. He'll be fine. The back of my hand wipes the salty butter from my chin. After all, Sonam's sons are looking out for him.

I lean against the wall. My eyes close for a moment. *Norbu.* A twinge of guilt tugs at my heart. Kind and gently Norbu, Sonam's eldest son, who taught me all about the ways of the wild horse. He's been so good to me, but I didn't get the change to thank him. He was already gone, searching for his father when I returned with the wild stallion. A shallow sigh slips from my lips as I pull myself up. When all this is over.

Dendup plops beside me. "You're hiding on us."

Tea sloshes over my skirt; a rude awakening, yet pleasant escape from my own pitiful thoughts. A lightness ever so subtle fills my chest. The genuine delight on Dendup's face as he sinks his teeth into the moist bread and washes it away with the creamy brew, the way this man rejoices in the simple things and never hesitates to express them. It touches my heart, time and again.

"So, how about catching the last of the horse races for today?" Karma gulps down the last of his tea. "We still have some light left." He tilts his head to the side, his eyes on me.

"Sure, why not?" The words are out before I know it.

Horse races. I hop up and smoothen my rumpled dress. I've no interest in the races, but I know how much my companions love to watch. It will be the perfect setting for me to bring up Yilhun Lha Tso. Considering the cheerful and relaxed atmosphere surrounding the races, what are the chances they'll say no?

"Let's go!" I swing the rich blue mantle around my shoulders, taken aback by my own audacity.

Who would have guessed? I do take after my mother, if only a bit.

Fourteen

Heralding the end of the day, the sun throws her last rays of burned orange over the shimmering peaks of Cho La. The great gathering of herdsmen, travelers, pilgrims, and other passersby, however, pays no heed to the pearly dusk edging in. The races are still in full swing, with no intention of ending soon.

Columns of pungent weisang curl straight into the blood red sky. Horse hooves pound the soft grounds to a pulp. Colorful scarfs rustle their silk in the crisp evening breeze, and the scores of tiny bells tinkle as the horses sway their heads—I'd almost forgotten what a spectacle the races are, a veritable feast to the senses.

My eyes widen as they catch the riders at full speed, scooping up scarves and shooting their arrows. My hand clasps Karma's forearm as I'm caught up in the frenzied enthusiasm. I'm drawn in from the moment we arrive.

Karma's arm draws around my waist. "Glad we came then?" I nod.

It's been a long time since I've witnessed an event like this. As nuns, we never attended mundane festivities, unlike the monks who are active participants in these events.

The red-robed monastics are present in large numbers. The races will not begin, nor will they end without their prayers and elaborate rituals. Most monasteries have well-reputable stables with laymen representing them in the races. Owning large storehouses filled to the brim with tea and other precious goods, breeding horses and other livestock, engaging in trade, even outside their own locality, being requested to proceed in all the important events—the monks to move in and out of this mundane word with such an ease.

My heart sinks as I think of the many small nuns' communities I spotted on this road. Often dilapidated, their tiny housings are crammed with sincere practitioners, determined to serve the Dharma, no matter the poor conditions. With the monks' religious practices being valued so much more, it's a different world for monks and nuns.

My thoughts go back to my sisters, my home at the mountaintop for so long. With its spacious buildings and filled stockroom, I never realized how prosperous my grandmother's monastery is.

Wahoo! A cry from the crowd yanks my wandering mind back to the grasslands. I crane my neck to see what the excitement is all about. The final of the arrow shooting.

With the horses galloping at full speed, the riders need to hit the target set in the middle with a single arrow. The crowd is buzzing as the last rider dashes over to the center. Hanging from his horse, his eyes on the prize, he twists his body and aims. With the crowd surging, I'm on my toes with them. The bow and arrow are stretched out in the rider's hands, his shoulder almost dragging on the ground. We all hold our breath. *Will he?* A collective roar rises as the rider straightens again and brings his horse to a standstill. I clasp my hands—it's a hit!

"Excellent shot." Dendup's fist shoots up in the air. "Let's go."

He pulls a khata out of his sleeve and he's off, disappearing into the spree of white scarves as the horse and rider are celebrated.

"We'll have to greet the winner." Karma turns to me. "He's a friend of ours. Wait here." He squeezes my upper arm ever so slightly for confirmation.

"Sure, I'm not going anywhere." And I'm not.

My shoulders drop. In all this excitement, I didn't bring up the purpose of my coming along. Yilhun Lha Tso. What now? My eyes go over the crowd. If I find some pilgrims, I could ask them about it. Maybe some monks traveling in our caravan?

A vivid indigo twirling towards me catches my eye. It's Lanying, striding as confident as ever.

"Hey sister," I say, as she's within earshot. "Enjoyed the races?"

And there it is again, that grin.

"Pah." She spits on the ground. "Look at them, blowing their own horn." She waves a hand towards the celebrated riders, her lips curled in disdain. "They're not half as good as they think they are. You and I, we'd outride them any day—if we had the chance." Turning her back to the party, she puts her hands on her hips. "Wouldn't we?"

I chuckle. "Not me," I say. "But you, for sure." I've seen Lanying ride, she's amazing. "Why don't you give the race a try, then?"

I glance over her shoulder, keeping an eye out for Karma and Dendup.

"Nah." Her eyes narrow. "I'm attracting enough attention as it is." She pulls up the collar of her coat. "Not good for the trade, and not good for—you know." She clacks her tongue.

What?! I jolt back my head. *The mischief!* Her eyes flash a playful blue as I meet them.

"Men don't want to be seen with a woman commanding them around." Her grin widens even more. "Mind you, most men love it—but only in the dark. They sure don't want to be seen in that position in the daylight."

I try to avert my eyes, but somehow she's got me. *What woman talks in this manner?* A man, yes, but a woman? I lean back, my toes curled up in my sandals.

"So, I've heard about you owning your own stables." The disdain in her face melts into an appreciative glance. "Impressive. Let's talk business then." She shifts her weight to one side and rests her hands on the handle of her long knife.

"Sorry." I draw back my attention. "I know nothing of the trade." It's true. My hands reach for my prayer beads as my eyes glide from Lanying's long knife to the ground.

"Yet." She crosses her arms and leans forward. "You know nothing of it—yet." Her voice lowers. "But you will, for there's many of us women doing trade, you know."

I shoot up. "Really?" That's what Sangmo told me, too. Foreign women. Ask Karma, she'd said.

"Sure, we just don't all look like this." She slides her slender hands over the sleek indigo of her cloak. "Many of us rule the trade from home and have front men on the road to represent them." She grabs my hands. "I mean, the road's not that comfortable, is it?" Her hand exposes the deep pink lashes on my palms.

This woman sees everything.

"And it can be deadly." Her eyes gaze at the Cho La. "Lost many good men to the roar of the mountain gods." Her voice trails off, and she lets my hands slip.

"So why are you on the road yourself then?" A slight shake runs along my spine. I pull my coat tight as the wind latches on.

"Can't stay home," she says. "Too depressing." A wry smile curves on her lips. "And I don't trust anybody with my trade. Been burned often enough." She shifts her weight to the other side. "If you want to be well informed, you've got to do it yourself." She pulls her gaze back in. The familiar mischief shows itself again. "The road might not be the safest place, but at least I'm getting a little pleasure out here."

And just as the evening breeze has cooled down my burning cheeks, her last racy remark makes them fire up again. *Why does she speak like that?*

"So, tell me." Lanying raises her eyebrows. "If it's not trade, what makes you take this road then, sister?" She draws nearer, and her cloak rustles as the festive crowd quietens down.

"Pilgrimage," I say without hesitation. My hands fumble with the prayer beads around my neck.

"Pilgrimage!" She rolls her eyes. "I'm not buying it, sister." She pauses. Her eyes pierce a bright blue through the descending pearly pink dusk.

"Well." My breath shallows. The iron first squeezes tight around my heart. By now my mind's full speed again. I clear my throat. I would love to tell her my true intentions—if only to get their heavy weight off my chest.

"And visiting family, I heard." Her eyes deepen to crescents of cobalt. "Looking for an uncle, am I right?"

I gasp. *How does she know?*

"Like I said." She raises her chin. "If want to know what's going on, you've got to be on the road."

How did she hear about Uncle? My mind's pointing towards the impossible—Karma and Dendup. They would never tell, would they? I bite my lip.

"You don't want to tell me—yet. I get it." She draws her cloak tight with a swish. "In the meantime, I'll keep an eye and ear out for you, sister." Her eyes dart over my shoulder. "Got to go." She ducks, draws the soft hood over her head and fades into the coral sky.

My heels turn in the soft grass. Dendup and Karma are heading my way.

"Sorry it took us so long," Dendup says. "Our friend won, so there's going to be a pleasant party tonight—and tomorrow." He rubs his hands, his face gleaming with enthusiasm.

A party. "Nice," I say. The corners of my mouth curl up, but my heart sinks. There goes my chance to visit Yilhun Lha Tso. There's no way they'll come to the lake if there's a party going on late night.

"Better head back then," Karma says, and slowly we make our way, joining the crowd to the caravanserai. With Dendup speeding ahead of us—the chang is calling—Karma tugs at my sleeve, drawing me in.

"Don't worry." His voice tinges hoarse from the cheering. "I'll make sure he's up bright and early to join us to Yilhun Lha Tso."

It takes me a moment before I realize what Karma's saying. *We're going!* I'm sure I must silly, but I'm not good at hiding my emotions—especially not my relief.

"Thank you," I say. "It means a lot." I turn to him with the biggest smile.

"Of course." He ducks his head a little, making sure I see that playful look in his eyes. "You are on pilgrimage, after all."

Fifteen

"**B**right and early," Karma had said last night. He kept his word.

It's early when our horses' hooves scramble through the hollow courtyard. Even the dawn hasn't draped her orange and red hues over the fading shades of the indigo night sky yet. As for bright, well, that's debatable.

While I took to my mat right after dinner, Karma and Dendup joined the party at the inn. By the look of Dendup, it must have been a good one. Eyes slit, shoulders slumped, hands clasping on to the pommel of his saddle, he's a washed-out shadow of the lively, talkative Dendup I know.

With the morning chill burning the palms of my hand, I wrap my scarf tight. I haven't heard Dendup utter his usual cheery good morning either. So much for the aftermath of chang. I spur on my horse and catch up with Karma, who is leading the way.

"You said early." I steer my horse beside Karma's. "But is this not overly early?" I turn, only to see Dendup's already falling behind.

"Early's good." Karma pats his horse on the neck. "The horses are well rested, and we'll reach the lake before sunrise." His eyes focus ahead to the fading dark, and a slight smile rises in the corners of his mouth. "Don't you worry about Dendup." His voice carries an amusing tone by now. "He'll pick up once we'll reach the lake."

With the clack of his tongue, Karma prompts his horse into a gentle canter. Without hesitation, the other horses, including mine, relax into the pace set by Karma's horse.

Before sunrise. That's soon. I pull the sleeves of my coat over my hands and shift back in the saddle. With only the comforting clatter of the horse's hooves to distract me, my mind turns to prayer. *Om mani padme hung.*

It's not long before the wind dies down and a fiery brim appears over the snow-capped peaks of the imposing Cho La.

"Over here," Karma leads us off the path, towards a small forest. For a few moments, it's night again, with our horses crunching their way up through the dense, shaded woodland. The dew on the needle branches sweeps a soft, refreshing trail on my cheeks, as if it wants to wake me up for what's coming. Ducking over the neck of my horse to avoid the last branches ahead, the forest shifts the surrounding shadows into an open space. As I raise myself again, I clench the reins and blink, for nothing could have prepared me for the magnificence hidden behind these trees.

In front of me, in all her glory, is Yilhun Lha Tso, a luminous diamond of icy deep turquoise, set in a sweeping plateau of golden sand, swaying cypress trees, and lush leas. My mouth goes dry and I freeze. My horse halts by himself at the sight of the lake. It's simply stunning.

"Come." Karma ties up our horses and beckons me to the shore.

As the first golden rays of morning sun caress the lake, her smooth surface reflects the cloudless sky in a spectrum of purple and mauve. Crystal crests sparkle along her waterline, mirroring the mountain glaciers whose melt feeds the lake. So clear, so calm. Her serenity sooths my soul.

Yet, a shiver runs up my spine as my eyes gauge the dark indigo in the middle of the lake. She looks so pleasant, but her unfathomable depth resonates a daunting undertow. Even the mellow morning light can't soften it—she's ferocious in all her magnificence.

"Now I understand our premature departure," I say, my eyes still on the silken blue. Soon this place will be crowded with worshipping pilgrims, their well-intended clamor covering the magical quietude of this immense force of nature. A surge of gratitude flows to my lips.

"Thank you." I turn to Karma. Though his gaze remains on the lake, he nods.

"I felt you would see her as I do." He meets my eye. "A frightening beauty. You know what's underneath there, don't you?"

I follow his gaze back to the lake and frown.

"Down the lake? No, not really." I focus on the deep indigo eye of the water, but her haunting depth hides it all.

My thoughts lead me back to the monastery, to my grandmother telling us about Yilhun Lha Tso. What was it again? For a moment, my mind's blank, but then it hits me. "Chakramsavara." With a triumphant smile, I turn to Karma. "Dechen told me that the mountains and rocks surrounding the lake have the divine form of the Chakramsavara mandala." My eyes glide over the lake and its surroundings again. "Well, at least for those who have the pure vision to perceive it..."

My voice trails off as I realize I'm not recognizing any of what Dechen envisioned here. A deep blue lake, yes, but not the dazzling, radiant body of Chakramsavara as he's depicted on the thangkas with his four faces and twelve arms. Not his ever-present consort Vajrayogini either. Nothing. I don't see any of it.

My shoulders drop as my heart sinks to the bottom of the infinite azure. Another confirmation of what I already know and fear—I'm still far from a pure vision.

"You mean the wrathful Chakramsavara?" Karma's eyebrows turn up, and his eyes dart over the lake again.

I nod, even though I know he can't see me. Silly me, did I really think I could see what Dechen, an advanced practitioner, said I would?

"Oh, hell no." Dendup's voice croaks from behind us. "It's worse." His pitiful yet amusing appearance shakes me right out of my gloomy mood. A ruffled mob of hair above a crumpled chuba, tiny beads of red in an ashen face, a stumbling stride—I can't suppress a chuckle. It looks like Dendup's still wrestling and last night's chang is winning.

"Worse?" Karma smiles from ear to ear as he observes our companion staggering towards us. "What could be worse than an enraged deity?"

With a sigh, Dendup leans against one of the enormous boulders on the shore. "A scorned woman, of course." He waves his hand over the lake as he sits down on the rocks. "Everybody knows that."

A wink and a sneaky smile in Karma's direction follow. Dendup's making fun. *Good.* Means he's coming back to his former self again. I turn to Karma. His jaw s set, and it's obvious he's ignoring the last remark.

"A scorned woman." I pause. "Interesting." I make a deliberate point to catch Karma's eye, but he's pretending to study the lake again.

"Yep, it's Dugmo, the unfaithful wife of King Gesar who's down there." Dendup shifts his weight to make himself comfortable. "Can't believe you don't know that story, sister." He glances up at me and rubs his eyes before continuing.

"Dugmo was one of King Gesar's wives. I think she was the first one even." His hands rummage through his chuba and draw out a small bottle. "She went off with another fellow for a while—maybe for one night, I don't know exactly, but King Gesar was not pleased, as you can understand." He unscrews the top and puts the bottle on his lips. His face relaxes as the liquor hits his palate. "Gesar banned her from his palace." He wipes his mouth and gives me a meaningful glance from under his furry eyebrows.

The color is coming back to his drained face.

"So Dugmo travelled all alone, came to this lake, and fell in love with it." He points his head to towards the water and closes his eyes for a moment. "So much so that she couldn't leave this beautiful landscape anymore. She sunk herself beneath the lake to stay forever and a day." He rubs his eyes again.

A contagious grin comes to Dendup's face as he ends his tale. "Hence the holy lake of the fallen soul, for a fallen woman she was." He screws the top back on the bottle and puts it away with a rumble.

"You're quite the storyteller, Dendup," I say. "A fallen woman at the bottom of a holy lake." I sit beside him, my arms pulled around my knees.

"And not just any fallen woman," Dendup says. "A fallen queen." He glances over my shoulder at the lake. "Now, you would think that tale deserves me a fresh cup of tea, wouldn't you?"

His breath reeks of stale booze, but he's my elder. How can I refuse?

"Sure." I jump up, but before I get the chance to gather some loose twigs, Karma stops me.

"Nordun, no." He shakes his head, his voice soft. "You go ahead. The rest of the pilgrims will be here soon." A twinge shoots up my arm as his fingertips stroke my hand. "We'll stay here." He looks over at Dendup. "And have a good rest." Dendup grimaces, his head between his hands.

"From here, we can see most of the lake." Karma takes my hands in his. "You'll be safe." And with a little squeeze, he lets go, urging me to the shore. "Go."

An inviting breeze rustles from the deep blue, carrying the sweet scent of morrow. Karma's right. I turn my face towards the mauve-streaked sky. Soon a golden warmth will shred the pallid veil of dawn.

My fingers wrap themselves around my prayer beads and the hallow words flow from my lips. *Om mani padme hung.*

Slowly, I start walking.

My sandals sink in the silty shoreline. A surge of gratitude lifts my heart.

How fortunate to be here, right now.

How fortunate I am, indeed.

Sixteen

And as the world awakes, the sun guides me around the holy lake. A place of true worship, carved Mani stones and piles of rocks, stacked and draped with prayer flags, bedeck her sandy shores. "When you have nothing to offer, offer rocks and imagine they're precious gems," my grandmother used to say.

I crouch down. My fingers select the smoothest pebbles around. With the glittering peaks of the inescapable Cho La in the corners of my eyes, I stack the stones in a pile, paying homage to the spirits of the sky and mountains. *Om mani padme hung.* May they grant us a safe journey over these mountains.

My thoughts turned to prayer. I circumambulate the lake's smooth turquoise surface, purifying my mind of negative karma and collecting merit for all sentient beings. Now and again I stop, relishing this precious moment.

The swift breeze in the warming air carries the zesty smell of the cypress trees all around. The flutter of a pair of back-necked cranes echoes over the immense silence of the mysterious blue. These fragments in time pierce the taut fabric of my being with a terrifying yet thrilling clarity. It's in these moments that I'm offered a glimpse into my own clear nature of the mind.

Wet sand curls between my toes as I spin around, hands out to the side. My mind empty, my body weightless, and my being filled with gratitude—this is all I ever want to be.

The sun's rays have reached the plateau as I'm halfway down the lake. From here, I can see my companions seated under the swaying pines. Red robes dot the other side of the shore—the first monks of our party have arrived too. A slight heaviness stretches across my chest. *I always thought I would go here with my sisters.*

I sink on one of the craggy boulders with my sisters in solitude, my dear Pema and Tsomo, on my mind. So often we talked about all the holy places we would visit together as soon as our studies were done. They are in retreat now, advancing their practice with our former abbess Dolma. Three years, or even more. So good of them, and how I miss them.

My fingers fumble with the red string the sisters left on my wrist. A reminder that they're always with me, always taking care of me. They're the ones who told Karma about Uncle's spell on Mother. They knew because they have the gift to see beyond the human realm. And they told Karma to keep me safe.

Karma. A tingle runs up the nape of my neck. Would Pema and Tsomo still have chosen him if they knew what he's up to now? They probably know. I pull up my legs and throw my arms around my knees. Somehow, my sisters always know.

The cloud of bustling maroon on the faraway shore blurs in the background as my eyes glide over the lake. Pema and Tsomo would be able to see Chakramsava's radiant blue body transforming the polluted rivers of delusion into holy waters. They would see his four faces representing the four doors of liberation, and his twelve arms being the twelve dependent-related links of this samsaric existence. I blink. They would see it, but I don't. I rest my face on my knees. The soft wool prickles against my chin. And I probably never will see it—I have chosen a different path by myself.

My eyes on the water, my mind's drawn in by its unfathomable depth. The lake's so still, no ripples to be seen. Like a mirror, reflecting everything back in its natural state. My mind empties, and I'm sinking. My thoughts float away on the blue hue, and I let them. If only I could silence the restless inner chatter that rips through the shallow of my mind. If only I could cast away the fearful doubt that muddies the razor-sharp clarity my mind naturally possesses. To be as peaceful and unobscured as this lake, that's what I wish—and not just for a moment. I know it's possible. I've witnessed my grandmother, many of our senior sisters, their minds as clear as the crystal teardrops hanging from the branches after the night freeze at dawn. I know it's possible—just not for me.

The muffled sounds of my fellow pilgrims approaching from afar pull me out of the blue. My mind resurfaces. I lift my face to the sun, her warming rays washing over me. Still, how fortunate I am to be here, to be able to generate all that merit now. *I have chosen a different path.*

A tiny tug on my heart reminds me of my other intention, the one I'm trying so hard to ignore right now. I don't want to think about it, for when I do, paralyzing doubt creeps in, pulling me right back into that dark place of worry and fear. "Whatever aims you have, these will be achieved," the ngakpa said. All good is foreseen, so there's nothing to doubt. I take a deep breath to steady my thoughts.

Blinded by the bright beams, I rub my eyes and look over the lake. My companions are still there, unmoving in the shelter of the woodland. *Are they discussing their plans for Uncle right now?* The iron fist around my heart tightens as I keep my eyes on the two of them. Dendup's such a jolly character and Karma is patient, kind, and his touch so tender. How can they even think about such an evil act? Will I be able to I prevent it all? If so, how?

My breath shallows. A struggle won't be the answer that I know. And I won't be able to talk them out of it either—they're too determined. Who would listen to a woman, anyway?

I smoothen my skirt, my palms warm and sweaty now. *How?* The iron fist around my heart squeezes even more. My mind is being pulled in all directions, pondering and wondering the how of this situation. I can't push through, and I can't fight my way out of this—not with my persistent thoughts, and certainly not with Dendup and Karma.

My temples throb. All this thinking ahead, it's not doing me any good. There's nothing I can do right now. I wipe my heated face with the back of my sleeve and take another deep breath. *Focus.*

I make my way to the lake and dip my hands into her pristine waters. A crisp cool spreads through my body as I run my hands across my face into the back of my neck. Little drops trickle their way down my spine and slowly the heated conversation in my mind is calming down.

Act from a pure heart. Tara's words echo over the lake. Cool water seeps through the back of my shirt. *It's only from a pure heart that good things can be done.* Tiny dangling driblets on the edge of my lashes cast the illuminating light of morning like sparkling stars all around. Yes, a pure heart. I let the realization sink in. I need to keep my heart pure and my mind clear. Nothing good ever comes from worry or fear. A pure heart secures my path to truthful actions. A calm mind makes me see clear to wherever my heart guides me. All I can do in this very moment is set my highest intention—and be patient. Very patient, for Lhasa's still a long way.

And while these thoughts nestle themselves in the corners of my mind, I let out a yawn. My stomach grumbles. Time for tea.

"Here, sister, here!" A flappy hat fans my face, two little hands attached to it. "Take it, you're too warm." It's the little girl from the inn, the one who was so kind to give me tea when I was wiped out. The hat waves in front of me. Her face beams with the brightest smile I've seen today.

"Thank you," I clasp her tiny middle. "That's so much better."

She places the hat on my head and giggles as its limp brim drops over my ears.

"I think it's too big." She tips the front of the hat up and peers into my face. "It's my mother's." She turns and points at the steady stream of pilgrims that has almost reached us.

"That's fine." My fingers lift the hat a bit. "I'm good now, so let's give it back to her."

One hand on the hat, the other on the girl, I wait for the party to catch up with us.

With the invoking hum of the pilgrims all around, my body seems to float as we circle the second half of the lake. Completely at peace, I reach my two companions, who have made themselves quite a comfortable picnic under the trees.

"Tea?" Dendup's all smiles again as he handles me a steaming cup. The little girl, still at my side, pulls a stale crust from under her raggedy coat.

"Oh, we can do better than that," Karma says, and he hands her a chunk of buttered flatbread. Her beady eyes devour the bread and she mumbles a "thank you" before she delves in.

"Good kora?" Karma pours the girl some tea in his cup.

"Very good." I nod and wipe the butter from the girl's chin. "But surely we're not done yet?" I wink as I try to catch Dendup's eye.

"Huh?" Dendup grimaces. "Not done?" He scratches the top of his head.

"Well, now that we're here." I laugh as Dendup fishes a wooden mala from his pocket. The polished beads flash an auburn gleam as he swings the string around his wrist.

"I just did a whole round, right here," he says. "Surely that counts for something?" He veins a serious look, but the sneaky grin in the corners of his mouth gives him away. Even the little girl's not falling for it.

"Nice try, Uncle," she says. "But I think these beads are shiny and new, they have never been counted around." She grabs the string from his wrist, her infectious smile matching Dendup's smirk.

"You're so right, little sister." Dendup puts on his quasi-disappointed face. "I'm sorry. Will you forgive me my teeny tiny lie?" His head bowed, he peeks at the girl from under his bushy eyebrows. She puts the beads right under her nose and squints.

"Maybe," she says. "If you go to kora with me and sister." She clutches my hand. "Sister does a great kora. She knows her prayers so well."

My heart melts from the look on that tiny face. So spontaneous, she radiates an unbridled delight we adults can only envy.

"Well then," Karma says. "If you and sister do kora so well, I think Dendup and I can't stay behind." He slaps a protesting Dendup on the shoulder. "We can all use a bit of good merit-making, for sure." And with those words he clears the cups.

So around the lake we go again, now with the four of us. And I'm surprised as both Dendup and Karma turn out to be skilled stackers of stones. While mulling a vast variety of mantras under their breath, they build the most spectacular rock piles, reverend homages to Yilhun Lha Tso and her sacred surroundings. And as regards to kora, little sister and I agree—it's one of the best we've ever done, especially after Dendup decided his wooden beads were much better suited around little sister's neck.

As the first shadows of the majestic Cho La turn the lake from a clear turquoise into a deep indigo hue, our party heads back to the caravanserai.

Karma leads the way with little sister holding on to the front of his saddle. Dendup follows closely with her slightly older brother, jousting his way back on one of his pack horses. Generous, kind, and gentle, these men never cease to amaze me.

Clearly so devoted to the Buddhist faith, yet determined to kill a man.

How do they justify their paradoxical behavior, if only in their own mind?

Seventeen

T here's something that happens to you when you visit a holy place—to your body and your mind. It leaves an imprint. Not only a karmic one, but a physical one too. I feel it the moment my eyes open. A lightness in my body and mind, an agility in my limbs that I've never had before—and it's not only the good night of sleep that's brought it on.

While most pilgrims stayed to spend the night at the lake, we went back to the comfort of the inn.

"There'll be plenty of nights without a roof ahead," Dendup said, when I asked him why. "Too many nights under the open sky is a punishment on the body."

And while I would have loved to have spent more time at the lake, I'm grateful now—the warmth of the hearth this early morning is a pleasant welcome.

My companions are already up as I wake between two empty mats. With my body as light as a feather, I hasten to make three prostrations. As I fold my hands in prayer, I notice the deep pink streaks on the palm of my hands. The nasty lesions that festered a few days back have closed. The skin's already reforming her familiar lined pattern. Even the burning sensation is gone. I stretch out my hand and trace the ruddy lines with my finger, inspecting them closer. How amazing this human body. How it heals and adapts to its new circumstances.

I crouch to fold my blanket. The stiffness that used to settle in my limbs after a day's ride is gone. "You'll get used to the saddle soon enough," Sangmo told me. But to be honest, it took my body a long time to adjust to the riding. I've had aches and pains ever since I left the monastery many moons ago. My heart skips a beat at the thought of my home on the remote mountaintop. My body's reached the point where it's suited to serve my new life as a lay person now. I'm praying, however, that my mind won't mirror the usual laxity of a layperson's mind. My highest intentions are still the same—to serve all sentient beings the best I can in this lifetime.

The earthy aroma of freshly brewed tea draws me to the kitchen like honey to a bee. It's packed, and I can't see my companions, but that's fine. By now, I know how these kitchens work. The trick is to sit as close to the stove as possible, so you can catch the servants' eye as they go around in full flight. It works, and in no time, I've got a cup filled to the brim and a slab of buttered bread in front of me.

As the salty spread melts on my tongue, my stomach grumbles. I didn't notice how hungry I was. It must be from all the walking yesterday. I blow the fatty foam to the side of my cup and let my thoughts drift to Yilhun Lha Tso. As the warm brew rinses the brine off my palate, my whole being is filled with the comforting blend of wholesome fare and intense contentment. A good kora it was.

"Sister!" A small voice calls out from the doorway.

It's the little girl who came with us last night. Her parents stayed at the lake, but this cheeky one begged Dendup and Karma to take her and her brother for a ride on the horses. Of course the men couldn't say no, the softies. "Sister, they're waiting for you." Her tiny hands above her head beckon me to come.

I wash the last piece of bread down with my tea and follow the patter of her footsteps into the hallway. She's already disappeared as I step out.

The courtyard's as crowded as the kitchen, with the muleteers securing their loads. It's into the Cho La mountain range from here on, with the crossing of the highest peak expected in a day or two. My feet on the threshold, I peer through the mist that covers the mass of bags, packs, mules, and men. The huff of my stallion comes from the other side of the courtyard. There it is, all saddled up and ready to go. Next to my horse stand Karma and Dendup, their backs to me.

I stroll their way, my hood turned up to ward off the morning chill. As I reach within ear distance, my feet somehow stall. Their heads bent together, their gestures intense, Karma and Dendup appear to be in a heated discussion. There's a third person with them. Karma's tall statue is obstructing my view. The dim morning light isn't helping either, but my eyes spot a pair of man's boots—foreign boots—shuffling up dust opposite my two companions. Their jerky behavior alerts my mind. I slide my hood back a little and perk my ears.

The veil of dawn muffles their words, but as soon as the stranger's accent hits my ear, my stomach tightens. The man's voice carries a snaking, gnawing edge. I yank the hood back over my head and pull it tight. My jagged fingernails hook the black furred rim. Every muscle in my body tenses. I don't know what's being said, but I know it's not good—and I'm sure I'm not supposed to hear this.

What to do? I shiver, my feet frozen to the ground, my knees weak. With my mind on full speed, I shift back in the shadows, making sure I stay out of the men's sight.

"Found you!" A girl's voice echoes with a cheerful yell, and two tiny hands latch on to my leg. I stumble, but pull off a smile. It's little sister again, saving me from a most tricky position, even though she doesn't realize it.

"You sure did," I say. With a deep breath out, I kneel at her side and put my trembling fingertips on her shoulders. From the corners of my eyes, I see Karma and Dendup, their attention turned to me and little sister now.

There's another thing I spot too—the stranger's boots rushing out of view, the gleaming buckles disappearing into the crowd.

"You're here." Dendup scratches his head. His eyes dart from me over the crowded courtyard and back. "Been waiting long?" A halting smile cracks through the veneer of his pinched lips.

"Nope." I try my most casual tone. "Just here." I meet his avoiding eyes from under my drawn hood. "Sorry to have kept you waiting." My heart's pounding. A slight heat rises in my cheeks. Do they know?

"That's fine," Karma says. "We're just getting ready ourselves."

The casual tone of his voice should reassure me, but as I lift my chin towards him, the long, leery look in his narrowed eyes says it all. *He knows.* He knows I saw them arguing with the stranger.

His stony stare sucks the air out of the awkward silence between us. I clench my fists, expecting a lashing of words which is undoubtably going to follow from him, but to no avail. The only thing coming from his lips is a quiet, mellow smile.

I flinch. Did I misread Karma? Then he bends towards me, enough for the first rays of dawn to thaw his icy stare into a tender forest green. He knows alright.

My heart skips a beat as he smoothens the creased rim of my hood, caressing my flushed cheeks ever so lightly with his fingertips. He knows, and he doesn't mind—he trusts me. A warm glow spreads across my chest. He trusts me with the implicit understanding not to mention what I witnessed. Not to Dendup, and not to him.

My shoulders sag, my fists unfold. All I want to do now is slide my hands over his and hold them against my face. But I don't, of course, and I wrestle myself out of his captivating glance.

Sharp sand crunches underneath as I spin my heels.

"Let's go then." I untie my horse with a nonchalance that strengthens my airy tone, but my insides cringe. Why am I still so awkward towards him?

My hands clasp the manes of my stallion. He gives me a quick leg-up. I cast my eyes down. What a silly girl he must think me to be. My mind feverish, I surrender. I'm trying hard, but I just don't know how to handle all of him. I'm treading unknown territory here while he's got the advantage of a seasoned traveler.

"No need to hurry, love." His voice is barely audible, and his hand rests on my calf. "It's still a long way to Lhasa." With a loving but oh-so-cheeky smile, he slides his hand down, and I can't help but laugh at him, but mostly at myself.

The sky opens to a purple blue. The caravan moves out of the sheltered town onto the open planes. And while the milky rays of morning light dispel the shadows of the frosty night, they don't resolve the fragments of the harsh foreigner's gnaw lingering in the back of my mind. Who was that stranger, and why did Karma and Dendup not want me to see them with him?

I fold back my hood and raise my face to the surging sun. My fingers slide the jade beads around, invoking the support of the mother of all Buddhas. *Om Tara.* I mean, I know I'm in good company with them, but an extra helping hand won't hurt, will it? *Om Tara.* Especially when she's a force above nature.

It turns out to be another day of pleasant riding for us. The rustle of tall grass in the warm breeze, the rich, balmy smell of earth churned up by the horses' hoofs, the lush valley leading us up to the mountain range is invigorating to body and mind. Spending the night under the open sky turns out to be so much more comfortable—and calmer—than I feared. As there's no inn in sight, the caravan spreads itself out in the hardy grass at the foot of the Cho La. Mules and men scatter around the small bonfires ignited to mark our ground against the prowling predators.

Finding the comfort of company, provisions go around, and tales of wonder and amazement drown the crackling glow of the flames. With a slice of moon and a thousand stars against the vast blue sky and my thin mat secured between Dendup and Karma, deep sleep immerses me as soon as I crawl under my blanket.

Only the wind scratching through the tops of the frozen grass gives away the coldness of the night. With my blanket tightly wrapped, I sleep through the frost and Dendup's usual loud snoring. I must have been in deep sleep, for it's only when little sister puts her icy hands on my cheeks and giggles in my ear that I awake.

The pungent scent of wood smoldering and charred pine needles hits my nose. I sit up. Rubbing the sleep out of my eyes, I notice the empty places beside me. Where are my companions? A quick glance around and I spot our horses, already packed, and there's Karma and Dendup, taking their time with their tea. While the world's already in full swing under the pasty morning sun, I've slept right through the buzz of the rising caravan. I hop out of my blanket and clear my mat.

"Why didn't you wake me?" I say. With flushed cheeks, I tie my gear together. I've been sleeping while they were working—not good.

"Ah, figured you needed it." Dendup winks over the rim of his cup, his voice a mix of comfort and cheer. With a sigh, I sit next to him.

"Thanks," I say, as Karma hands me a cup of tea. "I did."

Slowly I wake up, sharing the tea and a crust of bread with little sister glued to my feet.

"Weather looks good enough." Karma's eyes are on the stately Cho La, her chiseled peaks like sharp teeth biting into the pink caked sky.

Dendup nods. "It's a long trek." He swigs the last of his tea down. "And you, little one." He pinches little sister in her scrawny leg. "You better stay close to your ama and apa today or Mi la tse tse will take you away." His voice low, he peers at the girl from under his furred eyebrows.

"You know he lives up there, and he loves to play." Dendup points at the Cho La and Little sister's eyes widen. Her small hands grip tight around my ankles. "Listen to your ama or apa now, or you will never see them again." His voice takes on an even more gloomy tone to emphasize the gravity of the matter.

Mi la tse tse. I laugh at the sight of Dendup's quasi-frightening face. He's trying to scare little sister, and it works. All children are afraid of Mi la tse tse, the hairy monster that lives in the mountains. He loves to play with children and lures them with sweet treats away from their parents, never to be seen again. How many times did my father try this trick on me? It worked too—it's a great tale to keep unruly children in line.

"Mi la tse tse is up there?" Her hands squeeze my ankles even tighter. As little sister's eyes meet mine, the fear in her eyes melts my heart.

"He sure is." I put my arms around her shaky shoulders. "But you're a good girl, aren't you?" I glance at Dendup and grimace. He shouldn't scare her like this. "You stay with your ama and apa and everything will be fine." Her woolen cap slides to the side as she nods. "Good, so go now. We'll see you tonight." And off she is to her parents, no doubt running as fast as her sticky legs can carry her.

With Dendup stamping out the fire, I'm checking my horse and gear again, securing it extra tight for today's trip.

"Nordun." Karma's voice comes from behind, and his hands slide around my waist. Before I get the chance to turn around, his strong arms lift me into the saddle. I gasp as my hands clutch the manes of my horse.

"A warning would have been nice." I straighten in the saddle. "But thanks."

My hand slides over his, resting on my thigh. A tingle shoots up my arm, straight through my body, and creates flutters in my stomach. My mind's all over the place—oh, how he knows to throw me off balance.

"Stay close today." His voice is low, and his fingers interlace with mine. "Keep between Dendup and me." I nod.

"I mean it, Nordun." His jaw sets as he lifts his chin to affirm the gravity of his request with a stern look.

"I will." Our fingers still intertwined, his thumb strokes my thigh and I sense his hesitation to let go. "I promise." I mean it. The weight in his tone leaves no suggestion for banter.

"Good." He drops his hand. "That's settled then."

My eyes dart over to Dendup. The pack horses are tied, and he's ready to join the caravan, steadily setting itself in motion.

"Let's ride in the front line." Dendup gestures to Karma. In one fluid motion, their horses line up with mine, spurring us all on in a full trot.

It doesn't take long before we're out of the valley, onto the slopes of the mighty Cho La. The lush green fades into parched gray under the warming sun. Our horses' hoofs scrape the barren rocks as the narrow path winds up towards the ridge. We're riding at a walking pace. In a single row, our caravan steadily climbs, like a sleek serpent determined on the prowl.

As the vastness of the sky comes closer, an eerie silence prevails. There's no more chatter of birds, only the sharp scratching of the wind against the rising bedrocks and the quiet hum of prayer.

The sun's gaining strength quickly at this height, pounding merciless at our head by noon. Her rays reflect on the scattered ice crusts. I draw my hood further over my eyes. Shifting in my saddle, I feel my body's strength draining away with the little trickles of sweat that make their way down my back. The heat and height weigh heavy on my shoulders. The lightness I experienced since Yilhun Lha Tso is erased with a single sun.

My stallion, however, prances as vigorous as ever. He despises his position, squished in single file, and huffs all the way, holding his head high. Alarmed by the clumsy scrambling of my horse's hoofs, Karma turns to check on me.

"He'll back down once we reach the snowline." Karma squints against the blaring sun. A glimpse of unease come through. "If not, we'll switch horses."

I loosen the reins once more. I'm sure I can handle my own, but he's right. No need to take risks on the steep mountain slopes. I shift back in my saddle to relax into the steady pace once more. *Om Tare.*

In the corners of my eyes, an orange frame simmers in the sun. Bluish gray wings slice through the breeze. A lone vulture circles the bright blue yonder. My gaze focuses on the path before us. Father's words of warning ring in my ear. "It's a dangerous place out there, Nordun, for many left but never returned." His hands had pressed on my shoulders. "The mountains are unforgiving, turning complete caravans into valleys of bones, all along the route."

A chill runs up my sweat drenched spine. Still, here I am. Father has faith in me and in my companions. *Om Tare.*

As the scattered snow crusts turn into an icy trail, we dismount and lead our horses by foot. Dendup's unleashed the pack horses by now, for if one falls, all fall. It's not that they can wander off, anyway. The trail's narrow, a path carved into the side of the rocks leading straight up to the solid vertical cliffs.

My stallion's strut has turned into a shamble. He's never walked on ice before. I chuckle as he presses his nose into the back of my coat. Relentless as ever, he's still determined to take the lead.

By midday, a surging gust swirls a few long-hanging clouds around the peaks. I drop my hood and turn my face to the shrouded sun. The arid breeze catches a few of my sticky locks on the side of my temples—finally some relief. My nostrils tingle as the crisp air clears my head and for a moment, I feel lifted again.

"Sister." Dendup's voice urges a warning call. "Buckle up." My gaze follows his hand, pointing to the highest peak. "Something's coming, real soon." My eyes dart over, my body tenses at the sight.

A gray mist has settled around the peak, and it's cascading down right before my eyes. My hands tighten the reins as the breeze becomes a shrieking wind, twisting its way towards our convoy. *Hail. Or snow?* I fasten my belt as a sudden bitter cold finds its way through the folds of my coat.

My hood pulled, I settle my gaze on Karma's stallion before me, my breath in sync with the silent stride of his hoofs. The first flakes of dusty white float down like feathers shaken out of a bird's nest, hooking themselves on the fur trim of my coat. It doesn't take long before the soft crystals harden into solid slivers of ice and the veiled sky above us rips open. A cloudburst of hail comes thundering down, cutting off my breath and my steps.

"Keep moving!" Dendup's command echoes from behind.

I gasp and stumble forward to regain my pace. My heart's pounding. I scold myself. Silly me, it's only hail. I draw closer to my stallion, the wisps of steam rise from his widened nostrils balmy against my hand. His head bend now, icicles are sticking to his unruly manes. Sensing the imminent pour down, it seems he's calmed down. His twitching ears give it away though—he's very much on edge. I squeeze my fists.

"We're good, you and me." A wishful whisper while I stroke his soggy nose, a solace directed at him, but intended to uplift my own spirits. It helps if only a little.

Ice above us, ice below us, my horse and I scramble on.

Eighteen

T he first small mani stones appear along the path. *Om Tare.*
Hacked into the side of the bedrocks, they're a sign we're
coming up to the highest point now. Almost there. *Focus.* My feet
sag in the sleet. Hail turns into snow, caking the front of my coat.
I slide the reins around my bent arm and fold my sleeves over my
numb fingers as far as possible. One foot in front of the other, my
breath shallows as the raw cold pierces my lungs.

I halt for a moment to turn my back against the gale. Coming
up for air, I peer down the path from under my hood. All I see is
shadows, moving like a funeral procession into a vast pale white.
I blink, my thoughts swirling over the long line of silhouettes that
are my companions. *Ghosts.* I'm walking amidst an ashen haunt of
roving spirits, risen from their funeral pile, and damned to walk
the bardo for an unknown time.

In a crystal surge, the pure luminosity of death flashes before
my eyes. Yes, we're ghosts, spirits inhabiting these temporal bodies,
destined to perish, whether we want to or not. Maybe today, on
this mountain, maybe some other time. It's not for us to decide.

I swallow my breath as the haunting insight lingers on in the
back of my mind. *Ghosts.* With my stallion's nose prodding my
shoulder, I draw my hood closer and face to wind. *Keep moving.*

My breath's sawing in my throat. My knees shake from the
strength spent. I raise my hand as Karma looks back. I'm still here.
In the distance, I see the shreds of prayer flags, their voices lost

in the wind. *We've reached the top.* And just as I'm about to step ahead, a vortex of shrieking air lifts around us, drawing up dense walls of opaque snow and pearly ice. Any effort to stay upright or even to stay put is spent, for the mighty Cho La has decided to reveal herself in all her force, leaving us all to wander in a world without end. My body beaten, I sag to my knees, ready to give in to whatever it is the mountain demands. *This place, this time—this is what the bardo is like.*

A sharp-arrowed ache shoots up my forehead as I draw a deep breath. This is the breach between death and next life, the in-between where our spirits roam after our bodies are spent and left behind. This is the vault in which all our fears and foes are stored, ready to be unleashed on us in a terror of delusions. And this is the moment where the mundane and the sacred meet, the moment where we have the opportunity to awaken. We either liberate or further entrap ourselves, depending on how we relate to it all. *This is it.*

A strange calm descends on me as I stare down at my hands, suspended in time. My breath cascades down in a white cloud. I raise my palms to the sky. My fingers catch the crystal pouring down. A rainbow of light reflects in each and every one of them. They blind me with their brilliance, and I close my eyes as warm streaks roll down my frozen cheeks. Humbled by the rawness of her elemental power, I lay myself down. My body melts into the enveloping cold. I surrender to Cho La. This is the moment where it all comes down to staying aware, staying present—in body and mind—with whatever manifests.

Breathe! A surge of adrenaline shoots through my body as a deep voice resounds over the howling wind. *Breathe!* I gasp. The taste of iron fills my mouth. Glass particles cut through my nostrils, down the back of my throat. Jolted back to the here and now, I grab the front leg of my horse and drag myself up. My body numb, but my mind vivid and alive, I slide my arm over my stallion's neck. With my face pressed against his frozen manes, I shiver and swallow the steely liquid that foams around my lips. Whatever arises, it's all an illusion. It's all in the mind. Keep breathing, keep moving. *Om Tare.*

"Come on!" My lips motionless, my mind forms the words. It takes all my strength to push on my stallion. He doesn't need the spur, though. When he senses my desperate touch, he drags me on, one cautious step after another one. Aimlessly we wander, going forward to wherever Cho La's whirling power demands. And as the vault of fears and foes cracks right open, ringing in my most vengeful nightmares to haunt me down. My mind turns to Tara, steering me clear from an untimely death—I've surrendered to survive.

Drifting in this frenzied white dome, fending off the eve-persistent phantoms that prey on my body and mind, I've lost all notion of time. It could have been one part of the sun, it could have lasted even a moon, I don't know, but all of a sudden it halts. Without warning, the sky rips open in the brightest azure and swallows the coiling vortex with a roaring thunder, leaving our beaten down convoy to emerge in an eerie, silent whiteout. The descending stillness crushes my spine, and I fall to my knees once again. Only this time, my face is turned to the sky. A prayer of gratitude flows from my lips. She has heard my plea; she has granted me mercy. *Om Tare.* I'm free.

Still on my knees, I try to catch my breath and lick the tiny trail of blood trickling from the corner of my mouth. My head spins as the clear air rushes down my chest. My body is open, my mind is clear. I close my eyes and sink my hands into the freezing sleet. I need to ground myself, for I'm weightless and floating into the opal expanse.

"Nordun." A voice pleads as two powerful arms lift me up. "Love, look at me." Cold hands on my cheeks, a warm breath stirs my lips. I open my eyes and sink into an ocean of emerald. "Nordun." It's Karma.

My lips move, a stale whiff from my mouth. "I'm good." The words pour out of my mouth in a gulf of heated iron, flowing all the way from the back of my breath. My stomach contracts and I gag.

"Spit it out." His one hand slides around my waist, the other pulls back my hood. My stomach turns itself upside down. Blood splatters in the snow. Instant relief settles through my body. "That's it." He runs his thumbs over my lips and wipes the traces of red of my mouth. I shiver, pearls of sweat form on my forehead.

"I'm good," I say, and sink back into his arms.

"Of course you are." He pulls me in, defying any resistance met. "You're about to conquer so much more than this." His lips graze the tip of my ear. His whisper carries an ominous edge. "You just don't know it yet." His muscles around me tense—for only a split moment—a tight ripple under the fur of his dense coat. Narrow slivers of green meet my eyes as I draw back. Before I can open my mouth, he slides my hood back over my head, leaving me no space to react to his puzzling remark.

"Nordun." Dendup pops up beside us, cloaked in white. His typical grin peeps from under his cap. "I see you're in excellent hands." With brisk strokes, he wipes the snow from his chuba and slaps Karma on the shoulder, his comical relief coming through. "And again, Cho La grants us a safe crossing." His eyes dart over the horizon. "Let's not push our luck and hurry, for we're nowhere in the clear yet."

With reluctance, Karma releases his grip, and I steady myself, rubbing some life back in my hands. Dendup's right, we're only halfway. Even though this meagre snowfall is nothing compared to the fierce blizzard we just survived, it's still a long way to safe shelter. My stallion shudders, as if to strengthen Dendup's words. "Yes, I hear you." My hands run over his neck.

With the front part of our caravan already on the move, I hasten after Karma, my legs remarkably light. Crossing Cho La's highest point, a gateway of shimmering white against a stark blue, a silver sun breaking through the last clods of creamy gray. Her stillness and silence halt me and I bow my head in reverence to the mighty Cho La. She has humbled me with her magnitude and honored me with her mercy. She has touched me with her strength and showed me my own. Nothing will ever be the same again, and yet it is for here we walk on, my horse and me.

A slender tongue of ice twists down. It's our path from the top. Shielding my eyes from the pearly sheen that's known to blind, I let myself fall into the rhythm of the descent. *Om Tare.* The ice melts into a shifty trail of loose rocks and gravel, leading us into the shadows of a steep-sided gorge. With the river raging beneath us, we slide down, our pace even slower than the crawl up this morning. I fix my eyes on the path before me, my hands pull the reins tighter with every scramble of my horse's hoofs.

"Easy now." My voice croaks a futile reminder as my horse's already on his edge, treading with the utmost care. Sweat veils my forehead, and the intensity of the trail prevails over the bitter cold. We straggle down until we reach the lower grounds at the onset of dusk.

As the first fires are lit among our scattered group, I saddle off my horse and sink down beside his bent head. "We've made it." I stroke his sodden manes. "We've come through." My fingers numb, I wrestle with the horse's halter.

"Here, let me." Karma's hands shroud mine. A painful tinge shoots through as they meet with his warm breath. "You get yourself to the fire. We'll take care of the rest."

With a thankful smile, I pull my hands up my soaked sleeves and dash down to the nearest blaze.

"Ah, good to see you, sister." Hands stretched to the flames, Lanying's voice resounds with genuine relief. "I knew you would make it." She swings back her hood. Sparks of fire reflect a thoughtful light blue in her eyes. "Here, come closer." With one hand around my shoulder, she pulls me in. "Get warm." Her hand rubs my back. "Many have not come yet." A gloom slides across her face and she turns to the darkened mountain range.

I flinch, the fire's heat blazes against my face. Of course, we were in the front group and we've only just arrived.

"Any idea how many?" I glance at Lanying, for I dare not look at our scattered convoy.

She shrugs. "We'll have to wait for the light to assess the damage." The pragmatic tone in her voice tells me she's been here before—many times. "You don't worry, sister, you're in good company." She looks over my shoulder. "Here're your two guards again." She spins her heels and draws her hood back over her head. I snatch her sleeve and hold it tight.

"Stay," I say, and grab her other hand. There's no need for her to run off like that.

"Next time, sister." With a hiss, she tugs herself free, and off she is, the tail of her long coat breezing behind her.

I blink and step back.

My mouth half-open, the words are on my lips. "Don't be foolish," I wanted to say. "No need to be avoiding each other like this." But she's already vanished amongst the swift shadows of night.

"Drying out a bit?" Dendup moves beside me, wringing his hands at the fire. I nod. My face and hands are ablaze by now. The heat's thawing my frozen bones. "Found us a suitable spot out of the wind." He points to a ticket of bushes, our gear already spread out. Turning my back to the fire, I wrap my coat tight. As warm as it is within the fringe of the flames, so bitter is the cold outside of it.

While a few muleteers keep the fires crackling, we retreat to our mats. Squished between my two companions, I crawl deep under my blanket. Cho La has pushed my body to its limits today, exhausting it with a deep sense of release, and I'm ready to fall asleep.

"Nordun." A whisper from Karma. "Look."

I peep from under the blanket. Karma's hand points to the midnight sky. I draw up a little; the breeze catching the top of my head. Amidst a thousand glowing stars is a flashing rain of fireballs—a cloudburst of fierce orange and fiery yellow pours down on the peaks of the Cho La.

"Wow." I can't suppress my amazement and raise myself up on my elbows. I've seen the sky streaked in fire before, but not like this. So fiery, so fierce. A smile curls on my lips—what a gift we are granted. What an auspicious sign the heavens have sent us on our journey.

I shiver as the bitter breeze chases me back under my blanket. I pull my arms out of my sleeves and rub my shoulders. The cold's having another go at me, latching itself onto my bones. Turning on my side, I pull my blanket closer, the coarse wool scraping my cheeks. If only I could get warm again. The woody fumes of the smolder still linger in the air. Maybe I should get to one of the fires for a bit? I duck deeper as my teeth clatter.

"Nordun." Karma's voice is gentle yet insistent. "Come here." His strong arms grip around me. With one heave, he hauls me into his blanket. "Open your coat." His fingers fumble with the strap around his chuba, but my mind blanks. I freeze.

"Come to me, my love." His voice is husky now, and I hold my breath as his hand slips underneath the fur of my coat. He opens the front and folds the sides away. My mind's jolted awake. Scrambling to make sense of this, my body tenses in all ways imaginable. "Trust me." He draws me closer and folds my rigid body into the warm, open space of his. He wraps our coats and blankets tight around and rests my head against his chest. "Breathe." And as his heart beats a drum in my ear, it releases a quiet warmth, a tender comfort that relaxes the very being of me.

With my body melting into his, a calmness eases my mind. I draw a deep breath and swallow the suffocating misgivings in me. *I'm good, we're good.*

My hands slide up with a slight hesitation but nestle themselves in the soft spot of his midriff.

With his fingers caressing my cheek, our breaths and beings fall into sync, and we drift off into the night under the watchful eye of the mighty Cho La.

Nineteen

The frost breaks on the surface of our blankets with a crisp rustle, but the bone-piercing cold hasn't touched me at all. Sheltered in the warmth of Karma's body, I wake, cozy and snug, my cheek still pressed against his chest.

"Good morning." With a gentle whisper, he releases his grip. "You're one quiet sleeper—you haven't moved at all."

I've slept in his arms. My breath quickens as my mind registers where I am, and I wince. *All night.* I pull up my arms from underneath, unable to meet his eye yet.

"Give me a moment. My arm has gone numb." He chuckles, slides on his side, and puts my head in the crock of his neck. "So that's better." He rests his cheek against my balmy forehead, his breath a tranquil breeze in the quietude between us.

I swallow, my chest tight. *How did this happen?*

"Nordun." A pensive pause.

"Hmmm," I clear my throat, but the lump of unease won't loosen from the back of my throat.

"You're not going shy on me now, are you?" He runs the back of his hand over my cheek and lifts my chin to meet his eyes. "Nothing happened, you know."

My breath relaxes, and I shiver. He's right. Nothing happened. Yet, the moment our gazes fuse and our breath meets, I know. *Something happened.*

My temples throb and my fingertips tingle with an unknown ache to touch him. I hold my breath as I run my fingers along the roughened edge of his jaw.

His head bends and touches my forehead. His eyes close as my fingertips stray on his cheekbone. The smell of him, so salty, so soothing. My mind has deserted me. I just can't let him go.

A smile buds in the corner of his mouth, and his hand covers mine. He presses his lips against the palm of my hand. His eyes open, and his gaze locks mine in a tender understanding between us. I come up for air, surfacing from a depth I've never been before. This man, so patient. Something happened, we both know it. Something happened to me.

"Karma." Dendup's raw voice jolts me back to the here and now. "Get up, quick."

I look up and freeze. Something's wrong. The cap pulled over Dendup's eyes can't hide his wrought expression.

"What?" My mind strung, I shoot up, only to be pulled back by Karma and the entanglement of our clothes. Calm as ever, Karma peels the layers away. A smile still graces his lips.

"Don't worry," he says. "Dendup tends to overreact." His sturdy hands pull me up and smoothen the front of my coat. "In case you hadn't noticed." He winks, but as he turns to Dendup, his smile fades into a frown. Dendup shakes his head.

"Cho La." He casts his eyes upon the arid mountain range behind me. "She's demanded the ultimate sacrifice again." His voice casts a worry. "She's taken a little one last night."

My stomach plunges. I stumble back. *The ultimate sacrifice. A little one.* Dizziness seizes me as Dendup's words spin on their axes in the vacuum of my mind.

"Wow." Karma steadies his arm around my waist. "Which little one?"

My eyes dart over the frosted fields where the front of our convoy stranded last night. Small groups scatter around the smoldering fires, slowly waking up to the break of dawn. The outer ring of muleteers and mules keeps their precious cargo close in the pale pink of the morning mist.

I crane my neck and I strain my eyes, but I don't see little sister.

"That one's brother." Dendup's words get lost in the echo of a desperate wail. It's little sister, running towards us as if she's being chased by the last shadows of a horrifying night.

"Sister!" Her limp little body latches itself to my legs with a heartbreaking sob. I crouch and throw my arms around her. A flood of tears breaks through.

"What happened?" I steady my voice and my mind. My hands wipe her heated, streaked face.

"Her brother went astray last night." Dendup stoops beside us and gently ruffles the nest of fuzz on top of her head. "He's playing with Mi la tse tse now." He pauses and heaves a deep breath. "And they're having a lot of fun together." His voice pitches as he turns to me. "Right, Nordun?" Little sister's head bobs up. Her teary look of bewilderment stares me right in the face.

"Really?" Her thin voice rips right through my heart.

I open my mouth, but nothing comes out.

Her eyes widen at the sight of my hesitation. Her knees fail and my heart plunges down at her feet.

I draw her close and hold her tight as the weight of grief crushes her birdlike body. Tears burn behind my closed eyes—so much suffering to bear at such an early age. I clutch her tighter to prevent myself from speaking, for it's better to stay silent now.

We both know Dendup's words are not true and some things are not meant to be said—their truth is like bindweed, choking the life out of everything it comes across. Sometimes staying silent is the best way to be.

So, I do the only thing I can do in the face of unspeakable suffering—I hold her.

Resting my mind in stillness, I hold her in my arms without reacting, without response, without any emotional disturbance, so anger and sadness have nowhere to latch onto in me.

I hold her in my heart and inhale her hot, dark and devastating despair in an even cool breath, while exhaling a fresh sense of cool, bright light beaming through the pores of my body.

I hold her until her breath falls in sync with mine and the wall she's trying so hard to build around her heart crumbles .

I hold her until our hearts connect, sharing the burden of her grief and strengthening her center so she can hold her own—for now.

Twenty

O ur convoy is sluggish to start today. Even the sun—spinning her shiniest, most golden rays through the vale—can't seduce us this morning.

With little sister calmed down, we take up our usual position—Karma in front, me following, and Dendup closing our line. Giving the grieving family some respite, Dendup swings little sister in the front of his saddle, which creates a big giggle through her tears. While whistling along with the chorus of the birds, he gives her the reins of his horse for the day. Needless to say, it puts a smile on the face of both of them.

The sun on our side, we ride into the green open valley towards Derge, but my thoughts are stalled on the merciless mountain and the little brother she claimed last night. With no body left, his steam of consciousness floats free now, roaming the death bardos for an unknown time. I wince. How confused and afraid he must be right now, finding himself in such haunting territory, all alone. *Om mani padme hung.*

As my mind forms the words of prayer, my fingers fumble with the red string on my wrist that my sisters left me. A small pang of regret stretches across my heart. If only I could get word to my sisters in seclusion. Their powerful prayers and offerings would guide the little one through his dark in-between, for no matter where the mind is, it will hear. *Om mani.* My eyes scout the horizon. There's no way to get any prayers done—the nearest monastery is still a day away.

I shift back in my saddle and draw my shoulders. We've prayed for so many of the deceased, my sisters and me. My heart still carries the words and the honest intention, for none of that hasn't changed. *Om mani.* For the benefit of all sentient beings.

With a sigh, I loosen the reins. Somewhere out there is a little one in need, and wherever he may be, he can hear me too. So my horse will have to lead us today, for I will pray and do the offering, from my own fragile mind to his in the in-between. I lift my face to the sky to receive her welcoming warmth and let the beads slide through my fingers. *Om mani padme hung.*

"Everything good?" Karma turns around to check on his following. I raise my hand.

Everything's good. When he throws me one of his wicked winks, I dare to meet his eyes and smile back at him. My heart makes a little leap. Cho La has taken a life, but she's also granted one—to me. The clarity I feel, the lightness in body in mind—it's true what Father said about ascending her peaks. If she doesn't demand your life, she cleanses your body and mind.

A surge of gratitude surges through my being. I close my eyes, seeking the stillness to be of solace again. The warming breeze plays with the silky fur of my collar, a smooth gaze against my face. A fleeting thought drifts by—one of a tender, precious life—and I return to my silent prayer once again.

With a mellow sun as our companion, and the bountiful valley providing plenty of fresh foraging for our animals on the way, the caravan doesn't take many stops today. I don't mind, for my prayer carries me through the day with ease. Dusk sneaks up on us before I even notice, chasing an orange red sun behind the western peaks. With our caravan spread out under an indigo firmament, Dendup lights a fire and the first twinkles appear.

"You did well today," Karma says as we tie down our horses for the night.

I nod. "My body's used to the saddle by now." I hoist my bag on our pile near the fire. "Finally." My hands on my hips, I stretch my back with ease.

"That's not what I meant." Karma slumps down against the bags. "Come sit." He gestures for me to join him.

"I heard you." His voice low, he rests his hand on my thigh.

"You heard me?" I raise my eyebrows and let my thoughts go over today. What does he mean?

"Your prayer, my love." His face softens and his warm hand covers mine. "All day around us."

My prayer. He hears my prayer, the silent words in my mind. How's that possible? My gaze draws to the fire, the orange tongues licking their way to the sky.

"But..." I turn, the heat of the flames gushing against my cheek. My eyes search and find his, fiery sparks reflecting in a green gleam.

Tiny wrinkles appear in the corner of his eyes. A smile draws up his lips.

How did he hear?

"Hey, lovebirds." Dendup's laughter roars above the flames, pulling me out of my wonder and right back in the now. "Who will fetch this old man some tea?" He wrings his hands and rubs his legs. "Or something else to warm the inside of me?" He plunks down at Karma's side.

I jump up and start rummaging through our bags. How unthoughtful of me to let my elder go thirsty. *Tea.* My hands find the right provision, but my mind's still lost for answers. How did Karma hear?

As Karma hauls the fresh water, I spread out what's left of our food. Even with my eyes cast down, I feel Dendup's gaze on me. As I glance up, he throws me a quick wink. My shoulders drop and we both burst into laughter.

"Sorry sister," he says. "I can't help it. You're just so easy to tease."

I roll my eyes. "You tell me," I say and hand him his cup and tsampa pouch.

"Still, we're doing better every day," he says. "Aren't we?" With a puff, he throws a bit of the fine flour in his mouth and chews it.

"Any chang left, by chance?" His eyes dart over our bags and I get up to see.

A fierce hiss escapes from the blaze as Karma bangs the kettle down the fire.

"Nope," he says and looks Dendup in the eye. "Tea is what's left."

I stall, my eyes on the bags.

"Ah well, it's Derge tomorrow morning." Dendup rubs his whitewashed moustache and sighs. Handing him the left-over butter, I crouch down beside Dendup again.

"At least there'll be some decent chang waiting there for me." His fingers mold the creamy fat into a little ball while he looks up to me, that typical tease on his lips. "And an entire day of rest for you youngsters to go about."

My toes curl in my sandals, and I still cringe, but only a little this time.

It's like Dendup said—we àre doing better, day by day.

Twenty-one

With Derge on our mind—and almost in our sight—our convoy has an early start. Determined to reach the town before the sun's at her highest point, the high-pitched yells of the muleteers echo over the shreds of grayish blue that cover the field. Their urging cries leave no room for lingering. Everybody's on the road by the first light of dawn.

My stomach grumbles, and a yawn escapes from my mouth. Breakfast wasn't on the men's mind this morning. My fingers probe the silky lining of my pocket. No tsampa balls left. I run my tongue across my teeth. I love my food and my cup of tea—especially in the morning.

All those times my grandmother caught me and my sisters with our hands in the tsampa bag, or sneaking a fresh fried khapse in the sleeves of our robe—a smile breaks on my parched lips. "A little hunger never hurt anyone," she would note with that stern voice of hers. Yes, she knew how to play on my guilt. Still, we never went hungry.

Another deep grumble from my stomach—it seems to disagree. I set my eyes on Karma's horse before me and lick my lips. The tea will taste so good.

The wind carries the sweet smell of the warming earth and a pink blush sweeps the sky. Spurred by the hum of the muleteers, we move through the morning with ease. It's not long before I spot the fluttering tops of the prayer flags in the woodland ahead, crowning

Derge's main monastery with fierce pride. As always, Dendup and Karma know their way around. Upon arrival, they lead us through the back ways to a small guesthouse nestled in the corner of town.

"Friends of ours," Dendup says, and it sure looks that way. We—well, Dendup really—are welcomed with open arms by the matron of the inn as we enter the courtyard.

"Just friends?" I slide the saddle off and look over my horse's back at Karma. I don't need the answer. His grin says it all.

"They're good people," he says. "Honorable people." He piles our bags as I tie our horses to the side. "We're far from our home and families. Good friends, trustworthy friends are what we need on the road."

I nod.

"They're pleasant company, you'll see." He puts his arm around my shoulders and walks me in. "And the tea is ever so agreeable."

I glance up. My eye catches a silver glint reflecting underneath his chuba as we step over the raised threshold of the inn. The iron fist around my heart clenches, my stomach churns. *He's wearing his long knife.*

Friends, he said, friends on the road, but my mind screams: *allies.* It's allies he meant. Allies in his quest to revenge my mother's death; allies in his quest to slay my uncle. Dizziness grips me. A sour taste fills my mouth. I stumble ahead.

"I got you." Karma's arms catch me on my way down the hallway. I shiver. His long knife flashes before me. *Focus.* My fingers dig in the wool of his chuba. I steady myself, my hands against his chest.

"I'm fine," I say and draw a deep breath. "Must be the hunger that got to me." A faint smile peeks on my lips, but I can't make it to break through. Karma's grip on me tightens.

"Tea's ready." He sweeps me to the kitchen where we're met with a buzz of clattering crockery and loud laughter. "Some food will do you good."

My body sags into a cushion with instant relief. The comforting smell of hearty thukpa on the stove settles my swirling stomach. And Karma's right—the tea is excellent, and the thukpa does me good. With every slurp of the spicy, meaty brew, I swallow my restless thoughts of friends, foes, and allies until my stomach's full and my mind at ease.

"Sister." A soft poke, an elbow in my side. I bounce up, my eyes wide, to meet Dendup's chuckle. I must have dozed off.

"The pilgrims are going to the monastery this afternoon," Dendup says. He licks the last of noodle soup from his bowl. "We're busy ourselves, but we figured you wanted to go?" Dendup's question is directed at me, but his eyes are on Karma opposite us.

"Yes," I perk up. "I would love to." My mind fuzzy, I rub the sleep from my eyes.

Karma shifts in his seat and puts his hands on his knees.

"We'll bring you," he says. "And collect you." He looks up at Dendup.

I nod.

"He's afraid you might stray on him again." Dendup leans into me and chuckles. A mix of tea and chang stains his breath.

Karma shakes his head. "Best to keep rest for a while, Dendup-la." His eyes flash a mean green. He swipes Dendup's cup and empties the rest on the floor beside him.

I wince as Dendup clenches his fists and bends over the table, ready to strike.

"Don't be a fool." Karma's voice is a low hiss. His arm shoots across and curbs Dendup's wrist. Their eyes clash in the dense space between the three of us. Dendup growls and his eyes bulge a nasty brown.

The stench of sudden sweat hits my nostrils. The swollen muscles in Dendup's neck rip through his reddened skin. Just when I think he's about to burst over the table, he lets out a roaring laugh and falls back, his body limp in the seat.

I gasp. Cups clatter and shatter the tension that was so tangible one moment ago into thin air.

"You're so right, my brother," Dendup says. He pulls his cap over his eyebrows and slouches further into his seat. "As always, you're so right." His mumble fades and within moments a steady snore escapes from under his lopsided cap.

My mouth open, I look at Karma. He shrugs and jumps up.

"Let's go," he says, and gestures at the door. "I'll take you to the monastery."

I turn to Dendup, deep asleep.

"Don't worry, he's in good hands here." The matron nods, her broad face gleaming in the heat of the stove. He's fine. I get up, my mind still going over what just happened here. The rage on Dendup's face, so not like the cheerful, kind Dendup I've gotten to know. A vague unease churns my stomach. *Allies. We're a bit busy ourselves.* My thoughts chew the leftovers of his words.

"You're good?" Karma's hand drapes around my shoulder.

"Yeah, sorry." I draw a deep breath. "Still drowsy from the meal and the nap." I slide my hand over his and straighten my shoulders. "A walk will do me good."

A steady stream of pilgrims guides the way, but the monastery can't be missed. Seated on a rolling hill amidst a luscious grove of green, it crowns the town of Derge.

"Do me a favor," Karma says as we halt at the enormous gate. "Stay with the others." His hand squeezes my shoulder. "No wandering around this time, promise?"

My smile meets his cautious look as I take my bag off his shoulder.

"I promise," I say. "I'll wait for you here." Giving him no chance to respond, I rush off, my sandals slipping in the dust. A little alone time for prayer and meditation, some real silence and solitude—this is what I've craved ever since Cho La and losing little brother.

The low hum of prayer buzzes in the courtyard, countless pairs of pious feet clobber down in rows. With a mass of monks, nuns, and pilgrims making their merit, this temple turns out to be anything but a silent place of solitude. Lined up to present my offerings, I raise myself on my toes, eager to set my eyes on the beauty I heard of inside.

The wide-open temple door behind me provides a grand entrance. A golden afternoon sun pours her rays on the enormous shrine. The gilded statue of the Buddha Shakyamuni, flanked by Padmasamhava and Buddha Jampa, towers on the shrine. It's clothed in the finest of silk and brocade. The shimmering of crowns, the most precious of gold, silver and gemstones, adorn their majestic presence. My eyes widen at the display of this magnificence.

Once inside, I'm absorbed in the heated stream of buoyant bodies, spinning the prayers of rattling wooden wheels and circulating the massive lacquered pillars clockwise with deep devotion. A vague sense of frenzy lingers around the crowd, unravelling the edges of my nerves. The air is thick with pungent shreds of smoke, stinging my eyes as they dart from corner to corner, looking for a quiet place to sit. To no avail.

"Sister." A determined hand grabs my elbow. It's Lanying. "Come over here." She turns on her heels and pulls me out of the rushed mass into the cool shade of the temple wall. "Too much ado, this place." She flashes a bright smile. "Better come to our sisters in the hermitage behind this high-and-mighty pretense." She hooks her arm through mine and marches me out of the gate. "They're waiting for us." I stop her mid-stride when I realize she's taking me to visit a nunnery.

"I haven't any offerings to bring," I say, my hand on my empty bag. Everything I brought, I gave to the monks. A sneer curls on Lanying's lips and she directs her head towards the temple.

"No need," she says. "Not like those greedy bastards." *Pah!* A curt spittle hits the gravel and I gasp.

"Lanying!" My hand over my mouth, I r and glance around for witnesses to this blatant display of contempt. Lanying just shrugs and hauls me on.

"Well, that's my opinion of them." Her voice cool, she strides us out of the gate onto a narrow path that winds around to the rocky facade behind the monastery. Right on ridge of the barren slopes, amongst a few swaying pines, my eyes spot a tiny hermitage.

A surge of delight opens my heart, a smile lifts my face. With its whitewashed walls hidden under the crimson shades of climbing creepers and its darkened rooftop topped with a myriad of weathered prayer flags, the monastery looks just like a bright bird of paradise, nestling peacefully on a dotted crest of green. What a little beauty, this place.

"Welcome, welcome." A toothless smile and open arms embrace us after the steep climb—the abbess has been waiting for our arrival.

"Ama-la." Lanying bows her head. I do the same. The abbess's fingers rest on the crown of my head, a thoughtful blessing. My cheeks flush, as I have nothing to offer her. As my eyes meet hers, I'm welcomed by the warmest of amber set in a thoughtful, frail face. Her thin, calloused fingers stroke my reddened cheeks and my vision blurs for a moment at the touch of so much grace.

"I brought my sister, Nordun, on her way to Lhasa," Lanying says. The abbess takes our hands in hers with a remarkably firm grip.

"We've been expecting you," the abbess says, a content smile on her lips. "Tea's ready. We've got a lot to catch up on." Coming up to the main building, she turns to me and directs her head to the crooked door on the left. "Our temple." She pats my hand. "We'll be over in the kitchen." She hooks her arm through Lanying's and off they go.

With a little spring in my step, I hasten to the door.

A hollow creak resounds on the thin timber paneling, a lengthened shadow spills over the worn wooden floor. I clasp my hands as I see her—her golden face lit by the orange glow of dusk. She's here, the mother of all Buddha's, seated in the heart of the temple.

My lips tremble, a sob slips from my breath. I fall on my knees, my hands pressed to my heart.

Of course, she's here—she's always here.

Warm tears streak my cheeks as I surrender myself to the mercy of Tara and sink into the silence and solitude I was looking for. *Om Tare.*

Twenty-two

It's only when I hear the swish of a robe that I'm aware she's sitting beside me.

"Ama-la," I say, and open my eyes. I bow my head, ready to get up.

"No rush." Her hand on my arm urges me to stay seated. She shifts on the flimsy cushion and closes her eyes. A great stillness descends upon her.

The contentment she embodies, the serenity she radiates—the memory of my grandmother pierces my heart with the arrow of longing. *Ama-la.*

My unruly mind slips away from me, desperate to escape to the safety of my grandmother, my monastery, my home on the mountaintop, so many moons ago. *Focus.* With a sharp breath, I draw in my aching mind and swallow my selfish desire to be anywhere else but here right now.

The abbess opens her eyes. A sparkle of deep amber reflects as her deep, yet kind, gaze probes me. "How are you, my child?"

My shoulders raise. My hands draw in my sleeves to seek the comforting touch of the silky fur lining. I open my mouth—what can I say?

"I'm fine, ama-la, thank you." I clear my throat. "I've been granted a new, precious life." My mouth dry, I swallow. "And although I struggled at first, I feel some ease has appeared in my mind over the last days."

A warm blush spreads over my face, for I know I'm not fooling either one of us. She leans in and nods as the faint clacking of her prayer beads encourages me to go on. I cast my eyes down on the cloud of crumpled blue that covers me.

"But I feel as if I'm still in the Bardo, the in-between." My cheeks burn, my breath grows hot and thick. "I've left the place I've known for so long—my grandmother, my sisters, my home." I heave. "But my mind." My fists clench inside their furry pouch.

My mind feels feverish and a stream of words is swelling, sloshing over the jagged edges of my hollowed skull. "It's like my body has stepped into the new unknown, but my mind is still stuck in between. Not knowing how to leave behind the old, not knowing how to be in the new." My fingernails dig into the palms of my hand, a pacifying pain amidst the burning agony of my mind.

"Yes, there is a shift in my mind, for there are moments of clarity, of ease, more and more, but I fear it won't last." I sob, the scorching lump of disappointment growing fast within my throat. "I fear I'll falter again and again in this world—that's me, that's my wayward mind."

There it is. I've said it aloud. I've uttered the words of doubt and disgrace and given my mind the upper hand—yet again.

The beads are silent by now, the abbess' hands suspended in midair. "Yes, your mind is anxious, my child, for it doesn't like change or distress." She rests her hand on my arm, and I glance aside as the weight of shame presses on my chest.

"It left behind a place of comfort." Her voice is steady, with a hint of sternness. "And it has not arrived yet to a place that has restored that ease." A tiny smile peeps on her pinched lips. "But you know very well that this will pass too, for all things are impermanent, nothing remains the same. Everything is always changing, from moment to moment, and so is our state of mind." She pauses. My hands release their sweaty grip and seek the coolness outside of the sleeves.

"Yes, ama-la." I bite my lip, and a tingle of shame shoots through me. "My grandmother taught me well." She did, for I fully understand that the meaning of impermanence. Our bodies, our families, our homes, and yes, also our state of mind—everything is always changing from moment to moment, nothing lasts forever. The memory of my mother floats before my eyes. Yes, I've known change ever since I was young. Yet, it has never touched me as profoundly as it does now. My insides wrench and my clammy hands clasp in my lap.

The abbess leans back a bit. A sharp rattle resonates on the wooden floor as her beads fall to the side of her cushion.

"We never know what is going to happen next." She jolts up and snaps her fingers. "Even in this fleeting moment, we're in a state of change and uncertainty, dying a little and becoming anew from moment-to-moment, Nordun-la. This is the nature of our samsaric existence, and this is where we have to build our home and put our mind to rest." The snap of her fingers rings around my hollow mind as I chase my running thoughts.

My face still heated, I look up to her. "But how, ama-la? This world.... It's so noisy, so full of distractions." My voice thickens. *Distractions.* I cringe and cast my eyes down again.

"I'm used to prayer, study, and meditation in the silence and safety of the monastery, and now... I fear my unruly mind will laps again and again and get the better of me." *Distractions.* Could my shame burn any brighter on my cheeks?

"Ah... this world is the best opportunity to practice, my child." Her hand taps my arm, a gentle pat to pay attention. "Standing in the midst of change, being pulled aside by distractions, and touched by the suffering of others." Her hand touches my face. "There's nothing you can control out here, only your mind, so if you can accept whatever happens out here—good or bad—that is the best practice."

Her eyes spark that warming amber again, but this time more fiery, more fierce.

"Let the noise be, let go of your expectations, and do not long for anything else, for this is samsara." Her voice swells, her hands raise. "Tame your mind. Let it be home to the noise, the distractions, and the endless suffering of all. Tame your mind—that's the supreme spiritual discipline." Her shrill laughter whirls through the air. It's a shriek of apprehension, yet a call to blissful understanding—and I get it.

My shoulders drop. A surge of joyous relief washes over me, cleansing the sticky, murky thoughts from my mind, rinsing the weight of shame from my body. Warm tears well up and escape from the corners of my eyes.

How silly of me to expect my state of mind to stay the same. Of course, it changes—it always has. Even in the monastery, moments of clarity lapsed into moments of obscurity—one state dying, the other becoming. And I always overcame obstacles and obscurations by keeping to the practice of the path, I always did.

My head spins, a lightness overtakes me. Being aware of dying and becoming, from moment-to-moment—that's the practice, that's the path.

My heart fills to the brim with delight. I will overcome again and again in this noisy, hectic world, for this is where the suffering is. This is where I choose to practice for the benefit of all sentient beings. I can't contain a giggle as the abbess's cool hands wipe my face. How childish she must think me to be.

"You've not chosen the easy path, my child." Her hand strokes my cheek as her eyes delight in mine. "But you're not alone in this. Tara, our beloved savioress, is always here." She puts her hand on her heart, a tender touch of deep devotion. "And so are we, your sangha of sisters." Her fingers tap my wrist where the blessing cord is tied.

I nod. The red string flares like a crimson beacon in my vision.

"Thank you, ama-la." My breath whispers with respect as I realize—Tara's shown herself to me, once again.

Her hands in mine, the abbess rises from her cushion. I hasten to get up.

"Time to join the others, they'll be waiting with tea," she says. "And undoubtedly with some amusing stories as Lanying has arrived." A muffled chuckle slips from her lips. "That girl..." She shakes her head and puts her arm through mine.

Together we walk into the afterglow of the day, our cautious steps turning into a stride as loud laughter lures us to the kitchen.

Twenty-three

"AAma-la!" A telltale grin escapes from Lanying's face. We must have walked in the middle of her telling a most entertaining story, for the circle of nuns in front of her is slapping their knees and holding their bellies with laughter.

The abbess waves her hand at the red-robed bustle scattered around. "Lanying!" Her voice pitches, her eyebrows draw down.

"Would you believe this bunch of boisterous nuns?" Her voice carries a restrained edge as her eyes flash from the nuns to Lanying. "You put all my disciplinary efforts to shame with your fantastic tales of faraway travels." She sighs, a stern stare on her face. "What to do with you all?"

A suspended silence crashes down on the earth-beaten floor as she looks around the row of bowed heads. I hold my breath, for I know this situation all too well. Catching my sisters and me over and over again in idle chats and futile amusement, I too outdid my grandmother's honest attempts to guide us on the path—far too many times.

Vicarious shame flushes my face, and I glance at Lanying, who still stands there, feet wide apart, hands on her hips. My mind boggles—has this woman no shame? A loud pang from the banged-up stove dissolves into thin air. My toes curl in my sandals. Could this situation be any more awkward? I cast my eyes at the door. My mind's already running down the front steps. Just when

I'm about to clear my throat and offer our apologies, Lanying bellies a loud laughter.

"You get me time and time again, ama-la." She leaps over to the abbess and throws her arms around the tiny woman. A brazen hug almost knocks the both of them to the floor.

Spotting a wide grin, the abbess cradles Lanying's face in her hands. "I did, didn't I?" She pinches her nose.

Relief soars through my body as Lanying's eyes mock me over ama-la's shoulders. *They're only joking.*

With a surge, the flock of red robes rises and buzzes around again, this time to make space for us in their circle, serving piping hot tea and fresh fried bread. And to listen to the end of Lanying's story, of course, which turns out to be only the beginning—the stories that woman can tell. She keeps us bound to our seat for many cups of tea with news from the borders and forgotten tales of long-lost kingdoms. And as we share laughter and food, thoughts and tales, I've never felt more at home, home amongst sisters.

"Told you these nuns have no pretense." Lanying's arm hooks mine as we skip out of the white-washed enclosure.

I nod, my head light, and my heart filled with joy. How good it was to spend time here.

I turn to the abbess for a last blessing. She stands in the doorway, her hands folded in her frayed sleeves. I'm about to bow my head when Lanying grips the abbess by the arm.

"Ama-la, so sorry, I forgot," she says in an unusually hushed voice. "Sister here is looking for her uncle." Her eyes dart over to me and back to the abbess, a deep blue glister shines through. "Did anybody of interest happen to come by these last days?"

I freeze, and the iron fist around my heart clenches tight. *Uncle.* My jaw drops. Lanying just asked ama-la about my uncle. She sure doesn't let it rest.

The abbess's hand sways in mid-air and with a waver she rests it on my shoulder. "An odd couple came by a few days ago." She pauses. "I noticed they were from the old way too."

My mind jolts at the possibility. *Uncle and Khandro-la?* Could it be my uncle and the ngakpa's wife she's talking about? My body tenses at the thought of it.

"They didn't hide it, anyway." The abbess shakes her head.

"The old way, huh." Lanying's voice sharp, she leans in. "What did they want?"

A sudden icy breeze whooshes around the first fallen leaves of autumn. *The old way.* I draw my scarf. This could be Khandro-la, but Uncle?

"Nothing much," the abbess says. "They brought us some offerings and spent some time in there." She points her head and all three of us turn to the tiny temple.

"Yeah, right, I doubt they were repenting their devious deeds." Lanying snorts, an icy smile curls around her lips. "Well, at least you're right on their trail." She raises her chin. "And with Karma and Dendup on your side..."

She doesn't finish her sentence. She doesn't have to. The proud f of assumed victory on her face says it all. Nausea churns my stomach. I dig my nails into the palms of my hand. *Not now.* I draw a deep breath and clear my throat.

"Yes, I'm on the right path," I say, my voice a thick blur. "The pilgrim's path to Lhasa, that is."

Lanying's eyebrows arch as I look her straight in the eye. *Not now.* I don't want my thoughts to wander to futures unknown. I want to be present and clear, and delight in merit of the pilgrimage like I have been able to do for the last few days. I turn my face to the auburn sky, the flaring orange amongst opal heralds the arrival of dusk. "We'll go down now, or we won't have much light left."

I bow my head to ama-la. A high chirp chatters from the slanted rooftop, followed by a loud swish around our heads. We both glance up at the same time to see a pair of grandalas swooping and gliding down. Their deep, almost eye-searing blue bodies tumble and soar through the golden-brown sky with sheer joy and the abbess squeezes my hands in hers.

"See that pleasure, that absolute delight?" Her eyes still on the birds, she lets out a sigh. "Take some of that with you, my child."

I meet her eyes—her soft gaze radiates that deep tranquility I know so well.

"Yes, we are always in the in-between, suffering under the impermanence and change, with no certainty to be found." She takes my face in her hands, the frayed edges of her sleeves brush against my jaws. "But why not replace the fear of loss of the old with the joyous delight in the new, in the new life you've been granted?"

My heart cracks open as my eyes meet hers, a sparkle of the purest love.

"Accept the death of the old, let it go, and rejoice in the new, the opportunity to change your state of mind to another possibility. Grow yourself, from moment-to-moment." She pinches my cheeks and chuckles. "And transform to adventure, for the desire to free others from suffering in this samsaric world..." She pauses as her hands slide down and grip my elbows. "Well, that requires a vivacious state of mind."

As her jubilant words pour straight into my heart, I freeze, and all is suspended—this place, my body, my mind. I'm halted in the in-between.

Swish. The next moment, a blue breath of feathers surges around the two of us. I blink. The diving birds rise with a last twist, and fade into the darkened mountain range. And I'm right back at the enclosure, my heart brimming with joy, my head bowed in reverence to the abbess.

Adventure. Delight. The abbess's words keep swirling in my mind—but there's not time to ponder. With the tails of our coats flying behind us, Lanying and I boot down the path as fast as the loose gravel allows us to. Halfway through, I stop to catch my breath. My hands on my knees, I take a last look at the hermitage, a flake of pristine white glistering on the edge of the teal shaded ridge.

Adventure. Delight. A quiver of pleasure brings gooseflesh to my skin.

"Come on." Lanying hooks her arm in mine again, pulling me on. "Almost there."

And we are. With no time and no breath left, we storm around the corner to the gate of the monastery.

"Well, well, look what just came down the mountain." The harshness of Dendup's voice stops us in our tracks. I hadn't seen him at all, but he's hiding in plain sight, leaning against the stacked stone wall across from the monastery.

Lanying pinches my arm. "See you soon for some real adventure, sister." She flashes that cheeky smile of hers at Dendup, and off she is. Her heels spin in the dust, leaving me behind with my snarly looking family member.

"Sooo." Steadying himself with his hands behind his back, Dendup raises himself from the wall. "Caught up with your new friend then, eh?" With a slight sway, he leans forward. "Karma sent me to fetch you." One hand against the wall, he lugs on the belt of his open chuba, his shirt crumpled and loose underneath.

I take a step closer. Is he...?

His eyes puffy, he snorts. "He won't be too happy to hear that." His putrid breath, a mix of chang and vomit hits my nostrils.

Drunk. Dendup's been drinking again, and it isn't sitting well with him.

"Just like he won't be too happy to see you like that." My words snap out before I know it. I raise my chin but cringe inside for disrespecting my elder like this. Still, he shouldn't be out here in this state. Our eyes cross, but I keep my stance. A sloppy smirk appears on his face.

"I won't tell if you won't." His voice turns almost apologetic, but his eyes gleam a playful cheer. I answer his smile with a curt nod. He knows I won't tell on him—I never would.

"Come on then." I take his horse by the reins. "Let's get ourselves home, unseen and unheard."

I haul myself in the front of the saddle. It takes Dendup a little more effort to mount, and I'm happy to notice nobody around.

"Just give him free rein," Dendup says, as I spur on the horse. "He knows his way." He slouches against my back. A slur follows. "We'll be just fine."

And we are, for we arrive at the inn with no Karma in sight yet, but with a matron in the courtyard, more than willing to put Dendup to bed.

Twenty-four

M y eyes scout the kitchen. Karma's nowhere to be seen. *Good.* I rest my head against the wall and doze off for a moment. The crackling fire of the kitchen stove almost lulls me to sleep.

As I slide the jade beads through my weary fingers, my mind wanders back to the hermitage. A deep calm stretches in my body. It was a good day.

"Hey." Karma's voice hovers above me. "Sorry I'm so late but..."

I open my eyes, and his tall, muscular legs are the first thing I see. He bends down and my heart skips a beat as he meets my gaze, as if I always forget how gorgeous he is. He leans in, his long loose hair brushing my hands as he searches the inside of his chuba.

"Here, I got you something." He pulls something red out from under his shirt and sits beside me, his hand on my knee. "Thought you might be interested." He passes me a slender, elongated package, wrapped up in red cloth.

"For me?" My eyes widen as I recognize the shape. *A book.*

I run my hand over the top, the thin fabric ripples under my fingertips. Yes, a book. Without hesitation, I untie the knot at the back. The folding fabric reveals a stack of long, brown pages, sown together in the middle with one single thread. My index finger and eyes join to trace the lettering on the first page. A smile comes to my face as I recognize the scripts. Yes, I can read it. My lips form the vowels and consonants of the first sentence.

Nice to meet you. My voice breaks. "What kind of book is this?"

I frown and glance at Karma. The first half of the sentence makes perfect sense, but the second half is all gibberish.

"You tell me." Karma laughs. "I can't read." His eyes sparkle, and his whole face contracts in one big grin.

I try again, my eyes on the page. "Nice to meet you," I read. Well, that makes sense. But then the second half of the sentence... my mouth forms the vowels and consonants. "Hen gaoxing jian dao ni." My mind searches in all its corners as my eyes fix on the words. The letters are familiar, but the sound makes little sense. *Hen gaoxing jian dao ni.* Still, something about that sentence—or cluster of words, really—is familiar.

"Hěn gāoxìng jiàn dào nǐ," Karma says, his voice steady and slow. *Hěn gāoxìng jiàn dào nǐ.* My lips mimic his words inaudibly. I focus even harder on the page, pressing my mind to make sense of it all. *Hěn gāoxìng jiàn dào nǐ.*

"Of course!" I shoot up, and our heads almost collide. "It's the Han language!" I've heard that sentence before, so many times. I just didn't recognize it on the page.

Karma nods. "It is." He slides his hand down my back. "So can you make out what kind of book this is now?"

My fingers run over the page, following the sentences. They are all in familiar script. The first half of the sentence is in my language. That I see. The second half is in my script, but the meaning... I look at the first sentence again. *Nice to meet you - Hěn gāoxìng jiàn dào nǐ.* The second half is the equivalent in the Han language but written how it sounds in my script. Now it makes sense.

"It's a phrase book." I look up in delight. "It's a book to learn the language the Han people speak."

He nods again, his eyes gleaming that soft green that makes my stomach flutter.

"So, tell me what's in it." His arm slides further behind my back. "I had to get it on good faith." He pulls me close.

"Well." I smoothen the first page and we read together.

First, I read the phrases in my language, then the phrases in the Han language. The first page has expressions of introduction and a list of food. This book is clearly written for the travelers and traders on the road—the next pages contain words and phrases helpful to visitors in a strange town looking for lodgings and asking directions.

Next up is a list of goods to trade, clothes, tools and weapons, and useful phrases to bargain down prices. We both laugh as Karma casually corrects my intonation, and together we make our way through the book.

Time falls away as my eyes devour the pages. My mind, open and eager, relishes in the learning of something new and exciting. This booklet not only gives me the opportunity to learn a new language, it also gives an interesting take on the problems one can encounter while traveling through the foreign lands like being robbed or being accused of stealing and even killing. Strange illnesses are mentioned too, as are vicious attacks of mysterious wild beasts.

"Om mani!" I put my hand over my mouth as I read of a monstrous beast that is said to gobble down men and mules in one go at the light of the full moon. "Did you ever come across this?" I look at Karma and hold my breath.

"Don't believe everything you hear on the road." He smirks. "Some people do like to boast about their adventures."

I shake my head. Who could ever make up a story about something horrible like this?

My eyes are drawn back to the book—only a few pages left to go. To my delight, these last pages deal with Buddhist terminology, an explanation of the Buddhist philosophy in simple sentences. As it turns out, even Lord Buddha has a different name in the Han language. It also deals with the respect one has to pay to the teacher and high lamas.

"This is wonderful," I say as I think of Lanying and the contempt she showed for the monks at the monastery. "Very helpful." I turn to Karma, my fingers running through the end of the book. "You don't mind if we finish this?"

He smiles and gulps down the last of his tea. "Not at all," he says. "I love seeing you like this." His hand caresses my cheek and I blush.

"Just a few more pages." I quickly cast my gaze back on the book and together we read.

My heart expands learning the strange words about Buddhism, the world I know so well. The last page is a bit of a smudged one. The writing seems from another man's hand. It deals with the arrival of a particular high lama, a master of the Buddhist religion. My eyes widen as they shoot ahead to the last three sentences. My voice falters. *What?*

To my horror, the sentences don't relate the proper respect one has to pay to a lama, or the correct salutation towards a respected teacher. No, they tell that this teacher is dear to many women, that he goes about a lot, and that he makes love, a lot. My face flushes as Karma tries to catch my gaze.

"What's it saying?" With an expression of genuine interest, his eyes dart to the page, then back to me. He has no idea. My fingers line the edge of the page.

"Eh…" I hesitate. The blush on my face creeps down my neck.

"You can't read it?" Karma frowns and peers closer at the page.

"I can…" My nail scratches the top corner of the page. "It's eh…" I take a deep breath in and speed over the sentences, giving Karma no time to correct my pronunciation. I stoop and as I finish, I keep my eyes fixed on the page.

An awkward silence pops up between us. Here I go again, still so uncomfortable with the ways of this world. I should be better by now, but I'm not.

The silence doesn't last long, for Karma bursts out in a snicker.

"I love it when you become shy like that," he says, and he pulls me in.

My warm cheek presses against the crisp, wrinkled linen of his shirt. I want to shrink even further, but I can't.

He lifts my chin and his eyes—full of mischief—meet mine. "Let's read these last sentences again, but this time real slow." He fs a frown. "For I will have to correct your pronunciation on that."

His lips pinch together as he suppresses what is undoubtably another burst of laughter and I cringe, but only for a moment. When I see my own reflection in the gentle green of his eyes, I can't help but laugh at my silliness.

Here I am, in the arms of the man whose body I laid mine to sleep against under the wide-open sky for the last two days. And now I'm too shy to read aloud these sentences about the supposed behavior of a lama I don't even know? I free myself from his tight embrace.

"I guess it's like you already mentioned," I say, trying to sound steady and sure under his tongue-in-cheek comment. "Some people do like to boast about their adventures on the road." My eyes fixed on the page again, I dig my nails in the palm of my hand and start reading the last sentences clear and slow, giving Karma plenty of time to adjust my intonation.

"See," he says. "That wasn't so difficult." His lips gaze my still burning cheek. "Now will you teach me?" He rests his hand on the book.

"To read?" I raise my eyebrows. "Sure, but sounds to me you're doing great without it." I lean back against the wall and put his hand in mine. He knows all the sentences in the book by heart.

"I do." He nods, a pensive shadow glides over his face. "But I always wanted to learn." He leans back beside me. "And now I've found myself the most kind-hearted teacher." His lips brush my earlobe. "And the rest of my life to learn."

My heart bursts open in my chest, and I feel my insides melt. *This man!* It's not his gorgeous green eyes or his tender touch on my skin—it's the very words he just said.

That night I lay my body to rest against his again.

Not out of necessity as the last two days under the freezing open sky demanded, but willingly as my longing for him grows deeper and deeper, and I'm beginning to hear the whisper of my wild, loving soul.

Twenty-five

The next day we fall into our familiar rhythm of long stretches in the saddle and nights in the open fields. From here on it's to Chamdo, the next major town for trade. The muleteers are keeping a good pace, much to the delight of Dendup, who's already stated more than once how fabulous Chamdo is, or moreover how good the food and the drink are over there.

Our days are filled with riding in the usual line, and little sister taking turns in the front of our saddle. She's a welcome distraction, with Dendup teaching her songs, me teaching her prayers, and Karma, well, I don't know what he's teaching her. He often has to catch her, making sure she's not rolling off laughing. I bet he's boasting about his adventures on the road to her, too.

Our early nights are spent huddled around crackling fires, under the darkest of an indigo dome, strewn with a million twinkling stars.

Since we've crossed the peaks of the mighty Cho La, other mountains pale at the comparison of her grandeur and majestic height. Still, the ranges we cross now are high enough and even so treacherous, demanding my utmost attention for some of the day. Fortunately, my mind's at ease and filled with prayer, like a pilgrim's mind should be, so even the tough parts of the path are not daunting obstacles for me anymore.

Yet there's a vague sense of unease dwelling in the corners of my mind, rearing its ugly head whenever I don't guard my thoughts diligently. I know what it is. It's the impatient part of me wanting to skip ahead to whatever plans Dendup and Karma have made for Uncle in Lhasa. It's the deluded part of me thinking I can control the situation by wondering and worrying. And I also know it's no use giving into that part of me.

Whenever the time comes, I'll know, and strength will arise in me—the ngakpa's divination foretold so. Nothing will harm me, as long as I keep faith in the essential goodness of others and act with my purest intention. His words have never rung so much truth to me than at this moment, for the pilgrim's mind is one of trust and faith, of taking whatever occurs in life as the path. And that's what I'm striving to be—a true pilgrim—for now.

"See, almost there." Dendup's voice behind me jolts me out of my thoughts.

I turn. A grin graces his face, undoubtably caused by the joyous company of little sister in front of him. He points to the right, towards the grassland ahead. I raise myself and peer in the distance. The noon sun reflects her rays on an endless row of gilded steeples popping out of the field. My heart leaps as excitement seizes me. The famed Kamaduo chortens, how I've been looking forward to seeing these wonders.

As if he senses my enthusiasm, my horse speeds up his pace and I'm not reigning him in.

"Go ahead." Karma motions as I pass him in full trot.

My eyes delight in the shafts of golden ahead, and I chuckle. *As if he could stop me now.* The horse's hoofs bounce in the damp grass. The warm smell of churned earth rises, and for a moment it feels like we're floating towards the brightest of all suns. With the whitewashed cylinders of the chortens in sight, I reign in my horse. Time to slow down. These holy stupas represent the physical presence of the Buddha and hold sacred items—they are to be approached with the utmost respect. Securing my horse to the poles intended, I walk on, my hands in prayer, my mind in full adoration.

"They are huge!" A small hand tugs at my sleeve. "And there're so many!" It's little sister, her eyes wide in admiration of the myriad of chortens lined up in front of us.

I frown—my companions sure caught up with me in no time.

"Yes, they are huge," I say and take her tiny hand in mine.

"There are over one hundred and thirty of them here," Dendup adds, and he takes her other hand in his. "Let's go to kora together...." He folds his cap in his chuba. "... and count all of them." With a firm step, he tugs us along into the stream of pilgrims, circumambulating the chortens, row after row.

Crowned by strings of prayer flags releasing their invocations in the gusty midday breeze, these ancient chortens are everything—if not more—I always thought them to be. Their solid square bases represent the Buddha's lotus throne and buzz with the sturdy, low vibration of the earth. It's as if they're urging us on, onto the Buddhist path with firm faith and fierce perseverance.

I glance at my companions. Little sister's face is in total delight. Dendup's expression is in total devotion, and I catch myself feeling amazed at his sincere expression. Sure, I've seen his dedication to the Buddhist path before, at Yilhun Lha Tso, but I still can't make any sense of it. There's only reason he's here today, and it's not because of these stupas. *Not now.*

I squeeze little sister's hand tight. My faint smile directed towards her, I promptly tell her about the chorten's cylindrical bodies, and the meaning of the golden tops, not to show off any of my knowledge but to steer my thoughts in another direction.

I could have spent the remainder of the day here, accumulating merit amidst the splendor of these hallowed chortens, but the prospect of reaching Chamdo by night is too alluring for the muleteers, including my own companions. Night has fallen already as we reach the town and I can't make out much of its buildings.

Like in Derge, Dendup leads us away from the caravan, into the backways, to "friends of us." The welcoming in the courtyard is as cordial as in Derge, with the lady of the inn already on the lookout.

"So lucky to have friends everywhere," I say to Dendup as we dismount from our horses. He must have missed the sarcastic tone in my voice, for he only has eyes for the matron, exclaiming that we'll be staying for at least a day or two. Karma on the other hand, has picked up on my tone and throws me a playful grin as he piles up our bags.

"Give the man a break," he says, his lips dangerously close to my ears. "Not everybody has the pleasure of laying himself besides a soft, warming body like I do every night."

Instead of the usual blush appearing on my cheeks, I break into laughter.

"You're right." I slide the saddle off, turning straight into his arms. "Who am I to judge?" And I mean it, for it's not up to me to criticize my elder, especially one that takes such good care of me.

That night, it's not until late that I feel Karma's warmth surrounding me. After we saddle off and have something to eat, Karma and Dendup go out for "some urgent matter" and I don't ask, for I don't want to know. My whole being is filled with gratitude for the merit I made today. Settling down in a corner with my phrase book, I doze off until Karma puts his arms around me and lays me down to sleep into the tender hollow of his body.

I had hoped to practice my newly learned phrases at the market of this town for today, but Karma has other plans. After a late, hearty breakfast of meaty thukpa and with no Dendup in sight, he urges me into the already sun-drenched courtyard.

"Come on." He hands me my saddle. "I'm taking you away for the day."

I step back, the saddle in my arms. "Where are we going?" I say, not knowing whether to worry or to delight. Dendup obviously hasn't returned yet, and now Karma, avoiding my question, seems to be in quite a hurry to get away. My eyes dart to our bags, still piled at the side of the yard.

"They're safe here," Karma says as he notices my concern. "I've got us covered." His hand slaps the small daypack around his shoulder.

I hesitate for a moment, but then slide the saddle over my horse's back.

"Sorry, boy," I say under my breath. "I know I promised you a break but seems like we're on the move again today." With a soft neigh, my stallion scrapes his hoofs and I mumble on as Karma gives me a quick knee up.

He laughs. "Did I just hear you make apologies to your horse?"

His hand rests on my knee, and I clench my reigns, caught like a kid with my hand in the tsampa bag. I dip my chin down. A glance sideways in his direction releases all the tension built up in me though, for as our eyes meet, I see nothing but genuine joy. No scheming to get away from here, no secrets or hidden agenda. No, there's nothing but pure contentment in the depth of his eyes.

My hunched shoulders drop—*you silly girl*—and I scold myself for being so suspicious of Karma instead of looking forward to being alone with him for a day.

"Yes, that's right." I slide my warm hand over his, still on my knee. "And I mean it, for our horses deserve a day of rest too."

A thoughtful look crosses his face as he pats my stallion's neck.

"It's not far," he says. "And there's plenty of shade and good grazing for the day."

I raise my eyebrows and shift back in my saddle.

"Now you make me curious," I say. "So, we're not going into town then?"

He hops on his horse. "Nope, you'll just have to wait and see."

With a smug smile he leads us out of the courtyard.

We ride out of town with the sun on our face, and a light breeze spurring us on.

Our horses' hooves clap in sync on the granular gravel, and I can't help but think: this day just might turn out to be so much more interesting than the day in the town I'd planned.

Twenty-six

T he morning sun is still far from reaching her highest point as Karma leads us off the gravel road onto a narrow, barely visible path down south. I halt my horse for a moment, my eyes skimming ahead into the heightened woodland where the arid pines sway their burnished tips on the gentle wind.

Karma gestures without turning, and I spur on my horse to follow him. In a slow but steady canter we climb for a while, past the warm and fragrant woodland, up the cooler, more barren mountains, even further. As we reach the highest point, Karma halts, and I stop at his side, eager to learn what's ahead.

I shift to the front of my saddle and throw my glance down the steep gorge below. A green-hemmed river runs through, slicing the valley in half. The far end's covered in early autumn orange and dark green. The side we're on is patched brown and scant of trees.

Karma points, and I bend to look closer, but I see nothing but sand and dust. Small piles of boulders are stacked in rows and on top of each other, and yes, I do detect a few large squared walls, carved out of what appears to be beige-brown stone. Karma's dismounted by now, and leads his horse down the winding path.

"Wait until we're closer," he says, as he answers what must be the most curious gawk on my face. "Almost there."

He goes ahead, a confident stride in his step. But as we get closer, I still can't make out anything of the peculiar, and uneven, collapsed silhouettes. We let our horses loose in the luscious side stream of the river where they reward us with a wild spray of crystal clear water, the iced drops a cool welcome to my perched lips.

"I'm sorry, but it makes little sense to me," I say, walking together amidst the stone shambles. My hand glides along the wall, dry grit crumbling between my fingers.

"Come here." Karma pulls me up on one of the heightened rectangles. "Now look around and tell me what you see."

My eyes run along the outlines of a walled square and another one leading into it through a small opening on the bottom. A narrow lane passes along it, opposite another crumbled, walled square, but on a different elevation, running into the adjacent hill. Then it dawns on me.

"It's a house, an old house." My voice pitches. "Or more like a few old houses together." I turn to Karma. "But it's nothing like the houses I've seen." My eyes dart over the structure again.

"They are houses." Karma says, and I crane my neck to catch his glance.

"But who lives, or rather, lived here?" I say as my mind tries to imagine this place alive, with people and no doubt a few animals. His hand slides around my waist, and he draws me closer. The shaft of his long knife presses against my hip.

"Beats me," he says. "But see that cave?"

I shield my eyes against the sun and stretch to see as he points at a narrow gash in a nearby hill.

"That's where they left their people behind."

I recoil. "You mean..." My words linger, for I don't want to voice it out loud—too gruesome.

"Yep, it's packed with bones," he says. "Human bones."

He turns and squeezes my side.

"But ancient bones, so don't you worry." A playful grin on his face, he runs the back of his hand across my cheek. "Whoever was here, they've left a long time ago."

His words should comfort me, but I can't stop the tiniest of quiver running down my back.

"How long, do you think?" My words are barely audible above the faint whisper of the midday breeze.

"Very long," Karma says, and he walks me down again, onto the alley between the walled structure. "They've even left a few things."

He squats, and his hands turn the powdered soil. Under his chalky fingers, the outline of a large, round pot appears. And another one.

I kneel beside him and peer at the pots. No, it's only one pot, but it has two bellies, and it's buried right here in the ground. Karma spits in his hand and rubs the partially dug-up pot with his palm. My eyes widen as an intricate pattern of twisted, zigzagged lines becomes visible around the sides of the pot.

"Amazing." I run my fingertips across the rigged, dark lines, careful not to shatter the fragile clay. "I've never seen anything like it."

Karma looks up. "This place is covered with it," he says. His hands rumble through the dust. "Here, look, I found this here before." A small, grainy bead runs across the palm of his stretched hand. "Here's a few more, with different colors, too." He puts three drab droplets of stone in my hand—reddish brown, black, and what appears to be a darkened green.

My face lights up—my curiosity's awakened by the sight of these trinkets that once must have adorned some young woman's neck.

"Just think about it," I say as I rub the beads with the hem of my dress. "Somebody has worn these, treasured these once." The colors become brighter now, but the beads lack the lustrous shine of the jewels I know. Still on my knees, I straighten my back.

"Now you u what I see." A content smile graces Karma's face.

We wander about the place together, from room to room, envisioning whatever must have played out here.

"I wonder where they came from." I say. "Or where they went." I dip the small pot Karma brought in the stream and scrub the dirt from under my ragged fingernails at the same time.

"No idea," he says as he blows on the dried grass to ignite the fire. "And I guess we'll never know." He plunks down next to the fire that's crackling enough to heat the water for tea. "It's not much, but it will do for the day."

He rolls up his sleeves and spreads out the bread, dried cheese, and some fruit from his bag. As he hands me a fresh peach, I can't help but notice the dark lined miniature deer head on his inner right arm again. Where before a strained unease would come over him whenever he caught me staring at it, his eyes now soften, and he pulls me next to him.

"Go on then," he says and stretches his arm. "I know you want to."

And I do. My fingertips trace the lines of the swirling antlers curling on top of the deer's head. So crisp, so clear, it's like they were etched into his skin only yesterday.

"I guess I'll never know where this came from, either." His face is devoid of any emotion, but his voice wavers.

"So you know nothing about it." I bite my lip and try to sound resigned, but the inquisitive pitch in my voice gives me away. I'm not buying this, not for a moment. Karma's too smart, too much a man of the world not to have at least sought more information about the marking on his skin.

"Well." His voice wavers again, and the fine lines around the corners of his eyes twitch a little. "I've been told they could be Mongolian."

I gasp. "Mongolian?" My fingers are still on his hands, and again I trace the inking, so delicate and fine.

"Yes, it's what Grandfather suspects." His voice low now, he takes a deep breath. "You see, when they found me, running around in the wild, I only had on a ragged shirt, nothing else." He pauses, his eyes dart off in the distance. "And when Grandfather, later on, wanted to throw away the shirt, he found two tiny silver bells, probably tiger bells, sewn into the hem of it."

Tiger bells. I raise my eyebrows.

"Bells from Mongolia, from a shaman," he says, and glances away.

"A shaman." My hand clasps his arm. "You mean a spirit healer?" My mind's at full speed now. I've heard of those foreign lamas engaging with the spirits.

Karma nods. My hand lingers on his arm.

"Somehow those bells got lost," he says. "I'll never know." His voice trails off as he stares at his marking, and I'm overwhelmed by an acute sense of loss and longing—his loss and longing for home.

My hand slides in his, our fingers interlace, and I rest my cheek against our hands.

"But you would like to know," I say, my voice soft and steady. "For there's always that subtle longing inside of you, and an elusive distance, always there, even when others seem so near." I close my eyes for a moment, and let our minds connect—I so understand him. I, too, have felt that profound, yet unknown longing. No matter how dear my grandmother and my sisters at the monastery are to me, it was the stables that called me home in my dreams, again and again, until I gave into it.

"It wouldn't be fair," he says. I open my eyes to his gentle voice and his hand caresses the edge of my jaw. "I owe Grandfather my life."

I release our hands and lean back, waiting for him to go on. The hiss of the water boiling over the pot interrupts the moment, and I jump to make the tea. But when I sit down again, it's still there, that intimacy, lingering between us in the balmy afternoon air.

"You think Grandfather would mind if you went looking for it?" I say, and I pop a piece of bread in my mouth, followed by a slice of juicy peach. Salty and sweet blend on my palate—oh, how I love that odd combination.

"Looking for what?" Karma dips his bread in the tea and gulps down the mush between his fingers.

"Home, I guess." I shrug. That's what I think it is.

"My home's with Grandfather," Karma says. "For he gave me my life." He pours himself a second cup of tea. "I would have died out there, on that road, had he not taken me with him." He stirs the hot brew with another piece of bread. "And when the others blamed me for bringing misfortune on the family, he protected me with his own life." His jaw tightens.

"I brought sickness and death with me upon my arrival, causing three of our good family men to die."

My heart sinks as his voice breaks.

"When the council decided it was me who had to be next, Grandfather threw himself in front of the knife they raised to slit my throat." A strange gloom crosses his face, a mix of hope and sadness. "So, how can I leave him?" He shakes his head and raises his chin, and a firm determination erases the sadness as soon as it arrived.

"I see." I slice the rest of the peach as carefully as I'm about to choose my words. "So you're in debt now with the family, for they—or rather, Grandfather—spared your life."

It's true, the family had every right to kill him then, for the deaths they thought his arrival had brought on.

"You know I am." Karma empties his cup in one go, a trickle of tea stains his shirt. "But I don't mind, for my life is good with them." A faint smile breaks on his lips, but it doesn't reach his eyes and my heart bleeds for the innocent, lost boy he once was.

"But you're never there." I lick the dribble of juice running down my hand. "Like a wanderer, always on the road, I hear." A cagey gaze meets my eyes as I hand him a slice of peach. In an instant my mind pierces his—*I see you*—and he blinks, knowing I'm on to him. Behind that sure facade, a restless spirit shines through. And as I keep his gaze on me, the icy cool hue in his eyes ebbs to the warmest shade of emerald green.

"I know," he says, and for a moment he hesitates, gulping the slice of peach down in one go. "But I never had somebody like you to come home to, did I?" He presses a loving kiss on the top of my head.

I laugh, for I get what he's doing. We both see it and it's fine. He let me see inside of him today, and that's enough for me, for now. Still, when I pour us another cup of tea, I can't help but wonder if he can settle with me—I know what the longing, the desire for home can do.

"Besides." Karma waves his hand around as he blows the steam off his cup. "You have to admit, the road can be a good place to be if you're in the company of somebody who knows the way." I can't help but agree.

"Oh, I do," I say, admitting that even for the horrendous journey over the Cho La, our trip has been good for me.

"And now that we've got the time..." My hand reaches in the inside of my shirt and I pull out the phrase book I'd been wanting to use at the market today. "How about you help me find my way too?"

And together we sit and read and speak in foreign and familiar tongues, until the sun throws her lengthened shadows across the pages, signaling our time to go.

"Thank you for being so patient with me," I say as we saddle our horses. The swirling stream soaks the hem of my skirt.

"No bother, you're doing great." Karma looks over the back of his horse. "Your words, they're good, very clear."

He loves teaching me the language, I can tell—we had so much fun with it today.

"Thank you, but that's not what I mean," I say. My voice soft, I bend down to strap the saddle tight. A little twinge of clumsiness shoots through my fingers.

"Then what do you mean?" He moves over to me and pats the neck of my stallion.

I clear my throat as I turn my heated face his way. He knows very well what I mean. Yes, I lay my body to sleep in his arms every night, but I've not given myself to him—yet. And he, being nothing but loving, tender, and patient, hasn't demanded any of it.

"Oh, Nordun." He laughs and shakes his head. "To take something precious by force, I've done that before." He reaches over and rests his hand on my cheek without a hesitation. "And it is no good." His lips pressed together, he raises his chin.

"A heart has to come willingly, it cannot be taken by force." His thumb strokes my cheek. "It is like I told you when you set this horse free at the stables, remember?" His hand slides down, caressing the edge of my jaw. "Deep inside the heart of all living things, there's a wild spirit that can never be tamed or taken by force. The heart of a being is always free, and it knows it."

I nod. I remember that day.

"The stallion came back to me, because he wanted to," I say. My fingers dig into the coarse manes of my horse. "And his wild soul decides to stay—from day to day." I hook my warm fingers in his.

"That's right, my love." His gaze casts down and he untangles our hands from the manes. "And so you will come to me, in your own time, precisely because I've set you free." His hand cradles my chin.

I gasp and hold my breath as he pulls me closer over the neck of my horse.

And when his lips graze mine ever so slightly, my heart is seized by a love so full and profound that I dare no breath out—I want to hold on to this feeling, if only for now.

Leading our horses behind us, we walk back up towards the orange brimmed ridge, his arm clasped around my waist.

My fingers twirl the stone beads in my pocket, my thoughts drift back to the moments between the two of us today. This day sure turned out to be so much more interesting that I'd planned.

Karma pinches my side and raises his eyebrows; he must have noticed the smile on my face.

"It was a good day," I say and turn to cast a last look down the valley.

It was, for it made me realize even more—there's no going back. From here on it's Lhasa, and whatever it may bring, I know I'm ready and willing to put my heart on the line.

Twenty-seven

T he dusk darkens to reveal a tangerine moon. The day at
Chamdo market has come to an end. Crackling fires light the
market square's stalls, from which the shouts of the traders push
the last of their day's produce onto the folks drifting back to their
dwellings and inns at the edge of town.

"Good to see you youngsters." Dendup's cheerful voice echoes
over the clatter of our horses' hooves as we rush into the courtyard.
He must have been waiting for us, for he's already hopping out of
the doorway as soon as we've turned the corner of the yard.

"Here, let me," he says and takes my horse's lead as I dismount.
"You go inside. You must be tired." He sounds a bit out of breath,
and a remarkably fresh smell of citrus surrounds him.

"Well, thank you," I say, happy to hand him my horse—my
throat feels bone dry and dust cakes my face. I could do with a wash
and a fresh cup of tea.

I skip to the basin at the back of the house and splash the icy
water until my cheeks tingle. So good. My eyes close, the cool drops
run down my neck.

Shì... Yīqiè shùnlì... A faint, snakelike murmur drifts from the
yard and I can't help but listen...

Zuò zhǔnbèi... It's Karma's voice, in the foreigner's language. I
can't make out which one. Who's he talking to?

My hands clasp around the metal basin, and I shiver. The water
has soaked the back of my shirt by now. I run my scarf through my

neck, the gritty leftovers from the road prickling my skin. My mind wavers, but my feet are already flying towards the yard, curious to see who's there.

I'm too late.

"Hey." Dendup's eyes shoot over Karma's shoulder as soon as he sees me. "You're not in yet..." An edgy smile curls his lips and he steps aside, shielding a swift shadow rushing out of the gate.

"No..." My voice trails off and I lean to the side, but Dendup mirrors my movement, preventing me from catching a last glimpse of whoever they're talking to.

"I freshened myself up a bit and then I heard you talking." Keeping my eyes on the swinging gate, I vein a relaxed smile, but my insides are anything but calm. "In a foreign language."

Tense glances drift between the two of them. *I wasn't supposed to hear this.* I shiver again. This time it's not from the cold.

"Just a trader." Karma turns on his heels. "Come, let's get you to the fire." His arm hooks around my rigid shoulders and he strides me into the kitchen.

Dendup's following in our trail. What can I say?

With the unease growing between us, we settle down, and the matron serves us a hearty meal. Even her cordial manner, her delicious thentuk, or even the roaring fire she's put on can't warm the bitter cold that's occupied my heart.

Dendup and Karma are making casual conversation. I know they're trying to lighten the air, but I can't.

Lies. My mind's swirling. Tears prick behind my eyelids. The steaming soup scorches my tongue as I slurp the brew down as fast as I can. A sour taste stains my mouth. Can I blame them? I have not been honest either, for I'm not only here on pilgrimage.

"I'm going to sleep." My voice croaks. I raise my weary bones, avoiding their gaze.

"Sister." Dendup's strong fingers clasp around my wrist. "Stay." His grip tight, he pulls me down. "We didn't mean to be rude."

I bite my lip and glance at him, his face a pleading look. My fist clenches. I'm fighting hard to hold back my tears. To no avail. My knees give in, and I cast my eyes at the wooden floor. He is my elder, after all.

"We..." Dendup's voice is subdued now, and he releases his tight grip. "We're family, and there're no untruth to be told between us, but..." He turns to Karma. "You tell her."

My heart beats against my chest, rapid and numb. *Tell me what?*

"Nordun, love," Karma shifts himself next to me, his voice a low whisper in my ear. "We're only trying to protect you."

I blink and raise my chin. "From what?" I swiftly wipe my cheek and settle my gaze in the distance. "Protect me from what?"

A heavy silence crashes upon us, and my shoulders drop. I already know the answer. They don't want to burden me with their gruesome plan and all that this will involve.

"Karma and I—we know what we're doing." Dendup leans in and rests his heavy hand on my arm again. "Besides, it's not of woman's concern, you know that."

I shake my head, and the iron fist around my heart tightens its grip. *It is of my concern!*

"There's no need to lie or cover up—we all understand what you're doing," I say and heave. "Or planning to do." I lean back, my face heated, my voice thick with emotions. "I might be naïve in the ways of this world, but I'm not stupid." *Regardless of being a woman.*

My eyes flash between the two of them, and even though my vision is blurred, my breath stalls as I detect the look on Dendup's face. It stirs something deep inside of me—genuine worry has replaced the tense expression on his face. There's an honest concern for my wellbeing shining through in the weathered face of this rough mountain man.

"No, you're not," Dendup says. "On the contrary." He waves his hand. "But the less you know of all of it, the better." His voice takes on a grave tone.

"By now Tennah—and most likely his sons—understand we're on to him." Dendup wrings his hands. "Your uncle's a devious man, sister, and we have no idea yet what he's going to do." He pauses. "Of course, we have our connections keeping an eye on him, but in the meantime, we can't be too careful."

The blood rushes to my head as I realize the danger Uncle still presents. He has killed my mother and he won't hesitate to... My mind blanks at the horrendous thought. *I'm such a fool.* Of course, Dendup and Karma are trying to protect me. That's what our men do. And they'll go to all lengths to... *What was I thinking?* I cringe at the thought of my selfish behavior.

"I'm sorry," I say. My voice halts. "I know you have my best interest. I don't mean to make things difficult for you." My apology's sincere. My eyes cast in my lap again, my fingers twirl the red string on my wrist.

"You're anything but difficult, sister." Dendup's voice is almost convincing. "But like I said, we want to keep you safe, and the less you know."

I nod and am met with an unexpected, pleasing smirk on his face. *Why's he smiling like that?*

"And it would help if you stopped wandering off on us."

What?! I shoot up as his smirk breaks out in a grin, filling the space between us with lightness and laughter.

"Me?" My voice pitches and I put on my most innocent face, but nobody—including myself—is buying it. They know about my trip with Lanying to the hermitage the other day. Dendup slaps his knees, and Karma pulls me into his side, chuckling all the way. No use hiding it anymore.

"It's like Dendup said." Karma's warm hand tucks the loose strands of hairs behind my ears. "There's no untruth to be told between the three of us." His fingers slide down my neck, and a tender touch lingers along.

"And there's nothing to cover-up either," Dendup says, as he frowns from under his bushy eyebrows. "For even in the darkest shadows of the night, the truth will always reveal itself." His gaze darts over the kitchen and stops on the matron, busying herself around the now smoldering stove. A swift spark ignites in his eyes. "Now, if you youngsters will excuse me." He jumps up and runs his fingers through the messy mop on top of his head. "I've got some wandering to do myself."

With a spring in his step, he shoots away from us, his arms already stretched out to the becoming lady of the inn.

I shake my head as Karma leans back and draws me next to him. What to make of a man like that?

"He's a good man, love," Karma says, as if he can read my puzzled thoughts. "And you did right not to tell on him."

I smile, and my body relaxes into his. Of course, Karma knew. He's been with Dendup on the road for so long, he knows of Dendup's relentless fondness for the chang.

"Still, no more lies, no more cover-ups." Karma's voice carries an insistent edge. "Promise?" He presses my head into his chest and his fingertips stroke the top of my hair, restful, content.

"Promise." A faint sigh slips from my lips as his heart beats a soothing drum to my ear. My body, now warm and cozy, is drifting into sleep, but I'm not ready—yet. There's one more issue that's been lurking in the back of my mind ever since we left the stables. Now's the perfect time.

"Karma," I say, trying to sound casual.

"Hmm..." A distant, yet attentive murmur responds.

I swallow to steady my thoughts, for the issue I'm about to put in front of him is dear to me. She is dear to me, and I've never been good at plotting like this.

"Remember when you told me this afternoon..." My voice wavers a bit. "About the heart that is always free..." I clear my throat. "And can't be taken by force, that you've done that before and know now it's no good?" The words cascade from my mouth, a rapid flow that leaves me out of breath.

"Yes." He veers up a bit. "I remember."

I curl my toes as I hear his voice deepen and feel a slight, yet definite, ripple under his skin.

"Well." I take a deep breath in. *Come on, get it over with.*

"If you know it's no good, then why force your sister's heart onto somebody? Why force her to marry a man she doesn't want?"

There, I've said it—for Sangmo. I sit tight, and I wait, as I would wait in the calm before the storm. I squeeze my eyes s and duck in anticipation, preparing for the wild tempest of arguments to thunder my way. The stroking of his fingers has come to a sudden stop and his hand rests heavily now on the top of my head.

I sit tight and wait as the soft drum of his heartbeat replaces the rapid pounding of my own heart in my chest.

Yet, I'm waiting in vain. His hand lifts, and his fingers resume the stroking on top of my head again.

No reaction. Well, not the blast I was expecting, anyway.

"You think I would force her to marry?" His voice calm, his fingers twist my hair around.

I peep through my eyelashes. "Well." I keep my voice and posture as small as anything. "That's what she told me..."

And that's what you're entitled to. My mind lingers back to my conversation with Sangmo in the room the night we picked out my clothes. She begged me to help her, to make Karma change his mind.

"Right." He pauses, and I dare to open my eyes again, as I detect no tension whatsoever in his demeanor.

"And you think I would succeed in marrying her off?" His voice picks up, still controlled, but there's an intense tone in it, one I can't discern. "Nordun." A chuckle, barely audible, escapes from his chest. "We're talking about Sangmo here, right?"

My body still on edge, I turn, and his fingers tangle deeper in my locks.

"Yes, of course," I say. "Sangmo, who else?" My eyes widen as he looks down at me. He doesn't even try to contain his glee.

"Oh, love." He bursts out in laughter. "In case you don't know Sangmo by now..." His hands wrap around my face. "I would make a fool of myself if I tried to marry her out, for nobody—and I mean nobody—can force that girl into anything she doesn't want to." He shakes his head.

"I'm afraid to admit it... but there's no way she'll ever obey a man... not even me." A quick frown shadows over his face, only to be replaced by a playful smirk. "But that streak seems to run in the women of our family."

My mouth falls open, and I want to reply to his last remark, right there and then, but my words stall and my body sags, flooded with the relief of what I've just heard. No marriage for Sangmo. My heart leaps as tears of joy spring in the corners of my eyes.

"Oh, thank you!" In a flurry, I swing my arms around his waist and bury my hands in the folds of his chuba. My head settles in the tender hollow of his neck.

Another chuckle escapes from his chest as his hands glide over my back, pressing me tight until I have to come up for air.

"You silly," he says. His fingertips wipe the strayed hairs and tears from my face.

"You knowI had to set Sangmo straight before we went—it's what brothers are supposed to do." His lips graze my forehead and move down the tip of my nose.

"But you terrified her," I say, as I recall her desperate plea for freedom, for a life of her own.

"I know," he says, and shakes his head. "But there's no harm in a bit of scaremongering, is there...?"

And as his lips taste mine, all my worries fade, for one last one, lingering one. But there is harm in it, for women like us, our fate is forever in the hands of their kinsmen. We'll always have our freedom to fear.

Twenty-eight

"Don't tell me this isn't the best tea you've ever had!" Dendup gulps down another cup of the steamy brew while I curl my bare feet against the stove. The chilly morning breeze caught me washing myself in the yard, sending me straight inside with a stern reminder of the early arrival of Autumn.

"Oh, brother." I peer at my ruddy toes. "I bet you say that to all the ladies." The tea is excellent indeed, but I'm sure it's the innkeeper's loving arms that attract Dendup to this guesthouse so much. He puts on one of his quasi-frowns, followed by the ever-playful glance from under his furry eyebrows.

"Now, sister of mine." His voice raises with his cup in front of me. "You shouldn't be thinking so ill of your elder, let alone speak like that." He pinches his lips, and a rueful smile curls from under his moustache. "But I'm willing to forgive you for your brazen manner, if you pour me another cup." He dangles the cup in front of me. The gleam on his face says it all—he had a grand night.

"So sorry, brother." I hasten to get the kettle. "I don't know what came over me." He leans back as I pour him another cup, feigning a meek smile. We're good.

"Now, before I forget." He rubs his moustache, waiting for the tea to cool. "A friend of yours came by yesterday."

My breath stalls, for the low tone in his voice predicts no good.

"Or should I say, a foe of yours?" Dendup points his chin over my shoulder, and I turn.

Karma steps into the kitchen, his long, wet hair dampening the neck of his shirt.

"A foe of mine?" Karma grabs a cup off the shelf. "Do tell."

I hold up the kettle, and his longing look meets mine.

"That damned woman, of course." Dendup's voice sneers, and Karma's eyes take on a dark edge, just for a moment. "She's nothing but trouble."

Lanying. My fingers clasp around the handle, and my knuckles turn white as I steady my thoughts—and the kettle.

"She said she'll meet you in the marketplace this morning." Dendup snorts. "Or else she'll come to get you here."

My eyes fix on Karma's cup. I pour and pour while my mind searches for the right words to respond. Feeling the men's eyes burn on me, I decide to remain quiet—for now—there's no way they'll let me go with her, yet.

"Let's eat." I sit beside Dendup, but not before I've piled more seasoned broiled meat on his platter with the thick spicy sauce he likes so much. I hand Karma a piece of baked bread, the sweet aroma of the melding butter complementing its salty, dense bite. And as the men satisfy their morning appetite, I sense their mood mellow with the abundance of mouthwatering dishes. *Good.* I sit back and relax.

I'm about to pour another round of tea when the rapid hopscotch of patter resounds in the hallway, followed by an elated cry. *Found you!*

It's little sister, her hands full with candied nuts and her face smudged with something pink and gooey, beaming her brightest smile.

"Here!" She skips over to me, hands me a few sticky nuts, and deposits the rest of them on the table before Dendup.

"For you." She licks her tiny fingers one by one. "And she says she'll get me a new chupa too!" Her eyes wide with excitement, she turns to me. "But only if you come with us, please." The giggle that follows her drawn out plea is the cutest ever, and I can't resist throwing my arms around her tiny frame, so full of life again.

"Says who?" Dendup's low, leery voice barks over the table, and I flinch at the brute tone. Little sister, on the other hand, is not impressed. She jumps over to Dendup and climbs on his knee.

"Our Han sister." Securing her spot between a stunned Dendup and a quiet Karma, she points her grubby fingers at the doorway. "She said she would wait in the yard."

Of course! I pull up my shoulders and turn away from my company, but it's no use. I can't hide the smile basking on my face. *She's good, really good.*

Swoosh! A sudden gush rushes through the hallway. The heavy front door slams into the timber banister. The rigid rattle of the iron hinges is followed by the swift thud of a pair of heels strutting along the solid wood floor. All our eyes are drawn to the doorway, and I'm sure it's her.

"Sisterrrr!" Lanying's voice reaches the kitchen before she does. Her coat swishes behind her as she strides into the room. "So good to see you." She throws her arms around my shoulders.

"Brothers." With a curd nod, she acknowledges Karma and Dendup, but barely—her eyes are on me.

"Soooo." She pinches my shoulder. "Are you up for it?" The glee in her eyes tells me it's already a done deal.

"Up to what?" Dendup's grumble has lost none of its brutal tone.

An icy-blue glints in Lanying's eyes and she turns her heels in that laid-back style of hers. "To town, of course," she says as she looks to Dendup with her face frozen in an ever-so-polite smile. "Little sister needs some new clothes."

She pouts her ruby lips at the little girl seated on his lap and flings a quick wink my way. "And we would love for sister Nordun to come, wouldn't we, little one?" Little sister shakes her head, her cheeks glowing a rosy red by now.

"And do you think our brothers here will let her come with us?" Lanying's eyes thin to crescents of sapphire and her voice pitches a sweet solicitation. I turn away for a moment. My smile's too obvious. We can all see what's coming next.

"Oh yes, please." Little sister's scrawny arms disappear in the creases of Dendup's shirt as she throws herself at his chest. "Can she come?" She stares at him with the big brown eyes of a baby fawn, the most innocent of looks I've ever seen.

Dendup's jaw tightens, and he puts his hand on the little girl's head, rubbing her wispy fuzz on top. I hold my breath as Lanying's fingers dig into my shoulder. *Om mani.* Will he?

"Who've you got with you?" Karma's quiet calm breaks the eager expectation between Dendup and the rest of us, releasing him from the decision that might shatter little sister's heart. While he addresses his words at Lanying, his eyes are on me. The hint of apprehension knots my stomach. He wouldn't think that I put her up to it, would he? I bite my lip.

"Two of my men." The sheer determination in Lanying's voice mirrors Karma's quiet confidence. "Trustworthy men, for I've h eard..." She doesn't finish her sentence—one does not speak of danger aloud.

"Trustworthy." Dendup's sneer slices across the kitchen. "You?"

I take a quick step back. My mind puzzles at his demeanor. Whatever happened between Lanying and my brothers, it clearly cut deep.

"Brother." Karma puts his hands around little sister and hauls her on his lap. "Why not let the girls here have their day of fun?" His expression is so subdued, I can't read what he's thinking, but my heart skips a beat at his words of approval. My toes scrape along the jagged timbers.

"It'll be straight to Lhasa after today, some hard travel and not the best of roads." Karma adds to his argument and the rest of us look on in high hopes. A swift glance from under my eyelashes reveals the slightest of inclination from Dendup's head.

"Oh, go on then." His face wrenched, Dendup utters a grumble from under his breath. "Who can refuse a cutie like this?" He tickles little sister until she squeals with delight. "Just make sure..." He hurls an obstinate look at Lanying, tinged with an edge of clear worry.

"I will." Lanying affirms her hasty reply with a whirl from her cloak. "Come on then!" She opens her arms for little sister to jump into and off they are, while I hasten to pull on my socks and sandals. Dendup's sour look makes me want to fly after my sisters, but I must acknowledge my elder's consent.

"Thank you, brother," I say, my voice muffled as I smoothen my dress. "That's very generous of you." My head bowed, I hear his huff. He's still grumbling and my feet itch to get out of the door.

"Promise you'll be careful." Karma's hand demands my waist as he strolls me down to the yard.

"Stay close to Lanying's men." He halts at the doorway and presses his warm lips on the top of my head. "I trust you."

I open my mouth to assure his faith in me, but he's already striding back to the kitchen, the thud of his boots echoing a staunch goodbye through the hollow hallway.

"And that, my dearest sister," Lanying says as we walk out of the gate into town. "That is how we deal with our men." A clever smile rolls from her lips as she tosses her long locks back in the breeze and takes little sister's hand. "Always familiarize yourself with their weak spot." She lifts a single eyebrow. "And use it to your advantage." With a big swing she puts little sister on the shoulder of one of her men, the girl shrieking with joy. "And you little one, you deserve the best chuba in town today."

I shake my head as my thoughts churn over Lanying's former remarks.... *weak spot... advantage...* A little tinge of disquiet prowls my mind. She's one skillful woman, that's not to deny. Still, something in her words doesn't sit right with me.

"Now I don't know who dresses you." Lanying hooks her arm through mine. "But little sister's not the only one in need of some sprucing up."

I raise my eyebrows and gaze down. What's wrong with my clothing?

"Love the color on you but the cut..." She shakes her head. "It won't do anymore." I shrug. The resolute tone says it all. She's got her mind made up and I'm down for another coat.

As the day unfolds, it's not only another coat I'm privileged to as Lanying proves to be the most generous sister to us. Guarded closely by her two men, she steers little sister and me to what seems to be the best tailors in town. Her sense of style is impeccable and under her watchful eye, we get dressed in a luxury my body has never met.

"Now this is your color." Lanying's approving hands glide along a roll of the brightest cerulean silk wool. The hue reminds me of my poppy coat, but held to the light, it's so much more vibrant, like a slice of the highest heavens, cut straight out of the blue sky. Before I know it, I'm poked around and measured by the eager seamstress, while Lanying's sorting for the costliest fur for the lining.

"Just because we're on the road," she says, a pensive look in her eyes. "That doesn't mean we have to compromise on comfort or style—ever." She pulls little sister near, and slides her hand over my hips, stretching the thin fabric of my underdress to reveal my curves. "What do you think, little one? Isn't she the most gorgeous thing ever?"

The two of them burst into laughter, while my cheeks burst into flames. My hands clasp across my chest as my eyes searches for a way out, but I'm literally pinned down with nowhere to go.

"You know, sister." Lanying's gaze drifts over to little sister rolling around the fur. "You better own your beauty, for that's your actual worth in this unjust world." She takes a step back and glances her approval at me. "Nearly there." With a stern voice, she directs the timid seamstress to a cut that's way closer than I would have picked, but I don't object, for I'm grateful for her company and her kind advice.

My hands run across the fur Lanying has picked, a hue of sabre black, scintillating like the darkest obsidian in the rich golden of midday sun. It's not all Lanying's words I'll take to heart, but I know she's right at one thing. Physical beauty sure wields power in this mundane world—it's what all girls from an early age on know to be true. But it also enslaves the one who dares to depend her worth on it, as my grandmother used to say. For beauty of the body is fleeting, fading with the years of our impermanent existence.

The mind, on the other hand, that's the only thing that will prevail, sustaining us in this life and the countless lives that follow. The quality of our mind, that's our real worth, for it's our only sole reliance, and therefore the only matter to truly treasure. The prodding of eager fingers at my rigid limbs and waist to get the right cut jolts me out of my musings, right back into the tailor's stall.

It's not until our clothes are ordered and our hair is decked out with a few corals and turquoise beads woven through that Lanying is satisfied with our appearance. Much to the relief of her guarding men, she declares it's time for lunch. Settled in the nook of the small inn she has selected, I lean in as she orders the food in the language I'm curious to learn. To my surprise, I recognize a few of the words she pronounces so elegantly, so clear.

"So, you're taking an interest in my language then?" Her face lifts. "Good, for you should get to know more of this word, and the language is an excellent way." She cradles little sister on her lap, the girl's eyes drawn from exhausted elation this morning.

"Karma got me a phrase book." My hands search my shirt, but Lanying waves her hand at me.

"Now, sister." Her voice lowers, and she leans in closer. "I speak a few languages myself, so I know what I'm talking about." She puts her delicate hand on mine. "If you want to learn the foreign language, then you must take a few lovers in the foreign tongue" She leans back in her seat, her hand squeezing mine. "I can recommend it." I feel my jaw drop and bounce up in my seat, my mind alarmed at her words. Did she just suggest...?

"Ah, there's our food." Lanying shuffles the plates around as little sister bobs back in her seat, no doubt awakened by the aromatic bouquet of aniseed, cinnamon, and other sweet spices filling our table.

"And by the time you're done with Karma." Lanying flings her head to the side. "Which should be soon." She pauses. "I'll find you a few suitable lovers, ones that can fulfill all your needs. Trust me."

No way! My mind balks at the ideas she's suggesting, but she won't have any of it. Adding a reassuring chuckle to her argument as she fills the plates and gestures for us to eat. As the thick sauce of meat hits my palate, the most delicious of velvety sweet and sour smothers my protests and seizes all my objections for now. *This food!*

"See, I told you so," Lanying says as she detects my savory delight. "Something foreign to taste is just what you need." *Om Tara.* My mouth full, I can't help but laugh. For this woman, she's something else. "And not only for pleasure, but for your trade, too." I raise my eyebrows at her words. "Foreign connections of the right kind are worth their weight in gold." She licks a little juice from the corners of her mouth. "Trust me, for it has done my business very well." With a satisfied sigh she leans back, her eyes gleaming at the sight of little sister still digging into the delicacies.

"I'll come to visit you at your stables." A content hiccup escapes from her lips as she puts down her empty cup. "And we'll expand our ventures together." She adds a dismissive wave from her hand. "Once this pilgrimage of yours is over."

With a gobble I swallow the piece of fat chicken that's suddenly lodged itself in the back of my throat. "I guess you know all about my pilgrimage by now," I say, my voice dim. There's no question, she knows—but how much?

"Oh, I do," Lanying says, as she polishes little sister's grimy cheeks with the hem of her sleeve, covered in grease. "And from what I hear, our brothers have got it all wrong." She turns to me and wrinkles her nose. "It's not your uncle you should be worried about..." A bleak grin appears on her lips. "It's that woman, she's got him under her spell."

No! Her words drain the blood right out of my face and my hands clasp the edge of the table.

"Sister!" Our little companion cries out to me. "Are you alright?" Her lips tremble as she sees my dreaded expression. I hasten to put on my friendly face and mask my fear behind a faint smile.

"Of course, little one," I say, my voice steady and clear. "Just a piece of chicken bone that got stuck here." I put my hand on my chest and swallow until her face lifts again and she tucks herself right back in her seat.

"No need to worry yourself." Lanying's demeanor is unusually quiet and calm. "Once we're in Lhasa, your brothers will take care of the situation." I follow her glance, scanning the room, the warm orange glow of the late afternoon reflecting on the rich amber of the polished benches. "They're good like that, especially Karma." Her voice trails off and my heart sinks at the sound of his name. She must have sensed it, for she puts her hand on mine and shakes her head. "We'll leave it to them, for it's what men do. You'll all be home safe before the big snow falls."

I want to believe her so badly, but my stubborn mind's throwing out the maddest of thoughts. Good at what? Taking revenge? Yielding the knife? I shiver as tears burn the rim of my eyes.

"Sure." I gulp down my last tea in a desperate attempt to drown my ominous thoughts. "We'll leave it to them." A profound silence brews up between us, and my mind keeps on screaming at me. *It's what men do.* But honestly, who am I trying to convince here, thinking we will leave it to them?

One look at Lanying tells me she's not buying it either. The blue in her eyes darkens to a raven black as she dips down her chin, almost unnoticeable. Her fingers tighten around mine and right there and then we seal our silent pact. Our minds settle in an unspoken agreement.

We both finish our food, but a bitter taste has taken over my palate and I need to wash it down with plenty of tea. Little sister's appetite turns out to be larger than her tiny frame and we'll leave it to her to clean all the plates.

"And now..." Lanying draws out her words, as she throws her arm around little sister. "Are you ready to collect your new clothes?" The girl practically bursts with excitement and jumps from her seat.

"And sister's clothes too!" She grabs my hand and pulls me with her, hopscotching all the way to the tailors.

There's no doubt about it, Lanying's pick of the vibrant, rich blue and close cut is spot on. To my surprise, it's not only a coat that's been tailored to my frame. Awaiting me at the jumpy seamstress, there's also a matching sleek dress and a pair of soft leather boots to go with it.

"Oh, come on." Lanying sighs as I put up a small protest. "You can't be my friend and not look your best." She smoothens my hair after I've changed and approves the new outfit with a cocky smile. "Our brothers will be in for a surprise." She tugs the fur at the sleeves.

"Beautiful!" Little sister claps her hands as I twirl on demand. The entire outfit, it's so comfortable, it must be because of its immaculate fit.

"We are beautiful," I correct little sister, who's hopping up and down in front of us, too excited to stand still in her new chuba. "And I don't know how to thank you, sister." My cheeks glow with gratitude. I bow my head to Lanying, for I honestly don't know. It's only now I realize I still go around like a female monastic, empty-handed, with no silver, or coins, or anything else to trade. *Somehow I have to change that.*

"Don't be silly," Lanying hisses in my ear. "And don't you ever bow your head to me again." Her sudden warm embrace takes me by surprise. "We are sisters."

"Sisters," I say, and my heart spills over as I hold her close.

"Just one more thing." She puts me at arm's length and looks me straight in the eye. "Promise me, sister, they won't tie you down, for you are the one that governs your destiny. You are the only one that directs your fate." She chooses her words with consideration, and I lean back into the rows of twirling wool. "They have their ways, oh so subtle, but be sure not to fall for their tricks." Her voice stifles with emotion.

"Like today, allowing you to come with us, giving you just enough leeway to think you're free..." She pauses and draws a sharp breath. "But trust me, they'll reign you in—crushing you harsh and underhanded—whenever they want to." Her round face hardens. "And when you least expect it." She pinches her lips together to a cruel, pallid pink and my heart bleeds for her. It's clear she's been there, beaten and bruised, and still bears the scars of those who tried to own the very piece of her she'll never give up.

I dig my fingers in the itchy wool and raise myself to hug her once more. "Promise," I say, and I anchor my arms on her hips.

"Good," she says, her eyes strangely mellow and filled with an inner glow I've not seen in her before. "Now let's get your gorgeous self back to our brothers before they trash the town looking for you."

And thus we walk home with the sun on our back and the overwhelming joy of new friendship found in my heart.

Twenty-nine

"See you later, sister." Lanying and the little one wave me off as I slip through the gate. With the late midday sun licking her crimson red tongue all along the charred mountain ridge, I'm right on time. A quick glance around the courtyard tells me there're no new arrivals today. It's going to be a quiet evening for a change. *Good.* I hop over to the front door and put my shoulder against its hardened wood.

Those wretched officials... As soon as the door is ajar, Dendup's harsh voice comes through... *greedy bastards, they are...* I sigh. Seems his mood hasn't picked up since I left. Pulling the bundle of my old clothes near, I tiptoe across the hallway. Alas, the squeaking of my new leather boots gives me away.

"Nordun!" Generous as ever, it's the matron's voice calling out to me from the kitchen door. "Please, come on, tea's ready." The cordial smile widens as she sees me, and an approving glance crosses her face. "Now look at you, all done up in new." Her hands anchor on her hips. "That was long overdue, if you ask me."

The cheerful wink that follows puts a flush on my cheeks and I find myself stuck in the doorway. A sudden unease twitches at my insides.

"Come." Her welcoming arms pull me into the kitchen, where the sweltering stove blasts my already heated face. "Got delicious candied fruit from our brothers."

She nods to the men in deep conversation around a low table in the back. It's Karma, Dendup, and another man I've not seen before. I tug the sleeves of my new coat; my mind tosses and turns. Will I go over... or wait?

I don't have to decide, as the matron already does.

"Have some for yourself, too." She puts a plate loaded with sugared fruits and nuts in my free hand, directing me to serve the men.

As soon as I'm in their sight, the conversation goes quiet.

"Brothers," I say and bow my head to the table. Dendup's drink floats somewhere in midair while Karma's face freezes in a bewildered stare. I hasten to steady the plate on the table, my mind struggling with what to say or do. He must have sensed my discomfort, as Karma folds his hand around my elbow and draws me in.

"I see you had a good day then." He twines his fingers in mine.

Dendup grumbles. His drink has spilled by now—his hand didn't make it to his mouth.

"That darned woman again," he mutters under his breath.

I shrug at his pinched expression and rush a hand through my hair. *Too much.* The dress, or the hair, or both—it must be too much. My eyes follow my fingers, fidgeting with the furred lapel of my coat.

"Not good?" I take a deep breath before I dare to glance down at Karma and cross my arm over the sleek belt around my waist. One glance in his twinkling eyes says it all.

"More than good." He gets up and runs his fingers along the edge of my collar. A wistful smile peeps through the corners of his mouth.

"Sorry sister." Dendup's hands shoot up the air. His tone is still harsh, but his clumsy gestures make it clear— his apology is well meant.

"I can't stand that woman making a fool of us today—twice!" His mouth twists and it looks like he's about to chew up his moustache. "First this morning, using the little one so blatantly to get her way, and now..." He spits out his words and takes a big swig from his cup. "Like we can't afford to clothe our own." He frets as his cup lands with a loud bang on the table, right next to his clenched fist.

"Looks like we're done here." Karma spreads his fingers around my waist. "So, tell me all about your day." I breathe in relief as he whisks me away from Dendup's ire and the stranger's leering look.

With the matron serving us a refreshing cup, we settle down in our seats. My unease dissolves even more as the perfect blend of rich tea, salty butter, and a pinch of freshly ground tsampa hits my palate.

"I should have seen this coming." Karma runs his palms over my sleeves and squeezes my forearms. His eyes settle on me in a deep emerald gaze.

"Seen what coming?" I can't grasp what he's getting at, but he just shakes his head, urging me on.

So, I tell him all about the bracing buzz of Chamdo town, of the many fascinating faces and their foreign tongues, the enticing and exotic produce in the stalls and the endless choice of vibrant colored cloth at the tailor. I go on about the cute, new outfits for little sister, the boundless generosity of Lanying, and of course I don't forget to mention the close safeguarding of her men.

Karma smiles and sips his tea, his hands doubled in a steeple under his chin.

"So," he says, quietly interrupting my excited account. "You didn't have to yield your knife, then?" His eyes draw down the drapes of my coat and leaves me to stumble over my next sentence.

"How?" My hands shoot to my side. It's still there, buried between my underdress and shirt.

"Oh, love," he says, as he catches my baffled face. "It's impossible for women to hide the straight blade of a knife on their body." His hand searches my hip, and he leans in closer. "Especially with those gorgeous curves of yours." His lips blow a playful chuckle in my ear and I squirm.

"She took great care of us." My voice sounds almost apologetic. How do I wrestle my way out of this?

"I'm sure she did." Karma leans back, his hand still on my hip. "But she can't be trusted." The faint lines around his eyes tighten as he looks me in the eye.

"Whatever happened in the past," I say and straighten my back. "That's between you and her." I meet his stare to reinforce my words. I mean it. I don't have a clue what happened, and I will never ask. My hand slides over his and our fingers lock on my side. "It has nothing to do with me."

Karma's face softens as my fingers caress his.

"You are wrong, my love," he says, his voice a tinge hoarse. "For everything of me has to do with you now."

A dark glint shoots through the deepest of his eyes, just for a moment, and I blink.

"I don't need to know." I shake my head. "Not now." My heart beats faster as my hand rumbles through my coat. Where did I put it again?

Karma raises his eyebrows and leans back into his seat, observing me quietly as I pull a string from my pocket.

"I got you something," I say. "Or rather, I made you something." I stretch out my hand and show him the thin leather strap I salvaged from my old dress today. Dangling on it are the three clay beads we dug up yesterday, their earthen colors deepened with a bit of oil. In between the stone drops, I've strung two exquisite jade beads of my mala, their viridian luster a striking green glow in the palm of my hand.

"It's a reminder," I say, and I feel my cheeks flushing again.

Karma leans in and cups my hand in his, his breath a balmy stroke on my palm.

"A reminder?" His eyes glide over the beads and he folds our hands.

I nod. "These are your reminder of the road, your favorite place to be," I say and slide the earth-toned drops through my fingers. "The excitement of meeting new people, the adventure of discovering foreign places..." I glance up and smile as he's gone quiet, a pensive look in his eyes. "But most of all, the alluring strength of the mountains, drawing you back with their promise of freedom—time and again."

The far-off look in his eyes confirms what I've observed ever since we met.

"These two are your reminder of home." My voice hesitates as my fingers twirl the jade beads on the string. "Your heart is always free to roam, to go wherever it needs to be."

My own heart's hammering against my chest by now and deep inside I want to run and hide, but my desire to share my truth with him is so much stronger. I take a deep breath in and close our hands, the leather strap lacing between our fingers.

"This is a reminder that—no matter what happens between us—you'll always have somebody to come home to." Slowly, I draw our hands in, holding them close to my heart. "You will always be home with me."

An ease folds over me and I bow my head as the vision of our joined hands blurs. I mean every word I said. *No matter what happens.* Love changes, for people change, as easily as the wind changes direction. But never will I allow hatred between us—I will always be someone for him to come home to—only him.

His warm lips press on my forehead and his hands guide mine around his neck. I tie the strap while he holds me without voicing a single word.

As he lays my head against his chest, our breaths move in sync and I close my eyes, knowing I did right today.

No matter what happens, I believe in the innate goodness of all beings.

No matter what happens, I will follow the wisdom of my heart.

Thirty

"Hey, sleepyhead." Dendup's cheerful voice pulls me out of a deep slumber. "Time to get up, sister."

I open my eyes to the empty mats beside me and see they've done it again—Dendup and Karma snuck off early to prepare our horses and let me sleep in. They're good like that, and while I'm usually embarrassed by it, I'm grateful now.

A big yawn escapes my mouth as I stretch my limbs. The excitement of yesterday with the crowded town, its buzzing stalls, the endless fittings of garments, and Lanying's more than candid talk left me exhausted. I must have passed out once my head hit the pillow—or rather Karma's chest—because the memory of anything after the sumptuous dinner of yesterday evening is absent.

Not fully awake yet, I hasten to clear the mat. My blurry eyes catch the red string on my wrist as I bend to make my prostrations.

"First tea, then talk," my sisters used to say in the early morning. *Pema and Tsomo.*

The thought of my dear sisters tugs at my heart, and my mind lingers back to the mountain, to the twin sisters, one brilliant mind born into two human bodies, so alike yet so different.

My hands roll the blanket tight. The clatter of dishes on the far side of the kitchen prompts me on—no time for reminiscence this morning.

Rattling off my morning prayer, I repack my bag with only shifty shadows and muffled pother surrounding me. From now on, it's a stretch of hard travel to Lhasa. Dendup reminded me of it yesterday evening, raising his so-called last glass with a pained look.

Ah well, knowing Dendup, he'll find comfort on the way.

Securing the last strap on my bag, I follow the enticing aroma of zesty thukpa, drawing me to the stove like a moth to a flame.

"Made it extra spicy." The matron serves me, a bowl filled to the brim with a smile that warms my heart. The stay at her home has been good for me; my body's well rested and fed. But Lhasa's calling.

I squint as the whiff of pepper hits my nostrils. The matron wasn't joking. Carefully, I blow the steam to the side. My eyes close for a moment, relishing the quietude all to myself with only the hiss of the wood stove around me.

"Ready for Lhasa?" Karma's arms lock me in from behind. His warm breath strokes my cheek. I lean in and rest my hand on his. *This man.*

"Ready," I say. *Lhasa.* Something deep inside of me stirs, a renewed awakening of purpose on this pilgrim's path.

"Let's go then." Karma throws my bag over his shoulder. He turns and the side of his chuba gets caught, exposing the shiny shaft of his long knife as he strides out of the door. I flinch. The silver glints, a potent reminder that he's also on a journey, albeit with a purpose so different from mine. I've been hiding it, that terrifying truth—banishing it to the furthest outskirts of my mind. Yet somehow it always rises and roars again—it's the real reason I'm here. *Not now.* My legs waver. The taste of sour thukpa hits my palate.

"Come on, then." Karma's far voice jolts me towards the hallway, the unnerving flicker nonetheless clear in my vision. *Not now.* With a deep breath I follow his swift shadow into the courtyard, where the dim morning light is my alley, hiding my sudden unease. Our horses are saddled and ready, scraping their front hoofs as if to urge me on.

A quick leg-up from Karma and I'm on my prancing stallion. *Om Tara*. With my prayer beads clutched in the palms of my hands, I settle down in the saddle—and in myself—reigning in my excited horse and my unruly mind at the same time. And so we join the caravan, a long trail of waxen silhouettes waiting at the edges of the still snoozing town of Chamdo, ready to ride into the onset of a purple-hazed dawn.

It doesn't take us long to fall into our routine again, with Karma in front, Dendup closing our line, and little sister gracing us with her joyous company from time to time. Our long, often scorching hot days in the saddle are followed by short, freezing nights on either wet grasslands or hardened sarsens, both a dread to our bones. I'm in good company though, with my brothers always finding the best spots to lay our weary bodies to rest.

Nevertheless, these mountains are hard on the body as Dendup fervently reminds me, crying out loud about his aching back every morning before the first cup of tea. I can't disagree with him on this one, but then again, my nights are spent in the comfort of Karma's arms, making the journey so much more bearable.

With my mind turned to prayer for most of the time, I delight in gaining the merit, traveling thought this hallowed landscape of sacred mountains and revered lakes. Yes, the road is wayward and unpredictable, but that's what I'd imagined a pilgrimage to be—like our life here spent in samsara, taking whatever occurs, our trials, our good fortunes, and our hard conditions. So, while Dendup grumbles about another mudslide, leading us to detour, I try to view the setback as another lesson in letting go of resistance and resentment, with varying degrees of success.

Nature with all its wildness proves to be a brilliant teacher, giving me all the training my unruly mind needs. The treacherous trails with loose gravel and dense vegetation, the unpredictable weather changing from scorching sun to blistering rain in an instant, even the unexpected encounters with animals—the wild out here demands a ruthless mindfulness of staying fully present.

Ominous piles of bleached bones—human and animal alike—stacked all along the trails serve as a morbid memento of our own inescapable impermanence and unheralded death out here. To survive this journey, I need to be with all that happens in this very moment, needing to keep my mind exactly where my presence is—in the here and the now. And that's just the right training for me, as my thoughts love to travel ahead, always have—envisioning all that's waiting beyond the horizon, all that my eyes and mind are not yet able to distinguish.

I have plenty of time to observe myself and my companions on these long rides, and I must admit, with all the instruction on life in the monastery, Dendup, and especially Karma, have the better of me. First, I thought them so confident, so at ease in the wild because of their experience out here, with this trail. Now I know it's not their familiarity with these outer circumstances, for even the trail changes within the shortest of time. It's their being, so wholeheartedly present amid everything that makes them so at home with themselves, wherever they go, whatever they do. Whether it is lighting the fire, packing our bags, arriving at an unknown place, even riding the long stretches and the winding tracks, they're in the awareness of everything, in every stumbling step our horses take.

"You can't afford to let down your guard out here," Dendup told me during one of our many nights around the fire. "These mountains, they're like a cruel mistress, demanding your full attention and sending you her immediate wrath if you so much think about as going astray." And while Dendup loves to orate his many—often gruesome—tales of the mountains with much verve, Karma and I sit and listen, tangled in the quiet intimacy only we share.

This journey with my companions, the closeness between us and the vastness of the landscape we travel together, it does me good—like a pilgrimage is intended to do. There's a clarity that has pervaded my mind, like the golden shafts of the sun moving along the planes we ride, illuminating what I already knew, but was never able to actually grasp. As I turn my face to the raveled shreds of opal and pearl lingering around the mountain ridge in this early morning light, I now truly realize it's the same with my wayward thoughts—just little shifting shadows, that's all.

"It's onto Nam Tso from here." Karma's warm voice jolts me out of my usual morning musings over the comfort of a cup of tea.

Nam Tso, the holiest of lakes today. How fortunate I am on this pilgrimage, surrounded by the blessings of these sacred places, gaining the merit for the benefit of all.

For a split moment in time, I hear Grandfather's voice in Karma's call, urging me on from afar. *This family is your sanctuary, my child.*

Yes, how privileged I am to be in the company of my trusted brother and my beloved.

How blessed I am with this family as my sanctuary after all.

Thirty-one

"There they are—my gateway to riches!" Dendup jumps off his horse and slings the lead around the nearest tree. Throwing his hands in the air, he's off to the lake and her smooth, silken shore.

We've made it to Nam Tso and the holy lake is everything my grandmother told me it would be. Set between the towering peaks of the sacred Nyenchen Tanglha mountains and the bountiful grasslands of the Changtang, she's an alluring gem, a mesmerizing jewel, drawing me in with her miraculous shade of deep, rich turquoise.

In all her splendor, it's not the mysterious blue hue that entices Dendup to speed off like a madman to her shoreline, though. It's the two massive standing stones beside the water—the famed Yilbin stone measuring many men high—that have captured his imagination.

"Dendup's quick today." I pull my eyes from the captivating blue hue to the two buff sarsens covered with a myriad of colorful prayer flags. Dendup's already on his knees, prostrating himself in front of the stone pillars, imploring them to bestow him with wealth and success in the trade he intends to do on our way.

"The closer to Lhasa…" Karma shakes his head and ties our horses. "Come on, little one." He swings little sister on his hip and takes my hand at the same time. "Let's ask the door-god for good fortune."

Together, we stride to the lake to join Dendup in his prayer for prosperity.

With the sun already at her highest point, the clear azure dazzles like a brilliant solitaire between her green and blue surroundings. I squint and pull my hat to shield my eyes from the intense sparkle.

"She is gorgeous, isn't she?" Karma scouts over the lake, seemingly unaffected by her powerful glare.

I nod. With several secluded islands dotted across the mysterious surface, Nam Tso is the perfect sanctuary for the practice of meditation. It's no wonder many monks—and some nuns—travel across the winter ice to spend the entire summer in mediation here, only able to get back to the shore again when the first ice of winter freezes the shallow again.

"Sorry we won't be able to circle her all today." Karma points to the west, where a rocky trail starts round the gritty coastline. "We'll do the shorter kora, along with the sun. You're good with that?" He turns to Dendup, who has retreated to the sheltering pines in the company of our horses.

"You youngsters go and make some merit." Dendup waves his hand and leans against the tree. "When you're back, you can make me some tea." A little chuckle slips from my lips as I see the content cheer on his face. Apparently, the wish granting ritual for fortune was all he had in mind for today.

With little sister hopscotching along, we join the humming stream of pilgrims, circling the lakeshore with its piles of ancient mani stones and sun-bleached skulls of yaks.

"We'll come back and spend a few days here," Karma says, as he sees my longing look towards the craggy caves settled deep in the nearby cliff face.

The very sight of these caverns surges a profound sense of awe through my being. *Om mani.* It's here that the Buddha himself and Padmasambhava, the second buddha, meditated so many centuries ago.

"Let's sit for a moment." He pulls me next to him on a big bolder to relish the view of the hallowed caverns. With the soft click of my prayer beads resounding the silence, my body settles against his, and my mind relaxes into quiet gratitude. So many blessings on this journey.

"Soon we'll reach Lhasa." I hear my voice drift from afar. "I can't believe how fortunate I am to witness the most holy Jowo Shakyamuni Buddha statue."

My mind stirs. What did I just say? *Lhasa.* My fingers clasp my beads tighter as my mind drifts ahead.

"Don't, love." As if he senses my sudden uneasiness, Karma's fingers draw around my neck. "Don't go there."

I sigh. *He knows.* Somehow, he knows.

"I suppose I can't talk you out of it, then?" My words are steady but my mind wavers. I can try.

"You can't." He tosses me a hasty reply. "The family has decided." His body hardens as the muscles in his arm ripple under the crinkled cotton of his sleeves. "We've already let it go once; we can't do that again." His voice lowers.

"We?" My hands on the boulder, I raise myself. "They can't do that again, you mean." My voice pitches. "Karma, that was so long ago." I shake my head. I've heard it all before.

My grandfather Rapten eloped with my grandmother when they were still young. My grandmother's brothers hunted them down at the family camp, killed Rapten one dark night and took my grandmother, who was pregnant by then, home. Somehow, grandfather's family didn't seek revenge. Why, I don't know, but seems they've been sorry ever since.

"The family won't back down," Karma says. "There's no choice, not this time..." His voice fades as he casts his unsettled gaze over my shoulder.

"That's not true!" I jump up, surprised by the boldness of my own voice. "We always have the opportunity to choose." I catch my breath as the words roll from my mouth. "You, me, we all have a choice." My face flushes as the sweltering afternoon heat gets the better of me.

With an icy calm, Karma turns his gaze on me, his eyes a distant, frosty green. "So, you want the family to forgive?" He raises his chin. "Be weak and let the crime go unpunished?"

I cringe as his harsh stare slices through my flesh and bones, exposing the deepest of my core in one clean cut.

"Yes, I do." I say, my voice a conceding whisper. "I want to let it go." A sob escapes from the back of my throat.

"Uncle will be punished." My voice blurs, but somehow my mind is crystal clear. "For the bad karma he created will come to fruition." Choosing my words with care now, I take a deep breath in. "We might not witness it in this life, but his punishment is already delivered by the law of karma, the law of cause and effect."

My body sags against the hard boulder, my palms scrape its arid, chalky surface. "He will have his punishment, but it's not for us to deliver. We will only do more harm to our family and to ourselves."

There, I've said it. Declared my truth. My heartbeat throbs against my aching ribs and I look up, expecting the worst in the silence that just crashed upon us. I was wrong.

Instead of coming down on me like a stroke of lightning in a thunderbolt, his eyes have softened into the shade of a lush forest in the midst of summer.

"I see you don't have the desire for revenge, my love." His voice mellow, he pauses and leans in. "I've heard your silent prayers on the whispers of the wind." His hands reach for my rigid hands and his fingers brush the opal shale from my bruised palms.

"I've felt your innermost devotion in the caring, generous touch of your hands." He shakes his head and looks away. "But I've chosen to fulfill my duty to the family, as I've done so all my life." His hands drop mine, and clench into fists.

"So, don't ask again." With a brisk turn, he strides off into the spiraling stream of pilgrims at the shoreline.

My vision blurs as I swallow the bitterness that has flooded my mouth. *Silly me.* I press my hands to my aching ribs and draw a deep breath. What did I expect? That my words would change his mind?

I knew they wouldn't. Even the ngakpa's divination said so. The only way is to act from the truth in my heart. Well, I just did. I said what was in my heart and where did it get me? My limp limbs sink back into the bolder. I close my eyes to let the disappointment pass through the hollows in my heart.

"He's nothing special, you know." A sharp sneer rings in my ears. "With his high and mighty attitude... you can do so much better." *Lanying.*

"Sister." A weak smile precedes my courteous greeting. She must have seen us arguing.

"Did you just challenge Karma?" Her hands on her hips, she pries my closed stance. "You're a fast learner!" She wrinkles her nose and lets out a shrill laughter.

I blink, not knowing how to react to her embittered amusement.

"You two really have it in for each other, don't you?" I say, and I straighten my weary back.

"Actually, he's not that bad." Lanying's eye narrow. "A bit too soft, if you ask me." Not letting me off the hook, she devours me with that sharp blue in her eyes.

"Well, I haven't noticed that," I say. My feet grind into the gravel. "He's quite vindictive when it comes to the matter with my uncle." My shoulders sag again, and tears burn behind my eyelids.

"Ah, sisterrr..." Lanying leaps over to my side. "That's good. Revenge is good." She crosses her arms over her chest and settles back into the bolder. "Revenge settles the score, so all will be in balance again." She rocks back and forth on her heels, and a hint of complacency peeks around her lips.

"You're wrong." My voice calm and clear, I turn to her. "It's not up to us ." I dare to face her. "We can't deliver the law of cause and effect; it doesn't work that way." A tiny spark of revolt ignites in my mind. Lanying's an intelligent woman—she should know better. "You're deluding yourself when you think you can."

"Maybe." Lanying's eyes narrow, and a devious sparkle shines through. "But it sure makes me feel better, knowing that I've settled a few scores in this lifetime." Her voice is almost a sneer.

"Really." I raise my chin at her. "And tell me, what good did that do you?" A surge of frustration floods my mind. She's acting like a fool, and there's no way I'm letting her get away with this self-deceit.

She looks away, and a grim twist appears around her mouth. "You think I was born this way?" The words spit out of her mouth and splatter with a vengeance at my feet.

"No, sister, I was made this way..." She pauses as her eyes flare up in a burning blue fever. "Or rather, I chose to become like this." Her words breathe fire by now, but her ice-cold, unmoving stance chills me to the bone.

"Had I not taken what was mine, I would have crawled into a ditch and died." Her nostrils flare as she turns away from her raging outburst, and a sad sigh drifts from her simmering breath.

I flinch as the devastating vengeance in my sister's voice cracks my heart right open. My mind boggles at the unexpected display of ache. This woman... *What a fool I've been.* Who am I to call her out like this? I swallow hard to suppress my surging shame and sorrow. What do I know of the hardship she must bear in this life?

"I'm sorry, sister." My voice small now, I grip her hand. "I really am." I blink through my tears. "But I don't want revenge." My sweaty palm slides off her hand, and I sense my sincere apology landing at her feet. Lanying shuffles, shifting her weight back and forth.

"I know," she says and glances at me, her eyes still like half moons of the brightest sapphire blue. "And I'll help you." She sniffs and tugs at the shimmering silk of her sleeve. "I've gone too far. There's no redemption for me to be found in this life, but you…" A remarkable mercy draws over her face. "I don't want you to get lost like I did."

Before I can open my mouth, she twirls around, ready to take flight. "So, I'll see you in Lhasa, sister." She speeds off, the long tail of her silken coat swishes along with her last remark. "I'll find you when time calls."

I'm left standing in amazement, as I always do when she vanishes like that… There's something about her that puzzles me, something not from this world. I don't get the chance to rack my brains about that. Little sister's on her way, all bright and wide-eyed.

"Tea's ready." Her hands flutter. "Brother told me to hurry."

I smile at her disarming innocence. I don't feel like joining anybody right now, especially not Karma, but who can refuse a package of pure joy like that?

"Coming," I say, and scoop her tiny frame in my arms. "I'm ready to drink the whole kettle dry."

I am—my palate's parched. Salty sweat crusts the corners of my mouth. I swing little sister around and her buoyant giggle reassures me I'll be fine with her on my side.

Although I'm apprehensive about facing Karma right now, the soothing cup of tea in the shade of the swaying pines dwindles the distance my words might have spun between us. The thoughtful way in which he clears a seat for me, his gentle touch lingering on as he hands me my cup—there's no trace of resentment over me speaking my truth in his manners. I shrug off my misplaced apprehension and lift my cup to Dendup. "Any tea left?"

Dendup stirs the kettle with a vengeance. "Seen you talking to that woman again." He frowns as he peers into the apparently empty pot. "Stay away, sister, she's no good." He throws me one of his dire looks.

"You really have no time for her, don't you?" My mind groans. *Here we go again.* Putting Lanying down on every chance he gets.

"What did she ever do to you?" I raise my voice, demonstrating that this time I want to know.

"Not to me," Dendup says, and takes a quick glance at little sister. "But to her entire family; she sold them all out." His words are a whisper to keep the little one out of earshot. "It killed her brother, her father, and who knows what became of that husband of hers." *Family? Husband?* I veer up as Dendup shakes the last drop out of the kettle.

"Death follows wherever that woman goes." With a bang, the pot lands on the ground. "You were a fool to ever get involved with her." He delivers his harsh words at Karma with a spiteful look on his face. "But at least you got out in time."

Karma turns his back on Dendup. With a careful nonchalance, he packs the last of our leftovers in a bag, leaving Dendup to grumble over the empty pot. I hold my breath as I observe the two of them, plotting through their strangely complacent silence. Seems to me they've been here before.

I keep to my corner, my mind chewing over Dendup's words again and again. Selling out her family, a husband, it all sounds so foreign to my ears. Would she really be capable of something like that? I'm dying to know the whole of Lanying's story, or at least the story as Dendup believes it to be, but I'd better let it rest—I don't want to shatter the fragile peace between the three of us. *Not now.* I sip my cup.

As night appears, cloaked in a dark cobalt blue, we roll out our mats at the higher, secluded shores of Nam Tso. The cloudless sky brings a bitter cold and despite the words between us today, Karma bends his body to shelter mine.

Nestled in the comfort of him, I marvel at my longing to be with this man, a longing becoming strong so fast. As my body finds its place in the tender hollow of his chest, I let my thoughts go over the day—and what a day it has been.

"Nordun, love." Karma's fingers run on the top of my head. "Promise me you'll stay out of it." He slides his hand down my neck, and his thumb lifts my chin.

Confused at what he's suggesting, I open my mouth, but he presses his fingertips to my lips, a tender yet determined touch.

"I hear your quiet resistance growing in the silence," he says, his voice a dense whisper in my ear. "I hear it rising, in everything that remains unsaid." He pulls me closer and grazes my forehead with his lips.

"But you'll have to leave it, love." He presses my head against his chest, his heartbeat drumming his steady request in my ear. "Promise you'll leave it to me and won't ask me again."

My mind blanks for a moment, my hands clenched against his chest. *This man!* How can he be so right about my innermost thoughts? How can he know the hopes and dreams swelling inside of me with fear and delight at the same time? As his hand slides along my burning cheek, I close my eyes and search for an honest answer.

"I won't ask again." My reply seems to reassure him as his breath evens and his hand drops to my shoulder.

He's content but I know it's only for now, for soon he'll understand the true meaning of the words that just slipped from my lips...

I won't ask again, but when the time comes, I won't leave it to him.

Thirty-two

There it is, rising in the valley below us—Lhasa, land of the Gods.

I halt my horse for a moment to savor the memory of this view for a lifetime. Lhasa, land of the Buddha—the very name of this place has always sounded so magical to me. Built by the first great dharma king, Songtsen Gampo, many centuries ago, this blessed place is shrouded in tales of mystery and wonder. With magnificent monasteries and towering temples, it holds the holiest of holy, the Jowo Shakyamuni statute.

An overwhelming gulf of gratitude floods my being at the sight, and I can't contain my happy tears. *Lhasa*. We've made it.

A quick glance from the corners of my eyes reveals that the sight of Lhasa has touched my companions, too. Karma's lips move in a silent prayer, and Dendup has even taken off his cap, though he's been here so many times before.

The opalescent sky has opened up. A light drizzle welcomes us and moistens the fertile valley plain as we descend upon it. I raise my face to the fragile midday sun, and I thank the gods for sending such an auspicious sign our way.

"Hear that, sister?" Dendup steers his horse beside mine and holds his hand around his ear. "That's the call of great tea, decent food, and fortunate trade." His lips smack aloud, no doubt already relishing the taste of it all.

"But first we give thanks." I vein a stern look. "Let's not forget we have been granted such a smooth journey now, brother." I reign in my horse a bit, as it competes with Dendup's stallion, wanting to be always in front.

"Of course, sister, of course." Excitement has taken Dendup's eyes. "First, we give thanks." He shifts back in the saddle and pulls his cap back over his furry eyebrows.

As soon as we arrive in Lhasa, it's the same routine again as in any other town. Dendup takes the lead and steers us away from the caravan, into the winding alleys, towards a smallish inn. The only difference is that this guest house seems to be right in the buzzing middle of Lhasa, and not on the quieter outskirts as the other inns were located. A broad smiling matron welcomes us—well, Dendup—into her open arms and into the packed courtyard.

"I know you're dying to visit the temple," Karma says as he swings our bags to a pile. "So, I'll take you whenever you're ready. Our brother's got other engagements." He nudges at Dendup, already engaged in conversation with long-lost friends.

"Is it that obvious?" I've been trying to contain my excitement, but the surge of adrenaline rushing through my veins ever since we entered the gate, it's just too much. The sudden lightness in my body makes me bounce around the yard with every step I take. My pulse is quickening, the rapid beat urging me on to rush to the most revered of all. "I'm sorry." My fingers fumble around, inspecting the front legs of my stallion. *Looks good.*

"Not sorry, love," Karma says, and he squats beside me. "This place, its sacred sites all radiate an exceptional energy." He lifts the hoof of my horse and scratches the dirt away. "That's the pull v in your body right now." He raises himself. "It's a true blessing to be here for all sentient beings."

My hands still on my horse's leg, I close my eyes to sink into my innermost being. I don't have to search. There it is. My insides vibrate with an alertness, an aliveness I've never felt before. It pulses on the beat of my heart, floats in every vein of my body, and rests on every breath of air swirling in my lungs. A warm glow envelops me, and I immerse myself in this beautiful feeling, this all surrounding, soothing sense of home. Karma's right; it's an absolute blessing to be here.

"Come." With roaring laughter crowding the courtyard, Karma's hand slides down my back, pressing me to haul our bags to the quietude of the inn. Dendup's favorable position has secured us a private room this time—simple but sufficient and safe.

A few splashes of water at the back of the kitchen do the trick to clean me up, and we're off to the temple.

"Please stay close." Karma draws me in as we join the surge of pilgrims rushing to the shrine. The drizzle has cleared the dust of the town, revealing the vibrant colors of lush green creeping against whitewashed walls, and silken rainbow banners releasing their inked invocations with a fervent swish into a rose blushed sky. With the low hum of prayer surrounding us, the atmosphere is laden with an eager anticipation, sending tiny shivers beneath my skin.

"Ready?" Karma's calm voice pulls me back from the frenzy, grounding me right at the temple door.

I nod—I'm as ready as can be—and let myself be lifted by the stream of circling devotees. As though carried by an invisible force, I'm drawn into the holiest of the temple, to the life-size statue of Jowo Shakyamuni, carved by the celestial architect Viswakarma in India, in the lifetime of the Buddha himself.

I blink as my eyes turn from the late midday in Lhasa to the eternal time of nirvana, for this is what it feels to me, entering the highest of the heavens. What better fortune is there to be granted than witnessing this sacred image sculpted from his life portrait and blessed by the Buddha himself?

My vision surges to the ceiling, for there it is, the golden radiance of Jowo Shakyamuni Buddha, his two outer eyes gazing in mercy upon us pilgrims, and his inner eye resting in awakened wisdom.

I stretch my hands in prayer and lower my numb limbs to the earth-beaten floor.

It's only after many prostrations that I dare to set my eyes on the statue in front of me again. The splendor of it all—the bejeweled crown adorning the Buddha's head, the brocade robes draped around his stunning golden and ornamented throne, the giant gemstones embellishing his neck and elongated earlobes, the dazzling appearance—is simply overwhelming. Pearls of cold sweat bead on my forehead, running down my temples and neck. A light-headedness takes over, my knees give in, and I drown in the shattering of dark.

"I got you." Karma's firm hands seize me from behind. He yanks me to the side and steadies my back in the sturdy folds of his chuba. As his hands wipe the clammy veil of my heated face, I resurface into the twilight of the temple.

"Let's get you out of here." Karma throws an insistent arm around me, but I resist, pulling his sleeve tight, my vision till blurred.

"No, please." My voice wavers as I straighten my back. There's no way I'm leaving without circumambulating at least three times. "Let me go kora, I'm fine." I throw him a pleading look as my fingers dig into the felting wool of his coat.

He shakes his head at my dogged determination.

"Yeah," he says, trying a tone of consent to hide what the frown on his forehead reveals. "But we'll go together." He opens his arm and leads me back into the swirling tide of prayers and chant. "I'll follow you."

So we circle, around and around, and I feel better with every step. The lightness returns to my body, and a crystal clarity sweeps the left-over silt from my mind. As the shadows lengthen within the golden rays cascading through the temple door, the stream of pilgrims keeps swelling. It's at the end of the day that all come seek sanctuary here, hoping to find a glimpse of their own personal reprieve.

"Love." Karma points at one of the wood benches at the side. "Sit here and wait for me a moment, I see an old friend." I nod and slide on the low seat—*Om mani*—with my mind steeped in prayer.

The beads flick through my fingers, and I settle my gaze on the red dots among the pilgrims. A tinge of regret tugs at my heart as the devout monks and nuns pass me by. So many of them. Who would have thought, me sitting here, in the holiest of holy, dressed in lay woman's clothes? Not me!

Heavy incense stings the back of my throat. I swallow. It's still not easy to admit my next thought. I'm not only dressed in lay woman's clothes; I am a lay woman. Albeit by choice, and it's precisely this truth that strengthens me—I made the choice of my own free will. I'm here as a lay woman because I chose to serve the dharma this way.

My eyes glide up to the gilded shimmer of Jowo Shakyamuni Buddha. So, I'm here. What now? The back of my head rolls against the timber banister. A strange calm descends on me. Somehow, I expected a sense of anxiety, or at least a rattling unsettlement, arriving at this destination. There's none of that. A deep relief settles within me. My eyes dwindle into the passing blur. So many people.

With a jolt, I shoot up. *No way!*

A gush of adrenaline sends my mind on high alert. I crane my neck for the passing man who just now crossed my vision. *It can't be.* Without thinking, I shoot into the circling swarm.

Heated bodies pack against mine, stifling me with their briny stench of sweat as we push around the shrine. Spurred on by my intense desire to be sure, I shove the bitter nausea to the back of my throat. I must know.

My eyes spy ahead to find him in the mingle of unruly mops, beaded tresses, naked skulls, and long scarfs. *There he is!* Broad shoulders, a head full of graying curls, striding with that wild, yet sophisticated air I know so well. *It's Sonam!*

I raise my hand, trying to slice through the sluggish mass, but my attempt yields no result. The crowd's too dense. With a last effort, I throw myself to the side. This will be faster. My panting breath's running out on me, and I skid along the polished timber of the banister. I can't let him get away.

"Nordun!" A powerful tug pulls the tail end of my coat, bringing me to a sudden standstill. "Where did you go?"

I turn, baffled by the instant halt. Karma. His voice echoes in my ears, but somehow his presence is a distant distortion. Bewildered, I look back for the familiar figure I thought I saw, but he's nowhere in the crowd. Sonam's gone.

"I..." I bend over, hands to the knees, to catch my breath. "I...." I pull myself up at Karma's sleeve and wring out my words out of my heaving breath. "I saw Sonam." I gulp.

"You what?" Karma grabs both my arms and leads me out of the temple into the orange, charred dusk of the evening. "You saw what?" He keeps me close as his hands smoothen the sticky strands of my hair behind my ears.

"I saw Sonam," I say, still out of breath. "You know, Sonam from Zinzin..." My eyes try to catch his, but he keeps his gaze over my shoulder.

"Sonam?" A careful smile curls his lips and he draws his gaze back in. "You must be mistaken." His hand slides along my cheekbone in an unsettling caress. "We're in Lhasa, not in Rongdrak." At last, he rests his eyes rest on me. They absorb me into an opaque veil of green, a dense, dark forest with no shade to be found.

I shiver as I've never seen his eyes like this.

"You must be tired, love. Let's get some tea and a good rest," he says, his voice soothing. I let him lead me into the winding alleys downtown and pull my scarf tight.

"You're probably right," I say.

The weariness of the long day's settling in my bones and my mind's a perfect mess. Arriving at Lhasa, beholding the most holy Jowo Shakyamuni—it's all been good, but also overwhelming.

Karma's firm arm pulls me along in deep thoughts. My stomach clenches at the thought of his imminent troubles, so I'll let it rest—for now—but my thoughts keep running back to that tall, broad man striding along in the temple.

It was a long day, but my eyes didn't deceive me.

That was Sonam. Here in Lhasa. That I'm sure of.

Thirty-three

"What took you so long?" Dendup jumps in his seat, his sulked face a flush, his hands fluttering in stupefied gestures.

I halt at the doorway of the kitchen, taken aback by his abrupt outcry. The image of Sonam that has walked with me ever since we left the temple is erased in one swift swipe. Sure, dusk has fallen, but Dendup knew we would be at the temple. Karma pulls me along his resolute stride and before I know it, we're sitting across an agitated Dendup.

"Missed us then?" Karma's sarcastic tone reinforces his tense glance at the table full of sweet reeking cup. *Chang.* My eyes shoot from the scattered dishes to Dendup's reddish blotched nose and stained cheeks. Is he drunk?

"Hmff..." Dendup grimaces and for a moment, it looks like he's going to eat his moustache—again. "We need to talk." He waves at the matron. "But first we eat."

My stomach grumbles in agreement. Good. I sit back, reassured. He's not too drunk and whatever's on his mind can wait until after dinner.

At Dendup's order, the matron serves a chunky thukpa that seems to invigorate all three of us. Smacking the last bit out of the bowl, Dendup starts grumbling again. His hands draw over the table.

"Listen, I said no secrets between us, right?" Dendup's eyes glare from under his frown, and I freeze.

Secrets. My stomach knots as the last gulp of thukpa attempts to find its way back up my throat.

"And sister, when we set off," Dendup says, turning to me. "You promised you would do as we told you, didn't you?"

A taste of bitter bile fills my mouth, but I nod. This is not good. *He knows.* My mind bounces in all directions, a heat spreads from my chest up to my neck, drowning my cheeks in a fiery blush. He knows my real reason for coming along to Lhasa. *How?*

"What are you on about?" Karma's voice interrupts my frantic thoughts. "We've been to the temple and back." He rests his gaze on me, as calm as ever.

Dendup waves his hand again in annoyance. "I know, I know." His fingers spread on the table and he leans in even further. "I'm just saying it's time." He pauses, and I hold my breath.

Time? I push the sour taste on my palate back and clear my throat.

"What time?" I'm lost as my thoughts run out of options.

"Time for us to bring you to safety, sister." Dendup leans back and draws his hands around another cup. "You tell her." He points his chin at Karma, who's kept his gaze on me all the time.

"Safety?" I raise my voice. "What safety?" My eyes shoot from Karma to Dendup and back, my mind following in their trail.

"Nordun, love." Karma leans in and rests his hand on my arm. "The next few days..." He pauses, the tiny lines around his eyes deepening. "It's not safe for you to be out here, not with us." The meaningful glare in his eyes says it all. My eyes widen as a sharp blow shatters my ribcage, leaving me breathless and gasping for air.

"Don't." My eyes widen and I put my hands to my mouth to smother my thoughts, but it's too late. A gruesome portrayal of death and deception slashes across my mind. "Please don't say it." My whisper is hardly audible. I shake my head.

"We're not..." Dendup reaches across and wraps his huge hand around my other arm. "Your uncle, he's a dangerous man. We don't know what he'll do." His voice takes on an almost fatherly tone, and genuine concern shines through his rugged facade.

"That's why we'll take you to a secure place," Karma says. "A place your sisters asked me to bring you." He shifts next to me.

My sisters? I blink.

"It's only for a few days until..." Dendup's words freeze midway as he sees me cringe. He averts his eyes, but not before showing me the twinge of remorse that flickers through.

I raise my hands.

"Wait." I turn to Karma. "My sisters, you said?" My thoughts stumble over Karma's words. He nods.

"Pema and Tsomo." His hand gently strokes my back.

My mouth opens, but my mind stalls. *How?* I sag back in my seat and cast my eyes in my lap, the red thread on my wrist a blurred line in my vision. *My sisters again.*

"Better we go now." The tone of Dendup's voice leaves little room for arguing.

My fingers fumble with the knotted string. Karma and Dendup—they're sending me off, and my sisters told them to. Where's my part in all of this? I raise my weary head and nod.

"Yes, better go now." I look at my companions and can't help a little smile curling in the furthest corners of my mouth. Their stupefied stares are almost comical to me. They must have expected a pleading reply from me, begging them to let me stay. Well, if there's one thing I learned from being on the road, it's picking my battles wisely.

So, we walk the streets of Lhasa again, Karma and me, but now in the soundless shade of the night. His hand holds me tight, as if he expects me to run off at any moment.

I glance at him, my feet struggling to keep up with his stride.

"It's close," he says, as if he wants to convince himself this whole situation is fine. I can almost touch the reticence, floating like pallid slivers of fog between us.

"I'm good." My breath streams out like a sheer silvery puff. I pull my scarf tight. I still have no idea where I'm going, but I'm keeping a close eye on the twists and turns we take.

I'm a total stranger to Lhasa right now, but I want to make sure Lhasa's not a total stranger to me in the morning.

"Here it is." Karma halts in front of a narrow gate, leading into one of the many inconspicuous wooden houses lining the road. My hands glide along the cold iron of the bolted doorway and I sigh. That's secure alright.

"Nordun, love." Karma's words are a hoarse whisper in my ear. "Promise me you'll stay here until I get you." His thumb strokes the edge of my jaw, and his lips tentatively graze my forehead.

"Promise me." His strong arms grip tighter, and I nod.

"Don't let anyone lure you out of here." He slides his hand under my chin and tilts it to meet his dark gaze. "Not little sister, not Lanying." His heated breath caresses my cheeks. "Stay in, love, and stay away from her." His voice lowers, and an ominous apprehension ignites in the depth of his eyes. I lean back and raise my eyebrows at the sudden change in his face.

"But..." I stop as he puts his lips to my ear in a hushed hiss.

"I tell you." He secures his arm around me, and his hand digs deep into my hip. "She's not capable of caring about anybody but herself." His sneer smolders with resentment. "She can't be trusted. I've experienced that firsthand, believe me."

I flinch at the ferocious intensity of his tone. What is this?

Clang! The next moment, we both jump at the bolt snapping of the gate, swinging open on its heavy hinges to a crack just wide enough to sneak through. Karma clutches my hand and steps into a dim courtyard.

"Ama-la." Karma bows to the stately silhouette standing in the doorway ahead of us. "Thank you for receiving us." A tall shadow floats towards us, revealing herself in the fiery glare coming from the open kitchen door.

"You are most welcome." A soft yet unwavering voice resounds in my ears and I freeze.

Unable to move, I can only stare. Before me stands the spitting image of Tsomo, my beloved sister in seclusion. My mind boggles. That elongated face, those almond-shaped eyes, slightly older, yes, but exactly like Tsomo's eyes.

"Please, come in."

Even her voice...

I blink, and my eyes settle on the collar of her maroon robes. Where are my manners? "Ama-la." I bow, not knowing what to say.

"Please, from our families," Karma says, as he offers his bag to her. "With so much regard." A shadow shoots from the gate to receive the offering.

"That's not necessary." She waves her hand. "We're most happy you've come."

Karma ignores her protest and places his bag in the rushing guard's arms.

"I have to go." He bows his head. "As you understand."

The woman nods and extends her hands in a blessing.

"Nordun, please." Karma turns to me, his eyes blazing the softest of summer green again. "Don't forget your promise."

The back of his hand glides gently across my cheek and rests on my parting lips for a reply, but the words won't come. My mind hasn't caught up with what's happening.

It's not until the steely clonk of the sliding bolt resounds in my ears again, and a loving arm leads me into a cozy kitchen, that I find some sense in this all.

"At last we meet." The woman pours me a cup of tea in the empty kitchen. I look up, my face in a total daze. She laughs. "I see Karma hasn't told you then." She puts the kettle down and sits with me.

"I'm Palmo, your sisters' aunt." My hands wrap around the steaming cup. "You'll be staying with us for a few days." I nod. That part is obvious to me by now.

"I'm sorry," I say, and look at my trembling hands and my teeth clatter. "I'm a bit..." I choke, and my throat fills up with an emotion I can't explain. It's a sweltering heat, shattering my frost-bound bones, and it sucks the life right out of me.

"It's fine," she says, and throws her wool scarf around my shivering shoulders. "You've had a long day, a long journey." She folds my hands in hers, the most caring embrace. "First you'll sleep, then we'll talk."

Her arms hurdle around me. She leads me to a plain room in the back of the house and puts me to bed under a pile of itchy wool.

As soon as she closes the door, my body sinks into the squishy mat, and my mind lifts to the wooden beamed ceiling. Instinctively I curl up, folding my body to lay it in the tender hollow of his, of Karma's, and the most intense longing rips through me. I clench my fists in shame as I realize how frayed and fragile my aspirations have become. With everything that's happened, and everything that is bound to unfold, all I yearn for now is to rest my head against the flat bone on his chest, and even my breath to the faint drum of his heart.

My fingers search inside the collar of my shirt. There they are, so soothing to the touch. I slip the strand around the back of my hand and press the cold jade into my cheek.

Please let sleep arrive and fill this aching void in me. I close my eyes. Om Tare.

Thirty-four

I t's not until the sun is set on her highest point, throwing her warming beams on the polished window ledge, that I open my eyes. *Oh my!* For sure, I must have slept through the sounds of the bell and the communal prayers that mark the new day at every monastery in the early morning.

I'm rested and refreshed. The drawn-out night has buried the crippling loneliness from yesterday to the uninhabited edges of my mind. It takes me only the blink of an eye to realize I'm a guest in this room and I slept late—ignorantly late. I fold the heavy blankets neatly aside and hasten to the hallway. My bare feet halt at the touch of the polished wood. What a luxury. I squint and look around. Where to go?

"Nordun-la."

She must have been waiting for me. A heat creeps up my temples as I bow my head in shame at the woman who received me with so much grace last night.

"Ama-la, so sorry," I say. What must she think of me, such a lazy guest?

"Oh, please." She chuckles. "We don't apologize for a well-needed rest here."

I glance up, and again I'm taken aback by the striking similarity, by how she looks like Tsomo—those eyes, that smile, even that stance.

"And call me Palmo," she says. She hooks her arm through mine and walks me to the kitchen where I'm served hot tea and crispy fried rolls with a savory filling by a wide-smiled nun, her face the shape and shine of a full moon.

"This is the best breakfast I've ever had," I say, clearing the second helping out of my bowl. "It really is." My fingers rub the grease from the corners of my mouth and Palmo waves her hand.

"Jomo here is a jewel in the kitchen." She nods at the nun pottering around the stove. "And an excellent practitioner as well."

The little nun hurries over to pour us another cup of tea, her shoulders hunched at the compliment of her abbess.

My toes curl as I notice Palmo's gaze going over my lay clothes. "I'm sorry." I cast my eyes down, and my fingers fumble with the edges of my sleeves.

"Don't." Her voice unusually fierce, Palmo puts her hand on mine and squeezes it. "And don't be apologizing all the time. It doesn't become a strong woman like you."

I glance up and shake my head. "I'm not that strong." I sink further in my seat.

"Nonsense," she says, and her tone dares no denial. "From what I've heard..." She pauses, a grin coming to her lips. "If you're anything like Dechen, you're a force to be reckoned with."

My eyes widen, and my jaw slackens at the mention of my grandmother.

"You know her?" I say. "My grandmother?" I hold my breath.

"Know her?" Palmo says, as she raises her eyebrows. "My dear, we're practically sisters—in our younger days, sisters in shenanigans, for sure." Her exclamation is followed by the loudest belly laughter ever, one that measures up to Dendup's typical roars. "You didn't know?"

I perk up, my mind aroused at the mention of my honorable grandmother, the virtuous abbess of our monastery, engaging in mischief. Palmo leans back and smoothens her robe, her laughter subdued now.

"Oh, I'm sure she won't mind," she says and looks up, her eyes full and bright with no doubt the most wonderful memories. "You're her own blood, after all."

She settles in her seat and starts telling all about their nightly ventures to the storeroom to snack on freshly fried khapse, their secret detours to the nearest village while pretending to cut long grass on the pastures, even their daring excursion with some of the village girls to the horse races which required a change in lay clothes. Her tales of antics and adventure swing me from merriment to amazement. Who would have thought this of my reverend grandmother?

"Oh, yes." Palmo's hand rests on my arm. "Dechen used to be quite a handful." She closes her eyes for a moment, reminiscing about their younger years together.

"Mind you." Her bright gaze has turned into a thoughtful, even distant, stare as she looks up again. "It's quite a miracle she turned out so well, for the poor girl was heartbroken when she was brought to us." Her voice falls flat and wavers. "They had shattered her spirit, crushed her being to the bone by taking her baby from her." She sips her tea with care. "And Rapten was a good man, an honorable man who had done everything to make peace between the families." Tears fill her eyes. "Not to mention the day the terrible news reached us of your mother's accident... years later..."

Her voice trails off, and I choke at the thought of the enormity of my grandmother's grief. How much suffering can one bear?

"But then you came." A renewed sense of pleasure graces Palmo's lips. "And with you, so much happiness." She wraps her hands around her cup. "Palden did good bringing you to Dechen instead of those spiteful relatives of hers." She wrinkles her nose.

"Oh, I gave her a lot of sorrow, though, being such a wild child." I laugh as I recall my grandmother's stories about my boisterous behavior.

"Oh, Nordun." Palmo reaches over to me. "She is nothing but proud of you, even now." She points her chin at my lay clothes, and I cringe.

"Don't!" Her eyes flash a warning at me. "Don't ever be ashamed of the choices you make." Her voice stern, she pinches her lips. "Your grandmother immersed herself in the dharma as a monastic, knowing it was the only way to save herself from a life full of bitterness and resentment. She didn't have a choice. You, on the other hand, with a father like Palden..." She sinks back in her seat.

"Your life is a wide-open, ready to be explored with a boundless curiosity, and from what I've understood, you're doing great." She sniggers. "A female horse master, that sure must please Palden too."

I feel my face stretch and I can't help but gloat a little. It's so good to hear these words from her.

"But let's focus on the task at hand." She looks over my shoulder and gestures for Jomo to fill our cups once more.

My pulse races. *The task at hand.* I bite my lip and my eyes sink into the thick swirl of clotted cream on the top of my cup. She just recalled my mother's death as an accident. What does she know? I take a sharp breath in.

"Did you know?" My voice sounds frail, as my heart's so small. "About my uncle?" My vision resurfaces from the milky brew, but is still too weak to face her.

"Word came to me, yes," Palmo says. "And the family's intentions are apparent."

I nod and glance up to see Palmo's hands wrapped around her cup, a translucent shine coming through her blue-veined knuckles.

"But I also se Dechen raised you well." Her voice soft and steady, she looks at me from over her cup. "That's the real reason you're here, isn't it?" She spins her cup around again, letting the fatty foam settle on one side. "To prevent this useless killing?"

My quickened pulse relaxes, and I raise myself, realizing there's no hiding from the truth in her eyes. This woman knows it all.

"It is," I say. "But now that I've arrived, I'm not sure how."

Her hand dismisses my concern.

"There's no use pondering the how, Nordun." Her alert eyes soften with the tone of her voice. "Once you've figured out the why, the how will follow." She pauses and takes a sip of her tea without averting her gaze from me. "Trust your heart, and you'll be fine." She continues to taste her tea, giving each sip the utmost attention.

Trust your heart. I nod as my mind settles with hers in the quiet contentment descending upon us.

"Why not do some offerings to ensure a fortunate outcome?" Palmo sets her empty cup next to mine on the table. "Jomo will show you our prayer room."

Yes, prayer is what I need right now.

I follow the small nun to the back of the house with a spring in my step. A proud smile stretches across her face as she swings open the door, and a delightful scent of floral notes, peppered with a light hint of spice, floats our way.

With my feet at the threshold, I savor the aroma—so delicate and different.

"We make our own," Jomo says and urges me to step in.

My feet sink in the heavy wool of the carpets. My eyes drown in the abundance of natural light, bathing the room in the softest shades of pink, and blushed rose.

I take a few steps towards the shrine and lower myself three times before coming up for air. The beauty of this place is breathtaking. It's not the elements that are different, for the gilded Buddha, the elaborate offerings on the shrine, the detailed thangka's, it's all there. It's in the way this room has been arranged, from the gradient tones in the color scheme, to the matching textures of the fabrics—everything is put together with utmost care and thought.

I turn to take in the different thangka's, and my eyes settle on a few unknown depictions. I lean in to examine the unfamiliar deities.

"We used to circle the other way, you know," Jomo says, answering my unspoken curiosity. "But it doesn't matter which way we circle, samsara's still samsara." With a cheeky smile peeping through on her loving face, she hastens out of the room, closing the door behind her in her own quiet manner.

Still in wonder of the unexpected beauty, I sit on one of the mats and slip the jade beads from my neck. Ignoring the desire of my unruly thoughts to churn over Palmo's every word, I close my eyes and turn my mind to prayer. *Oṃ tāre tu tāre ture soha.* As my breath settles on the rhythm of my beads, my heart fills with a deep silence and my mind opens in the vastness of space.

I don't know how long I've been sitting in prayer when a sound of a bouncy pitter-patter pops in my ears, followed by the smooth stride of squeaking leather.

No way! I turn to see the door fly open and my suspicion is confirmed—little sister hops over the threshold, followed by a gloating Lanying.

"We looked all over for you!" The little one throws herself in my lap and latches her sticky arms around my shoulders in the snuggest hug.

Lanying halts at the doorway, flashing that triumphant grin of hers And I feel myself freeze for just a moment.

"Told you I would find you." She anchors her hands on her hips, and the silver of her long knife thunders a cold lightning bolt through the warm hued room.

I clutch little sister tight as my thoughts turn to the worst.

"It's time then?" My voice falters and my fingernails hook in the flimsy fabric of little sister's coat.

"It's time," Lanying says, and she turns on her heels. "But first, tea."

Thirty-five

"I I found out where they are." Lanying comes straight to the point as we sit down in the shade of the wide pine in the middle of the courtyard. "Hiding in plain sight, the idiots." She stretches her long legs and leans back against the papery white bark.

"Sisters, please." Jomo rushes from the doorway, a tray packed with tea and goodies in her hand. Sensing the serious nature of our conversation, she pinches little sister's cheeks and squints. "Come on, skinny chicken, let's get you inside and put some fat on those scrawny bones of yours." Squealing with delight, the two of them dart to the kitchen.

I push the tray between us and glance at Lanying. Her fingertips sway the dense whorls of verdant foliage above us.

"So, you saw them then?" I say. My eyes dart from the tray to the edge of the yard and back. Tightness pinches my ribs, and a heavy pit nestles itself in my stomach. *She found them.* My mind lays silent with all thoughts suspended at Lanying's claim.

"I didn't." She sinks her teeth into a dried date and tears its golden-brown skin from its pearly middle. "But my men did." She smacks the reddish flesh with contentment, flicking the velvety pit between her long fingernails.

I take a steeling breath and raise the teacup to my mouth. "Good." My lips form a to-quick smile and I try to look at her while avoiding her eyes. I've failed.

"They got to you." She takes another date and rips it to shreds before she pops it in her mouth. "Karma and that Dendup, they told you about me, didn't they?" Her voice hammers with a stone-cold certainty through the humid afternoon air.

I guzzle down my tea to hasten my response, but she's already ahead of me.

"Well, it's all true." She settles her aloof stare on me. "I sold out my entire family." Unmoved, she swats a fly from the tray.

My teacup floats somewhere between my mouth and my lap, and all I can do is stare at her. *It's all true.*

"But why?" My voice wavers. Do I need to know?

"It was them or me," she says. She slices another date to the bone with her polished fingernail. "And I made sure it wasn't me."

I shiver at the hint of complacency in her voice.

"You know, sister." Her eyes narrow on me. "Few girls have the luxury of growing up as sheltered as you have." She squashes the fleshy fruit between her fingers.

"Spending most of his sorry existence in the whorehouses, my father was all too happy to encourage my brother to stick his tiny prick in every hole he could find, including mine from as young as I can remember." She wrinkles her nose and swats her hand at an imaginary fly.

"And when I was about ripe enough, he sold me off to that filthy old swine to be humiliated in all the worst ways you can imagine." She glances at me and sighs. "Well, you probably can't, and that's a good thing."

As the immensity of her personal disclosure hits me, my thoughts go into hiding. I feel myself staring at her, but cannot focus.

She takes another sip of tea.

"It took me years to prepare, but I did it." Her voice has toned down to a low whisper. "I tricked my brother into imprisonment, but the lowlife killed himself, a fate which conveniently destroyed my father." She sucks in her cheeks.

"And that nasty husband of mine?" She pauses, and a slight smile curls around her lips. "Well, I got his sorry ass sold into slavery—he deserved a fate far worse than death." She leans back, relaxing in the stunning silence her words have spun between us.

My hands clutch my cup, the earthen rim presses hard onto the flat bone of my chest. I open my mouth, but my words drown in my throat as the hideous hurt of her confession sinks in. I meet her eyes, and the sudden, saddened blue in them smudges between us.

"So, you see, sister," she says and tilts her head to the side. "I wasn't joking when I said I'm beyond redemption in this lifetime." She rests her gaze on the toes of her boots, rocking her heels in the brittle gravel, back and forth, back and forth.

With a shudder, my mind rises, stirred by her last words.

"You might think you're beyond redemption." I weigh my words before I let them slip from the back of my tongue. "But you're not, for it's not what you've done that matters. It's what you do now." I put my cup aside and catch her gaze. "You told me you choose to be this way, to take the law into your own hands, remember?"

She presses a date between her tight lips and chews it with a vengeance. "For sure I did," she says. "There was no way I was going to wait it out for some karmic law to settle the score." She rolls her eye and spatters the pit before her feet. "I don't possess the patience of a mule, merely enduring the heavy load and brutal punishments imposed on it."

She lifts her chin at me and her eyes bear the brightest of peacock blue. "No, mine is the patience of a warrior, who despite the cruelty suffered and wounds sustained never relinquishes the quest for a glorious victory." She bares her teeth into a hard grin, and I can't help but shake my head at her tone of hollow pride.

"Lanying, you decide how you want it to be." I lean in to strengthen my words. "You made your choice before, with reason, and you can make another choice again—just as easily." I rest my case as a wistful shadow draws around her eyes. She sighs and my heart sinks. I've failed—for now.

"I adore your innocence, sister," she says. "I really do." She places her hand on mine and interlocks our fingers. "It's something I never had the pleasure of tasting myself." Her long nails scrape my fingers as she turns our hands into a fist. "And probably never will, for once our tongue is scorched by the fire of vengeance, it's scarred and devoid of savoring anything so sweet as innocence ever again." She tips her head back and closes her eyes. Her fist drops in her lap.

My fingers grip hers tighter as I swallow hard to stomach the bitter reality of samsara. My mind fevers with the thought of my grandmother's ordeal related to me just this morning, and now my sister's. My heart shudders. *The things some men do.*

"But let my past doing not deter you of my help, sister." Lanying's fingers slide from mine. "You'll need it, for that woman, I heard she's a sly one." She jumps to her feet. "We'd better get a move on." Her eyes dart to the gate.

"Now?" I raise myself and smoothen my hair. "Outside?" My voice pitches, and Lanying laughs.

"Well, they will not come to us, sister," she says. "So yes, outside." She waves her hand at the entrance. "My men are waiting—one will bring little sister home; one will come with us." She turns on her heels like she always does, and sniggers. "And you're more than welcome to take one home afterwards, just for pleasure. I trained them well."

Thirty-six

Torn between my curiosity and my promise to Karma, my mind's stalling and so are my feet—but only until Lanying's men stride in. With their broad shoulders and burly frames, their very presence erases my hesitation at once. My eyes glide to their side. If needed, they won't hesitate to swing the daunting long knifes hanging from their hips, for sure.

"We're only going to see today," Lanying says. "Making sure we've got the right snakes and sniff out their lair." Her words clear the last lingering trace of qualm. Sure, this sounds sensible.

With Palmo nowhere to be found, I leave a quick notice with Jomo and step out into the streets of Lhasa, in the wake of Lanying and her guards.

As soon as the gate closes behind me, I pull my hood over my eyes. A brisk dust swirls on the late afternoon wind, powdering the roads with fine grains of shale, caking my face with a sheer veil of grime. The orange sun is already fading in specks of ivory and amber, submerging the town in the long-drawn shadows of a sluggish sunset. A faint thunder claps in the humid distance, an ominous foreboding. I draw my elbows to my side.

My eyes fixed on Lanying's heels, I follow close, skidding through the town's center. The low hum of prayer swells in the winding backstreets; we must be close to the main temple. A look up confirms my suspicion; we're at the rear end of the shrine, a crisscross of frayed prayer banners topping its scaled stucco walls.

"She's in here, that serpent of a woman," Lanying says, and points at the narrowest of alleys with only one tiny door cut into the darkened wall. "It's not the best of inns." She grins. "But I've got it covered." With the flick of her hand, she orders the guard to stay put on the corner. "Stay close." She turns into the alley, pulling me along by my sleeve.

"Wait!" I freeze as my thoughts speed ahead of me, halting at the doorway of the inn. My pulse surges, a muffled rush ringing in my ears. "What are you doing?" My voice lowers to a hiss. "You can't just go in."

She looks back, a frown drawing on her forehead. "Of course we can." She shrugs. "I know the place, trust me."

With a determined stride, she heads for the door, leaving me no choice but to hasten behind her to the inn's obscure entrance.

"No windows." I hold my breath as her knuckles rattle on the hardened door. She smirks.

"What is this place?" My eyes shoot from the bolted door across the dim wall and back as I try to rein in my erratic thoughts. Without warning, a sunken grinding resounds from the iron latches, and the door creaks open. A low rumble of hushed rumors and subdued laughter floats ahead of the penetrating vapors of spirits and spiced grub. My feet won't move. Everything in my body screams to run, but Lanying's already in, the tail of her coat a waver to trail behind. I clench my fists and duck for the door.

"Where do you think you're going?" A strong hand grips around my elbow and pulls me against the coarse plastered wall. Another hand clasps hard at the belt of my coat. Darkness surrounds me as my hood falls over my eyes. A surge of adrenaline tenses every muscle in my body, and I gulp a big breath.

It takes me only a split moment to realize. *Karma!*

I heave, my heart hammers against my ribs. With a jolt, I pull my hood back and tear myself away from his taut grip.

"You promised." His sneer bites right through me, and my shoulders shrug under the crushing weight of his justified rebuke.

My mind's spinning. He's right, but there's no time. My eyes fly to the blackened entrance.

"Lanying!" With a desperate turn, I grab the lapel of his coat and face him. Under his bleak stare brews a thunder green.

"Please," I say. "She's in there." My words falter as my feet stumble towards the door.

"And you're not." His fingers delve into my upper arm, and his voice smolders with the onset of an outburst, ready to ignite.

"Leave it!" With a shriek, Lanying appears at the doorway, motioning her rushing guard to a halt. "You're good, sister?" She bares her teeth and bounces her fierce gaze from me to Karma and back.

"Don't," Karma says, his voice so unnervingly calm it draws a quiver through my spine. "Get away from her." He hauls me in. "Now." His arm gouges around my middle, and his fingers harden into the soft parts of my spine.

Lanying jumps to my side and anchors her hands at her side. Her feet wide apart, her heels dug in—she's ready to lash out.

"Please," I say and recoil at the outrage on both their faces, the raw resentment laying so bare between the two of them. "She's only trying to help." I raise my voice in vain.

"Leave it, sister." Lanying spits her words at our feet. "He'll never get it." She takes a step back and raises her hand at her guard. "You know where to find me." She throws me a curt nod and storms off, her guard trailing in the dust of her heels.

I blink as my mind speeds down the alley. Where's she off to?

"Don't even try…" Karma raises his hand, and his arm relaxes in the curve of my waist. From the corner of my eye, I spot the heavy door. Without a faint creak, it shuts again, its heavy ledges a silent security for whomever resides inside. A thick lump nestles in the back of my throat and I cast my eyes down. What now?

His hand tight around the back of my arm, he steers me out of the deserted alley onto the main street, where the rush of pilgrims pushes us on to the temple.

"Honestly, Nordun." He halts at the gate, and I draw my back into the grid of steel. "What were you thinking, going after her like that?"

I look up, and his seething anger looms over me. *He knows.* My thoughts scatter. He knows I was after the ngakpa's wife. He knows she's in there.

"I'm sorry," I say, but my words are hollow. He shakes his head.

"I wish you were." His voice has softened but still carries an alarming edge. "You're too stubborn for your own good." His hand draws over his face.

"I can't help it." Tears rim my burning eyelids and his face blurs in front of me. I clench my fist in front of my mouth. "I just can't."

"Damn it, Nordun." He clasps the back of my neck and pulls me in. "You've got to stop it right now, or you're going to get yourself killed."

His chest rises with a heavy sigh, and I bury my heated face into the coarse wool of his chuba.

I know he's right, but I can't stop.

His hands cradle my face, and his lips press a desperate kiss onto mine.

I can't stop, and he knows it.

Thirty-seven

A thunder bolt crashes through the sweltering sky. The sudden gale scatters the billowing clouds of a purple and pink twilight and carries the tidings of a storm on its way. My hands search for my hood, but Karma pins me between his shoulder and arm, and strides us onto the main street, away from the temple crowd.

"Wait, please." I halt as my hands tangle in the furred rim of my collar. "Just let me..." Wrestling the folds of my hood, my eyes shoot ahead, and I gasp. *It's him!* I leap back with my hands still hovering over my head.

"Sonam!" Broad shoulders, a head full of mad curls—Sonam is marching right by us.

"Nordun!" His eyes fever with bewilderment as he stalls his stride and turns. "What...?" He dives to the side and grabs my hand. "Why...?" A wide smile breaks on his bemused face as his eyes take me in from head to toe. "Look at you!"

My cheeks flush at his audacious attention, and I rush my hands through my hair before I draw my hood.

"Karma, good to see you." The two men greet each other with a pat on the back. "Dendup?" Sonam scouts around.

"At the inn," Karma says, and his hand slides behind my back, taking hold of my belt.

I pull my sleeves over my hands and steady my thoughts. No surprises here between the two of them. I glance back up at Sonam. *He knows.* He knows why Karma's here. But why is he?

Sonam's smile turns into a puzzled frown as he sets his eyes on me again. His eyes go over to Karma.

"Don't ask," Karma says under his breath. "Worst mistake ever."

I pinch my lips at his words as Sonam's laugh roars in my ears.

"I could have told you," he says, and shakes his head. "She's every bit like her mother."

Suddenly it dawns on me. *That's it.* That's why Sonam's here. *My mother!*

"But tell me, brother," I say, and slide my hood back a bit. "What brings you here while your entire family is looking for you?" *There.* I don the sweetest of smiles.

Karma's arm freezes around me. His fingers turn on my belt.

"Not here," he says, and points with his chin to an alley. "Let's go."

Without loosening his grip on me, he leads us to the inn where Dendup's sitting snug in the company of the lovely matron. Not at all surprised to see Sonam, he greets him with regards and raises his cup to his friend's health.

As pleasantries are exchanged, and the matron serves us our tea, I dare to bring the issue up again, for my mind keeps on pressing. I need to know.

"You got us all worried, brother," I say and turn to Sonam. "Disappearing like that."

In my peripheral, I see Karma and Dendup exchanging a knowing look. Sonam just leans back, an amused grin on his face.

"I'll tell you my story, sister," he says, and pinches my arm. "If you tell me yours." His eyes gleam with a mischievous spark. "There's no way these two here would take you to Lhasa of their own free will, not with the matters they've got to attend to." He nods at Karma. "Although he might."

I can't help but laugh. There's no way to outsmart Sonam.

"I will," I say, and cross my arms over my chest. "You first."

Sonam nods and gulps down his tea. Dendup leans in, his cup to his mouth. Karma stays unmoved, but the shallow lines around his eyes deepen ever so slightly. *Interesting.* I thought they already knew.

Leaving his usual bold gestures behind, Sonam tells—his voice flat—how he planned to go see my father as word had reached him of Uncle's foul play.

"I needed to see him, to help him." His tone heavy, his eyes gaze into nowhere. "I had let him down so badly after Lhamo's death." He rubs his moustache. "But somebody got to me, making sure I was arrested on the accusation of smuggling." A wry laughter escapes from the back of this throat. "Me a smuggler, what a daft idea." He extends his empty cup to Dendup, who pours him a drink from his flask.

"But as all things can be bought, so too can freedom." Sonam takes a guzzle of chang and wipes the clear trickle from the corners of his mouth. "I did send a message to Zinzin." He spreads his hands on the table and looks at me. "But I guess it took a long time for the words to reach." My eyes fixed on Dendup, my mind absorbs every bit of the story. *So that's what happened.*

"I had to come as soon as I realized the severity of the situation." He turns to Karma. "I'd heard the family would send you, as was to be expected."

My stomach pits as Karma nods. His vacant stare meets mine and my heart fills with sorrow at his empty look, the staunch indifference with which he takes up his horrendous chore.

"Palden's my best friend." He wrings his hands around his cup. "And Lhamo..." His eyes soften. "I needed to take care of this, for the both of them." He drowns his eyes in his cup, guzzling every drop with determination. A quiet sadness sinks over me as my thoughts go from Karma to Dendup, and the destructive deed they have devoted themselves to.

"I understand," Karma says, and nudges Dendup, who's dozing off in the corner. "Let's eat some more, then we'll talk." He gestures the matron for a round of extra spicy thukpa. "And I'll take you back to your place." He slips his warm hand in mine without looking at me, but his thumb rubs the inside of my palm—he's onto me.

"So, Nordun," Sonam says, his smile refreshed on his face. "I hear you did Palden proud." He raises his cup to me. "I never doubted you, sister." A slight flush creeps on my cheeks again, and I pull up on my knees as Karma's hand slides away.

"I had a lot of help," I say, and shift back in my seat.

"Speaking of help." Sonam leans in. "Where's Sangmo? You two were practically inseparable when we met." I take a quick glance at Karma, who has gotten up to go over to the matron.

"She couldn't come," I say, and clasp my hands in my lap. Sonam raises his eyebrows.

"No way." He pours himself another cup of Dendup's flask. "She'd love a trip like this. What kept her?" He takes another swag of the chang and I swallow.

"Sonam." I hesitate, for maybe I shouldn't. "She's with child." My words roll out of my mouth before my mind's made up. Sonam's drink spills as he chokes on the bittersweet chang.

"She what?" He wipes his mouth with his sleeve and snorts. "She's not!"

I lean in. "She is." I suck in my cheeks. "Sonam, you know Karma." My eyes flash over to the stove. He's still there. *Good.* "Why...?"

He raises his hands. "She came onto me, Nordun," he says, and draws his hands over his face. "I swear." He sighs. His shoulders stooped, he leans heavily on the table.

"She's a pretty wild thing, you know." He rubs his forehead, and a wistful smile curls around his lips. "Pregnant... if Zinzin hears of this..." His voice trails off and we both shoot up as the matron arrives with steaming bowls of thukpa.

"Hears of what?" Karma sits down and looks up at Sonam.

I bite my lip as Sonam puts the singing hot soup to his mouth.

"Of Sangmo having Sonam's baby." Dendup stretches from his corner and yawns a foolish grin. I clench my fists. *The idiot!*

"Of what?" Karma's hands stall. His brimming bowl lingers dangerously above the table. His knuckles whiten as he lowers his soup.

"Your baby?" He looks at Sonam, his voice seething with an alarming chill. Sonam glimpses at me, and we both hold our breath.

"And you knew?" Karma's icy stare pierces right through me. *Om mani.* What to reply? Fortunately, somebody's ahead of me.

"Well, you obviously didn't." Dendup sets his bowl down with a bang. "Right?" He looks straight at Karma with a lopsided smile plastered under his reddish nose.

I press my lips tight as Dendup's hoot bellies over the table, but I can't help the tiniest of twitch curling around my mouth.

"I'm sorry," I say, my voice a whisper. "But you never asked."

Well, that response sure doesn't help my situation, as Dendup and Sonam now both burst into a roaring laughter. With my cheeks on fire, I stare into the steaming soup, its spicy aroma a sting in my eyes. I duck my head at my daring reply. *That is not me.* Since when have I become so forthright?

With the hilarity between those two dying, we drink our soup, its peppery zest leaves a stale taste in my mouth. Karma's appetite seems to have vanished too; his bowl stands untouched.

"I'll bring you to Palmo's." His eyes brood with a dim glow. I nod and bid goodbye to my brothers.

"Go easy on her," Sonam says in a muffled voice, and he extends his hand to Karma. I draw my hood as Karma's hand on my back urges me out the door.

We walk in deafening silence, with Karma striding in the moonlit middle and me scurrying in the fragmented shadows aside. My heart has fallen to the bottom of my boots, and I struggle to keep up.

"Karma, please," I say, as we halt at the gate, but he looks away.

"No, Nordun," he says. "Not again." I glance at him, and his hollow stare pierces through my chest like the sharpest arrow sent with a vengeance from afar. I close my eyes and I let the bitter pain move through me. I did that, I caused my own agony.

As the gate swings open, Karma rushes in. A muffled conversation settles between him and the guard while I'm left outside the gate.

"In case you're thinking about leaving again," Karma says. "I paid this man a handsome sum to keep you in." He steps outside.

My eyes grow hot, and I stare at the ground. Those words just dashed all my hopes of making amends tonight. I clench my hood and duck my head, ready to shoot through the gate, but Karma's hard hand pulls me in.

"Don't you understand?" His voice breaths a burning whisper. "All I want is for you to be safe." The hard iron of the gate lodges into my side as I push him away with all the strength I can find. I bolt for the door, the gravel groaning with a loud protest under my fleeing feet.

As I hear the latch slam behind me, I stagger and let out a sob.

There's no way I'm ever going to be held captive. Not by him, not by anybody.

Thirty-eight

F ighting my tears, I tiptoe through the dark hallway. All is
  quiet. *Good.* My lips move in a silent prayer. If I just can get
to my room without being noticed, I'll be fine.

"I've been waiting for you." Palmo's calm voice echoes from the
darkened kitchen.

I shrink towards the polished banister and hold my breath. Now
what? Her tall shadow appears in the doorway. "Won't you come
in for a moment?" As silently as I entered the hallway, I move into
the kitchen. Palmo sits at the stove. The soft smolder lights her
loving smile.

"Ama-la," I say, and bow my head to hide my burning shame and
tears.

"Oh, Nordun," she says and chuckles. "You look like one of my
juniors, waiting to be reprimanded after being caught with their
hand in the tsampa bag." Her slender hands hold my heated face.

As soon as I'm met by the grace in her eyes, the floodgates of my
heart break open, and a stream of hot tears engulfs me.

"Now, my child." She draws me near the fire and sits with me
until the storm has passed, leaving me empty and anew.

"You didn't expect it to be easy, did you?" She hands me a warm
drink, a pure green tea with honey that sooths the raw inside of
me. I sniff.

"I never expected anything, really." My eyes still sting with
the disappointment of the day, and with a burning throat, I tell

her everything that happened, including my own inconsiderate, unkind actions.

"And now all I feel is a harrowing ache tearing through my being," I say, "And I can't breathe, it pains so much." My hand holds on to my heart.

She nods. "That is the hurting of your tender heart," she says and puts her hand on mine. "The hurt of a heart that has opened itself to the world." Her hands slide down my lap, enveloping my other hand with the warmest touch. "And that is good, Nordun, for it's a heart that flows with tenderness, encompassing all joy and all suffering; it's a compassionate heart."

I let her words rest between us as salt stains my cheeks.

"And now you have a choice," she says, and tips her head to the side. "You either let the hurt harden you, shutting down, closing off, and becoming rigid and indifferent to the sorrows of samsara." A fiery amber ignites in the depth of her eyes. "Or you remain open to care for all, the suffering and the joy, no matter what, and let yourself be led by your compassionate heart."

She sips her tea, and her eyes keep glowing over her cup onto mine. My fevered mind surrenders to her truth and the enormity of it all—to the realization that I don't have a choice—or rather that I've already made mine.

"But how?" I say, and my voice breaks. "How, when my heart feels so small, it wants to run and hide?" My eyes close, my fists clench. I so desperately want to know.

"Courage, my child." Palmo's voice is steady and clear. "The courage to trust the knowing of your heart, time and time again, in the full understanding that all sentient beings possess an innate goodness." She sighs. "Even though it is thickly obscured, and they have no way of knowing, it is still there."

I open my eyes to the serene glow of her wisdom, steeping her in the most delicate of hues of golden and blue. I blink.

"Courage, my child." Her voice resonates from the distance, a rumbling thunder echoing from the mountains afar. "When you are trying to help sentient beings, you will encounter difficulties. You must make your decisions and take the consequences." Her words roll in on the speed of lighting, and I bury my face in my hands for the clap to crash through. "You must have courage, Nordun. You must have a warrior heart."

I shudder as her words come thundering down, for it brings me my deliverance; the acknowledgement of the truth I was searching for. My hands slide down, drawing the veil of confusion, of the doubt I've been hiding behind. I've made my choice not so long ago, and now I'm ready—with all my heart—to fully follow through.

Clarity has returned to my vision, and Palmo pours me another drink with zest.

"You'll need it tonight." She nods at me, understanding my unspoken words.

"The guard." I say as my mind speeds ahead, already far beyond the gate. Palmo snickers.

"You don't think anybody in this house can be bought, do you?" An amusing smile curls her lips.

"No, Karma's generous donation will provide our lamps with the finest of butter for a very long time." She straightens her back and stretches her legs. "That, my dear, you can be sure of."

I shake my head. *This woman!*

"In fact, it's this very guard that will escort you to your sister," she says. "Whenever you're ready."

And thus, I walk with her blessing, straight to the gate where the watchman is waiting.

A slice of silvery moon has chased away the thundering clouds, illuminating the dark sapphire sky with her most brilliant opal luster.

I look up in wonder as I step onto the deserted main road—how quickly the shadows have vanished. I draw my hood—the vast open sky holds a biting midnight cold. With an empty mind and only the footsteps of the guard to follow, I set course to my sister. I'm sure I'll know what to do when I get there.

The guard knocks on an anchored door, and a small shutter slides open. Muffled words are exchanged, and the window closes again. With a deep screech, the heavy latches release their grip, leaving a crack open for me to slide through. I duck, and the next moment I'm blinded. Total darkness surrounds me as I stumble through.

"Last door on the right." A harsh voice resounds in the gloom, and I steady myself against the cold stucco of a hallway. My feet shuffle forward, and my hands search their way along the coarse plastered wall. Muted voices and stifled sounds hide behind the closed doors as I pass, while my eyes familiarize themselves with the dim.

At the last door, I halt, and my mind works again. What now? I lean in and put my ear to the thin timber frame. A familiar giggle comes through and I breathe a sigh of relief—she's in.

My knuckles prompt the door.

"Lanying." My voice is a whisper I'm sure she won't hear. I spread my fingers and push the door. It opens, and a soft streak of light lands on my feet. I step in, not at all prepared for what I'm about to behold.

"Sisterrrr!" Lanying shrieks, and her head pops up from under a heap of blankets, a wide, wicked smile on her face. She throws her long loose locks to the side and rises, her slim frame naked and proud.

"I suppose you won't join us?" She pulls the entangled layers on the bed and I freeze. A smooth, white body, rounded and curved, slides from under the covers, clinging on to a single sheet around her waist. *A woman.*

I can only stare as Lanying licks her lips in amusement. "Pretty, eh?"

She raises her eyebrows and grins as the woman slips past me, her undisguised shame shoving me out of her way. "No need to rush out," Lanying hollers. I turn my eyes away, my hand in front of my mouth. *A woman.*

"Oh, come on," Lanying says and sighs. "It's not like you haven't seen a naked woman before." She sits on the bed, her body still uncovered as I meet her provocative stare. My hand drops, my shoulders sag, and a hard lump chokes in my chest.

"I have," I say, my voice thick.

I blink, and my mind blanks as it registers what my eyes see. From her slender shoulders to her slim tights, her entire torso is covered with the pearly shine of serrated lacerations. *Scars.* The fearsome reminders of the most hideous abuse are branded on her body.

Lanying bares her teeth in a grin.

"I wasn't joking when I said it was them or me." She pulls her dress from under the bed. I swallow and move closer, while my mind runs off to hide from the sigh of so much suffering.

"I'm so sorry." My words get stuck. "I..." She waves her hand while looking for her trousers, shaking her long knife from the shaft of one of her boots.

"You've done me a favor by turning up like that," she says. "I was getting bored with that girl, anyway." She twists her long locks into a bun and secures them tight behind her collar. "I'm sure you've got something far more exciting for me." She jumps up and beckons me on the bed. "Do tell, I'm feeling quite adventurous tonight."

So, I sit down and tell her all that happened since our unfortunate parting this afternoon, including the futile attempt of Karma to keep me in. Lanying wrinkles her nose.

"I warned you," she says. "He's no different." A pleased gleam locks in her eyes. "He's tried the wrong woman, though." She throws her arm around my shoulder. "You're doing me proud." I suck in my cheeks, and erase the Karma I know, the man with his gentle green gaze and his tender touch from my mind.

"So, I need to see my uncle," I say. "Tonight." I clench my hands into fists, only to release them again the next moment. Lanying shakes her head.

"They won't do anything tonight," she says. "That family of yours, they'll wait." She dangles her legs from the side and wiggles her feet.

"How can you be sure?" I glance at her from the corners of my eyes.

"I know Karma, and I know of his ways." Her voice wavers for a moment. "He's good, really good."

I turn and frown. What does she mean?

"Karma has the patience of a predator," she says. "He doesn't rush." Her eyes narrow. "He'll spot them, those snakes, and he'll observe." She bends to adjust the straps on her boots.

"He'll leave them be for a while, allow them to feel safe, and then..." She sucks in a sharp breath and my stomach clenches.

My fingers grip around the edge of the mat.

"He's excellent with the knife." Lanying turns to me, and her eyes widen with an eerie admiration. "I've seen very few men who can wield a blade like he does." She straightens her back. "Sure, he has plenty of experience with that vindictive family of yours. Even so, it's in his blood, for sure." She lifts her chin. "You know about it, don't you? His Mongol descent?"

I stare at her, my mind taking in all she says. A predator. Plenty of experience. It's in his blood. A raw fear rips through my heart

"Yes," I say. "I know." I close my eyes as her words rush through my veins.

"So, what are we doing tonight?" Lanying's voice bounces off the bed.

I shift my weight on the mat and wait for the tingling to return in my numb fingers and toes.

"That's a good question." I open my eyes as while she fastens her belt, I tell her about the spell and that all I want to do is to get it back. "And warn them, so they'll go."

She pinches her ruby lips to a whitened line. "A spell..." She leaps to the door, swings it open, and lets out a low hiss. Within no time her two men come stumbling in, one after the other, half dressed and clearly not amused. A heated conversation in the foreign tongue follows, in which Lanying clearly has the upper hand.

"Yes, she carries a pouch with her." Lanying turns to me. "Never lets it out of her sight, it's bound to be in there."

Another intense discussion, mixed with some indecent gestures on Lanying's side unfolds before me, and ends abruptly with Lanying stamping her feet and the two guards speeding off, most probably to their room to get dressed.

"I suppose your uncle's not very open to reasoning." She plants her feet wide apart. "So, we'll take my men to encourage him to move on." A smug smile dons her face. "And leave that serpent to me."

Her hand glides down and strokes the silver shaft secured to her thigh. "There's a special place for the vilest of women like her, and I'll take every pleasure in showing her the way."

The gleam in her eyes mirrors the cold flash of her blade as she draws it—just for a moment—then it's gone.

Thirty-nine

With two fully dressed guards and an excited Lanying, I roam the darkened streets of Lhasa again. The two men lead the way, surprising me again with their swift, agile movements while their frames are so stocky and broad. As it turns out, Lanying ordered her men to follow the ngakpa's wife ever since we parted, reporting on her every step and breath.

"I can't believe they stayed in town all this time," she says. "The fools." She hisses and points at an inconspicuous house at the end of the street. "There, in the back."

Every muscle in my body tenses. My eyes shoot ahead, and the wiry shadows of my company lengthen as they've already turned the corner. *Focus.* I slow my breath to order my erratic thoughts.

The bitter midnight air bites at the edges of my nostrils. A gush of arid wind grates the tip of my nose. I pull my hood and clench my hands, my palms slippery with fear. *Courage, my child.* Palmo's voice resounds in my head, so steady and clear. *Courage.* If only I knew how.

Lanying's head appears around the corner. A pitched whistle calls me on.

"They're here," she says. "But they're not alone."

I skid next to her, my back slams against the roughened wall.

Her chin points at a raised window above us, and I turn on my toes. It's too high, but I don't need to look. I cringe as I recognize the low vibration in the muffled voices coming through—it's Sonam; he's already here.

My eyes fly from Lanying to her men and back. She nods, her eyes squinted into the crescents of a dark indigo moon.

"Karma's there too." She draws a sharp breath. "Didn't count on that." Her hand clenches under her silken coat, and my eyes widen with fear.

"You're not seriously thinking..." I flinch as she bares her teeth.

"No use. We'll have to outsmart them." Her eyes dart up to the window, then to her men, standing ready at the door. On her curt nod, they position themselves next to us, their faces staunch, their hands resting on their long knives. She barks at them in short, tense whispers, their heads unmoving in sync.

"Hmmm." She turns on her heels. "This is what we'll do." Her hand tugs at my lapel. "You go in and sweet-talk them, a heartfelt plea to let your uncle go." I frown, but she flicks her finger at my cheek. "I know you can." Her eyes flash to her men. "And act as if you came alone."

She draws me in, her hand behind my neck, and her lips breath a certain danger in my ear. "Now listen up. Get Karma as far away from your uncle as you can, and make sure you'll stand between them at all times—I don't care about that snake." Her hand slides down my collar, tugging again at my lapel.

"My men will snatch your uncle and take him away as soon as there's a chance. Sonam won't be a problem, and if so, I'll deal with him myself." She releases my coat from her grip, but her stare won't let me go. "Just make sure you keep yourself close to Karma, for he won't put your life on the line. That's for sure."

My mind went silent as soon as Lanying started talking, absorbing every word from her mouth.

"This is crazy," I say, and my thoughts spin, envisioning the worst outcomes possible. I clench my elbows in a desperate attempt to stop myself from shaking.

"You can do this." Lanying's fingers dig into my shoulders. "We'll be fast, in and out."

At her sign, the two men set themselves beside the door and fix their eyes on me.

"I can't," I say, but as if entranced, I drift towards the door. My hands shake as I put my hand on the iron hinge. I slam my shoulder in the door and my knees sag.

With a jolt, my limp body tumbles in, and I scramble from falling. For a moment, all time suspends in a frightening silence as I raise myself and stare into the bulging eyes of Tennah, my uncle.

"Nordun!" Sonam's voice roars in my ears. "What the hell...?"

A resolute hand seizes my belt from behind. I turn and shrink away.

It's Karma pulling me in.

"I told you to stay put." His eyes seethe an unnatural calm and his nostrils flare in anger. "You..." He hesitates, and I take my chance, my mind running at full speed.

I tear myself away and fling myself between him and Sonam, who's tied my uncle with rope.

"Please!" My desperate cry fills the room. In one glance I assess the situation.

Sonam and Uncle are next to the fire, and I'm facing Karma with my back turned to them. Khandro's squished into a corner. *Where is it?*

My eyes fling around the room, searching, and settle on the table. There it is—the pouch with the spell.

Khandro must have followed my darting gaze, as she leaps over to the table, her hands extended in an anxious grasp.

My eyes widen as Karma draws his knife and turns towards her, a whirl as swift as the wind. Panic soars through my body, and I duck under his arm to the table. I snatch the bag as the blade slashes into the table, drawing splinters as it's raised up again.

Clutching the pouch against my chest, I thrust myself back at Tennah and heave as Karma draws in his knife.

"No, please." My voice resounds a raspy prayer now, and my knees give in under Karma's restrained stare. My mind bolts in desperation as his fist clenches the sword handle tight. *Bang!* The heavy door blasts open, Lanying's men storm in, and the chaos is complete.

With Karma and Sonam drawing their knives to attack, Khando squirms her way past me. She lashes out. Her fingernails claw and tear the pouch right out of my hands. A crimson red flashes before me. She's drawn my blood.

I wince, and the bag rips. A thin piece of parchment slips out among the commotion.

She shrieks and her frame dives for the paper. My bloody fingers snag the page before her eyes and crumple it into a wad. I topple back, and my head hits the hardwood–but I crawl up before she throws herself at me again. *The spell.* There's no time, there's no choice. With one decisive throw, I sling the paper into the hungry fire.

The instant the inked wad hits the flickering flames, a blaze erupts with a violent crash. Blistering tongues of red-hot smolder lick up to the ceiling, and the putrid stench of decay surges through the room. A loud rumble roars from the blaze, and I stumble back.

There, amid the flames of smoke and smudge, a giant serpent roars its monstrous head.

My body freezes, and horror floods my mind. It's *back!* The snake, the demonic apparition that visited me so many moons ago, is back. A wave of nausea hits me as the serpent rocks back and forth.

Its fiery eyes seize me, and with a terrifying hiss, he rises, ready to strike. *Om Tara!*

"Sister!" A shriek pierces my ears, and a flash of silver strikes from the corners of my eyes. I dive to the ground, and my mouth fills with the taste of steel. I come up for air, my hands slithering on the splintering floor.

A bloodcurdling growl thunders from the blazing bellows of hell as Lanying's sword slashes through the mighty viper's coiling neck, striking its head off in one clean cut.

With a harrowing howl, the serpent comes crashing down, shreds of foul reeking gore surge through the billowing air, and columns of deep, ashen black whorl from the fire. Within the blink of an eye the entire room's ablaze from the floor to the ceiling; a burning barrage of scorching splinters and blackened soot comes pouring down.

I scramble up within the thick veil of smoked heat, tears streaming my face, and throw my hands over my head. My mind on edge, I bolt for the door, but an anguished wail stops me in my tracks. I turn.

There, right behind me, writhing like a maniac across the floor, is Tennah, his twisted body engulfed in a frenzied orange flare.

In one strike, I haul the small knife from under my coat and tear the rope. His smoldering limbs drop limp to the ground. His twisted, blackened face wheezes for air. Another surge of my knife rips through the front of my coat. I tear off the stiffened silk to smother the flames.

"Here!" A heavy blanket flies through the air. "Roll him in." Lanying lands beside me, and our rapid hands wrap the wool tight.

"He's too heavy!" Lanying yanks the rolled blanket but falls to her knees. Her face flings to the ceiling. A loud cry echoes through the smoke.

I wipe the grime off my stinging eyelids, and her guard rises out of the thick smolder from behind. In less than no time, he flips the wrapped body over his broad shoulder and shoots away.

"Come on!" Laying's hands grab my arm and drag me along.

We're not going to make it! My mind screams as burning beams crash from the ceiling, and a rumble of ashen soot and fuming rubble comes plummeting down.

A violent draft surges from the affront, propelling me straight back to the ground. With a last desperate push, I scram for the door, my feet thrashing the crumbling lumber.

"Sister!" A powerful arm scoops around my waist and lifts me up to the light. Together we tumble out of the blazing fire, into the dark streets of Lhasa.

A huge hand extends, and I clutch it to scribble up, my mind dazed, my body shattered to the bone. It's Lanying's man—he's seized me from the fire. I heave and gag. A warm gush of blood splatters in front of his feet. Cold sweat breaks on my face and I falter, sinking down, falling further, my head light, my body a dead weight.

"Come!" The guard bends his wide back and throws me over his shoulder, his hands bury deep into my thighs.

My vision blurs, and all commotion fades as he speeds off, carrying me on his back.

There's only the smallest of voice remaining, ringing in my ears—Courage, my child, you must have courage—for it never left me since it was said.

Forty

I should have let him die. My hands wring the washcloth again and again. Cool, clear drops of water drip from my fingers. Down my cheeks linger the hot, salty driblets of grief. His body scorched, his face burned beyond recognition—they brought him to the monastery, to the nuns who take such a great care. They brought me, too. Lanying must have instructed them to.

"Sister, please," Jomo says. She takes the wet cloth from my hands. "Now you take rest." I shake my head. The wretched stench of burn, ash, and soot clings to my hair, to my clothes, to me.

"Nordun, she's right." Palmo's calm voice reasons me to the door.

I must clean myself up, and rest, and dress my wounds too, but I don't want to. I want to be with the suffering, draw it out and let it wash over me.

This. I close my eyes and let the burning tears cascade deep down the hollows of my sunken heart. This was not what I had intended. Yet, this is how it is.

So, I wash myself, and let Palmo discard my ragged, charred clothes. She hands me a plain dress, and I slip it on. She sits with me in the kitchen, and I drink the tea and eat the food. She prays with me over Uncle's injured body, and I return to this world.

"The burns are bad," Palmo says. She has sent for the best amchi in Lhasa. "He will be scarred, maimed for the rest of this life, but he'll survive." She takes my hands in hers, still seated in prayer. "You did good, Nordun. He's alive." I shake my head.

"But his face," I say, and my voice despairs at the sight of his ghastly, blackened appearance. "He might never see again." It's true. Uncle's face is burned beyond recognition, and the amchi isn't sure about his eyes, his vision, yet.

"Still, he lives," Palmo says. "And we'll care for him the best we can." Her slender hands smoothen the thin sheet covering Uncle's wounded frame.

"Never forget how precious this human existence is, my child, how valuable it is to be born with all these human endowments, having every opportunity to practice the path and gain the merit needed in this samsaric existence." Her prayer beads tick a steady pulse, affirming the truth of her words all around.

"Tennah lives, and come time he'll turn to the Dharma again, I'm sure." The grace of deep faith rests on her face. "The condition of our body, whether it is sickness or old age, it is never an obstacle for the mind to practice, pray, and generate a better karma for our next life and the ones to come after that."

I nod. Even though I have never witnessed them myself, I've heard of the great practitioners who found their path, their strength, and deepest devotion amid the gravest of illness and misfortune.

"So," Palmo says as she opens the small window and lets the lazy afternoon sun set on the polished ledge. "You did good. He still has time." A fresh breeze slips in, dispelling the suffocating stink of festering flesh and healing herbs.

"And let's not forget that you've prevented a man from taking a life." Her amber eyes catch the mellow light of the midday, reflecting a golden glow as she turns to me. "You've lessened the karmic retributions of those who are blinded, of those who cannot see the grave consequences of taking life."

My face flushes, and the warmth spreads all the way to my chest. She's talking about Karma.

"That was part of your intention, wasn't it?" Her silhouette glides away from the window. "So, you did good." Her hands take mine again, enveloping them in a comforting embrace.

My eyes rest on the suffering laying naked and raw, so bare in front of me, and my breath shallows.

"Then how come it all feels wrong?" My voice chokes. "Like I failed?" I clasp our hands tighter and bow my head in despair.

"Because, my child, you envisioned another outcome." Her hands fold over my head and slide down my cheeks, holding my face close to hers. "You expected the result to be something else, something it's not." She lifts my face. "You know that expectations only set us up for disappointment." Her voice carries a sharp edge. "There's only sadness and resentment in that painful space, in that vast void between our wants and what really is."

My thoughts poke around her words for their true meaning, and my eyes search hers—I feel lost, adrift. Yes, I expected another outcome. One where Uncle got away after my warning, unharmed and free. Not this one, where he lies lying crippled and mauled by fire, stripped of all his human dignity in front of me.

A flash of silver passes through my thoughts, followed by Karma's cold and hardened stare. I close my eyes to banish the image from my mind. For sure, I did not envisage that. My heart shrinks in the painful recognition of his cruelty and of him, who I think of as my love. Was my heart mistaken? Have I been so wrong?

"I'll tell you again, Nordun, but you already know." Palmo's soft voice prompts me back to the room. "You did good, for all rests on the point of our intentions." She lowers her hands to my shoulders. "And your intentions are good. They are pure." She wipes my face with her sleeve, and I nod. The words won't come, but I move my lips in silent gratitude, anyway.

"Now, I'd rather you rest," she says. "But there's someone here to see you." She urges me gently to the door and my feet stall.

"Don't worry, it's Sonam," she says, as if she feels my hopes pass and my fear rise. "He's waiting in the kitchen."

His open arms, his genuine warm smile—it's all Sonam, hugging me tight at the doorstep.

"Nordun, sister," he says, and pulls me close to his wide chest. "You had us all worried sick." I swallow my disappointment as the wool of his chuba burns on my scraped cheek. He releases his grip and puts me at arm's length. "Not to mention the way you floored us, pulling that stunt on us last night." He shakes his head. "You are truly your mother's daughter." And he pulls me in again.

Jomo serves us tea, and Sonam tells me of his version of last night's events. How he and Karma got away from the burning house, as Lanying's men carried Tennah and me away.

"So, you didn't try?"

Sonam shakes his head, and his eyes avoid my empty question.

"Once the house caught fire, there were too many onlookers," he says, and stares in his tea. "And now the two of you are under Palmo's protection, so..." A tiny wink comes my way. Being in the monastery offers a sanctuary for both Uncle and me. We're fine.

"And Khando?" My mind searches and my fingers trace the reddened scratches on my hands.

"Didn't see her again," he says. "For all I know, she could have perished in the fire." He swirls his cup around, steam vapors from the rim.

We sip our tea in silence, and my mind searches for the right questions to ask.

"I'm sorry I didn't come sooner," he says, and takes a sip of his cup. "But we were seen at the house, so we had some explaining to do, Karma and me." His smile is wry. "You know how these damn town officials are."

I don't, but I nod anyway, my mind alerted at the mention of Karma's name.

"Karma?" I ask softly, as if I don't really want to know.

"Last I saw him was at the inn with Dendup." Sonam shrugs. "It's been quite a night—and day." He meets my stare, and he rubs his smudgy moustache; a sorrowful twinge comes to his eyes.

"Oh sister, I'm sorry," he says. "But know he's a good man." His hands wring around his cup. "A loyal man."

A sour taste gulfs at the back of my throat. *Good. Loyal.* My lips pinch.

"Loyal to the family." My voice sounds as bitter as can be. "Loyal to their spite."

Sonam sighs, a wordless admittance.

"Well, yes." He hesitates. "They saved his life when his own blood had deserted him, left him out there to die."

I shake my head. *That's what they say.* I blink as the startling thought takes flight in my mind. Where did that come from?

"Karma's loyalty to the family, it's very strong," he says. "The family took him in and raised him as a brother, and even a son."

My hands clench into fists, and my torn nails dig in the thick of my palms.

"They might have raised him as a son," I say, my voice a whisper now. "But now they treat him as their slave." I release my hands and draw a deep breath.

"Karma doesn't see it that way," Sonam says. "He's grateful to the family who considers them one of their own." He raises his cup to Jomo and thanks her for pouring another refreshing green tea. I let mine go cold.

"Although I always had my doubts," Sonam says.

He takes another approving gulp of his cup, and I raise my eyebrows. Doubts?

"If he really considers himself to be one of the family." He takes a fresh peach from the plate Jomo has put in front of us and inspects it well.

"Why do you say that?" I lean closer and take a peach, too. It rests unattended in my hand, my mind too occupied with Sonam's words.

"Nothing I can put my finger on," he says. "Just a hunch." He sinks his teeth in the fleshy peach and shrugs. "It's probably nothing."

I lean back, pretending nonchalance, but I'm not buying it. I've felt the same.

We sit and eat—well, Sonam mostly—and talk for a while. It comforts me to have Sonam so near.

"I'm here for you, sister." He hugs me as he leaves in the early onset of dusk, the sky all streaked, beribboned in orange, yellow and red. "I let your father down badly after Lhamo's death, but I won't do that again." He gives me an extra squeeze and strides out of the gate.

With a heavy heart, I turn back to the room where my uncle lays. I sit with him in prayer and attend to the changing of his gauzes. His soft moaning slices through my jaded body and settles in the fragments of my shattered bones. Can this suffering ever heal?

"Nordun, please," Palmo calls to me from behind. "Enough."

I know she's right. My body is caving in, desperate for sleep, but my mind won't rest, for it fears the night to come.

Palmo puts me to bed, and I close my eyes, but as I dreaded, sleep won't come, staying far from my room. It's not the horrific events of the night before that haunt my thoughts. It's him and the agony of being alone with my love for him and having with no place to go. I curl up and pull the blanket tight, my beads close to my chest. *Om Tare.* Please let it pass. Darkness surrounds me. *Om Tare.* Let it pass. I drift off.

"Sisterrrr." A slight pull on my blanket, a high hiss in my ear. "Move over."

A smooth rustle of silk slithers beside to me, a slender chilly hand slides in mine. I flinch and back away against the wall before I realize.

"Lanying!" My eyes discern her wide grin from the shadows, and it's only now that her voice rings through. "What..." Her giggle bursts out from under the blanket.

"I always forget how cold the Lhasa nights are." She rubs my hands vigorously against my arms, and I freeze at her icy touch. "Don't worry sister, I don't prey on the weak." She chuckles. "No struggle, an effortless victory—that's not my idea of fun." I can't see it clearly, but I'm sure her grin reaches all the way across her face now, and her eyes flash that daring twinkle.

"Well, that's not entirely true," she says, and sighs. "And you're not weak either." Her voice changes, and a melancholy drifts through. "You sure did me proud, Sister." She squeezes my shoulders and shifts closer to me. "The way you threw yourself at his knife." Her tongue clicks in approval.

"Did I?" My mind alerted, I try to go back to last night. "I... don't think so."

In my memory, I only stood between Uncle and him.

"You did," she says. "You're my hero today." She wiggles beside me. "And your actions made me think." She pauses, her warm breath stalled on my cheeks. "About choosing something better...."

I feel a smile breaking on my face. "I did?" I clench her forearm, my heart delighting in her words.

"Well, yeah," she says, "But you know, I'm only thinking... so..." She shrugs and I don't mind. I know it's a start.

"I'm sorry about last night," I say. "About barging in on you like that, I had no idea..." My voice goes quiet as her pearly lacerations come to my mind.

"Does it matter?" She pulls the blanket snug. "Is there ever an excuse for the wrongs I've done in this life?" She whispers now, her voice flat, and I wonder about her expression, but I can't see it.

I close my eyes and search for the answer inside. My heart heaves. I want to tell her that sometimes we do the wrong things for the right reasons, as it is exactly what we humans think we do. For the one who walks the Buddhist path, though, no hurt or suffering is ever an excuse for harming other sentient beings, let alone taking a life in reprisal.

"I don't know, but there must be a limit to the suffering we humans are able to bear." I choose my words with care, for who am I to say?

"For sure." She shivers. "It's either break or be broken with that family of mine." And I think of Karma, and his loyalty to the family, and my heart cracks open—for him and for her.

"Well, at least you helped to save one life last night," I say, and turn to her. "And that's a good start." I rub her freezing hands.

"That's one way of looking at it." She shivers again and blows her breath on our intertwined hands. "Damned sister, aren't Lhasa nights cold without a lover on our side?"

She chuckles again, no doubt sporting that familiar grin on her round face.

"It is, sister," I say, because I can't deny it. "It sure is."

Forty-one

Waking up next to Lanying is a treat the next morning. I dreaded the new sun to rise, but this day might turn out to be good after all. With her candid humor, Lanying has all nuns—including Palmo—rolling with laughter, even before prayer has been done. She always knows what to say, what's on the edge, and what to leave behind. How I wish I had that gift.

I raise my eyebrows as she points at the big bag in the corner of the kitchen.

"There's no way a sister of mine will be seen in that." She rolls her eyes at my plain dress.

Quickly, I glance around. Good, beside Jomo, all nuns have gone to morning prayer. My hands go through the bag to find the finest wool and velvet, stiffened silk and satin, fur trims, soft leather boots, and an intricate embroidered belt. In heavenly hues of blue, of course—Lanying's decided that's my color. I don't know how she did it, but she brought a brand-new outfit for me.

"I told you." A smug smile curls around her eyes. "We never compromise on comfort or style—ever." She runs her hands through my hair and wrinkles her nose. "Let me take care of this, too." And while I sip my tea, she does my hair, with beads of turquoise and a few corals. She tips her head and clacks her tongue. "You gorgeous thing."

I wave my hand. "Oh, stop it," I say, and get up to pour more tea.

"He won't know what hit him." Lanying winks at Jomo, whose beady black eyes shine with the amusement of watching us all along. I turn on my heels and stare.

"What do you mean?" I say, and my pulse races. My face flushes even more.

"He'd better come around today." Lanying smirks her famous sneer. "To stay away like that, the idiot." She pinches her lips, and I take a deep breath.

What if he does?

"You think he's gone after Khandro?" I say. It's not easy admitting my frightened suspicion, but I've seen that cold, hard look in his eyes.

"Nah." Lanying shrugs as she gets ready to take off. She sneaks a little something to Jomo, she's good like that.

"Any idea what happened to her?" I empty my cup and gather the rest of the dishes.

"Nope." She straightens her back and leaps to the door. "And I don't care. For all I know, she could have perished in the fire." She twirls around, her hand a wave. "See you soon, sisters." She's off before I get the chance to thank her—again. For the clothes, the hair, but most of all, for her company last night. I needed it more than I ever thought I would.

"Please, let me." I take the bowl and bandages from Jomo's hands. It's time to dress Tennah's wounds again. "You nuns have been taking turns all night." I bow to her as she melts my heart with that precious face and endearing smile. "I will do the day."

The zesty essence of crushed herbs stings my eyes. I can only imagine what it must feel like for Uncle on his raw and open wounds. I swallow the sadness that rises from my chest and let it pass before I enter the room.

There in the darkness, he lies. So still, only a faint rattle resounds from his chest. My hands work fast to lessen the agony they bring. My eyes blur to shield my heart from the face of suffering, from the horrible truth. Once done, I open the window and let the light pour in. With it comes the joyous call of a twite finch, its sweet voice serenading the day in fast trills and rolling twitters. The morning breeze adds her sweet, heavy scent of the last days of summer, and for a moment, all is well.

I settle next to Uncle, my face to the sun. The beads roll through my stiff fingers. The red scratches have thinned, bluish bruises have broken through, my hands are healing. *Om Tare.*

My fingers halt half-way through the prayer. I never heard him come, but I know he's here. The smell of warm earth and fresh green drifts from behind in the room. It's him. I turn on my seat.

"You've come." I say, and my heart leaps. How his quiet presence takes me by surprise. His face seems somehow thinner, his eyes sunken, but it is there—that beautiful emerald glow in his eyes. It's a dark glare this morning.

"I needed some time," he says, and moves towards me. I get up and wrap my beads around my wrist, hiding my trembling hands.

"Palmo told me he'll live." He points his chin at Tennah, deep asleep, but his eyes keep me in his gaze. I nod.

"Will you let him?" I try hard not to avert my eyes, afraid of what I might see, but his stare stays unmoving.

"Will you leave me a choice, then?" His tone deepens, and there's a tension in it I'm not familiar with.

"Not here," I say and move past him to the door, my knees weak.

He follows me through the hallway outside. Jomo comes rushing after us and presses a tray with tea in my hand.

"It's always good time for tea, sister," she says and throws me an encouraging smile. For a moment, I feel my face lift.

We sit furthest from the gate, with the silvery shadows of the morning between us. The twite finch has ceased her cheery tune, and the morning breeze has hushed. The air has turned dense with the promise of rain to come—not now, but sometime soon.

I raise my cup to rinse the sticky dryness that has latched at the back of my throat. Karma turns, and I hold my breath as his strong hand steadies mine.

"You are one hell of a woman, Nordun." His voice is quiet, yet restless. "The way you threw yourself in front of your uncle." His mouth twists and his eyes lighten ever so slightly. "I could have killed you, you know?" His thumb traces the thin lines on my hand, and his fingers slip between mine.

"But you didn't," I say, and let my words rest between us as I release my breath and our hands slip away.

"No, I didn't..." He hesitates. "I was wrong." He casts his eyes down. "I was wrong to lock you in." He looks up, his eyes a feverish gleam. My pulse speeds up.

"I heard your silent prayer, but I tried to smother it. I've felt your deep devotion in the loving touch of your hands." He pauses, and his firm fingers fold into mine again. "But I tried to bind them and take your freedom from you." He leans back, still cradling my hand in his. "I stifled the very thing that brings me joy and I did everything love is not supposed to."

My mind has gone silent, and my heart holds my breath. *This man. These words.* I search for his eyes to meet mine, to tell him it doesn't matter, because he's here, with me, right now.

"Still, here you are," I say, and put my cheek against our hands, still searching for his eyes.

"I am." His voice e, and he looks up to answer my gaze. Relief washes over me as the dark glow lightens into a lush summer green. "Though I should have come sooner." He presses a gentle kiss on the palm of my bruised hand.

"You should have." I close my eyes and let his breath caress my face.

"But you scared the hell out of me, my love." His voice is an urgent whisper. "With your naïve, yet stubborn ways." He presses another kiss on my hand before he lets go. "I so underestimated you."

I open my mouth, but he puts his fingertips to my lips, and I draw back, my face flushed.

"Please hear me out, my love." He leans forward. "Because I don't think I'll ever be admitting it again." He drapes his hands on his knees.

"You listened to the call of your heart." His eyes narrow to crescents of the lightest viridian green. "I was there with you when you took up that courage, leaving everything behind, not knowing where to go or if you would ever come back." He sighs.

"I should have known how strong you are, but I've felt your doubts, flowing like the tide, so closely under your skin, and I thought we would be fine, that you'd let go." He pauses and pulls in a deep breath while I sit and listen.

"I was a fool to look away from what is so clear." His eyes settle on the front of my neck, on the delicate silver conch shell he gave me at the start of our journey. "You are the courageous one of us, Nordun. You are willing to risk everything for what you believe in—even your life—and I failed to admit what I knew all along."

I blink as his words float between us, and the momentary shadows of the morning surrender to the highest of midday suns. Dryness has shriveled my throat with a coarse grit. My hand raises the cup, and the cold tea jabs a quick punch at my stilted thoughts. My heart so full and my head so light, how my whole being longs for him—his mind so beautiful, and his insight so clear, seeing me for who I am, even though I haven't really grasped it myself.

"I underestimated you." He leans closer. "But then again, I don't have your strength of faith, and I doubt I ever will." A wistful smile curls around his lips. "My compassion doesn't stretch beyond the narrow borders I've set around my heart, and as for forgiveness, well..."

We both smile at his silent admission and he takes my hands again, this time drawing me close, into that sweet lingering smell of the mountains at the height of summer.

"But you still scare the hell out of me, Nordun." His voice carries a raw tinge, the smallest of a reluctance coming through. "Exposing my weakness, calling me out in such a blatant way."

I raise my eyebrows, not knowing what to make of his last sentence.

"I'm sorry..." My words stumble and he laughs.

"No, you're not." His eyes—the viridian green so vibrant now—pierce through me. He leans back a bit, still holding my gaze and my hands.

"Remember at Nam Tso, when you told me I had a choice, and I told you I had made mine?" I take my mind back to that day at the lake, when I asked him to let Uncle go.

"I do," I say, although the bitter disappointment I felt that day of him walking out on me is nothing but a vague remembrance in my mind; it has no hold on my heart.

"I wasn't truthful to you, nor to myself." His jaw sets and his gaze drifts away. A sudden slack breeze blows the loose strands of his long manes back, sweeping them lightly against my cheeks.

"I make my choices out of the fear of losing a family that is never really mine, anyway." He turns back and releases my hands, sliding them back to my lap. "I don't choose with the courage of a free will." His hands brush the entangled strands from my face, his and mine. "And you, my love, made that so clear." His fingertips stroke the edge of my jaw, his breath, warm and balmy, meets mine.

"I'm sorry," I say again, and I don't know why. Maybe it's for the hurt I feel in him, the pain of longing, that strangeness of being out of place.

"Ever since we me, that first night," he says, "I knew we were bound, as your dreams call out like mine." His hands slide down along my arms, his thumbs rub the insides of my wrist.

"And as our lives collided, and I held your body close, my dreams..." His voice trails off, and in his eyes moves a sadness in gray-green, like the color of sage and moss at the onset of winter.

"Your dreams have awakened," I say, an urgent whisper. "I know, for I hear them calling out at night, in strange tongues and the brightest colors, when the moon is the nearest and stars all aligned."

So many nights, when I was nestled in the tender hollow of his body, his heart drummed the strangest rhythms in my ears, and his mind surrounded us with the most elusive visions of wide open spaces and clear blue skies and vast planes. At first, I thought they were mine, and I feared new nightmares had come. But then the deer hoofs clapped, and the eagle spanned its wings, and I knew they were his.

"They have," he says. "More alive than ever before." He rests his hands on my knees.

"And they will keep coming," I say. "And along with them that distant longing inside, as it did with my dreams too." I clear my throat as the memory of them still haunts me.

"And then it grows, that small yearning, into a louder noise," I say, and my words roll out like a thunder from my breath. "And you can't make it stop, even though you try so hard, running from it as fast as you can." I catch my breath as my mind tries to grasp what just came out of my mouth. I hear myself talk, but I'm not sure it is me.

"Yes," he says. He looks up. "That's exactly how it is."

The midday sun lights the sadness in his eyes, ebbing from winter gray to a warm summer green, and a cold grips my heart. He's turned a corner; he's said it out loud. He gave a voice to his inner longing, and now it's out here, and he can never put it back again. He just doesn't realize it yet.

"The louder it gets, the faster I run." He leans back a bit. "But you, my love, have stopped me in my tracks. I'm done racing around in circles." His hand goes up to the beads I tied around his neck, three for the road and two for coming home.

"You see me with all my fears and flaws and are not afraid to be brutally honest with me." His strong, warm hand reaches out, and I grasp it with mine, all clammy and cold. "How could I ever run away from that?" He pulls me close and rests his cheek on the top of my head while the ground sinks beneath me.

I'm lost, drowning in the frightening knowledge of what the longing will do. For one day, it will come down screaming at him, suffocate him with restlessness, and beseech him with an inner rage. A bitter anger will turn towards himself and the word. He'll never be free until he willingly follows what's calling him—and he doesn't realize it himself.

"But your dreams," I say, and I close my eyes to his tender touch. "They won't leave you alone." I bury my face in the collar of his chuba, and let the comforting trace of the earth, and the sun, and the mountain grass cover me. I don't want to tell him, because I will lose him, even though he has never been mine. But I have no choice but to love him, and genuine love does not cling. It only wants to set free. I look up, my hands against his chest, my heart shrinking with an ache.

"Your dreams, they'll stay to haunt you." I steady my voice. "And the longing will drain you from the inside, flooding the void in your heart with rage and regret. It will turn you with a bitter contempt to the world, and most of all to yourself if you let it be." A sob escapes my throat, even though I try so hard to stay calm. "It won't let you settle, not with yourself, and certainly not with me."

His hands cradle my face and lift it up to meet his. "What are you saying, my love?" His eyes widen into mine, and I flinch, casting mine down on his hands.

"You'll have to go and follow your heart," I say, "Like I followed mine." I heave. "I've seen what's calling you; it's that land faraway." My voice is so faint now, it's only a murmur. "And it's calling you home." My last words leave me breathless. I didn't see their real meaning, but now it's so clear.

"Don't say that." His muscles tighten around me, and his voice is a plea. "Don't tell me to go and seek those who left me behind to die."

I close my eyes. A faint thunder claps in the air, and a voice cries out in my mind. *No, we didn't.* I've heard it before, the desperate call, but never so clear as now. It's the voice from his dreams, urging him to come home. It's the one only I seem to hear.

"Let me make my own choice." His lips search my mouth, and his hungry breath meets mine. "Let me make my home with you." As our mouths and minds fuse, all my reason falls away. Oh, how I want this man.

"But please don't choose out of fear." I withdraw with a gasp and the voice of his dreams fades away. How can I ever let him go?

"So, you think I choose you out of fear?" His fingers spread on my cheeks, and his thumbs stroke my lips. "Oh love, you tell me." A playful grin curls in the corners of his mouth.

"What man desires a woman who lies to his face, sneaks out behind his back, and then throws herself in front of his knife?" He pauses, and his smile draws all the way up to his eyes. "Surely you can't deny me some courage for wanting a woman like you?" He tries hard to suppress an outburst of laughter, and I cringe. *This man!*

"I can't deny you that," I say, and look up. "But I don't want to change myself either." The most intense blush covers my face. Did I just say that? Was my mind speaking out like that?

"I know." His face twists in a semi-frown. "I guess I'll learn to deal with that." His fingers brush the loose strands of hair behind my ears, his fingertips a cool caress in the back of my neck. "Now tell me you'll ride home with me when all is settled here, with Dendup and me."

Dendup. I clear my throat.

"I hope he's not too angry." I slide my fingers over his and draw them to my lap. "And that he shares your opinion about letting Tennah be." My eyes glance over the courtyard, the coo of a lone dove sounds in the distance.

"Oh, don't worry," Karma says as he straightens his back. "I'll deal with that." He jumps on his feet, his boots a scuffle in the arid sand. "But for now, it's best if you stay here."

I nod.

"I'll come back tomorrow and take you to the holy places around." He stretches his hand for mine and pulls me up, his eyes flashing that emerald twinkle again. "For you are on a pilgrimage, after all."

I smile. What can I say?

The guard swings the gate, and quickly averts his eyes as Karma thanks him and passes through.

"Karma, wait." I hurry after him, my feet on the iron threshold. "Do you know what happened?" My voice pitches. "To Khandro?"

Karma turns around and shakes his head, but he doesn't speak.

"Did you...?" I hesitate and bite my lip. I don't want to speak the words out loud.

"No, I didn't," he says. "I'll give you my word." His eyes dart from me to the guard and back. "For all I know, she perished in the fire." His hand on my shoulder gives a tight squeeze to strengthen his words. "I'll see you tomorrow." He strides away, his heels crunching in the sand. There's no looking back.

Swirls of milky gray and darkened light drift over the courtyard. The high sun struggles to poke through. I shiver as I run to the door. A gush of warm wind churns up some gravel and I fasten the latch tight as the first drops of rain splash from above.

He came, Uncle is safe, so all is well.

So then why won't this sense of disquiet leave me alone?

Forty-two

Dusk arrives early, cloaked in faded coral and pearly gray, and hailed by dull pitter-patters on the mud floor and flattened roof. I draw near the stove in the company of sweet Jomo and wrap my hands around a cup of steaming brew. A faint cold dwells in my bones.

"So, he came." Palmo sits beside me, her slender hand on my arm.

"He did," I say, and stare at my tea.

"But all's not finished," she says, "For you would not be so quiet if it was." Her fingers slide over her beads.

I shake my head. I want to tell her all is well, but I would be lying. My eyes burn and I turn away.

Jomo closes the door on her way out. The wind lashes out at the rain, its drum a rapid beat against the earthen walls.

"What is it that still rests on you?" Palmo's voice probes the depth inside of me. And as I face her, my words rise and I tell her all about his beautiful mind, his crystal-clear insight, and his desire to stay with me. Her gaze deepens, the warm amber a trusting glow. And then I tell her about his wild dreams and the voice calling out, the one only I hear. And how it scares me the way my own dreams did.

The beads slow their pace as Palmo nods and shifts her weight. Her silence urges me on.

"It will leave him restless," I say. "It won't let him settle, and certainly not with me." My voice chokes. "For I've awakened his dreams. It's through me they come alive." I clench my hands, and Palmo's beads halt.

"Why does it happen? And why doesn't he hear it?" I sob and push my fist in front of my mouth, my face burning with shame. I shouldn't let myself go like this, but I can't hide it. Her eyes see right through me. Silence is still upon her, but it pervades as a gentle smile draws around her lips.

"Because, my child." She leans in and her beads slide across my lap. "When we open the gateways of our heart and truly let love in, it can unearth the deepest of things inside of us." Her hands are a cool touch to mine. "As much as love lavishes us in its warmth, its passionate embrace, it can also reveal the deepest of our wounds and our insecurities, unleashing all those demons we never knew that were within." I blink and let my thoughts unwrap her words in my mind. In the distance, the rumble of thunder resounds.

"And that is what is shown to you," she says. "That is what you see, and what you hear." My eyes widen as the meaning of it all stares me right in my face. Of course, he doesn't hear the voice. It's the memory of her, and it's too painful for him, so as little boys do, he turns away. So the voice seeks me, the only one who he has let in.

"I know he doesn't listen when I speak of it." I turn to Palmo. "So how can I still make him hear?"

Her eyes twinkle. "You want him to hear what's calling him?" she says, and I nod. "Then do as he does and lay your heart close to his ear." Her hands draw me in. "And reveal your inmost truth to him, the one your body whispers, but your mind refuses to hear."

I duck my head and flinch at her truth. My entire face flushes with shame. She laughs and lightning flashes across the room. The tide has turned, the storm has come in.

Murky puddles latch their scourings onto my soft leather boots as my feet fly over the sodden gravel of the main street. A fierce gale pushes through the darkest of violet sky. Warm rain soaks my silken and fur coat, but nothing can hold me now. My heart flutters like a wild bird caught in a cage, ready to flight as I arrive at the doorstep of the inn.

"He's in the kitchen," the matron says, as she opens the door with her smile. I rush in, but he's not there, and I stare into the eyes of a bewildered Dendup.

"Sister," he says, and rises from his seat. "I..." He hesitates, I bow my head, and a little rain drips down. The stove crackles in the quiet collision between us.

"I'm sorry, but..." I look up and hold my breath. He nods and points to the hallway.

"He's either at the horses or in the room." Dendup sinks back in his seat, a puzzling smile across his face.

"Thank you," I say, and my feet find the hallway. My eyes burn but lead me right to the back. I lay my head against the thick timber, and my nails catch a splinter as I run my fingers down the door. He's in.

My hands tremble as I push the door open. It resists with a creak, but there's nothing in my way. He's there, his shirt open, his hair hanging loose, and he looks at me and I look at him.

"My love," he says, and his eyes widen with the most brilliant of green. He knows why I've come. There's no need to tell. The door shuts behind me and I move towards him.

"I..." He wants to speak, but this time it's me who silences him as my fingertips linger in his heaving breath.

"I don't need a promise," I say. My voice is a delicate whisper. "I only want you to come home to me for one night."

My icy hands seek the warmth under his shirt, and I shiver with fever. My hair soaks the thin cotton stretched over his chest.

His cheeks brush the wet strands of hair from my face, and his hands search for me with desire. My coat falls, a damp thud to the ground.

The night envelops us in a smooth velvet indigo as he caresses me in all those places only his mind has been. And as he comes to me, I let the thunder roll in the bluest of skies and the eagles soar over the wide-open planes, and the wind cries of a mother calling her son home.

I know it, even before I open my eyes to the break of the new day. It's not the heat radiating from his skin that's missing, or the gentle crook of his neck where I rested my head for so long. It's the absence of the warm earth and churned meadows, of mountains and sun, and the last day of summer that rips through the hollow inside of me.

I curl my broken body at the memory of the night I knew would end, but now wished it never did. I open my eyes to the knowing he's gone, and traces of salt mark the sadness down my cheeks, on my lips. *Om Tare.* How it hurts.

My feet find the floor, and I open the window. The dawn comes blazing in on a haze of bronze and burnished orange, carrying the sweet scent of ripe berries and the airy tune of a serin finch. It's so still inside of me, yet something has awakened my senses. I've opened to love, and although it aches, it's an enlivening kind of pain.

My hands run across my breasts, still tender from his touch, and I am amazed again. How well he knew my body—so much better than I ever have. I close my eyes and swallow the last taste of the night. I made my choice—I loved a wild soul and set him free.

I hesitate, but make my way to the kitchen. The matron's wide arms draw me to sit next to the fired-up stove.

"Tea's ready in a moment." Her gaze carries a twinge of sympathy. Of course, she already knows. Dendup sits opposite me. His moustache holds the crumbs of yesterday's bread.

"I'm sorry, sister." His fist slams the table between us. "The idiot." His heavy sigh breaths across the stink of chang, but his eyes are clear and spitting fire. "I don't know what got into him."

I know, but how can I tell him? I showed Karma what called him, and his only choice was to go. I shrug and the fresh tea cleans my palate from the tinge of resentment I harbor.

My teeth sink into the fried fritters, the chewy pork a welcome distraction from my empty thoughts.

"Me too," I say, and the tears behind my eyelids burn again. "I'm sorry for all the trouble I caused you, brother." I put down my cup. "I will explain and try to make amends with the family." He waves his hand.

"I should have known, for he's a loner and his flings always have a bad ending," Dendup says, and I cringe at his words. "But I never expected him to leave like this."

I did, but I'm not going to tell.

"Listen, sister." He leans in and puts a fatherly hand on my arm. "Whatever happened between the two of you, and with Tennah..." He pauses, and it looks like he's about to chew off his moustache, but he's not. "Your grandmother raised you well, and you did what you were taught to do." A dry smile comes through and he draws his hands across the table.

"Even though we don't always see eye to eye on these things, she has my deepest respect." He leans back and sinks his eyes into his empty cup. "I guess I've got some explaining to do when we get home."

I nod, and my mind draws the curtains, wanting to go back to the night.

"I'll come with you," I hear myself say, and his dark look blurs from under his furry eyebrows.

"You better." His gloom twinkles a faint wink. "We'll leave in a few days." The brisk trudge of boots resounds through the hallway, and he points his chin over my shoulder. "Sonam and I will wrap things up as soon as we can." A broad hand rests on my shoulder, and my body sags as a steady arm pulls me in.

"Let me bring you to Palmo's," Sonam's voice sounds in the distance. Cold sweat beads on my forehead and remains of fritter and fat fight their way up my throat. I jump up and stumble through the kitchen. I'm just in time to make it to the back of the yard.

"Oh, Nordun." Sonam scoops me in his wide arms.

I fight my tears but lose the battle. If this is what I wanted, then why does it hurt so much?

Relief washes over me as I find only Jomo in the kitchen. Her smile usually does wonders, but this time I sneak to the back, to my room. My body shivers under the blankets, my mind searches for the end. I thought all was finished, yet I've got one thing left to do.

Lanying. I'll have to see her tomorrow, and not only to say goodbye.

Forty-three

"I'm sorry." It's the first thing out of my mouth as I hear Palmo's muffled voice coming from above. The thick wool sticks to my cheeks, and I pop my clammy head from under the blankets to meet her placid smile. I can't believe I've been sleeping the day away.

"Now listen." Her voice takes on a strict tone and I duck my chin to my chest. "You really have to stop apologizing like that." I glance up from under my lashes.

"I told you before, it doesn't suit you, and is totally unnecessary." She shifts on the bed. "Apparently, you needed your sleep after the events of last night."

She knows I went to Karma. My face flushes, and I'm sure it's the brightest it's ever been.

"You did well to take a rest." The blush spreads to my neck and chest, and even my earlobes are on fire by now. "We can't work for the benefit of others if we don't keep ourselves healthy and sane." Palmo's determined hands take mine. "Come with me to the temple. It will do you good."

I nod, and slip from under the blankets, the wooden floor a warm touch to my toes.

The low midday sun bathes the main street in a mellow mix of orange and ochre. A hint of rich golden glitters through. The calming cool after last night's storm has eased the strain of the arid air, lightening it with a crisp breeze. All is winding down, even the crowds usual droning like frenzied ants towards the temple have relaxed their pace.

It was good to come here, circling around and around. The soothing smell of incense, the devout hum of prayer, it steeps me in the familiar, returns me to what I've always known—life as a nun.

My fingers slide over the beads, my lips move with the chant of words, and the thought enters my mind. *Maybe this is where I'm supposed to be.* But I let it drift. My heart knows it's not.

"Found you!" A tiny hand tugs on my sleeve. It's little sister, her face all smiley and smudgy with her mother on her side.

"That is so good of you," I say. "Because I'm leaving soon." Her eyes widen. I run my fingers through her wispy mop, and we step aside.

"That soon?" Her lower lip trembles, and her cheeks turn rosy red. "But..." A sob shakes her tiny frame, and I throw my arms around her.

"But you can come and visit me," I say, and squeeze her tight. "And we'll ride the horses all day long." That does the trick. A blurry smile breaks on her face.

"Yes." Her voice a cheerful yell, her mother hushes her. "And Han sister too." She slashes her hand through the air—she's so fond of Lanying's long knife.

"Did you see her today?" I straighten her stiffed silken jacket, all crumpled up from the back. She shakes her head.

"I did the day before yesterday." The mother bends to me, her voice low. "Very early in the morning." Her hand points at the door. "Saw her at the edge of town, near the meat market, you know, where the big caravans leave." I nod. Just what I thought.

My dear little one and I say our near tearful goodbyes.

The sky has turned a violet hue, with streaks of magenta running through. The heavy smell of ripe sweet plums hangs in the air. Brash bellows resound from the sellers pushing their last produce to go. The evening breeze has left us the promise of a night filled with peace.

Palmo's arm hooked in mine, we walk home and my mind's almost at ease. Still, I need to see Lanying, maybe even tonight.

As if she has sensed my feet stalling at my thoughts, Palmo presses her hand on my arm.

"Take the guard with you when you visit your friend," she says without looking at me. "She doesn't live in the safest of places." A teeny chuckle chimes in my ears, or at least, I think it does.

"Thank you," I say, and for a moment I hesitate. "I'd better go now." The thought of her won't leave me alone tonight, but the truth of her might be worse to bear.

The anchored door, the small blinded shutter, the same routine—but now I don't wait for the voice; I know where to go, but not what to expect. My hand rests on the doorpost, my knuckles rattle the timber and a shuffle resounds from inside. The door flings open and a swirl of snow-white flutters up.

"It's you!" Lanying's in the doorway, clad in the strangest of robes, all silken with frilled ribbons running through. "Never seen a kimono?" She flaps her wings and twirls. Strands of her raven hair flow like the most fragile of pen strikes in a slow motion.

I step back at the flurry of so much fabric yet so much left of the body exposed. The silk, it's as thin as rice paper I once saw. No, it's thinner—it's completely sheer.

"As you probably guessed, I'm expecting somebody else." She grins. "Or rather some bodies else." One of her eyebrows draws up. "But it's always good to see you, Sister."

Before I can say anything, her hands draw me in and the door shuts. She spins and I sit on the bed.

"So, tell me, Sister." She pours a drink. "What did you do to make him leave like the wind?" She turns, her eyebrows a frown. "Not that I mind, you know. You can do so much better." The corner of her mouth draws up and her gaze takes me in.

My mind blanks for a moment. That's not why I came here. I had it all rehearsed, but she throws me off with her brash question, and the mention of him. I shrug.

"Never mind." I avert my eyes and wave my hand at the cup she offers me.

She steps nearer.

"And that, Sister," she says as she peers into my eyes. "That is why I don't do love." She plops down next to me; her arm draws around my shoulder. "It leaves you vulnerable, exposed." She shakes her head. "It's no good."

I blink to sharpen the blur, and it helps.

"I'm fine." I straighten my back and turn to her. I force a smile, but she doesn't mind.

"Of course you are," she says in that cheeky tone of voice I've come to know. "More than fine, and you should stay tonight." Silk rustles and cascades, her hand slides down my back. "The company I'm expecting..." Her ruby lips pout. "Well, let's just say they'll make you feel a lot better."

I cringe.

"Lanying!" I shake my head. "Do you ever...?" Her mischievous laughter drowns out my intended disapproval.

"Sisterrrr." Her voice hisses in my ear. "No woman ever benefited from denying herself the pleasures of the body." Her arm slides over mine. "On the contrary, it does you good, makes you feel alive." Her eyes glint a deep sapphire blue and I close mine, for I find it hard to admit her last words.

It makes me feel alive in a way I've never felt before. My fingers tingle as I fold them around the edge of the mat, and I push the painful admission away.

"That's not why I came," I say and take a deep breath to face her again.

"I know." She dangles her feet and takes a sip of the sweet-smelling liquor. "You're leaving tomorrow, but no worries, I was going to see you off." *Tomorrow.* I lean back. A cloud of fluff and white follows.

"Since you seem to know it all." My voice pitches ever so slightly. "How come you still don't know where Khando has gone to?"

There, I've said it. My fingernails scratch the mat, and my breath stalls for a moment as a sly smile curls around her lips.

"You got me there," she says, and sucks her cheeks in. She hangs her head and her face disappears behind a curtain of raven black.

"Only because the three of you slipped up." My voice is solid and sure. "You all had the exact same answer when I asked." *She could have perished in the fire.* "And you almost had me believing it." I shake my head.

"So, you come to me?" Her long locks fly around and set her face free.

"You were seen at the meat market the morning after," I say. "And you are the only one I deem capable of it." I lean my head against the wall and rest my case. There's no forcing her; she'll either tell me or she won't.

"Hmmm, you are good." Her mouth twists in a red line. "I didn't see that coming." A wry laugh escapes her. "So, I guess you already know."

My heart sinks, but I need to hear her say it.

"Did you really?" I say, my fingers spread out on the mat.

"I did, sister." She turns to me with the calmest gaze ever. "I told you, there's a special place for women like that, and that's exactly where she went to." Her voice is flat, and there's a light wheeze in her throat. "And let me tell you, she wishes she was burning in hell now, as this place..." She sizzles her tongue and her eyes spit a fire. "It's everything she deserves." An eerie content comes over her face. "And as it happened, the last load to the East was just leaving that morning. How convenient."

Lanying's laugh tolls in my ears and I cast my eyes down, not wanting to see her gloat in her self-perceived triumph. She kept her word. She brought Khandro to a place far worse than the burrows of hell—she sold her off as a slave.

A wave of cold punches the air out of me and my mind numbs with the thought. A muffled cry echoes from a room near us.

I'm too late. My hands go limp. There's nothing left for me to do here.

Lanying gulps down her liquor. I sit up and steady my breath. My heart thuds in my chest.

I'm too late. I tried my best, and I failed. No use staying on.

I hug Lanying goodbye with the promise we'll meet up at the coming of Spring.

The guard leads me through the dark night.

All I can do now is pray. *Om Tare.*

Forty-four

I t's a small convoy this time, with an unusual mix of rough traders, vague officials, packed horses, and armed men we're joining to head home. The shaded morning mist weights down the weisang that's lit, white shreds swirl low around our horses' trampling hoofs. Two red robed men chant their prayers, but their devout voices are lost in the restless roars of our company. We're leaving Lhasa, and we're leaving now.

"No mules or pilgrims this time, sister." Dendup steers his horse beside me.

I don't mind; I understand. Dendup and Sonam want to get to their families as soon as possible. They've got some explaining to do.

We ride out in a single line, and soon find our own pace again. With Sonam in front, me as a second, and Dendup closing our row. It doesn't take long and my stallion's at it again, challenging Sonam's horse for the lead position. I smile, as some things never seem to change.

My thoughts go back to this morning when I woke up in a panic. My body choked, my mind overwhelmed with dread, like in a bad dream. Only it wasn't a dream, I realized as my fingers touched the empty void in my chest. I'm going home without him and I don't know how—not yet. But being on the road will help, as its familiar rhythm puts that part of my mind at ease. The other part—the part of him—I'll have to deal with before I get home.

I look up to the pallid sun, struggling to get over the rusted mountain ridge afar. There's time. Settling to the back of my saddle and I relax the reins of my horse, scraping gravel, ready to bolt.

"Go on then, tire yourself out." With a jolt, he balks and takes off in clouds of grit and dust. I let him run, for he'll calm down by himself and return to the group.

So we travel and they try, Sonam and Dendup. They really do, but there's nothing that can lift my spirits for now, let alone my sunken heart. Passing through the landscape, set with the markers of him and me, the memories won't leave me be.

Lake Nam Tso, the cerulean jewel set amongst crystal peaks where he walked out, making his choice so clear; the dusty ruins near Derge where he let me see inside of him and spoke of freedom and longing; the starry night at the mighty Cho La, where he folded my rigid body into the warm, open space of his. Like scavenging ravens, they pick the flesh of my bones until there's nothing left but my shattered heart, raw and exposed.

At night I hurdle around the fire with Dendup's cheerful talk and Sonam's genuine care. We even have a few honest conversations, despite the strong liquor flowing in the men. They make me laugh, sharing their take on women and all. Like how I come from a long line of "feisty" women, as Dendup calls is, with no exception to the rule. And they even share some confessions they—in hindsight—I think never will admit again. Like Sonam's love for my mother and his cravings to be set alive.

"She was the one for me, Nordun," he says. He takes a sip of his flask and I drink his words, as I remember so little of my mother. "Stunning, like you, with the most gorgeous smile I've ever seen." The caster stays close to his lips.

"But I was not the one for her. Your father was." He takes another gulp. A small trickle drips down. "Never regretted letting her go; one cannot keep that's not meant to be." He sighs and turns to me, a sad smile hides under his bushy moustache. "You'll be fine,

Nordun, you did the right thing." I nod, but the tears burning under my eyelids say otherwise.

"You'll find a good man who'll make you smile again, like I found my Zinzin." His hand weights heavy on my forearm, and his words on my mind. I catch his distant gaze and pull it in.

"I know," he says, and shakes his head. "Sangmo." His voice trails off. "I'll try to make amends the best I can." I squeeze his hand.

"That would be good, to try," I say, and my thoughts go back to that night before I left, when Sangmo picked my clothes and told me she didn't want a marriage, only her freedom. "She's not demanding." Sonam's smile turns into a gentle grin.

"Y." His hands draw over his face. "And I should not have given in to her, but man, how that woman makes me feel alive, and I need that, Nordun, I do, time and time again." He puffs a deep breath and my cheeks flush at his candid confession. And then he gives me a wink, which makes my face burn even more.

To feel alive by the touch of the other, I know what Sonam means now. It's in all my senses—he is in all my senses. He awakened me and left me behind, gutted with a harrowing longing for so much more.

Yet, the endless days in the saddle are strangely soothing to my soul. The vast mountains stretching into the endless blue sky, the turning of the leaves from fresh green to the richest red, the sweet smell of ripe berries and dried cut grass, and the billowing clouds carrying the call of the birds above—the wild is so nourishing to all my senses.

But at night my mind turns to him, and the way his hands prepared my body to be his with the most tender of touch. It drowns my very being, sweeping me away with the ravishing desire for what's never going to be again. And I curl myself into a ball, until the feral yearning that grips me subsides with the arrival of dawn, every darkened night again.

I've chosen to survive the only way I know how—I've chosen to surrender. To stay present and sit in the eye of this raging storm, for it will pass—it has to.

It's the universal principle of impermanence—everything's always changing—and it's settling me amid this emotional chaos.

We always have a choice and I made mine.

And as the new day breaks again, I turn to the recognition that I have given it my all for the benefit of all sentient beings, and somehow that's something beautiful even though I can't fully comprehend or explain—not yet, but it makes my life all the more richer and larger as a result.

I've made the right choice for me.

Forty-five

The sun is not at her highest yet when the three of us halt on the hill. My stallion scrapes his hoofs on the barren rock, eager to boot down, but I need a moment to take it all in.

My fingers clench the reins, and in my throat swells. There beneath, nestled in the barren frames of the trees, lay the stables, the home I left so many moons ago, when the tidings were still lush and fresh with green. Thin shrills of white and gray curl up from the yard; they're expecting us today.

Sonam turns his stallion—he has to go. We already said our goodbyes this morning when we saddled up together for the last time, but he insisted on riding with us to the gate. Another day and his family will welcome him. His horse gallops away with a short wave of goodbye.

"You ready, sister?" Dendup bares his teeth and grins.

"Ready as can be," I say and spur on my horse. My horse's hoofs clatter in synch with the drumming in my chest. I know Father will wait at the gate, without a doubt, and I hope Sangmo too.

I'm not disappointed. We're greeted by the two of them with a swirl of white khatas from Father, and a tear of welcome on Sangmo's face.

"You've been gone too long." Sangmo hugs me, her rounded belly sticking between us. I cradle her face in my hands. She's beautiful and glowing. Being with child does her good.

Father holds me without a word of welcome, and I too am too choked up to utter a word. He draws me in, and I bury my face into the folds of his chuba. All is good. I've come home.

"Tell me the tea always tastes better at home." Steam gleams Sangmo's face as she pours me another cup of her milky brew. My nose wrinkles.

"I missed you too," I say, and we both laugh, as that's what she meant to say. My eyes glide around the kitchen. The tight plaster on the white-washed walls, the shine on the new timber shelves, the perfect arrangement of polished kettles, the bunches of herbs hung to dry along the wall. This place looks amazing. She sees me and shrugs.

"I hope you don't mind. I changed a few things," she says, and I clasp her hand.

"Mind?" I try not to laugh, but the curling tips of my mouth betray me. "I'm delighted you're choosing housekeeping over horse keeping." I pinch her fingers. "It suits you, now that you're becoming a mother and all."

She chuckles. "I know." Her hand rubs her protruding stomach. "I've gotten so big!" And I can't deny it, she has. "But I still ride, and I will until the very last day." And that too, I can't deny, for she probably will.

Together we sit, eat and talk, and Dendup agrees with Sangmo—there's no better tea like home. Father pours Dendup another cup with a few drops from his own flask. And after all the pleasantries are exchanged, the tea has made place for chang with the men, and the sun is throwing her afternoon rays through the windows. It's time for the inevitable to be addressed.

Dendup skips his usual ornate tales and gives Father and Sangmo the bare bones of our adventure. Uncle's in care of the nuns, and Khandro disappeared, that's the result. And how it came to be? Dendup shrugs.

"Well, probably a candle that got tossed over in the struggle," he says and chews his moustache. "The place was on fire in no time.

There was nothing we could do." His flimsy gaze darts over to me and I shrug, too.

"I wasn't there," I say, softly, and I avert my eyes to Father's scrutinizing glare.

"That's the story that reached us, alright." Sangmo's fingers pick a dried peach. "But it's good to hear it from you all in person." She pops the shriveled fruit into her mouth. "You know how people are." Her face becomes a grimace. "Spreading stories around." All four of us nod, and the silence becomes palpable, as we haven't spoken about the one missing yet. Karma.

"Did you hear from him?" Dendup's the brave one to bring it up. He spreads his fingers on the table and looks around. Father shakes his head and Sangmo gets up to rumble around the stove. The clatter of copper crashes through the kitchen.

"We were told he went to look for his kinfolk," Father says. "And the family gave his permission." The brownest of Father's eyes meets me in a velvety glare.

He went back to ask permission. My mind boggles. Why then did he leave so soon?

"We are his kinfolk!" Sangmo's voice resounds a raw plea, and a kettle bangs on the stove. A sob follows, and my heart hurts for her heart, as broken as mine. For the brother she lost, the brother she needs now more than ever, the brother she might never see again.

I close my eyes and draw a deep breath. How we humans hurt each other without ever wanting to. My hand seeks my string of beads, and my mind searches for the two I gave away. Where are you, my love? And most of all, are you safe?

We retreat to our rooms early, as the blood-red sun sets behind the hills. All is well here, and even better than that. Father's a changed man—his posture upright again, his eyes bright and clear. He's looking better than ever, and he attributes his renewed zest for life at Sangmo's presence and constant push to step into his role again—the horse master of a renowned stable, a force to be reckoned with.

"She makes me do the work," he said, his voice full of wit. "Ordering me around like that." He snaps his fingers, and of course, Dendup is all too eager to agree.

"That's what they do, these women of us." Dendup roared his cheerful laugh. "You should have known this by now." Sangmo even hit them with the raggedy cloth in her hand. Yes, Father and Sangmo in this place, they're doing well.

Sangmo's made a fabulous home for herself in Uncle's old quarters and is longing for me to join her, sharing snacks and stories until deep in the night. This evening I must pass. I crawl into bed in my tiny old room at the back of the house—the room I used to sneak out of as a child, and the room I now seek comfort in as I dread the night to come again.

Tiredness has set in my bones, and all the stories we had to recall have made my mind is weak. I close my eyes and clutch my beads tight.

Om Tare. Let darkness fall soon.

My prayers are heard.

***

I don't need to open my eyes, for I know he's here, and it's not a dream.

The scent of sweet earth, of blooming mountain meadows, and of the warmth of the sun in summer floats along. A quiet calm has come to the room.

I let my eyes adjust to the dim dawn not quite shining through yet, and to his silhouette sitting on the side of my bed.

"You're here," I say. I take a deep breath. My heart surges in my chest.

"I am," he says. His face is a shadow, but the green in his eyes shines so clear. His hand moves near, stroking the strands of my hair strewn overnight on the pillow.

I sit up, still dazed, but as his fingers slide into mine, the haze in my mind lifts.

"I needed to come," he says, and his lips caress the tips of my fingers, leaving them balmy with the warmth of his breath.

"But you'll go again." My voice is so small, for I don't want to say it. I want his hands to draw me close and explore my bare skin again, and for his hungry lips to follow in their trail.

"I am." He unfolds our hands and presses a kiss in the palm of mine.

Take me with you. My heart whispers, but my lips stay unmoved. Instead, my mind speaks.

"I know you have to," I say, and my words tear right through the tender core of my being.

"I do." His lips linger on my hand, and he hesitates to let go. "That's what you showed me, that night." His eyes turn a moist green and lock me in. "That incredible night." He pauses. "I'm sorry I wronged you again, my love." A sorrow slides across his face

"What do you mean?" My hands reach out, I so want him near. My fingers rest on the raffles of his sleeve.

"You gave me a choice, and I left," he says. "And again, I denied you yours, for I didn't ask you to come."

My breath stalls. His words hit my chest. My hands tremble and I clench them into fists.

"No, you didn't," I say. "And I never expected you to." I swallow my own bitter truth. I never expected him to, and maybe that's why he left.

He shakes his head, and his eyes search me again, and I see a flicker of doubt, a hint of fear shining through.

"You see, my love." He unclasps my hands and rests his on my forearms. His pulse rushes through his veins. "I grew up in a place that never felt like home, so I've grown comfortable being on my own." Slowly, he leans back and sighs.

"I made the mountains my home and being alone became my second skin." His fingers stroke the inside of my wrist, and my eyes are drawn to his mouth.

I shiver, his words so honest, his insight so clear. How I long for his touch, and for his heart to be mine.

"And then you came, and I knew we were bound." He raises his hands and cradles my face. "But I carried my aloneness with you. And when you let me hear my mother's call, I left, not wanting to burden you with my past and thinking I could go back to before, to being alone." His fingers spread on my cheeks, so feverish they burn.

"But something happened within me and I can't go back to how I was before—it feels lonely—as I've never felt lonely before." He closes his eyes and his forehead touches mine, the earthy scent on his salty skin so near.

"You happened within me, my love." His voice is hoarse now, and his lips search mine. "You shared my dreams, and you showed me I am not meant to be alone, for I am now, and I don't want to be."

And as his breath meets mine, I sob, and my hands reach out to dig my nails into the strong of his wrists.

"Then ask me." My lips leave a tiny trail on his chin. "Ask me, even though you know my answer."

For a moment, his muscles tighten, and he draws back. His hands slide in my lap.

"Come with me." His eyes shine a dark gleam. "In the understanding that I will fail you, but that I'll try to do better, again and again." His hand slides behind my neck and his fingers tangle in my long locks.

"Come with me, my love." His voice urges now, and his other hand strokes the edge of my jaw. "Come on the road with me, the one I've never gone before, and be my home so I can be yours." His words stall on his breath, the same way I hold mine.

I don't need to speak, he already knows, and his eyes flare with the most brilliant of emerald green. I bury my face into the crook of his neck as his hands draw me near, to the call of the mountains, and the warmth of the sun on the last summer's day.

And as he lays his body next to mine, again, I'm amazed. Who would have thought I'd be going once more, with this man, now my love, now so near?

Not me, but I should have known, really. I already made my choice—a long time ago—to care for all beings and do whatever it takes. I just didn't know if I could.

As the early dawn breaks in golden and orange, the sun rolls her rays through the tiny window and warms our skin.

A soft, yet nippy breeze follows through, carrying Palmo's truth on her whisper.

Courage, my child, you must have courage. My heart quivers ever so slightly. Her words have never resounded so clear.

I've opened my heart to the world without armor. I've laid myself down to care for all—raw and exposed.

And when time calls, I won't hesitate; I'll do it all again, no matter what.

I have what it takes to stand in my truth—I have a warrior heart.

Glossary

Ani / ani-la: Tibetan term for nun.

Bardo: Tibetan Buddhist term for the intermediate state or gap experienced between death and the next rebirth. Tibetan Buddhists believe this bardo can take up to 49 days; so prayers and other ceremonies are performed every day for 49 days after death. The term bardo also refers to the gap or space experienced between any two states in which the old reality is lost and a new reality has not formed yet.

Bodhisattva: enlightenment-being who has vowed to dedicate his/her life to the sake of all beings.

Butter tea: traditional Tibetan drink made by boiling strong tea and adding milk, yak butter, and some salt. Traditionally Tibetan people have Tibetan butter tea and tsampa roasted barley flour) together for breakfast.

Chuba: ankle-length, crossover robe that is adjusted at the waist with a long sash and pulled up to different degrees according to sex, rank, or region.

Dakini: a "sky dweller" or "sky dancer," the most sacred aspect of the feminine principle in Tibetan Buddhism, embodying both humanity and divinity in feminine form. The dakini appears during transitions: moments between worlds, between life and death, in visions between sleep and waking, in cemeteries and charnel grounds.

Divination: Mo, or dice divination, is an ancient predictive technique that is part of the Tibetan culture. The Tibetans consult *Mo* whenever making important decisions about their health, their family, property, personal matters, spiritual practice, friends and relationships, business, and travel. The answers of a divination come in the form of statements, advice, and instructions regarding practices or prayers suggested. While there are different forms of Mo divination, the form the ngakpa uses in this book (two six-sided dice with Tibetan letters on) is described in the book Mo: The Tibetan Divination System (2000) by Jamgon Mipham (published by Snowlion).

Dri: A female yak

Dzomo: A female crossbred between a Tibetan yak and a domestic cow.

Gen / Gen-la: Tibetan word for teacher.

Karma dakini: a specific dakini appearing to the Buddhist practitioner to mirror one's delusions, energize one's meditation practice, and activates one's realization.

Khata: traditional ceremonial scarf made of silk. The khata symbolizes purity and compassion and is presented on many ceremonial occasions, including temple visits, births, weddings, and the arrival or departure of guests. Most khatas are white, symbolizing purity, auspiciousness, and prosperity. There are also khatas in other colors: blue referring to the sky, green symbolizing water, red representing the space of protective deities, and yellow signifies the earth.

Khatvanga staff: ritual instrument held in the crook of the left arm of advanced Tantric Buddhist practitioners during ceremonies. The staff symbolizes the triumph of wisdom over illusion.

Kora: transliteration of the Tibetan word "Skor ra," meaning "circumambulation" or "revolution." The kora is performed by the pilgrim walking around the sacred site in the circumambulation in a clockwise direction, according to the traditions of Tibetan Buddhism. By circumambulating with the correct motivation, a person can purify their negative karma and can generate the seeds of enlightenment.

-la: the suffix "la" is a term of respect which can be affixed to the end of a title, as in ani-la (respected nun) or gen-la (respected teacher) or can be affixed to the end of a personal name, as in Ghedun-la.

Lama: Tibetan term used for a respected monk or high teacher.

Mala: a string of 108 prayer beads, one for each of the delusions (or worries) that afflict human life.

Mani stones: stone plates or rocks that are carved with the Tibetan Buddhism six-word mantra *Om Mani Padme Hum* or other mantras. Mani stones, or Jewel stones, as they are called, dot the entire Tibetan landscape. They are placed near monasteries, beside villages, along roadsides, along rivers and along long walls.

Mantra: phrases of words and syllables recited as an aid to concentration on a beneficial state of mind, in order to protect the mind from negative states. Mantras are spoken aloud or sounded internally in one's thoughts, and can be repeated continuously for some time or just sounded once. In the Buddhist practice, specific mantras like the Tara mantra (*Om Tare Tu Tare Ture Soha*) or the mantra of Avalokiteshvara, the bodhisattva of compassion (*Om Mani Padme Hung)* can be used to bring the mind greater compassion, better clarity or deeper understanding.

Momos: a type of steamed dumpling with a meat or vegetable filling.

Prostration: placing your body flat on the ground, face down, in a submissive position. Prostrations are often performed before meditation or teachings, and believed to be a eans of purifying one's body, speech and mind.

Sentient beings: term used in Buddhism to refer to the totality of living, conscious beings.

Sky burial: technically not a burial but a death ritual which entails taking the body to a designated site in the mountains, the charnel grounds, where it is left to feed vultures. The custom is known as "jhator" in Tibetan, which means "giving alms to the bird." The Buddhists in Tibet believe that the soul is immortal and death is only the beginning of a new life. Instead of letting the body vanish naturally, it is better for almsgiving to another kind of life and liberates the soul from the body, enabling it to gain entry into rebirth.

Tara: female Bodhisattva, known as the "Mother of Liberation," and representing the virtues of success in work and achievements.

Thangka: Tibetan silk painting with embroidery, depicting a Buddhist deity, famous scene, or mandala.

Tsampa: ground-up, roasted barley flour. Traditionally, the tsampa is mixed with tea and a little butter from yak's milk.

Thenthuk: hand-pulled noodle soup whereby the dough is not modelled into noodles, but is flattened and added only when the vegetables and meat are well boiled.

Weisang: ritual of burning branches of pine, cypress, and juniper trees to pray for blessings and offering gifts to gods. Weisang is done on many occasions, such as celebration of birth, wedding and harvest, warding off attacks by enemies, ensuring safety on a road trip, fending off illnesses, eliminating any evil, purify the air and attracting good luck.

Yak: long-haired, short-legged domesticated cattle, probably domesticated in Tibet and introduced wherever there are people at elevations of 4,000–6,000 meters (14,000–20,000 feet) in the Himalayas - China, Central Asia, Mongolia and Nepal.

Author's Note

Half-way through writing *The Horse Master's Daughter*, I already knew—there was going to be a sequel. Originally I'd intended *The Horse Master's Daughter* to be a standalone story, a gift to Nordun, my Tibetan niece whose father (my brother-in-law) refused to let her ride a horse. However, in the unguarded moments between writing Nordun's story and living in the mundane world, my mind was already flying ahead, spinning new tales, new

adventures for Nordun. Suddenly there was so much more happening on the page than I'd foreseen. The little tale I had in mind became a first full-fledged historical novel, and the seeds of a sequel had firmly planted themselves within me.

A pilgrimage to Lhasa was the obvious next journey for Nordun—pilgrimages have long been an essential part of the Tibetan Buddhist way of life. Buddhists from across Tibet have travelled to sacred sites in Tibet, Nepal, and India for more than 1,300 years, and although travel is restricted for Tibetans these days, pilgrimage is still going strong within Tibet. In fact, while visiting my in-laws in Tibet, I came across pilgrims every day. In fact, while talking to people about pilgrimage, it seemed like there was no adult—monastic or layperson—who had not undertaken at least one pilgrimage in his/her life.

In Tibetan, the word for pilgrim is *gnas skor ba,* which translates to "one who circles a sacred place." Pilgrims can get to the site of their pilgrimage by any means they see fit, but once arrived, one must walk on foot around the sacred site (circumambulate).

Within Tibet, pilgrims flock to man-made like monasteries and stupas, as well as to natural sites like lakes, mountains, and caves. The most famous man-made side is the temple known as Jokhang, in the city of Lhasa, the capital of Tibet since the 7th century. The Jokhang temple was built in the 7th century, and holds the famous statue of Sakyamuni Buddha that Nordun so reveres in *A Pilgrim's Heart.* The statue was brought to Tibet on the occasion of the wedding of the Tang Princess, Wencheng, to the Tibetan king, Songtsen Gampo, in 641 AD. These days another famous site is the Potala Palace, a fortress in Lhasa that served as the winter palace of the Dalai lamas from 1649 to 1959.

Natural sites such as the lakes, mountains, and caves are plentiful across the Tibetan Plateau. Long before the introduction of Buddhism in Tibet, the mountains and lakes were regarded as territorial gods, and many mountains and lakes have kept this sacred status. Nordun visits a few of those lakes on her way to Lhasa with Lake Nam Tso, *the heavenly lake* being one of the most famous lakes. This sacred lake incorporates five small islands. In the past, at the end of winter, pilgrims would walk across the frozen lake to one of these islands with food and supplies, and spend the summer there meditating, unable to return until Lake Nam Tso froze again the following winter.

By going on pilgrimage, Tibet Buddhist accumulate merit and blessings, and hope for purification of non-beneficial karma collected in their past. The pilgrims perform several rituals such as circumambulation of the sacred sites, prostrations along the way and at the sites, chanting of prayers and mantras while walking, and stacking stones at the slopes and shores of sites. These rituals, like mantra chanting and stacking stones, are also engrained in the daily lives of the Tibetan people. I've witnessed my family members and villagers—young and old—mumble their mantras while washing, cooking, and harvesting, and many times they would quickly but meticulously stack a few stones as we walked the mountain paths, or crossed a meandering stream.

The Tibetan Buddhists believe that the rituals and pilgrimages not only add merit to their personal karma but also are beneficial to the entire community and beyond—to all sentient beings. And it doesn't matter to them whether they pray and perform rituals together, or as an individual, in a temple, at a holy lake or in the privacy of their home, the benefits are always for all humankind.

So a pilgrimage it had to be for the sequel. After all, tracking across mountains, circling holy lakes, and accumulating merit for all, it is the perfect journey for Nordun to complete her transition from nun to lay woman, and an exciting, thought-provoking trip for you, the reader, to experience the magic and mystery of Tibet and its capital Lhasa, Land of the Gods, which unfortunately are out of reach to visit in person at the moment.

The *Nordun's Way* series is set in the time of the Mongol Empire and its Qa'ans. If you would like to know more about this historical setting and how I came to this choice (which I've explained in the author's notes of *The Horse Master's Daughter*), please visit my website www.elleslohuis.com

As a historian, I always want to do justice to the times and the people inhabiting the times. Also, for *A Pilgrim's Heart,* I did extensive desk research and consulted experts in the field. Besides desk research, I also wanted to do
in-depth field research. It was my big wish to go to Lhasa myself, but due to visa restrictions it was—and still to date is—not possible for me to travel the road Nordun took to Lhasa. Fortunately, I spent three magical months in Kham with my Tibetan in-laws and their friends who have travelled the roads to Lhasa through the mountains and shared their many tales and anecdotes with me.

I always come across amazing artifacts, places and people doing desk- and field research, like the beads Nordun gave to Karma after their visit to ancient ruins. Visit my website to see how I've placed these facts in the *Nordun's Way* series, and get your copy of the beautiful hand-drawn map of Nordun's travels that I've commissioned here.

Not much is known about the exact villages/settlements and their names in Tibet at that time. Therefore, I have taken the liberty of incorporating some of the villages/cities that exist in Tibet at the present time.

This brings me to a last note on facts and fiction—transliteration. For readability purposes, I've used the (phonetic) Romanized transcription whenever Tibetan terms, personal names, or place names are mentioned, and I've transcribed the Chinese terms, personal names, and place names in pinyin.

Elles Lohuis
Almelo, 2022

Acknowledgments

A warm thank you to my extended family in Tibet. For welcoming me into your home, and showing me how to live life with a courageous heart at all times.

Thank you to Dawn Ius, rock-star writing coach and editor extraordinaire. For letting me write and roam to find my voice, regardless of 'The Rules'.

Thank you to Kirsten, my bff. For calling me out when I'm trying to hide, and picking me up when I falter.

Thank you to Daleen, my accountability partner. For reminding me to follow my joy.

Thank you to Julie, my Dharma sister. For embodying the truth of compassion and forgiveness in daily life, and sharing the Buddhist teachings with earnest enthusiasm.

Thank you to Janneke, my fairy godmother. Yes, it's only ever a work of the heart.

And most of all, thank you to Tsewang, my husband. For your love knows of no boundaries - how blessed I am.

Echoes of Home

Nordun's Way Book Three

"Sometimes, even good hearts take the wrong path to do the right things."

When Karma asks Nordun to help him find his long-lost mother in Mongolia, she doesn't hesitate. Even if she fears he might never return home with her.

Joined by old friends and family, they set off on the treacherous trade roads to the far east, crossing rickety bridges and traversing narrow rifts, to where the Mongol warriors' cries roar on the battlefield, and victory is granted to those who deem themselves Gods.

As they uncover the traces of Karma's precarious past, suspicions arise between the traveling companions. Nordun knows the secrets she's harboring—but what are the others hiding?

When they reach their destination, a terrible truth unfolds and Nordun loses everything she holds dear. Now even her precious faith has deserted her—where will she find the strength to fight for what she believes in?

Read on for a sneak peek at ECHOES OF HOME.

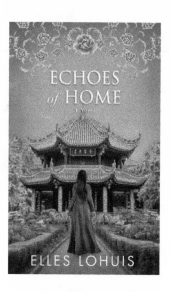

CHAPTER 1

Tibet, Eastern Kham
The Year of The Wood Rooster—1412 (1285 AD)

Dawn has broken. She basks the kitchen in pale hues of purple and pink, the stove murmurs a mellow good morning. It's my first time waking at home after a long and eventful pilgrimage to Lhasa. All went well, and all should be well on this fine fall morning—except it isn't.

"Let me get this right." Father's voice sounds eerily calm as he takes his seat opposite Karma. "You left my daughter in Lhasa without a word, disappeared for many moons on all of us, and now you're back, asking my Permission to take her to the jaws of hell?"

My empty stomach clenches. That subtle dark tinge in Father's voice—it's the reaction I expected. He's my father, so it goes unsaid. Besides, the facts are not in Karma's favor, and Father got them all right—except for one.

My heart goes out to Karma, sitting opposite Father, his head bent, his hands on his knees. I knew he would leave me in Lhasa. After all, I let him hear his mother's voice, her desperate call for her long-lost son to come home to her. How could he not give in to his mother's plea?

"Yes, Palden-la." Karma's manner mirrors Father's calm. "I am asking you for your permission." He looks up. A faint ray of morning sun catches his eyes and reveals the rich shade of emerald in them.

Karma, my love.

We'd gotten so close on our journey to Lhasa, but I had to let him go. Little did I know our parting would hurt so much. His absence ripped right through the tender hollows of my heart, leaving it raw and exposed. I would do it all again—even though I didn't expect him to come back to me.

"I made a grave mistake by leaving." He straightens his shoulders. "I betrayed your trust, the family's trust, but most of all, I betrayed Nordun." His eyes search and find me as I sit at his side. "I shouldn't have left like you like that, my love."

I wring my hands around my cup and nod. "You're here now." My heart is his, no matter what happened, and he knows it.

"I'm sorry for all the grief I caused." He puts his hands on the table and faces Father. "I'm willing to do whatever it takes to set this straight, Palden-la."

Father's eyes narrow on Karma in a harsh stare, and I bite my lip. This is not looking good. Father shakes his head.

"I trusted you with my daughter." A sharp edge rims his voice. "Abandoning her like that. What the hell were you thinking?" Bitter blame soars over the table at Karma, and I cringe. Father's going to fly off the handle any moment—for sure, he will.

Heavy boots resound in the hallway, rapid thumps paired with a few rough huffs. A sharp outcry roars from the doorway. "He wasn't thinking, the idiot!"

My spirit lifts—it's Dendup, my trusted family elder, who came with us to Lhasa. With his shirt wide open, and his chuba slung across his chest, he lurches into the kitchen in his typical boisterous way.

"You fool!" He charges at Karma and takes him in a mean hold, saving us all from Father's expected show-down. "Disappearing on us in the middle of the night," Dendup croaks.

For a moment it looks like he's going to wrestle Karma, but then his face bursts into a rowdy laugh. "At least you've got the decency to come back." He throws a cheeky smile my way. "Knowing we're going to give you hell, right, sister?"

A fierce heat flushes my cheeks, flaring all the way up to my temples. Dendup teased me all the way to Lhasa and back, and I'll never get used to it—silly me.

Dendup squeezes himself on the other side of Karma and gives Father a curt nod. I tear myself away from the looming silence and hasten to pour the men tea.

"What were you thinking, taking off like that?" Dendup slurps his tea with delight while our cups stand untouched. He's a master at savoring the pleasant in a tense situation like this.

"You've been trying to hide it on me, but I know you've been wanting to search for your blood relatives for a long time—why now?" Dendup's cup lands with a bang on the low table.

Blood relatives. The sheer contempt with which he utters that word makes me shudder.

Karma shrugs, and I wring a cloth between my hands. How to explain?

"It's me." My voice is thin, but the words grab everybody's attention. "I told him to go look for them."

Karma's eyes flash at me and Dendup jumps in his seat. Father doesn't even blink. I wish he would.

"You?" Dendup snorts over his tea. "Why?" Foam sprays from his mouth, and I bow my head.

Dendup's been nothing but good to me, and I never told him, not once. So many times, he comforted me on our way home, thinking Karma had left me for no reason. My fingers fray the fringe of the rag. What must he think of me now?

"It came to me that Karma's mother is still alive." The words slip from my lips, but I don't know how to tell them more. For sure they would not understand? Only Karma does, for we share our dreams, he and I. We're bound by them, but how to explain?

"I told him that night in Lhasa." I fling the cloth next to the stove and sink down at Father's side. "So you see, he had to go."

Karma's hand moves across the table and his eyes lock mine in a tender hold.

"I took off too hastily," he says. His restless gaze darts from me to Father and Dendup. "But I didn't want to burden any of you with my obscure past—or my uncertain future." His fingertips brush against mine.

"Uncertain it is, as these kinfolk of yours are brutes." Dendup's face twists in a grimace. "We've all heard the stories, butchering everybody who stands in their way."

Karma's jaw sets, and I slide my hands over his. Dendup speaks the truth. Karma's kinfolk came from the North over our mountains and established a truce with our tribes a long time ago. Seems we have been fortunate, though, as the tales of their conquests in other lands speak of a cruelty that can only be whispered. Ruthless plunder and vicious slaughter of boys and men alike, of young girls and women violated and enslaved until death, and of entire settlements and even monasteries burned down to the ground. These men have no mercy, it seems. Still, it has no bearing on my love, as he grew up on Grandfather's side of our family, and has only known of our way.

"But surely, their Khan has turned to Buddhism now?" I try, but Dendup's scornful laugh swipes my argument right off the table.

"Buddhist or not, their ways are barbaric." Dendup's smug tone says it all.

Of course, he's right, but how conveniently he seems to forget the reason he and Karma went to Lhasa. They didn't go on pilgrimage. No, they went to hunt down and kill my father's brother—on orders from the family to avenge my mother's death. Luckily, they didn't succeed—but they sure came close.

I rest my head against the wall. He seems so calm, so quiet, my love, but only I see him for real. Regret and restiveness cloud in the far yonder of his eyes. How my heart longs to hold him close.

"Dammit, Karma, I've cursed you all the way from Lhasa to here." Dendup sighs and rubs his bushy brows. "Hell, I even cursed you getting up this morning for pulling a stunt like that."

I can't help the brief smile peeping through my lips. He sure cursed Karma—all the way.

"But I've known you since you came to the family, being no taller than my knee's high." A grave shadow falls over his face. "We've been on the road together a long time and you've proven to be a real brother—more than that. You've proven your loyalty to the family over and over again." My ribs tighten and my mouth goes dry.

Loyalty to the family. How neatly Dendup places these tricky words. Karma never mentioned it, but Lanying, my sister from the Han side of the mountains, explained it to me. Loyalty to the family means executing the family's orders, and Karma's done more honor killings than anybody ever had to.

"I can't stop you from venturing out there, you're too damn stubborn, like me." Dendup's sneer is snarky, that's for sure, but there's an airy undertone sounding through.

"I guess the only way to make sure you return safe is to come with you on the search for those kinfolk of yours." His arm slides over Karma's shoulder. "Besides, it's time we conquer that side of the mountains once again in favor of the family's trade."

Karma shoots up, and my heart skips a beat. Father still doesn't move.

"You are?" Karma's voice soars with surprise, and I don't know whether that's good or bad. All I'm thinking about is how Dendup's company will strengthen my case for going, too.

"I am." Dendup's tone is persistent. "But first we prepare." He slaps Karma's shoulder and hands me his empty cup with a shifty smile.

I gather the other cups, still full with lukewarm tea. It's a done deal for Dendup—but for me? If only Father would say something, anything. I don't dare to look.

"Winter's coming and the mountains won't let us pass." Dendup's all reasoning now. "We'll leave some time after Losar."

Father sips the cup I poured. Still, there's not a word from his lips.

"That's great." Karma beams a smile at Dendup. "But I'm not leaving without my love." He bows his head to Father, but there's still no reaction from his side.

"I'll wait for you." I swing the kettle. Steam hisses as tea slushes on the scorching stove.

"I'm not leaving without Nordun." Karma lifts his chin and looks Father straight in the eye. "Tell me what it will take to get your permission, Palden-la."

I have to give it these two, the two men I love most—they're quite a match. I hold my breath as the stony silence between the two of them submerges the kitchen in a suffocating solidity.

With reluctance, Father shifts in his seat. "I'll think about it."

His response release my trapped breath and I gasp for air. He'll think about it. *This is good.*

"Nordun and I will go to the ngakpa this morning." Father sits back. "He deserves to know what happened to his wife in Lhasa firsthand." He rests his hands on his knees.

The ngakpa. An iron fist locks around my heart. It was the ngakpa's wife who provided my father's brother with the snake spell that killed my mother. The two of them fled to Lhasa when their devious play came to light this summer. Now Father wants me to tell the ngakpa how Karma and Dendup hunted them down. *This is not good.*

"We'll be back by midday." Father gets up. "We'll talk after that." He moves out of the kitchen without saying another word.

"I'm sorry, love." Karma jumps up, and I freeze.

I don't want to go. His hands hold mine.

"All of it?" I blink and he nods. Of course, all of it. It's all or nothing for us now.

My feet stumble through the hallway. My mind cries out. *What a fool I've been.*

For only a fool would expect Father to be satisfied with the vague account I gave him of our Lhasa adventure yesterday. Just as only a fool would expect him to let me go with Karma in search of his mother and kinsfolk.

After all, what father *would* let his daughter go off with her lover to the far grasslands of Mongolia like that?

***

Ready for more?

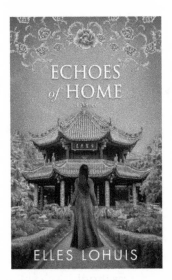

ECHOES OF HOME (*Nordun's Way* Book Three)

Join Nordun in her search for far-away kin as she finds that the definition of family isn't always in the blood—it's in those who treasure you for who you are, no matter what.

Get your copy now.

About Author

Elles Lohuis is a historical fiction author based in The Netherlands. A voracious reader and ever inquisitive explorer of far-away lands and foreign cultures, she holds an MA in History, an MA in Business, and a PhD in Social Sciences.

After working for nearly thirty years in international business, education and research, she left her academic position and private coaching practice behind to write all those novels smoldering inside of her.

Elles writes books that enthrall, engage, and enrich you, to sweep away to distant places and times gone by, opening a window to a world and its people that nowadays seems wondrous, foreign, and fascinating—but was once typically ours.

At the moment, Elles is back on base to complete her first historical fiction series *Nordun's Way*, a heartrending heroine's journey, sprinkled with nuggets of timeless Buddhist wisdom.

Connect with Elles and receive more sneak peeks of her writing, research, travel, new releases, and special offers at www.elleslohui s.com or scan the QR Code

And download your copy of the hand-drawn map of Nordun's travels, specially commissioned for the *Nordun's Way* series books 1, 2 and 3 here.

9 789083 240831